THE NOT WIVES

CARLEY MOORE

FEMINIST PRESS
AT THE CITY UNIVERSITY
OF NEW YORK
NEW YORK CITY

Published in 2019 by the Feminist Press
at the City University of New York
The Graduate Center
365 Fifth Avenue, Suite 5406
New York, NY 10016
feministpress.org

First Feminist Press edition 2019

This book is supported in part by a grant from the
Shelley & Donald Rubin Foundation.

This book was made possible thanks to a grant from
New York State Council on the Arts with the support of Governor
Andrew M. Cuomo and the New York State Legislature.

This is a work of fiction. All of the characters, organizations, and events portrayed in this novel are either products of the author's imagination or used fictitiously.

First printing September 2019

Cover design by Suki Boynton
Text design by Drew Stevens

Library of Congress Cataloging-in-Publication Data
Names: Moore, Carley, author.
Title: The not wives / Carley Moore
Description: First Feminist Press edition. | New York, NY : Feminist Press, 2019.
Identifiers: LCCN 2019008696 (print) | LCCN 2019009870 (ebook) | ISBN 9781936932696 (ebook) | ISBN 9781936932689 (pbk.)
Classification: LCC PS3613.O55454 (ebook) | LCC PS3613.O55454 N68 2019 (print) | DDC 813/.6--dc23
LC record available at https://lccn.loc.gov/2019008696

ADVANCE PRAISE FOR *THE NOT WIVES*

"A provocative and well-told story about chosen community, friendship, and human frailty."

—*KIRKUS REVIEWS* (starred review)

"A terrific literary novel about what it means to belong to yourself while trying to be a part of something bigger."

—*INDEPENDENT BOOK REVIEW*

"*The Not Wives* is gritty, sexy, *very* queer, literary social realism that's up-all-night compelling—just what I want from a novel set in NYC in the time of Occupy, with its sprawling cast of adjuncts, bartenders, poets, single parents, little kids, homeless teenagers, and serious organizers embroiled in various romantic and economic complications. When we say report back, this is what we mean!"

—ANDREA LAWLOR, author of *Paul Takes the Form of a Mortal Girl*

"Carley Moore exults in portraying the grit, drama, confusion, and ecstasy of her diverse characters' daily lives. *The Not Wives* is not just for not wives; it's for all of us struggling with how to be human—falling in and out of love/lust, parenting children, teaching young adults, protesting corruption, and just getting by—amid the ongoing clamor and bewilderment of twenty-first-century life."

—LAURA SIMS, author of *Looker*

"In *The Not Wives*, Carley Moore puts her considerable powers—introspection, humor, empathy—into the service of fiction, creating a landscape of achingly authentic female lives that we rarely see given such literary treatment. A compulsively readable novel with deep roots in our gorgeous, messed-up world."

—MICHELLE TEA, author of *Against Memoir: Complaints, Confessions & Criticisms*

"I was in dire need of a queer, sex-positive mom in literature—and then the gift of *The Not Wives* showed up. Here are the wives and not wives so many of us are, have been, have loved, might be. I couldn't put this extraordinary book down; it offered so much solace, recognition, and hope."

—LYNN MELNICK, author of *Landscape with Sex and Violence*

With seemingly effortless prose, Carley Moore paints a rich portrait of three deeply compelling women navigating the polarities and confining norms of modern-day life."

—ETAF RUM, author of *A Woman Is No Man*

"Set in a gentrified New York of wealth and insecurity, *The Not Wives* is a novel about precarity in the time of Occupy Wall Street. 'We are all falling apart and keeping it together,' Carley Moore writes, conjuring the activist spirit but also the trap of the status quo. Self-awareness is not enough, *The Not Wives* tells us; the question is how to dream without complicity, how to turn guilt into action. This is a feminist novel for our times—slutty and principled, dedicated and unsure, it dares us to feel everything."

—MATTILDA BERNSTEIN SYCAMORE, author of *Sketchtasy*

"*The Not Wives* is at once dark and bright, deeply serious and dryly funny, timeless and of a particular time. Moore's ability to weave relationships out of the bleakness of the 2011 political climate is unparalleled. This is a story about so many things, but at its heart, it is a tale of love and family that will grip you until its final pages."

—SOPHIE LUCIDO JOHNSON, author of *Many Love: A Memoir of Polyamory and Finding Love(s)*

"Audacious and exhilarating in its candor, *The Not Wives* captures the heady mix of pleasures and agonies necessary to turn one's life in a new, truer direction. Carley Moore attends to the complexities of urban living and activism with riveting clarity."

—IDRA NOVEY, author of *Those Who Knew*

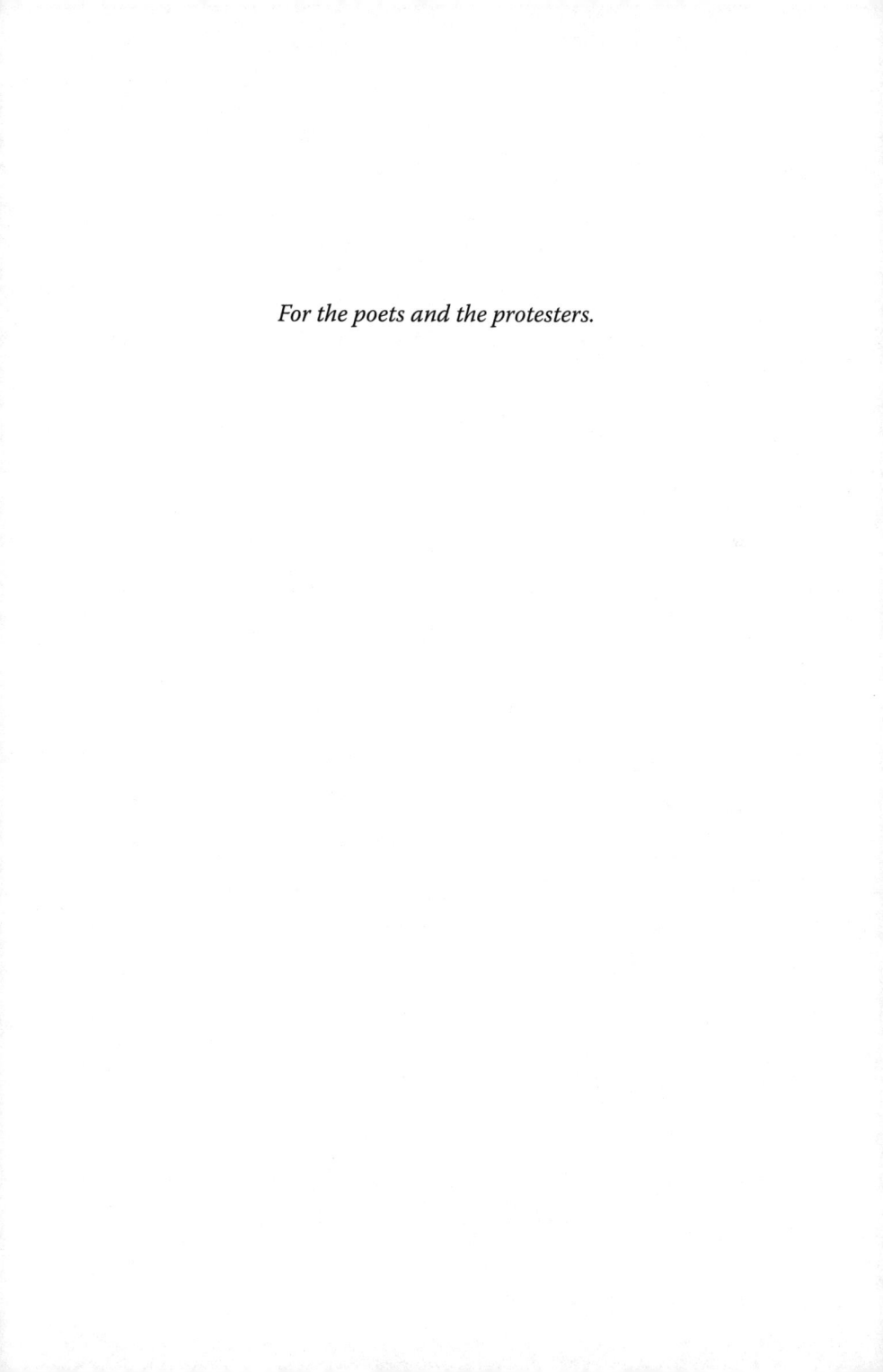

For the poets and the protesters.

PROLOGUE

She swung one leg and then the other over the lip of the rooftop. The leafy canopy of trees swayed back at her. She tried to focus her eyes on the individual leaves, the branches holding them up, and the birds who made homes there.

But she couldn't. She was dizzy and her eye sockets pulsed with a static, sticky ache.

You suck.

You're a failure and a whore.

The voices again. The ones that had driven her out to the roof. To see the view? To jump off? *You need air,* she told herself. *You want to be higher.*

She looked up at the sky. Just one or two stars. Crisp crescent moon. *A fish hook,* her mother used to say.

She stared down at her feet and clutched the scratchy asphalt of the roof tighter.

It was as easy as sliding into the deep end of a pool. An underwater swim through the midnight sky.

She heard the roof door open behind her. A voice calling. She didn't answer. She'd wait until it was close enough. To witness? To stop her?

"Watch out for the dead bird," she said as she turned her head around. It was a warning. It was the best she could do.

PART 1
SUMMER

YOUR MASCOT

Perhaps fucking was a road map for those of us who no longer believed in directions. Or maybe it was just another way to get lost. If nothing else, it got me free drinks and a bedroom-eyed view into the apartments, bars, and neighborhoods of a new New York—one that was building glass condos next to brick housing projects, replacing bookstores with twenty-four-hour gyms, offering its homeless cash incentives to leave the city, and opening stores so fancy I sometimes couldn't tell what they were selling. *Um, is this a café or a barber-shop? Do you sell fedoras or honey made from Brooklyn rooftop bees? Both? Great.*

Where were those mythical rent-controlled one-bedrooms in South Williamsburg and how much did they cost? How do people find curtains big enough for those giant green glass windows of their new co-op apartments? What was it like to walk the quiet night streets of Bed-Stuy after getting spanked hard by a man who called himself a wolf? Were there actually any single men still living in Park Slope? Did a father of three who had a studio in the same building as his ex and kids and who was starting a digital media firm have time for a girlfriend? How would you describe the decor of a railroad apartment in Red Hook shared by three men in their forties? Was the owner of that organic hair salon really as crazy on a date as the lesbian network said she was?

South First between Hooper and Grand. $914.

The internet.

Exhilarating.

A couple, but they were teenage boys, living with their parents.

No, but he kept trying.

Bench press, ticket stub, beer cup, early modern.

Crazier.

Fucking, it turned out, was still the most reliable way to split myself in two, especially since I'd mostly given up on drugs, and good fucking was the closest to unlocking the doors of perception as I thought I might get. The orgasm's rush of dopamine opened me up, gave me purpose. Sometimes, while riding some stranger's cock, I imagined myself stepping out of my body like a person out of a mascot suit where I was fake cheering for my life.

Like every indie girl who grew up in the nineties I took a lot of acid and still smoked pot whenever someone offered it to me, but those tripping days were over. I was afraid of the psychic revelations I might have on acid, and I couldn't bear the time commitment, the stomachache, the jaw-clenching comedown, so I fucked to better see myself. Even when the fucking was bad, I saw important things that my body kept secret from my brain, which was too busy lesson planning or writing sentences for a revealing personal essay or keeping track of the week's obligations on a giant Staples wall calendar that I stashed in a drawer because its paperness made me feel old. Sometimes I saw that I was actually quite sad or that I was, in fact, very drunk. Sometimes I believed that the extreme tilt of an Avenue A sidewalk was a bad metaphor for how the city was trying to slough me off, and like most renters and artists and teachers, I could fall right off the side of it and wind up in New Jersey or Long Island or Westchester if I wasn't careful. Sometimes I understood that it was time to go home and clean the kitchen and to vacuum up the sequins my daughter had sprinkled over the "forest" in her room. Other times, I saw that I liked myself after all these years, and so I could actually bear to disentangle my limbs from that smoky, bearded man who'd grown up in Bay Ridge and was a bartender without any dreams, and walk home in the middle of the sweaty night and eat pasta over the sink at two a.m. and feel just fine about it.

Because there are found objects along forgotten paths. Because a pilgrimage is a journey with its own sacred rituals. Because I believed in walking on my own. Because I no longer understood the complex algorithms and intimacies of couples. Because I had broken my home. Because it had turned out this way. Because one day, I looked up from the couch and he was gone.

STITCHED TOGETHER

He showed me his scars—the four-inch one along his arm and the six-inch one across his belly that snaked down to the waistband of his jeans. I saw where the needle had entered and exited his skin, and I traced my finger back and forth along the stitching of his stomach.

"Don't," he said. "It feels weird."

We'd met at a bar in East Williamsburg. A first date. Some shots. We talked mostly about bands.

"I think we have the same nose," he said, and rubbed the tip of his against mine. I breathed in the smoke from his one-hitter outside the bar and then I followed him home.

I moved down to his waistband. I undid his belt buckle and tugged at the zipper.

"I was lucky," he said. "I lived in a good neighborhood so the police came quickly. My neighbors came out with blankets and they waited with me. My cat, Cleopatra, even came out and licked my face, and I was lucid enough to say to my girlfriend, 'Who let the cat out?'"

I liked this story and the way he told it. The faraway look in his eyes as he remembered almost dying. I saw that he was a broken person like me, and so I slid my dress over my head and put his cock in my mouth.

I had my own scars—the deep seam where my belly button would have stayed if I hadn't had a hernia—but I'd never been shot or had a gun in my face. My grandma left Cuba in 1946 and married an Army colonel thirteen years her senior so that her children might pass for white. All of those cold Swedes on my mother's side—the way our pale skin burned and freckled in the sun, bruised at the slightest pressure. The privilege of that burn.

I remembered the one time I'd been stitched up. The doctor, who pulled Sasha out of me and untwisted the umbilical cord from her neck, sewed my torn vagina with a needle and thread. The birthing mirror was still there and so I could see it all, until the doctor moved it away with a flourish and a laugh: "No new mama needs to see this!" I was numb from the epidural and holding Sasha, who was struggling to nurse, but I marveled in that clinical way you sometimes can when you're high on drugs and adrenaline, at what doctors could do—the simple hands-on work of it. Sometimes it was just a needle and thread, stitching a body back together again. *The body is a cloth, a stitched-together garment*, I thought as he slid in and out of me and tried to stay hard.

"Stop looking at me with those eyes," he said.

"What eyes?" I said.

"Sometimes I just can't, I have to rest," he said, and flopped down next to me.

"It's okay. I don't mind," I lied. I looked around his room. A big TV stacked on top of a dresser. The giant poster of Sun Ra. Several old turntables on the floor. I was happy he had a bed.

"How long have you lived here?" I asked.

"Since 1998. The landlord is an asshole, won't fix a thing, but it's rent-controlled."

"Lucky. How much do you pay?"

"914 a month," he said. "But I've been out of work for a year, so I'm behind on rent." He sat up on his elbows and squinted in the dark at me.

"Sorry, I didn't know."

"Lie down on your stomach," he said, eager to change the subject.

I touched myself while he fucked me, but I couldn't come. I lay there for a while and then got up to pee. I didn't look at myself in the mirror. I didn't want to see my own face in the harsh, bare-bulb light of a stranger's bathroom. The bathroom hadn't been cleaned in a long while. There was no towel. I splashed water on my face and wiped it off with toilet paper.

"I'm going to head back to my place," I said when I walked back into his bedroom and started to root around on the floor for my underwear and dress.

"Just stay, Stevie." He patted the sheets. I was surprised he remembered my name. "Don't leave in the middle of the night."

"I'm a terrible sleeper. I just need to go home," I said.

"Fine, be that way," he pouted.

I hailed a cab outside of his apartment and wondered if I had the look of someone who'd just been fucked badly on my face. I said hello to the driver, called him "sir," and settled into the blue faux-leather seat. On the Williamsburg Bridge, the lights from the East Side did not comfort me like they usually did. I didn't feel lucky that I lived in New York, and that I had escaped the small town where I grew up. New York was cold and brutal in the same way it was alive and pulsing, and I knew that I couldn't count on it to take care of me because it never would. It wasn't a person or a dream. It was just a city, and in that way, forever indifferent to the people who lived in it. And so, I whispered at the skyline, "New York, my love for you is not unconditional. You can't kick my ass forever."

I nodded at the night guard in the lobby of the dorm where I had a faculty apartment, rode the elevator up to the seventh floor, and opened my door. I shrugged off my dress and stared at the clock. 3:45 a.m. I was still stoned from the one-hitter. I looked over at the comforter I'd left arranged in the shape of my body on the couch and jumped. It looked like someone was in there, still sleeping, but it was just the husk of my body from earlier that day, the woman who wallowed on the couch, and who was lately more passive than active.

My cat, Rudy, leaped up and rubbed against my leg. "You are very bad," I said to him, but we both knew I was talking to myself.

I walked down the hallway and into Sasha's room. She was a tiny hoarder. There were piles of beads, drawings overflowing out of her play kitchen cupboards, necklaces stacked up on her nightstand, old linty stickers reaffixed to her bedposts, and sparkly headbands all over the floor. On the blue Ikea kids' table by her bed, I noticed a pile of broken things—the heads and torsos of several Lego people, the slack loop of a stretched-out gummy bracelet, a legless stuffed-animal cat with giant eyes, and a Matchbox car with one missing wheel. *I should fix those*, I thought with a pang of guilt. I pressed her pillow to my face and breathed in. I smelled her orange detangling spray, but not her skin. I wanted to hold her, so that I could remind myself that I wasn't completely untethered. I wanted to smell her hair, her mouthy cracker breath, and the salty dip in the back of her neck, but I'd just washed the sheets and there was no trace of her.

I curled up against the pillow and choked out a tiny animal sob.

SCORE

"Smoke, smoke, smoke, smoke," a dealer cooed at them from the northwest corner of Washington Square Park. Like he knew they had money, like he knew they were desperate.

Johanna pulled the rumpled dollar bills out from her short pockets and dumped all of the change out of her sock and into Butch's lap. "Fuckers were greedy today. It took me twice as long," she said as she flopped down onto the grass next to him.

He counted the change, smoothed out the couple of dollar bills. "End of the month, people are tighter," he said. Johanna liked that he always had an explanation for what she'd already decided was random. These insights helped when you were homeless punk anarchists with a shifting code of ethics and semiserious drug habits.

"You're short," he said, and leaned over to kiss her chapped lips.

"No, I'm not," she said, brushing his lips away.

"I want to get the good stuff from the guy in Brooklyn, not that tourist shit," Butch said.

"I'm tired. Can't we just buy here?"

Butch sighed and pulled at his patchy beard. "You've got to do your share," he said. "Also, the shit is fine for you because you're a lightweight. I need the good stuff."

Johanna stuck her tongue out. "Can't I do something else for the dealer? I'm tired of begging today. It's degrading."

"Bad girl." Butch grinned.

An hour later, in a basement apartment in Bushwick, Johanna followed a tall white hipster into a dirty bathroom. He gave her a line off the tip of a key. She snorted it, sat down on the lip of the toilet, and pulled at his belt buckle. "It's big," she lied, and closed her eyes. He held on to the back of her head too tight, but she told herself she didn't care.

To Johanna, blow jobs were mostly transactional—gendered bitcoins in the dark economy she and Butch sometimes dipped into. She'd read sex-worker manifestos and she knew there were far worse ways to make money. *Once in a while, no biggie*, she told herself.

It was her choice. She did it for Butch, for both of them really. She loved him. He'd saved her from a small-town death. She'd never forget that.

Back in the park, high and full from the ramen they bought on the way back, she stared up at the trees in a hidden woodsy corner where they kept their cardboard box and sleeping bag, and then turned to look into Butch's dark, almost black eyes.

"See, sometimes it's really perfect," she said.

"Sometimes," he said. But he had that faraway look, like there was a plan she wasn't in on. "I don't want you to do that anymore," he said, rolling on top of her, pinning her down. The sound of the Friday night bongo circle behind them and the hot buzz of August heat. Tourists and students everywhere.

"What?" She didn't really want to talk about it.

"With that guy," Butch clarified.

"I can if I want to," she said, instantly defiant when anyone told her what to do. "Besides, you were fine with it when you wanted the good stuff."

He kissed her neck and shoulders and then rolled off of her again. He was spacey from the heroin and wouldn't be interested in fucking anyway. He turned away from her toward the fence that gated the park. "I'm ready for a revolution," he said as if he were talking to the squirrels and rats, not her.

"Me too," she said, and traced her pointer finger along his sinewy back muscles. He didn't turn back around, and so she got up and took their dog Tipsy to walk the perimeter of the fountain. She waded in and stared at the lit-up arch. She let anyone pet Tipsy who wanted to and didn't even ask for a dollar in return. She felt woozy from the lights and sweaty, and so eventually she sat down in the water and let it wash over her. Tipsy splashed next to her with her three good legs. She rubbed her finger along the scar on the inside of her left forearm—a coin-size burn from a cigarette lighter. She remembered the snaking coil of fire and the smell of her own burning flesh. Later, there was wound and scab and ridge. Topography. Map made out of skin.

"We're explorers," she said into the top of Tipsy's wet head. "We're hobos and runaways. We're totally free. Like Dean and Sal, we're on the road."

Never mind that Butch hated Kerouac. It was still her favorite book.

ETHICAL

"Hello?! I'm in here!" Mel shouted from inside the walk-in freezer. The safety latch was broken, and she'd forgotten to prop it open with an ice bucket. "Hey!" she shouted louder, and pounded her fist against the door several times.

"Oh, what'd you do, lock yourself in there?" The chef's voice from the other side. The owner hired him a week ago. His name was Carmine, and they'd been shooting each other significant looks ever since.

She set down the case of limes she'd come in to get. "Oh my god, let me out!"

"What do I get if I set you free?"

"I don't negotiate with terrorists." Mel laughed and then shivered. "Come on, it's fucking cold in here."

"Is that making your nipples hard?" he said, pulling the door open just a crack.

Mel wedged her foot between the door and freezer wall and pushed past him with her crate of limes. She tried not to look him in the eyes because she already knew they were brown with long lashes and that they would make her weak.

"Too soon?"

She turned around and shrugged. How to explain to him her complicated situation? She hadn't yet tried it out, though she'd rehearsed the words in the mirror. Above them the sounds of an artisanal farm-to-table restaurant and bar that was set to open in an hour. Chairs and tables dragging against the floor, shouting from the kitchen, waitstaff wrapping silverware in napkins at their stations, and Tommy the general manager yelling at Greta the hostess about a lost reservation. "It was in the fucking system! How could you lose a ten-top?" Mel wanted to help her—to pull aside this gorgeous twenty-five-year-old who had amazing, perfect tits and lips like a blow-up doll and give her some advice—but she didn't have the time. Collaborations and allegiances happened by accident and surprise in restaurants. This was one of those moments.

"I'm complicated," she said.

"I can handle you." Carmine walked closer to her and took the crate of limes out of her hands. Down here, in the cramped hallway stairs that led from the back of the kitchen and into the freezer, it was just the two of them.

"You think so?"

He put the crate down on the floor. "Definitely."

Mel pulled at the strap of her black tank top and pushed a strand of her hair behind her ear. *Here goes nothing*, she thought. "I have a girlfriend. We live together and I love her, but we are open and I see other people. But I can't like ever be *your* girlfriend"—she stammered for a second—"because, well, I'm taken."

"You think that makes you special, don't you?" He smirked at her.

She untensed her shoulders and laughed. "That's your response?"

"What? You think you're the only weirdo in this place?"

Mel stared at him. He was wearing his chef whites, checked pants, and rubber kitchen clogs. She saw the muscles of his arms through the cotton. She wanted his hands on her body—her back, her ass, between her legs, anywhere he wanted to put them.

"I just want to be ethical about this stuff."

"Ethical?" He laughed.

"Shut up."

"No, you shut up," he said, and took a step forward. He leaned in and ran his tongue along her lip and then pulled her closer. She opened her mouth wide and he slid his tongue on top of hers.

"Incoming!" the manager shouted from the back of the kitchen. Mel pulled away and picked up her crate of limes. The manager would freak out if he saw it on the floor.

"We almost got caught," Carmine whispered into her ear, and then he turned around and disappeared back up the stairs.

"Where the fuck have you been?" the manager shouted at Mel, more curious than angry.

"I got locked in the freezer and Chef had to save me."

"You gotta prop it!" He brushed past her. "Fucking Prince Charming, everybody is in love with this guy."

Back upstairs behind the bar as she cut limes and lemons, and stuffed the giant olives with blue cheese and garlic, she toggled back and forth between two images—one hot and one guilty. Chef's tongue in her mouth as he pressed against her in that cold hallway and Jenny dutifully at home with the dogs, wrapping a dinner plate in saran wrap for Mel so that she could have something healthy to eat when she got home at five a.m.

THE BRIDE

In my nightmare, Sasha is in the sliding car in front of me on the Wonder Wheel. I watch her scream and squeal, until the metal girder snaps off and she falls, cage and all.

In my nightmare, I lose her on the subway. I have her hand and then suddenly I don't. The doors of the A train slide shut and I shuttle away from her.

In my nightmare, we are homeless and living in a dumpster.

In my nightmare, I have two children, and we live in an apocalyptic high-rise on the edge of a teeming sea. They fall into an empty elevator shaft. Down into nothing I can see. Down into dust. Down into the end of the dream.

In my nightmare, all of the men are turning away from me, toward other women and other rooms.

In my nightmare, I am not gay enough and the lesbians kick me out of the Dyke March.

In my nightmare, I am naked in a pool. I am thirteen and everyone is pointing at my few pubic hairs and budding breasts. I can't remember how I forgot my bathing suit. *You stupid, stupid girl.*

In my nightmare, my father pounds on tables and grabs my brother by the neck.

In my nightmare, I do nothing.

In my nightmare, I am underwater. I can breathe. I have gills like a fish.

In my nightmare, my gills stop working. I am too deep to make it back up to the top.

In my nightmare, there are guns lying around on tables and in the streets. They pick them up. They shoot them.

In my nightmare, there are crowds that smother us. Protests gone wrong. Police on horses that trample small bodies. Stampeding populations. Streams of refugees begging to get in and out.

In my nightmare, there is a border guard. We never have the right papers.

In my nightmare, I am my junkie uncle. I die on a bench in Golden Gate Park.

In my nightmare, my brother drives his SUV into a wall. His blood alcohol level is .225.

In my nightmare, I fall and fall and fall and fall. There is no bottom to it, no floor to catch me, no dirt to break me in half or rattle my bones awake.

My clock radio, set to NPR, turned on. Clipped British voice of the BBC News Hour. *We've seen global protests this year unlike anything since 1968—Mohamed Bouazizi sets himself aflame, Tahrir Square topples Mubarak, austerity protests in Greece and Italy, Chilean students march against privatized universities, Los Indignados clashing with riot police in Puerta del Sol, and most recently, looting in London after the police shooting of Mark Duggan.*

I turned off the radio and looked out the window. Across the park, gleaming cubes of glass stacked on top of one another, a crane, and a makeshift elevator. Construction workers standing on red metal beams, suspended above the park, their sure steps across a bright blue sky. More condos I could never live in.

I left the apartment to meet Mel in the fountain. We didn't speak. Not yet. It was too hot. My phone said ninety-eight degrees. I felt like a hungover lizard on a hot rock. I could barely flick my tongue. She nodded and I nodded back. We stepped into the ice-cold water and sat on the steps.

"Rough night?" she asked, squinting at my face. Cool enough now to talk.

"Maybe I fucked him because he'd been shot six times," I confessed. She knew I'd been on a date.

"Jesus, was it any good?" She had on a long, loose black tank dress, with the straps of a red bra peeking out. I admired how casually sexy she always looked.

"Mediocre. He couldn't stay hard. I was kinda checked out."

"Awww, boner problems."

"He had a limp too, I guess from the shooting, and it made me want to take care of him."

"With your pussy?"

"Yep."

"You've always had a soft spot for losers."

"I identify with them, and I don't have to try very hard."

There were ten-year-old boys running around the circular steps shooting each other with water guns, five-year-old girls in tutu bathing suits on their bellies in the shallow water, two homeless punk teenagers with a pit bull on a rope sprawled out on the fountain steps, and the steady camerawork of tourists from all over the world.

"How's your chef?"

"He's so hot, I want to lick him," Mel said. "It's dangerous."

I wiped the sweat from my upper lip and splashed water from the fountain onto my hair. The dog from the punk teenagers wandered over to us and licked the back of Mel's calf. We both petted her. She was white with black spots on her back and around her eye.

"You're like a little cow dog," I cooed.

"Do you want to come live with me?" Mel scratched behind her ears.

"She's the sweetest dog." The girl from the couple walked over to us. She had on cutoff Carhartt pants and a grubby neon-pink tank top. Her hair was dirty blond, matted, and clumped in parts and braided in others. She smelled like Deadheads and wet hay.

"What's her name?" Mel asked.

"Tipsy," the girl said. "You can't see it unless she walks, but one of her legs is shorter than the rest and it makes her look a little drunk."

The dog kept at the salty palm of my hand.

"Are you guys a couple?" The girl looked back and forth between us. We got that a lot. We'd had one night together in college, a drunken but fun accident that we processed for a couple of weeks, and decided not to repeat.

"Best friends," we singsonged. We'd been saying it for years.

"You live around here?" the girl asked, shielding her eyes from the sun. There was no getting rid of her.

"Yeah, I teach at the University," I said, waving in the direction of the buildings that lined the park. I didn't tell her that I lived in a dorm. It was always hard to explain. People sometimes thought I had a room like a student or that I was a dorm mother.

"I live in Brooklyn." Mel gave me that look, like, *Do we know this person?*

"I'm gonna go there someday. To study social work."

"It's a good school, but too expensive," I offered. I thought of my students who'd left school in the last year because they couldn't afford the $50,000-a-year tuition. There were the ones who stayed too, and got deeper into debt. I had graduate school friends who had defaulted on their student loans and were now mired in bad credit and harassing phone calls. I dreamed of defaulting, of channeling my monthly $557 payment toward Sasha's nonexistent college fund. Instead, I dutifully paid those evil twin bitch aunts, Sallie and Fannie Mae, on the second of every month.

"But everyone wants to go there," the girl countered.

"Hype. Branding." I shrugged. I couldn't get into my own ambivalence about teaching there. I was lucky to have my contract faculty position and to have avoided the fate of so many of my adjuncting friends, but I still lived paycheck to paycheck. I had believed so fervently in higher education in my twenties and thirties. Lately, I wasn't so sure.

"You got a dollar?" the girl redirected.

I shook my head. "I didn't bring my wallet." It was true.

Mel reached into her tote bag and gave her a crumpled dollar. Tip money.

"Now you can keep petting my dog."

Her boyfriend, in worn black jeans and a Dead Kennedys T-shirt, walked over to us, pulled out a flyer out of his back pocket, and handed it to us. I scanned it quickly: *The People's General Assembly! It's time for the people to meet and to take the bull by the horns! September 17th, Occupy Wall Street.*

"It's time for a revolution," he said, and lay back down on the steps of the fountain.

"The working class is notoriously resistant to revolution," Mel said, just to be a pain in the ass, I knew.

"This is going to be different," he said.

"Look!" The girl nudged my knee with the back of her hand and pointed at the horizon of the fountain. Tipsy and Mel looked up too. "A bride!"

"People still get married," Mel said as if it were a marvel.

The girl rolled on top of her boyfriend. He lifted one of his hands up and slid it into the back pocket of her shorts. She giggled and kissed him and then sprung back up like she was in chaturanga and he was her yoga mat. He growled at her and nipped at her neck. Tipsy barked too—excited or protective, I couldn't tell. He wrapped his big hand around the back of her neck and kept it there like a collar. She tried to shrug him off, but his hand stayed, locked in place. He looked older than her by maybe ten years. Still handsome, but tired around the eyes.

The bride was a glittery thing on a sunny day, and the tourists trained their phones on her. The new sliver of condos gleamed behind her—the perfect backdrop, like an old print magazine photo shoot. The condos were wedged between the new campus center and an old church. The juxtaposition of old and new was temporary. Soon, I guessed, that church would be gone too.

She wore a cream-colored satin flapper dress, vintage or made to look vintage, with a pillbox hat and a matching Mary Jane pump with a big buckle. The groom held her by the waist and beamed. He looked like a hedge-fund guy—white, with perfect teeth, a full head of slicked-back hair, and a chin cocked permanently up. He always got what he wanted and his latest acquisition was an artsy wife. Should I slip her a note or whisper in her ear, *This, him, it, cannot be the only thing you do*? Maybe this bride already knew that.

I imagined them fucking in front of one of the giant new windows of their condo. They just bought it. They paid in cash. It was all theirs. There was no furniture yet. No curtains. The decor would be her first real job as wife, but that would come later. I stared up at the window and toward a construction worker who was shouting at another worker in Spanish. I squinted until the workers got blurry and the couple became my real-estate porn. I saw her naked, except for her silly pillbox hat, and squatting above his face. Her nipples pink and upturned. His mouth, a perfect *O* of pleasure, while he ate her out. She reached back and pulled hard on his dick. He gasped with delight.

"September 17th. Occupy!" the guy in the Dead Kennedys T-shirt broke my bridal reverie. I looked up. They were leaving the fountain with their dog and backpacks. The girl squinted in the sun at me and I waved goodbye back.

"We'll be there!" I shouted. I was pissed off about Wall Street, the housing crisis, and student-loan debt, and I knew that Sasha was with her dad that weekend. *Why the hell wouldn't I go?* I thought.

"We will?" asked Mel.

THE WIVES

The wives were at work. They had jobs in publishing and marketing. One wife was a doctor. Another was a lawyer. The wives were stay-at-home moms. The wives were tired. The wives were so busy and so bored, and all at the same time. They worked their co-op shifts and they started co-op nursery schools. The wives were curious about the lives of other wives. The wives did not care about other wives. The wives wanted a different apartment or they wanted new tile in the bathroom. They definitely wanted laundry in the building if they couldn't have it in the apartment. Some wives wanted to move to Maplewood. The wives complained on the playground—mostly by the sandbox and at the kiddie swings. There was something about the repetitive motion that lulled them into revealing things. The wives had picnics in the park with their children on blankets with cut-up fruit. They put sunscreen on everything. They loved an outdoor concert and a glass of rosé! They demanded brunch! The wives were surprisingly fit, although most of them felt fat. Some wives were fifteen to twenty pounds overweight. The wives had their dreams. The wives were writing it all down—in notebooks or on the backs of receipts. A lot of the wives were writers who didn't make any money or teachers who made a little bit of money. Some of the wives were rich—they had trust funds or inheritances or parents who gave them down payments and cars and tuition for private elementary schools. The wives had their dreams. The wives loved their husbands, but they had crushes on their therapists or their baristas or one of the stay-at-home dads or the artisanal-cheese vendor from upstate who they saw at the farmer's market on Saturdays. Some of the wives were queer and missed their girlfriends. The wives were shy. The wives just couldn't shut up. The wives were on BuzzFeed or Facebook or Snapchat or whatever. The wives had their own stash of porn; some of it was still on DVDs. It was private. Some wives were worried all the time—about vaccines and benchmarks and climate change. The wives did yoga and Pilates. It was never enough. The wives wanted another baby. The wives were infertile. The wives did not have babies, but they thought they should. The wives were at home. Some were at bars. They had their suspicions, but they kept them quiet.

SCHOOL

"Can we get a cupcake after?" I held Sasha's hand as I walked her to camp. I'd been up since five a.m. packing her lunch, showering, getting us dressed, and planning for my first day of class. My semester always started a couple of weeks before her school year, and I never felt ready.

"Maybe, let's see."

"That means no."

"Maybe means maybe."

"Mama?"

"Yeah, doll."

"Can we live at the beach when we can't live in the dorm anymore?" she asked. "At Coney Island, there were those pink buildings with seahorses on them. I want to live there with a bunch of other kids." Sasha hated that she was the only six-year-old living in the dorm.

I remembered our last trip to Coney Island.

"Sasha, not so far out," I'd said as she got knocked over by a wave, sputtered, and came up. I grabbed her hand and moved her tangled hair off of her face. She insisted that she could swim, but her two years of being carried across the pool at the Fourteenth Street YMCA by various teenage swimming instructors had yielded little more than a scary fearlessness and an ability to put her face in the water and blow bubbles.

"I know!" she shouted, and leaped up against a wave with glee. "I am controlling the waves!" I walked out to my waist, a little past the breaking waves, with Sasha. We hit a still patch of ocean and settled into it. I watched sticks float by and then a stray condom wrapper. "Ewww," I said.

"Look, a bag of Goldfish." Sasha pointed to the stream of garbage that was now flowing toward us. I noticed a tampon applicator and an empty baggie, and I stepped back to avoid getting hit by a juice box. The lifeguards stood up on their giant chair deck and whistled for us all to come in. "Sash, come on, we gotta go."

Even with the garbage, I loved Coney Island. The steel girders of the Wonder Wheel, the swinging cars that made my stomach drop, the way the beach was packed full of every different kind of body and every color of skin, and the impromptu dance parties on the boardwalk.

"Maybe," I said. How to explain New York City real estate to a six-year-old. It can't be done. "I'm not sure where we'll live, but it's going to be awesome," I lied.

At the mouth of the playground where the counselors waited, I hugged her. "I love you!" I watched her start to draw with one of her camp friends and then rushed back to campus.

I WALKED INTO the brand-new classroom with its three walls of glass windows and a blond wood seminar table in the middle. I was sweaty. To the right, at eye level, I saw construction workers in their hard hats walking across a newly finished floor in one of the luxury condos. Two of them were unfastening a giant bathtub from the jaws of the crane. If I wanted to, I could wave. The front wall of windows faced the tops of the trees, and the left windows looked onto the red brick of the campus library. The room felt like a floating cube and the table a walkway into the sky. I was used to teaching in cramped rooms with giant stains on the carpet and mysterious metal ladders in the center that led to nowhere. The classroom-assignment gods had been kind to me for once. I placed my finger on the table to steady my vertigo thoughts.

"So fancy," I said to my students, who looked back at me nervously. First-year students. I'd have to teach them how to talk to each other and to me.

I sat down at the seminar table and pulled out my notebook. "Let's start with some writing about ourselves. We'll share it. Oh, and let's have nameplates."

For five minutes, they folded paper and wrote their names in markers and pens, both in giant and small letters, and looked nervously at each other, like *Is this right? Is this what we do in college?*

A young woman with red lips and long, dyed-black hair rolled her eyes at me. I eyed the nameplate she'd made out of Sharpie and a piece of notebook paper. Emma. I ignored the eye roll. Two young men in baseball caps stopped slouching and sat up. The international students, all clustered together, smiled at me and nodded.

"Describe the last time you got caught in the rain," I said. "Keep your pencil moving, no censoring yourself, no fixing grammar, just go."

They started to write. I started too, but a half-assed version in which I was both there and not there, moving my pen across the page and also writing nothing that mattered to me. I wrote their names over and over again, so that I could memorize them. Noah. Emma. Clara. Yun Hee. Hye Su. Ren. Miranda. Alexis. Sam. Aleem. Nailah. Seth. Noel. Fein Yen. Xue (Michael).

"Let's find a stopping place, and then hear just a sentence out loud from everyone. No disclaimers, no explaining, just read what you have on the page. Let's think of it as a trailer, like at the movies. You know, the best part," I said.

Some of them read slowly and quietly, while others were giggly, proud, or monotone. It was scary, I knew, and they all had their performances for showing off or hiding out.

Their writing was good. I asked them to jot down favorite images and we gathered them on the board. *I was in my car and blasting my favorite song. The sky turned purple and then dark gray. In India it rains for a month. My sandals squished from being soaked. The band played through the thunderstorm anyway. I watched the rain from my window in Portland. I held my brother's hand while he splashed through the puddles. He took my clothes off because they were wet and I asked him too. The drops on my arm were heavy. The rain turned out to be hail.*

I passed out an essay and waited for it to make its slow circle around the table, I stared out the giant glass window. The fountain and arch in the distance. The park filling up with college students making their way to class, nannies and their preschoolers, and still the drug dealers in the far corner. I looked at my students. When I started teaching, I was a nervous twenty-two-year-old graduate student; now they were closer to Sasha's age than mine. I knew they were technically adults, but they looked so scrubbed and kid-like to me sometimes.

"Let's read this out loud together, taking turns. Aleem, you start and then we'll just go around."

And then I saw her. A body in the air. A navy-blue dress. A flash of girlish hot-pink underwear. Brown hair. Black boots with the laces untied. A bright-yellow backpack still on her back. A young woman. Falling in front of our window. A blot against the blue-screen sky of our movie view. Then gone. Papers from a notebook falling slowly after her.

A couple of my students saw her too. I gasped and grabbed on to the table. The woman with the dyed-black hair, Emma, ran to the window.

"Oh my god!" she said. "She jumped. She fucking jumped."

Another student got out his phone and walked toward the window to take a picture.

"No, put that away," I said. "Don't look, maybe . . . don't," I stammered as a couple more students ran to the window. "No pictures, no!" I yelled. "Her parents can't see her that way," I lowered my voice to try to explain. Somebody started to cry. Small choking sounds. "My friend in high school did this last year." Her nameplate said Miranda.

I picked up my phone and dialed the number for campus safety. My hands were shaking. "I'm teaching in the new building and a body, a girl just jumped or fell in front of the building."

"An ambulance is on its way. Keep your students in the classroom and away from the windows," an officer barked into the phone and hung up.

"You guys, come away from the window, please," I said.

"Everyone says our school is a suicide school. Here and Cornell," said one of the guys in the baseball cap.

"On the first day?" another student said out loud to no one in particular. I looked at her nameplate. Yun Hee. She'd drawn a heart near the last *e.*

"It's lonely here," another student said. Fein Yen.

I walked close to the window and made useless waving gestures to move them away from it, but I didn't look down. I couldn't bear to see her. Ambulance sirens roared from down the street. Footsteps in the hallway. "Come on, you don't want to see this," I said, more at myself than them.

"This is the sixth student who has jumped in the last two years," another student said. I looked at her nameplate. Nailah. She was right. I'd been at faculty meetings where we used the word *epidemic.*

I remembered the other horrible New Yorker sky images I kept tucked away—the plane cutting through the blue sky to hit that tower while we all stared up in disbelief, and then the papers from those offices billowing out into the East River and over onto Cadman Plaza in Brooklyn. Lost memos from forgotten people. I squeezed my eyes shut to erase the overlapping images. *A plane is not a girl. These are different papers.* Still, there was the trauma of falling, of watching people fall, that would haunt us all forever.

I sat back down. I got everyone to sit down. We couldn't read the essay. What could we do? The image looped in my head. Her brown hair. The dress. Navy blue, flying up like a cape. The flash of pink underwear. The school-bus yellow of the backpack. The papers. Why had she taken her notebook? Why was she still wearing her backpack? I couldn't unsee it. I had no idea what to say.

"This is terrible," I managed.

A campus police officer opened our door. "We're going to evacuate this building using the fire escapes in the back. Everybody out!"

"What is the homework?" a student asked me as we filed out.

"Read that essay, I don't know," I snapped. "I'll write to you guys later today."

"Go back to your dorms or your next class," the campus police shouted at us as we filed out the back door and onto the street.

I walked numbly away from campus, toward a nearby café. How could I teach the rest of my classes? I thought of her parents getting the world's most horrible call and that I was always afraid one of my students would kill themselves. I thought of Sasha's little shoulder blades carrying her backpack and I almost walked to her camp to get her. *Stay close to me forever*, I wanted to say. I thought of my uncle, the image I'd created in my head as a kid, of him falling backward off a balcony into the cloudless California sky. *An accidental fall. She jumped. They jumped because they had no choice.*

In the café, I ordered a tea and sat there staring at it. I wrote to my other two classes and canceled them. I texted Aaron.

"I saw a student jump. Her body fell in front of my classroom window."

"Wtf? She okay?" he texted back.

"I seriously doubt it. She fell above us. I teach on the seventh floor."

"That's fucked up. I'm sorry," he texted.

I sipped my tea. "That class is ruined," he added.

"Traumatized."

"I'll give you a hug tomorrow at the playground."

I stared at the screen of my phone. I wanted him to drop what he was doing and come and get me, but he wasn't going to do that. He didn't have to anymore.

"Okay," I texted back.

THE HUSBANDS

The husbands were at work. The husbands were stay-at-home dads. The husbands were on BuzzFeed or a porn Tumblr. The husbands had iPads and Kindles. The husbands were in other rooms. The husbands wanted more fucking and less guilty blow jobs. The husbands went out too much or not enough, worked too late or didn't make enough money, had beards or no beards. The husbands weren't sure about the apartments—their square footage, their down payments, their rents. The husbands quit their jobs. The husbands were fired. Some got better jobs. Some didn't. The husbands took care of their babies. The husbands were terrified something would happen to their kids. They were afraid of words like "depression" and "bullying." One husband cleaned a toilet while another husband looked on and said, "Huh, so that's how you do it?" The husbands made dinner. They washed dishes. The husbands were tired of talking and of beach vacations. The husbands loved the beach! The husbands thought therapy was a waste of money, but went anyway. The husbands threw their children into the blue skies of all parks. The husbands rode their bikes and went to the gym. The husbands got fat because of artisanal beer and grass-fed sausage links. The husbands were bald. The husbands had a lot of hair, actually. The husbands were a great big mystery. The husbands had their dreams. They liked the idea of brunch more than the routine of it. The husbands ate all the dark chocolate in the back of the cupboard and they weren't sorry. The husbands got drunk. The husbands egged them on and ate them out. The husbands were waiting at home. Some knew. Some didn't.

THE VISITOR

And then my dean sent me an email, summoning me to his office.

In all of the years I spent in school—from age five when I learned how to hold a pencil to age thirty-three when I finished writing a boring book called a dissertation—no one had prepared me for the petty machinations of my dean. His power, his budgets, his grudges, his ability to crush joy and creativity, his refusal to give praise, and his love of Charles Dickens. I hadn't read *Hard Times* since high school. Fuck did I know?

My last boss in graduate school, in the program where I learned everything I knew about teaching, was an occasionally punitive, but mostly brilliant daddy type, who believed writing essays was a path to spiritual and artistic awakening. He taught us to have ideas, praised our hard work, and made us feel like we mattered. He also believed in the power of women and rewarded us for speaking up. He wasn't a feminist, but he liked what women had to say and he wanted us at the table. It had ruined me for the rest of academia.

"Can you stop by my office this afternoon? My assistant, Elsie, has put you on the calendar."

After I left the café, I walked through the park, around the patch of concrete where she'd landed. The ambulance had taken her body away, but her blood was still there, staining the sidewalk. A crowd around the police tape. Candles and stuffed animals already forming a makeshift altar. Maybe she hadn't known it, but this park was already a graveyard. In the 1800s, prisoners were hanged from the branches of trees and buried where their bodies fell, and before it was a park it was a potter's field. The remains of almost twenty thousand bodies were underneath us.

I was sure he'd called me in to talk about her. I was a witness. Maybe she was one of our program's students. Maybe he wanted to make sure my students and I were okay.

"I have some bad news for you," he said, shutting his office door. He was in his midsixties, gray hair, gray expensive baggy suits, gray-white skin, all of him white cement, the color of the western New York sky I'd run away from. I'd heard he'd once been part of the Berkeley protests in the sixties, but now he pounded on podiums and called us traitors at faculty meetings when we asked for a living wage.

"I know about the girl," I said, staring at the collection of ancient pots he kept arranged on his windowsill. His was the only office in our program with windows.

He waved his hand in the air. "Not that, but it's a tragedy and a mess for the PR people."

"My students and I saw her jump." I pretended like I didn't hear the PR thing.

"I'm sorry you had to see that. My door is always open for students who need to talk."

I nodded, like I believed him. I'd recently seen him on the reclining bikes at the gym, pedaling slowly and reading the *New York Review of Books.* I was on the elliptical machine, listening to "Ms. Fat Booty" by Mos Def. We'd wisely ignored each other.

"It's about your apartment." He paused, picked up a book on his desk, and moved it to another spot.

My heart did a little flip kick turn. *Oof.*

"The University has decided to cancel the Profs in Residence Program. They need the apartments for more dorm rooms. They've asked me to tell you that you have to move out by the end of the year."

"But I am supposed to be there for another two years. Sasha is in school in the neighborhood. I don't have anywhere else to go. That's just three months from now." My heart beat fast against my rib cage.

"I know it's a surprise, and not something you planned for."

"Can you get me a faculty apartment in the towers?" I asked even though I knew it was pointless.

"You know those are reserved for tenured faculty. I can't do that." He put his hands up. *It's out of my control.* He might as well have made a *whatever* sign at me.

"This is bullshit," I said. "Whenever you call me in here it's for something awful. It's never good. Once it was to tell me that I couldn't talk with other pregnant women about maternity leave. Another time, it was to reject my proposal for funding for a journal of student writing. All I asked for was five hundred dollars! For students! Last year, I came in and asked for a raise, and you told me that the janitors deserve a union but not the contract faculty." I'd never said this much to him in one sitting. I spoke up at faculty meetings, but rarely face-to-face. Mostly, I tried to avoid him.

"Stevie, I don't run the program that gives you that apartment," he said.

I grabbed my bag. My face flushed with rage. I wanted to pick up one of his precious pots and smash it to bits. "They didn't give it to me. It was a job I applied for and I applied four years in a row until they hired me."

"It was a lucky perk for you," he said.

"It's an extra job I do so that I can have housing," I said it again.

"You had a good run." He picked up another book and looked at the spine. I took that to mean, *Get out. We're done.*

I slammed the door on my way out. *Temper. Temper.* I tried to control myself, but failed. I had to get out of the office and back outside before I burst into tears.

I cried as I walked back to my apartment. I kept my head down in the elevator, so that I wouldn't have to talk to students. I closed the door to my apartment and turned on the radio. For comfort? To hear another voice? To drown out the voices in my head?

Radical Islamic sect Boko Haram claims responsibility for a carbomb attack in Abuja, Nigeria's capital. Twenty-three people were killed. In Libya, rebels have taken most of the west of the country, including Tripoli, where hundreds were killed. There are reports of mass executions.

The newscaster burbled on. I stared past the water towers on the other side of the park. I needed to pick up Sasha soon and pull myself together.

The faraway places. The distant killing. The too-close death. I had a headache. I felt useless and complicit. A passive listener of the news.

In my nightmare, we are paperless, wandering, searching.

In my nightmare, the children get separated from their parents.

In my nightmare, there are camps everywhere.

In my nightmare, there are bombs.

In my nightmare, we are alone.

In my nightmare, I am not a good mother.

In my nightmare, I do not find shelter for us.

In my nightmare, I cannot free other people's babies from cages.

In my nightmare, I am falling, always falling.

In my nightmare, I cannot reach her and she falls too.

In my nightmare, there is never a net.

In my nightmare, I am the phoenix of anxiety and worry, and I destroy us all.

Something landed on the ledge of my window and I got up to look. A hawk. I took a couple of steps closer to the window, and she raised her wings as if she were about to take off again. I stepped back and she lowered her wings and stared through the screen at me. Brown-gray feathers, hooked beak, giant claws, and a body that was easily a foot tall. The mythical University hawks. I'd heard about them. Some biology professor had even set up a hawk cam. They had their own Tumblr.

Rudy, my cat, slunk in from the bedroom to let loose a guttural wail. The hawk turned her precise, predatory eyes calmly to him.

"She'll eat you," I said and scooped him up.

I took a half step forward. She flapped her wings again, but didn't take off. There was a dead rat in one of her talons, bleeding out. Long tail, white sharp teeth, and delicate rat paws. The second halo of blood I'd seen that day.

We stared at each other for a full five minutes. Me holding my live, squirming cat and her clutching her dead, twitching rat.

"Hello," I finally managed.

She blinked at me, and then she gripped her rat and flew away across the park.

CUPCAKE

Sasha licked the white buttercream frosting off the top of her giant red velvet cupcake. Of course, we were having a treat that day! If I'd taught my daughter nothing else in her six years, it was that sugar was a salve to all wounds. I'd eaten mine in the time it took Sasha to get hers out of the bag.

"How was camp?" I was still in my teaching outfit, sweaty in a dress and uncomfortable bootie heels. My ankles felt wobbly on the tilting Essex Street sidewalk where I'd picked her up.

"We went to Funtopia!" She beamed at me. "I killed six of my friends in laser tag." I'd been to Funtopia. I'd never had any kind of fun there.

"That was today?" Should it bother me that I didn't even know my kid had been to Queens and back in one teaching day? I had nothing useful to say about her as the budding killer of her closest friends. I told myself it was a video game and not live-action paramilitary training. How else was I going to make it through parenting in America?

"What did you do today, Mama?" she asked.

Oh, I watched a girl kill herself and I found out we're getting kicked out of our home, I thought, but said instead, "I met some of my students today. They seem cool."

I often wondered, *When is it possible to tell your kids about the shit you're dealing with?* Mostly you have to lie until you can't lie anymore and the world seeps in and shows its ugly business. I thought of my own mother telling me the secrets and lies of her marriage to my father at age thirteen, as I sat rapt on the toilet while she took a bath. I felt so special and lucky to be chosen as confidant. It took me twenty years to realize it was a trap.

Privilege was the shelter of stupidity, of not knowing, or having enough money to hide the world away, to damp it down, to exist above it all. Until. Until.

The sidewalk tilted and I stopped. Gray around the edges of my vision. New York finally was getting rid of me. I didn't want to go. I took Sasha's hand to steady myself.

"Can we find a bench?" I said to the remaining small tunnel of vision I had and to Sasha's hand which was warm and alive, tethering me to this concrete.

"There's one!" Sasha led me to one, and we sat down.

"I just need to rest for a minute," I said, and closed my eyes. I kept hold of her hand. She didn't wriggle free.

I'd come to understand that a panic attack is your heart when it hates you. It's a flashing light in the middle of the night that says, *Wake up! Wake up! Wake up!* It's all of the things you put on top of it to try to stop it: the booze, the lovers, the fucking, the husbands and wives, the babies. A panic attack is your fortress of shit, the moat of consumable goods that you wrap around yourself like a mink stole or an ankle monitor or a chastity belt or Spanx—all coming undone and spooling out away from you and then snapping back in your face. It's what your lungs do when they don't believe you because you smashed and stacked a bunch of feelings on top of feelings and they got out and collapsed like those giant Jenga games in certain bro bars. A panic attack says, *I can't, I can't, I can't.* It's not a recipe or an equation. It's the galaxy of blood in you surging backward to say, *Fuck no, fuck this, fuck!* That buzzing buzzing buzzing sound that David Lynch made with the cut-off ear in the beginning of *Blue Velvet.* It's your chemicals having a tantrum. Kicking and screaming on the street in broad daylight. It's you alone as a kid at three or five or eight or twelve in some small place telling yourself, *I'm safe, I'm safe, I'm safe*, when you're almost certain that you're not.

The sidewalk tilted more and the bench too. I thought of the things my therapist said and the pills I sometimes took to make them stop. They were in my kitchen cupboard. I kept hold of Sasha's hand. I had her, I did.

"Should we call Daddy?" she asked, small voice. We'd been here before.

"No, I'm okay," I lied, and we sat there until it stopped and the gray backed off and I was steady enough to get us back home.

HORSERADISH

Mel ran down the hallway that led to the freezer. During prep, she'd forgotten to bring up the locally brined cocktail onions and home-made horseradish that were ingredients in the new cocktail menu she was trying to memorize.

I hate fucking cocktail onions and I hate the douchebag that asked for that drink, she thought as she darted past Omar the dishwasher. "Guapa!" he called after her. She flipped him the bird and he laughed.

She leaned hard on the freezer door and kicked through.

Carmine and Greta the hostess. He had his hands firmly on both pockets of her tight white jeans and his lips on top of hers. Greta turned toward Mel and blushed.

"Whoa, okay," Mel said. Part of her wanted to close the door, unsee them, and pretend it never happened, and another part of her wanted to join in. Didn't she kinda want to fuck Greta too? Didn't everyone at the restaurant?

Greta reminded Mel of her first girlfriend in college, Mari. They'd been on the swim team together. Mari was a diver who could jack-knife her body ten feet in the air, and unlike Mel and the rest of the swimmers, she was petite, more curvy than lean, and had major tits that Mel couldn't help but stare at in the locker room. She wasn't a particularly good diver, but by that point Mel had given up on being a good swimmer. She and Stevie started hosting drunken dinner par-ties in the $300-a-month house they rented in their upstate college town. Somehow, they lured Mari over. She showed up in a *Ladies of the Canyon* witchy boots and caftan getup, and brought a bottle of wine instead of the usual box or jug.

"The grapes for this wine grew in the shade on a Tuscan hillside," she said as she breezed into the kitchen. Stevie rolled her eyes as she pulled a soggy quiche out of the oven, but Mel listened and let Mari pour a little in the mug she was using as a wine glass so they could both sniff it before taking a delicate sip.

"Shady?" Mel joked, and Mari wrinkled her nose. Mel read this to mean, *You're cute like a bunny. I will pet you later.*

That night, Mel found out Mari never wore underwear, and that her mother had a ton of money which was making her feel sad and oppressed. She played along. She'd grown up comfortably middle class, but this was more like offshore money, Swiss bank accounts, epically global.

"There's a trust fund she set up for me, but I can only use it for necessities right now," Mari complained, and Mel put her finger inside her to make her stop talking. She smelled like chlorine and oranges, and she came so fast that Mel didn't know what to do, so she made her come again, this time with her mouth. Within a month, they'd broken up. Mari was jealous that Mel lived with Stevie. Mel decided that Mari had no sense of humor. Still, they were out about their relationship, a first for both of them. They told the swim team they were girlfriends. They even held hands while walking through the quad, which made a couple of frat boys turn and stare.

And then Mel's stepmother called and cried on the phone. Her older sisters called too.

"It's Daddy," they said, and she hated them for still calling him that.

She stopped talking to Mari. She holed up with Stevie and drank tequila straight from the bottle she kept under her bed and did her homework and fucked random guys who she picked up at two a.m. in downtown bars. Six months later she met an international student from Germany, Andre, who she fell in love with and followed to graduate school in New York. For five years with Andre, she tried to pretend she wasn't bisexual.

Like Mari, Greta the hostess had that same rich, bored, haughty look that Mel sometimes still found alluring. She liked to make those girls messy with desire. Wet and open and fallen from their safe perches. If people wore T-shirts that summed up their deepest subconscious thoughts, Greta's would read, *I'm slumming it here because it makes me feel alive. Fuck,* Mel thought, *maybe mine would say that too.*

Carmine raised his eyebrows at her. "See, you're not the only one who's complicated."

"Mel!" the manager shouted at her from the kitchen. She'd left the bar unstaffed.

"Fuck, he's going to rip me a new one. I need the cocktail onions and the stupid horseradish." Mel gestured a *gimme* fist at Carmine and Greta. "Come on, help me!"

"We'll help you if you give us a kiss?" Carmine said.

Mel looked behind her to see if the manager was coming. She let the door slam shut. "You're both going to get me fired." She looked at Greta, her unlined skin and pore-free nose, her pouty, perfect lips. She wanted to bite them. She imagined cupping her hands under each of Greta's tits while she put her tongue in Carmine's mouth.

"Let's make a Greta sandwich?" Carmine egged Mel on.

"Do you like to be in the middle?" Mel asked, taking a step closer.

"Yeah, I do," Greta's voice got huskier.

Mel slid her hands into Greta's jean pockets and kissed the back of her neck while staring at Carmine. Carmine kissed Greta again and then Mel, while Mel slid her hands up around Greta's tits. "Is this okay?" she asked her.

Greta moaned, "Yes," and Mel imagined how wet she might be and that she probably wore a thong. She wanted to peel it off with her teeth.

Greta bent down in front of Carmine, her shoulder brushing past the crotch of his chef's whites, and picked up the jar of homemade horseradish for Mel. She kissed her full on the mouth and said, "Break's over."

Carmine took a step back and handed Mel the cocktail onions. "This is my favorite restaurant," he said, and the women giggled.

"What the fuck?" The manager yanked hard at the door and sent them all scurrying back to their stations with their heads down.

"You gotta fix that door," Mel called over her shoulder.

Back at the bar, she made the drink for the douchebag, who actually turned out to be quite sweet.

"Get lost back there?" He nodded over her shoulder toward the kitchen. He looked about fifty. Still had his hair. Fit. A not-stupid shirt.

"You have no idea." Mel laughed.

He left her a ten for a tip and took his drink to sit by the open wall of windows.

Mel wiped down the counter and found places for the horseradish and cocktail onions. She stared through the open wall of windows at the brownstones across the street. There was a kid and a nanny on a stoop and a sign for a psychotherapist's office.

She remembered Jenny not speaking in their last session, shut down and pissed off. Mel digging nails into the flesh of her own arm to keep from screaming, *It's not about you!*

"Even as you open up the relationship, you'll need to think about your own intimacy, how to preserve it, how to grow it," their therapist said.

"How?" Jenny and Mel asked in unison, their one moment of agreement for the whole session.

"There are lots of ways—things that are special for just the two of you. Dinners. Sexual experiences you share. Some couples like sex toys."

"How come you never give me a chance Mel?" the manager interrupted her therapy memory and leaned over the bar.

"What? I'm gay." Mel laughed to brush him off. He was the owner's son, an Adderall addict and a control freak, mercurial and difficult, but basically harmless. At least, that's what Mel told herself.

"Not always," he said.

"You're my boss." She laughed again, trying still to keep it light.

"So?"

"So, no."

"You'll change your mind," he said. He was barely thirty. Gym body. Wavy brown hair, the requisite hipster beard, a bump on his nose like somebody once broke it. She served his eighteen-year-old girlfriend silly cosmopolitans and appletinis.

"You think so?" she said to the air.

He'd already walked back to the kitchen to bother someone else.

NOTES

"It's your job to make the money and mine to score," Butch said as he hugged Johanna that morning underneath the cluster of tall pines by the northwest corner of the park.

"Scoring is easy," Johanna complained.

"No, making money is easy when you're as pretty as you are," Butch countered.

"That's not the point." She tried another angle. "Shared wealth. No division of labor. Workers have no assigned gender roles."

"Why did I teach you so much?" Butch pulled her closer. She felt his hard-on through his jeans. "It's hot when you talk like a Marxist."

"I just want to do different things. Why can't we make art and sell it or play instruments like the banjo and bass couple?" Johanna pulled away and felt for the top of Tipsy's head.

"They are not homeless drug addicts like we are," Butch pointed out.

"I am not an addict." Johanna still believed she was dabbling in whatever Butch did because he copped and fixed for her.

"I know, baby." Butch paused. He could tell she was testy and he was already feeling sick. He spent a lot of time getting her to work, and it made him tired. Sometimes he dreamed of finding a rich girl, someone who could take care of him. Still, he'd never forget the first time he'd seen Johanna, thumb out on Route 17, wearing ripped jeans and a crop top, with a ridiculous sign that said, *California or Bust?* He convinced his then-bandmates to pull over their rusted van and pick her up. It didn't matter that, at first, they'd passed her around. It didn't matter that she was always willing. He still fell in love with her. "You're right, we need to make changes. But for now, it's just a fact that you can make double what I make in an hour, so let's just do this so we can party, okay?"

"We could steal some instruments?" Johanna pushed.

"Damn it." Butch sat up on his elbows and glared at her. Sometimes he thought she just needed a good smack.

"Fine, whatever." Johanna found an old piece of cardboard in the garbage and made a new sign with the Sharpie she kept in her pocket. It was the only working tool she and Butch had if you didn't count their bodies, which lately she didn't.

Down on my luck. Lost my way. Anything helps, she wrote.

She found a busy walkway near the new construction and sat down with Tipsy. She tried to make eye contact with each person who passed.

"You got a dollar?" she asked them. "You got a dollar?" she asked them a hundred times until she had enough.

Tipsy barked and lunged for a pigeon. Johanna stood up and saw something falling out of the corner of her eye. Fabric, a blanket, maybe; no, a boot and arms in the air. It was a girl. Hurtling. Fast. Down. Down. Down. Down. Down. Down. Down. Down. Eight stories. She counted. Long brown hair flying up around her face. Dark-blue dress against a light-blue sky. Black boots. Laces in the air. *She looks like an inkblot.*

Her body hit the ground just seventy-five feet away. A sickening crash like a pile of wood hitting the floor of the nearby construction site. Johanna gasped. Tipsy barked. She took a couple steps closer. One of the girl's legs was twisted at an ugly angle. A trickle of blood pooling around her head like a crown in a religious painting. Papers falling slowly after her. A man in a suit rushed over, took a pulse, called an ambulance on his cell phone.

Johanna felt a lump in her throat and watched the papers still falling like tissues in the wind. The girl—*the woman*, she corrected herself—wasn't much older than her. Johanna stared at her yellow backpack. Her dress had gathered around her waist. The creamy tops of her thighs. Hot-pink underwear. Johanna couldn't look away.

Someone should cover her thighs, Johanna thought, but she couldn't go any closer. A siren wailed and then another. A cop showed up.

"Move back! Move back!" he shouted.

Johanna pulled at Tipsy's rope. He was sniffing everything, barking still.

Another cop. Walkie-talkie static and noise. The papers still falling. One landed close to her foot. Tipsy stepped on it and barked louder. She grabbed the piece of paper off the ground and shoved it into her pocket without looking at it. *A souvenir? A clue? A suicide note?*

She looked around. Nobody had seen her. The two cops were busy stringing yellow police tape in a large square around the girl's body.

The ambulance wailed to a halt in front of the nearest entrance, and she walked north to find Butch.

KICKSTARTER

"You just can't unsee it," Aaron said. We sat on a bench in Washington Square Park, staring off into the distance at Sasha who was swinging, kicking, and dangling from the rope monkey bars. The crane from the condo construction cast a wide shadow over the playground.

"We're going to have to talk about it," I said. "We have to process it as a class. I can't pretend that a girl didn't commit suicide in front of our class." I squinted behind my insomnia headache. I was up at four a.m. with a panic jolt. The girl falling through the sky, and me behind her trying to reach the hem of her dress. No parachute. No strings. And then the voice, my ego I guessed, that whisper-mouthed my fears to me while I slept. *You have no plan, no savings, and no place to live. The rental market is brutal and it's only getting worse. You could lose your job at any moment. You don't have tenure. You're not going to make it. You'll have to leave New York City and all of your friends and move back to western New York with your family.* And then the voice flipped like it was the B side of a 45. Same artist. Different tune. *Shut the fuck up. You're fine. There are homeless people everywhere and you have no right to be afraid.*

"You're good at processing." Aaron smirked at me, referring to all of the talking I made us do before we separated.

"Shut up," I said.

"You're still cute when you get mad at me."

"I'm not cute!"

"You're going to be okay," Aaron said, sensing my fear. I'd texted him the night before about the apartment. "You're the toughest, most resourceful person I know."

"Is that why we're still married?"

"Don't be like that."

"I have to start looking for apartments," I said.

"Realtors won't show you anything until a month before," Aaron said.

"God, I love the New York rental market." I stared up at the crane looming over the playground. "I hate those things," I said. "They fall on unsuspecting New Yorkers and kill us."

"Smart to have it hanging over a bunch of babies," Aaron said. "I went to Kickstarter headquarters yesterday."

"How come?"

"For the Antic. I went with Tomas so we could take a tutorial on how to raise money more effectively."

"Really?" I marveled at all of the things Aaron could do now that we were separated. He'd started an event space, a writers' room, with several twentysomething poets that had gotten a lot of attention. I hadn't visited, but Sasha had told me there was a printing press, which I assumed in six-year-old-girl-speak meant a copy machine. I was wrong. They found a working letterpress, and they were offering free letterpress classes. I was ashamed to tell anyone that such a thing made me wildly jealous. Did I want to take the class or teach it? Did I wish I owned my own letterpress or did I long to be part of Aaron's cool, hip thing? All of the above. Antic's existence made me accept that Aaron could do lots of things I hadn't believed he could, and that my enraged wife's view of him had been wrong. Or we'd held each other back. Equally painful, probably true.

A couple months ago, he'd texted me, "I just cleaned the tub." I had no idea why he was telling me this, so I texted back, "Cool." He'd been living on his own for six months in an East Village sublet with a claw-foot tub in the kitchen, a New York City that barely existed anymore.

"No, for the first time! I'm sorry I never did that when we lived together. It's hard," he texted back.

"Thanks for saying that." It meant something, these admissions of guilt and sorrow at our married selves.

"It's in Greenpoint. It's so beautiful, like light everywhere and open. No cubicles. I want to work there," Aaron continued.

I thought of Aaron leaving our department with its tight little walls, bad art, and bitter meetings. I wanted to get out too, but didn't want him to go first.

"Mama! Mama! Mama!" Sasha shouted urgently at me while dangling between two rope bars. Her fingers loosened, she fell to the faux grass in a heap, and then looked up. "Did you see? Did you see?"

I gave her a thumbs-up and Aaron shouted, "Do it again!" Between us, we had what we alternately referred to as the "Daddy bag" or the "Mommy bag" depending on whose apartment Sasha was headed to. It had a small mess of items in it that could not be duplicated—Tony, the stuffed fish who Sasha had slept with since birth; the prairie skirt that Sasha wore every week the second it came out of the laundry; and the Hello Kitty diary with a lock where she kept her lists (Birthday Party List, Friends and Enemies List, Castle Contents List).

"It would be fun to be part of something new that paid well." I looked over at Sasha, who had abandoned the rope monkey bars and was squatting near a pile of leaves. "Worm house construction."

"Could be for squirrels." Aaron took my hand, squeezed it, and held it, rubbing his big thumb along the inside of my palm. I looked down at our clasped hands. I missed his skin against mine.

"Don't say anything, Stevie," he said, as if he knew I'd ruin it by talking.

When we met, he had a beat-up Toyota Tercel, faded red from too many days parked in the San Diego sun, where he'd spent two aimless summers managing a youth hostel before he started grad school. He'd once said those were the happiest, saddest days of his life. He was lonely, but every week a new crop of travelers came to the hostel. He took naps on the beach and read books behind the hostel front desk. I remembered the electric jolt I felt when we first met, the drives we took to the grocery store or out to Coney Island, how even the simplest errand was magical with him.

Sasha ran over to us, carrying something in her hands. I thought it would be an old barrette or a hair tie, the usual junk that she picked up and wanted to take home.

"What did you find, doll?" Aaron asked and let go of my hand.

"It's medicine." Sasha set her lips straight. Serious.

We peered into her hands. A pile of pills. A bunch of leaves. A stash.

I knew at night this park still belonged to the homeless and the dealers, so the pile of pills in the playground didn't totally surprise me. More than anything, it seemed like a dumb hiding place.

"Whoa, honey, good job." Aaron looked around at the toddlers crawling through the fake grass. We came early to avoid the older kids who hogged the monkey bars and pissed Sasha off. It was 9:30 a.m. Soon all these toddlers would go home for their morning naps. I remembered those precious naps. Writing. Fucking. Whatever Aaron and I could squeeze in. Mostly chores. I wished there had been more fucking.

Aaron took the pills into his hand. "Sash, you saved those toddlers' lives."

Sasha beamed and then skipped away back to her worm fort. I followed and scanned the ground for more pills. Nothing that I could see.

I sat back down on the bench and peered at the pills with Aaron.

"They're definitely prescription."

"That looks like Percocet."

"We could sell these."

"Or just take them."

"You're going to throw those away, right?" A dad had seen it all and wandered over. He looked all business. A baseball cap. Baggy jeans. A big sports logo T-shirt. Like he threw money at strippers sometimes and had once been excited about cigar bars.

"Yep, just trying to figure out what they might be," Aaron said, and walked over to the garbage can.

"Fucking city," the bossy dad muttered. "You guys live here?"

"I do," I said. "He lives in the East Village."

"Oh, I thought you were married," the dad said. "You look married."

"We were," I said.

"We are," Aaron called over from the garbage can. Was he feeling possessive or just like it was none of this guy's business? I shot him a *WTF?* look, which he ignored. The dad frowned at us. Clearly, we were confusing.

"We're moving into one of those condos, and we're looking to make friends. I mean we haven't moved in, the construction is slow as hell, and probably even slower now that that girl jumped, but we come around on the weekends from Tribeca to try to get the feel of the neighborhood."

I didn't want to tell him that we would never be friends, and that the only married people I cared about lately were gay or about to be divorced.

"The feel is mostly drunk college students," I said. "With some old-school NYC park shit thrown in."

"I figured," he said, and leaned in closer to me. "Did you know the girl who jumped? I heard she was having an affair with a professor and she couldn't handle it and *poof.*"

I hated the way he said *poof,* like she was a magic trick. "I didn't know her," I said.

"I teach in the law school at the University. This is a faculty building. Well, for law-school faculty, and the president nabbed the penthouse apartment."

"Tenured faculty," I clarified.

"Not sure about that." The dad looked confused. He shoved his hands into his big jean pockets.

I pretended I didn't hear him. I didn't feel like explaining the elaborate class system that made up university life in the twenty-first century. Adjuncts at the bottom, unionized but so broke many were applying for food stamps; contract faculty like Aaron and me, who made just enough money to eke by as long as we had other jobs on the side, like mine in the dorm; and tenured faculty who made double what we made and had access to faculty housing in the four towers just south of the park, and now apparently this new sliver of luxury condos. For the most part, tenured faculty wouldn't be caught dead living with students in a dorm. I guess, soon, I wouldn't be either.

"Oof." He darted away to scoop up his toddler girl who'd smashed heads with another kid. Each kid howled with pain.

"God, two is the stupidest age." Aaron came back from the garbage can and we sat on the bench again. I didn't tell him what the guy said to me—I didn't want to ruin his day.

"The worst—no civilization or humanity. Pure id."

"Falling and crying all day long."

I saw the punk homeless couple from the fountain walking down the path across from the playground. They were moving slowly, their packs heavy on their backs. The man's mouth shaped in a shouting grimace. The girl two feet behind, head down, taking it or checked out, I couldn't tell, and the dog limping two more feet behind her. They reminded me of some biblical pilgrimage. A punk update on the holy family. Trying to find shelter. Their dog was their baby Jesus.

She looked over toward the playground, spotted me, and raised her arm in a slow arc of a wave.

I waved back. The guy didn't see me.

"Who are they?" Aaron asked.

"I met them in the fountain. They invited me to a protest." I remembered her pinned eyes and slurred speech. "I bet those were their drugs."

I felt around in the bottom of my purse and pulled out one of the flyers I'd been given.

Aaron brushed off the sand that lived in the bottom of my purse. "You going?"

"Why not? If nothing else, I can take pictures for Youth in Revolt."

"Maybe you can kick that bull in the balls while you're at it. Fucking late capitalism."

"It's killing us all."

"Except for that guy." Aaron raised his eyes in the direction of the dad who'd been talking to us. He'd placed his squirming kid on his shoulders while his wife packed up their thousand-dollar stroller and matching diaper bag. "He's doing great."

"Yep, he's totally winning."

BECAUSE

Because there was an air mattress. Because he asked me to lie down. Because I was fucked up. Because it was four a.m. Because I was a vortex of need. Because he kept touching me. Because he knew what he was doing. Because I was forty. Because of my shitty father. Because I was alone in my marriage. Because of what he said. Because of how he tasted. Because he was new. Because he didn't know anything about me. Because he couldn't seem to tell that I was a mother. Because when I told him, he didn't care. Because I wanted to feel alive. Because someone wanted me. Because I was desperate. Because I was a bad person. Because I wanted to be punished. Because I thought it would be a wake-up call. Because I read the statistics on cheating and learned that women did it even more than men. Because, therefore it was biological and inevitable. Because of Dan Savage. Because of my best friend, Mel. Because the couples therapy wasn't working. Because someone finally tried. Because I was at a bar. Because of the shots. Because of that one bump of blow. Because I knew what I was doing. Because I didn't. Because I had always identified with Anna Karenina and Madame Bovary. Because sometimes I pretended I was in a novel. Because sometimes this worked. Because I was bored. Because of the way his face felt against my breasts. Because he touched me. Because he didn't ask. Because he didn't find me surprising. Because he acted like I belonged. Because it was close to five a.m. Because Mel was asleep in the other room. Because nobody stopped me. Because my husband didn't care if I came home. Because I knew if I did, he'd ignore me and roll away from me in the bed. Because for too long he acted like nothing was wrong. Because he was depressed. Because I was depressed. Because we were always broke. Because we were overwhelmed as parents. Because of the miscarriage. Because of the IVF treatments, which turned sex into a commodity and a lab report. Because I was tired. Because it was dark and then it was light.

BAD GIRL

I hurried through the aisles of CVS and piled the stuff I needed into my arms as Sasha flip-flopped behind me—a jumbo box of tampons, hair dye, condoms, Midol, and tissues. *Can't spend more than fifty bucks*, I reminded myself. I'd have to put something back. I slid the condoms back onto the shelf, hoping Sasha wouldn't get curious and ask me what they were. *Did I really have to choose between debilitating cramps and safe sex? Um, yes.* I turned into the cat-supply aisle and Sasha trailed behind.

"Sweetie, can you carry the litter? We just need a few things before the students come over." We'd said goodbye to Aaron at the playground. Our big activity for the rest of the day was hosting a snack hour for students in the dorm.

She pulled it up by one end and wrapped her arms around it. "I got it," she said as it slid out down onto the floor. The bag miraculously didn't break open.

"Grab it honey?" I said. "Mama can't. I'm carrying too much."

"Why do you talk about yourself that way?" Sasha asked.

"What way?"

"Like why do you say, 'Mama can't,' instead of '*I* can't'?" she asked as she hoisted the bag back up toward her nonexistent hip.

"I don't know. It's something I did when you were a baby. Should I stop?"

I felt attached to this third-person construction. It allowed me to comment on my own mothering from a distance.

"No, it's just weird."

"Good weird or bad weird?" I asked.

"Both," Sasha said. "This bag is too heavy."

In the aisle next to us, I heard giggling and then a dramatic "Shhhh!" A dog barked and then whined.

Sasha looked up at me. "There's a dog in here?"

A woman's voice: "You weren't there. You didn't see her hit the ground. It was awful, but I couldn't look away. Her leg was twisted at this terrible angle and her skirt had flown up. I wanted to fix her underwear, but I couldn't go any closer because of the blood. You know how I feel about blood. The cops came and they started to yell at us to move away, and I thought 'Fuck you pigs!' but I didn't say anything."

"Baby, baby, let's get out of here." I recognized their voices. The punk couple I saw everywhere now.

"Just let me put the cough syrup down my pants and then later, I can drink it and forget what I saw," she said.

"You're too fucking loud," he said.

"Let's go pay." I pulled at Sasha's shirt to move her forward.

"He said *fuck*," she whispered at me.

"I know, it's just a word."

"A treat?" Sasha asked as we stood in line to pay.

"A small thing."

Sasha dropped the litter at my feet and brought back a king-size Snickers. I shook my head no. "Regular size." She came back with a giant bag of Starburst.

"Still too big."

She held up a Hershey's bar. "Perfect."

The dog barked again. I remembered her name was Tipsy.

"You can't have a dog in here," a CVS worker said to them.

I looked back down the aisle. I both wanted to talk to them and not. We'd both been witnesses to a girl in transit, passing out of this world and into another. I'd seen her fall from the sky and she'd seen her make contact with the earth. Somehow, I felt, this connected us.

The couple emerged from the privacy of their aisle and spilled into the front of the store near the line of us who were waiting to pay.

"She's my service animal," she complained, but she and the guy allowed the worker to herd them gently out of the store. Before she left, she turned around and flashed me the peace sign. I smiled back. *She must have gotten her cough syrup*, I thought with some misplaced anti-capitalist pride. During my first year of college, Mel and I got off on setting up shoplifting challenges for each other. I'd been the expert at stealing condoms from drugstores. I took them out of the box and hid them in my underwear. I was careful to always buy something when I lifted something. It had been a thrilling year of pranks that ended when I got caught at the grocery store stealing garlic. The butcher, who must have seen me from behind the two-way mirror, thought I was much younger than I was and dragged me to the front of the store by the ear.

"You see this girl," he said into the store's intercom, interrupting the sleepy shopping of several upstate mothers. "She's a thief and she's not allowed to shop here." The women stared at me blandly, bored by my petty crimes.

But it worked. He'd shamed me. I never stole again.

"Mama, you know that bad girl?" Sasha asked.

"Not really," I said, and we piled our stuff on the counter to pay.

CARJACK

The first time, Johanna was ten.

Her mother's boyfriend. Hands underneath the one warm blanket she'd snagged for herself. A gift from the school nurse, from Walmart. The Buffalo Bills logo.

As if she didn't know or wouldn't tell.

"Go away!" she yelled at him in the dark and he told her to shut the fuck up, but he left her room.

Her mother, hungover and bitchy the next day, made it clear whose side she was on. "Don't be a little flirt," she said as she ashed her cigarette into the garbage bag by the front door and missed.

For the next week, she set up booby traps. Tied twine to her door handle and attached it to a pan so she'd wake up. Shoved books against the door and later one of the mismatched chairs her mother pulled from the dumpster behind the office complex in town.

It was just a matter of time.

Their cabin didn't have enough walls, and the walls it did have were drafty. It was more shack than cabin really, but she and her mother pretended it housed them. Deep in the Pennsylvania woods. Inside felt like outside. Squirrels and bugs came in and out as they pleased. She'd kept a snake in her closet for a while until her mother found it and screamed at her about filth and a sidewinder that almost killed her when she was a kid in the Utah desert. Her mother had run away from her Mormon family and that act had first saved and then ruined her.

So when he came back for dinner a week later, she lit out while they made their way through a case of beer on the porch. Crawled out her one window and ran through the woods until she got to the neighbor's house a mile away. She didn't allow herself to imagine anything in those woods. There were no bears, no deer, no creatures, just her and the trees, and her backpack bumping against her back as she picked her way over roots and pine needles. It was a full moon. That's how she could see. She'd wrapped her Bills comforter around her neck and imagined she was a prize fighter with an enormous towel. Ready to fight anything.

Johanna knew they kept the car unlocked and parked behind their house. It was blue and big and smelled like a thousand cigarettes. The back door stuck but she yanked it hard three times and she was in.

In the morning, a woman opened the door and sighed, "Awww, honey," and then she was gone again. To call her mother? The police? She hadn't gotten far, but maybe she'd proven a point. She was not to be fucked with. She could leave at any time and she knew even then that her mother needed her way more than she needed her mother.

Johanna hopped up to the front seat and wondered if she could drive. She'd seen kids do it in movies. She was half asleep. It was an old car. She yanked at what she thought was the turn signal, but it was the gear shift. She'd put it in neutral. The car started to roll down the driveway and toward the busy road below. She panicked and pulled at the doors, but they wouldn't open. She pressed the pedals on the floor, but they did nothing. The car kept rolling, picking up speed. The driveway was long. The gravel crunched underneath the car's tires. "Help!" she called out, still yanking at the door handles. "Help!" this time louder and more urgent. A car zipped by and then a dump truck.

The woman's husband ran out the front door and toward the car, shouting, "Get out! Get out!"

"I can't," she shouted back.

He caught up to the car, pulled hard at the door handle and jumped in next to her. He yanked the emergency brake just as the back end of the car poked its butt out into the road. Another car swerved and honked to avoid hitting them.

"Fuck you!" he shouted. Johanna wasn't sure if he meant it for her or the car. He put his head on the steering wheel. "At least you're not dead," he said, but she knew it would be better if she were.

When she went back to school, her best friend—a boy with a pale, freckled face and yellow-green eyes and a hardcore chess obsession—told her, "My mom heard you on the scanner. Ten-year-old steals car."

After that, every time she ran away, she imagined her adventures broadcasting across hundreds of police scanners into the living rooms of everyone in her school. *Eleven-year-old hitchhikes to next town over. Twelve-year-old gets caught shoplifting condoms and tampons, sixty miles from home. Thirteen-year-old picked up on possession in Pittsburgh.*

She liked being on the rural news. The static, crackle, beep on the scanner made it official. And finally, like the posters of fugitives she stared at in the post office during a school field trip, she was a wanted girl.

BABELAND

"What about this one?" Mel took the giant rainbow cock off the shelf and pretended to blow it.

Jenny laughed and her face got red. "I forgot what going here with you is like."

Mel pretended to gag on the size of it and put it back down on the shelf. "My eyes are always too big when it comes to cocks. I think I can handle it, but when we get it home and you take it out of the nightstand drawer, I'll start whimpering."

"Do you have any questions?" a super chipper, super sex-positive femme woman with a septum piercing and a sleeve of old-timey sailor tattoos interrupted them.

"Just need a new dick," Jenny said.

"Totally. Well, these are all latex which means you can wash them with soap and water, and all of them, with the exception of the rainbow dick, work with pretty much any standard harness. We're also having a 25-percent-off sale on all harnesses this weekend," she said.

"Oh, let's get that silver leather one," Mel leaned into Jenny and pointed at the wall of leather harnesses, whips, and restraints.

"I like the one I have," Jenny resisted.

The saleswoman took a step back to give them space. "I'll be floating around the store but just holler if you need me."

"Actually, do you have any Asian dicks? Like, I'm Chinese American and I don't want a rainbow dick or a white dick or a black one, I want one that matches my skin color."

"So we have this new line of dildos that comes in an array of colors and some of our Asian customers have been interested in these two." The woman led them over to another shelf full of more realistic cocks and held up two, one in each hand, for them to look at.

Mel and Jenny each held a dick in their hands. "Oh, these feel like real skin," Mel said.

"Do they have to be so veiny?" Jenny asked.

"They are hyperrealistic, it's true," the woman said. Jenny wondered how she did it, how she stayed so unflappable and serious in the midst of so many questions.

"I like that it feels like a real cock," Mel said.

"You would," Jenny said. "And quit saying *cock*, it's a dick."

"Why do you have to be such a man hater?" Mel teased. She knew it was an old grievance—her bisexuality, her fluidity, the fact that she genuinely liked and sometimes loved men.

"I don't hate men. I hate the patriarchy," Jenny clarified.

"Me too," Mel said.

"It does kinda match my skin." Jenny held it close to her cheek.

"This is like the time I went to the American Girl Doll store with Stevie and Sasha," Mel said. "Everyone gets a doll or dick that matches their face!"

The woman laughed again and moved on to help another customer.

Their couples therapist had suggested they go to Babeland as a "sexy" activity, a way to remind them that they weren't just partners living together. Mel couldn't quite remember the last time they'd had sex—was this just a thing that happened to all couples after a while?

"You don't have to tease me for liking a more realistic cock," Mel said.

"Maybe we should just get a gold, sparkly one and pretend it's a cyborg," Jenny said, placing the dick she was holding gently back onto the display shelf.

"Cyborg sex could be hot," Mel set her cock down too, but poked at it one last time. "It really does feel like skin."

They walked back over to the rainbow dick and then toward the erotic books and into the "bridal" section, which had bachelorette party favors like tiny erect penis pacifiers and coupon books for sexual positions.

"I feel like being here means we've failed," Jenny said.

"It doesn't! We just need a little help and a new cock," Mel said, but she felt herself losing steam. She looked over at the saleswoman, who was helping a straight guy buy a vibrator for his "shy" girlfriend.

"I started seeing someone," Jenny said, looking down at a book of sex coupons and not at Mel.

Mel felt a hot surge of feeling in her chest—jealousy, betrayal, relief? She had no idea. "Why didn't you tell me?" They'd been talking about it in couples therapy, but Jenny still seemed on the fence.

"I thought it was just a one-night make-out session after one of my campus readings, but we've been texting and we had a drink in the city and I should have waited but it just kind of happened."

"Do you like her?" Mel willed herself to ask. She knew if the open relationship thing was going to work, she had to extend to Jenny what she wanted for herself, but she still felt jealous and scared. *I don't want to lose you*, she felt like blurting out, but she bit her tongue.

"Yeah, she's interesting."

"That's good," Mel said. "I want to hear more about her maybe, or not yet, or, I'll tell you when I'm ready?"

Jenny grinned and put her arm around Mel. "You are the coolest person I know."

"Of course I am. Now can we get the veiny cock?"

"Dick," Jenny corrected her.

AT HOME, MEL poured them each a glass of white wine and unwrapped the dick from its box. She set it up, standing on the counter, and they both stared at it and took sips from their glasses.

"Do you want to know more about her?" Jenny eyed Mel nervously.

Mel took a bigger sip of wine because she thought she might die of jealousy. "Nope. Not yet."

"She's just fun, but you are the love of my life," Jenny continued.

Mel put her hand on Jenny's thigh. "Babe, just shut up and fuck me."

They left the dick on the counter and wound up on the bedroom floor, the dogs barking and whining outside the door. Mel licked and sucked Jenny's clit. She forgot how sweet and salty she tasted. She stayed there with her flat, good, strong tongue until Jenny cried out, bucked her hips, and covered her face with her forearm. And then Jenny licked her and used her hand like Mel liked, and she pushed up against those radiating fingers until, until, until, until, until . . .

CAKE VERSUS FRUIT

"Hi, I'm Stevie. Welcome to my apartment," I said as I moved down the line of students snaking out my door and down the hallway.

"What's your name? Hi Rodney, hi Catherine, hi Deepak, hi Stella," I said, shaking hands and smiling.

"I read one of your essays online," Stella said. "I really like stories about music." She had a cute black bob with scissored bangs.

"Oh cool! Thanks!" I said. Sometimes they googled me. "Are you a writer?" I asked.

"No, I'm an economics major, but I hope to write on the side," she said. "My parents—I'm from China by way of Queens—they won't let me major in English or creative writing."

I nodded and took a deep breath. I felt the acute social anxiety I sometimes got at the beginning of the snack hour I held every month for students in my apartment, called Cake versus Fruit. I bought expensive fruit platters and fancy cakes on the University's dime, and we all hung out and then voted for cake or fruit on a dry-erase board convened by Sasha. It was silly, but students loved it. *You can't talk to everybody. You can't know the names of the 250 students in your building. It's okay*, I told myself.

"I bet you can do both," I said. "There are a ton of writers who have day jobs as therapists and doctors and clerks." Was this true anymore? I was thinking of William Carlos Williams and Fernando Pessoa, the poet doctor and the poet clerk. I knew therapists and nonprofit directors who were poets, but most of the fiction writers I knew had full-time teaching jobs, or were married to someone who made it possible for them to write.

She beamed and squeezed my hand. "You are so cute!" Did this mean I was ridiculous or like a granny to her?

I smiled back and scrunched up my face like I did for Sasha. My job in the dorm was equal parts professor and enthusiastic surrogate mom for homesick first-year students.

"Don't forget to write a postcard!" I let go of Stella's hand and shouted to the hallway of students. I'd bought a selection of cheesy NYC skyline postcards, nice pens, and stamps so that they could write to people they missed.

"Mama! I got a strike!" Sasha called out to me from down the hall. We'd recently bought a Styrofoam hallway-bowling set, and she was busy playing it with a cluster of students cheering her on.

"Nice!" I raised my fist in the air.

I stared out the giant hallway window that looked out onto the roof and park. It was a seven-story drop. I saw the jarring flash of underwear on that jumping girl. I rolled her name around in my head. Madison Reilly. It was a name from a TV show. The name of a girl who had it all figured out. *Your job, in this dorm and as a teacher, is to keep students from jumping,* I thought. *It's to make them care enough about something—writing, a book, me, my kid, a lover, a movie, a poem—so that they won't give up.*

"Excuse me," I said to the line of students, and squeezed back into my apartment. There were twenty students with their heads bent over postcards, sandwiched onto the couch, chair, and carpet that served as my living room, and thirty more pressed up against each other in the kitchen, against the counter island, and sitting at the dining room table. The room was hot and close, but they looked happy. *Nerds,* I thought with affection. The postcards had been a good idea. Later that semester, I'd planned to take them to see an exhibition of Black Panther Party photographs in Chelsea, to the Nutcracker ballet, and to make terrariums at a greenhouse collective in Bushwick, but now that I knew I was out, I felt myself going through the motions.

"This is so nice!" Chandra, the student from my floor, shouted at me above the din. "I love seeing how real professors live!"

"I'm not sure this is how we all live, but I'm glad you like it!" I said. It was going fine, and still I felt my face settled into a fake rictus of a grin. Should I tell them this was all ending, me here in this apartment? By the end of their first semester of school, I'd be gone. Would they remember me? Did they care? *Don't get too attached*, I wanted to shout. *I am a shadow. Here for now, but gone soon.*

I approached a group of students near the corner of my kitchen. "What are you guys talking about?" I interrupted. If I didn't force students to talk to me, many of them wouldn't.

"The girl who jumped," one said.

"I just get really mad at people who give up. It's such a fuck you to the rest of us who are trying so hard."

"I heard she was pushed."

"Did you know her?"

They all started to talk at once.

"I saw her fall," I said. "She must have been so unhappy," I added. My stomach churned at the obviousness of what I was saying.

"If I were going to kill myself, I would not jump, because it doesn't always work. You can just mess yourself up for life and still be alive. Pills are way better," one of the students said. She was tall and model-thin with a purple velvet choker pressed tight around her neck.

A small tackle at my waist. "Mama, who got pushed?" Sasha asked holding one of her Styrofoam bowling pins.

She'd been listening.

"A student got hurt and we're just talking about her," I said, trying to keep it simple.

"Is this your daughter?" the students cooed in unison.

"Yeah, this is Sasha," I said.

"Can we bowl with you?" they leaned down to ask her.

Sasha nodded yes and ran back out into the hallway like it was a totally normal thing for a six-year-old to bowl with eighteen-year-olds in a dorm.

COUGH SYRUP

"Lovey, how about your bed tonight?"

"But I'm going to miss you too much, Mama. Our five days go too fast." Sasha went straight to it.

"I miss you too. Do you know that?" My phone chirped and I looked quickly at the screen. I'd already downloaded an app for my phone that would send me rental listings. *Spacious Sun-Filled Top Floor Studio at the Forester. $1,350.* I hadn't told Sasha about the apartment. I couldn't bear to break it to her yet. She'd had so much change in her life in the last year.

"I guess so." She pushed a long strand of light brown hair behind an ear. It was 8:30 p.m., her bedtime, but we were in my bedroom, standing next to my bed, on the cusp of our usual back-and-forth about where Sasha would sleep. She had her own room, and flower-quilted bed, but she preferred the vast terrain of my king-size bed. I was never one of those smug co-sleeping parents who giggled proudly as they regaled the Music Together class with stories about finding their two-month old nestled unknowingly at the bottom of the bed, and I'd never joked over a playdate's afternoon glass of chardonnay about sneaking in a quickie while the baby gurgled his way through the night on the other side of the futon. I'd always taken some old-fashioned Dr. Spock pride in the fact that at five months, Sasha slept through the night in her own crib, in the glorified closet that Aaron and I used to call her bedroom. Now, at six, Sasha paraded around my bed naked and groped my breasts in the night like a tiny tyrant husband. The parenting blogs I'd read said it was common after separation and divorce for kids to start sleeping with their parents. Half the blogs said it was psychologically damaging, while the other half said it was fine as long as everyone was comfortable. The data, like so much about parenting, was inconclusive.

Sasha jumped up and down on the bed.

"Sash, no jumping. It's winding-down time. We're starting tonight in your bed, okay?"

Sasha shot me a panicked look. "It's too dark in there."

"You have the nightlight and the hallway light."

"But I'm always thinking in there."

"Thinking is okay."

"It keeps me awake."

So tired. If we stopped talking, we could both crawl into my bed and be asleep in five minutes. I could set my alarm for five a.m. to send emails and prep for class. Besides, based on the apartment listings my phone kept sending me, we'd be living in a studio in the far reaches of the Bronx until she graduated from high school and ran screaming to college to get away from her mother. "I really don't care."

Sasha beamed at me. Victory. I pulled down the duvet and we wriggled into the bed.

I woke up with a thud, a kid-size-thirteen heel against my head. "Ouch!" I said, and moved away from Sasha's body. She'd turned herself around and her feet were where her head should've been—only not on the pillow, but in my face.

"I hate this," I said out loud to the room. Sasha kept sleeping.

I walked out to the kitchen and looked at my phone. 4:03 a.m. I knew I'd never fall back asleep. I scrolled through the headlines on my news app.

President Obama launches a three-day, five-city bus tour to hold town hall meetings and talk about the economy and jobs.

A silent Mubarak faces the court in Cairo.

Former GOP candidate Donald Trump calls President Obama incompetent for not withdrawing from Iraq sooner.

It was a bad idea, but I got my computer and arranged myself in my couch blanket nest and started to look at old Facebook photos.

I found Sasha at six months wearing her Obama Rocks! onesie with red tights and a white tutu. I went further back through my albums and found pictures from my baby shower. *God, I got so big!* I thought. *I should have dyed my hair the whole time.* I looked so sad in those pictures. I wished for the hundredth time that I could have had a happy, easy pregnancy. I went even further back and found a sweet picture of Aaron and me in Rome, eating some life-changing pasta at a crowded bar with big happy grins. *So young!*

I stopped looking at pictures and hesitated for a second. I walked over to the cupboard and rooted into the back of it for the prescription codeine cough syrup I had from last spring's cough I couldn't shake. I took a big swig and lay back down on the couch. I felt its pleasant buzz and warming of my chest.

I found his Facebook page. The DJ from that terrible, wonderful night, when I threw the final hand grenade into my already dead marriage. I hovered over the Like button, but I didn't press it. *Have some self-respect!* I told myself. My head felt woozy from the cough syrup. I scrolled down. Hayes. *That was his name,* I reminded myself.

I'll be at Gold Star on the L doing my 90s show, every Sunday night starting at 10.

I stared at the lone fuzzy picture of him, tall and hunched over his computer, his long hair covering his face. I couldn't remember what he looked like. He was shapes more than anything else. Angular hair. Square jaw. Triangular shoulders. Something stupid thumped in me. Desire, I guess. I shut my laptop and slid it on the floor.

I put my phone on top of the computer and closed my eyes. The cough syrup was working. I slipped off into a dreamy, warm sleep. Calm. I was so rarely calm.

It's all fine, I thought, and then it was dark.

"Mama, Mama." Sasha's small hand on my shoulder. "Why did you leave the bed?"

"You kicked me," I said, and squinted at the sun coming through the windows.

"No, I didn't." She was naked as usual, totally confident and comfortable in her skin. I loved that about her.

"Yes, you did," I pushed. "It wasn't on purpose, you were asleep. But it woke me up."

"I would never do that." She pressed her forehead into mine and kissed the top of my nose.

You're gaslighting me, I wanted to say, but instead I kissed her nose back, got up, and made breakfast.

DIVE BAR CELESTIAL

"That school makes people jump, I swear," Mel said. "The cost of it is deadly, and then you factor in all that crazy millennial shit, how bonkers social media makes them, and how much they're still umbilically attached to their parents. Why aren't they all jumping?"

"Um, they kinda are. Suicide is the leading cause of death among eighteen- to twenty-five-year-olds," I said.

We were two drinks into the night. I had just told her about the suicide. I didn't say that the girl falling was my new panic dream and that I couldn't walk into that classroom without wanting to vomit. I couldn't really talk about it, other than to report it, as if it were a headline and I was merely reading off a teleprompter.

"Can I read your OkCupid inbox?" Mel asked.

"It's a terrible shitshow." I slid my phone over to Mel. I knew it gave her a vicarious thrill.

Mel read out loud. "I'll bite or maybe just nibble. Having fun this fall? Good morning sunshine. Did I catch your eye? Yet? I wish you all the best on this lovely Monday afternoon. Hi. Hello. Wanna talk? Nice description—and you are beautiful. Smiley face. I like the lips. Say yes to me. Where do you live? Wow. I like your eyes. Hope we can talk. I'm Matt. Do you have Gchat or Skype? I need you tonight."

"It sounds even worse out loud." I sipped at my whiskey.

"God, they write such dumb shit." Mel leaned forward on her stool and tried to make eye contact with the bartender. She slid my phone back down to me. "Did you meet the boner-problem guy there?" she asked.

"Yep, it's just sifting through a pile of terrible guys to find one that is maybe not so terrible," I said, and looked around the bar. Twenty- and thirty-year-olds sitting in clusters on the couches near the doors, staring into their phones. Repurposed wood for the bar. The tin ceiling still intact and tin gold stars affixed haphazardly along the walls and ceiling. The effect worked. Dive Bar Celestial. One bathroom in the back and a DJ booth tucked into the corner by the one window. Dive bars were trendy. Some people thought of them as a pushback against gentrification because they at least resembled the old thing, but really, they were just another brand or style of bar in the city: Wine bar. Tapas bar. Dive bar. Beer hall. Beer garden. Gay bar (though there were fewer and fewer of those). Hookup bar. Artisanal cocktail bar. Burlesque bar. Banker bar. Sports bar. Barbecue bar. At least with a fake dive bar, you could leave things shitty and unfinished and call it a style.

I thought of all the real dive bars I'd known, loved, and occasionally been afraid to enter: Mars Bar. Milanos. Trash Bar. The Coal Yard. A place called Kokies in the nineties where you could conveniently, of course, buy cocaine. I stared across the street at another shiny new condo, this one made out of rusted slats of steel and timber with a gym and a bank in its lobby. Kitty-corner was an old building, a municipal-looking courthouse with a pink Head Start sign affixed to one of its pillars. Across from that, a community garden. One of the last in the neighborhood. I was so grateful for those New Yorkers in the seventies, the Green Guerillas, who took over abandoned plots of land when the city was falling apart and no one wanted to live here, and made vibrant, eclectic gardens.

"I want to have my own bar," Mel said.

"Your bar would be so fun, and you'd treat your staff really well," I said.

"I wouldn't sexually harass them at least," Mel said. She got the bartender's attention and he brought them another round.

"You might a little," I joked.

"Does he know you're coming?" Mel asked.

I eyed the DJ booth. Hayes was hunched over his computer. "He told me he deejays here, like way back when we had our stupid night, and said I should come anytime. But I was Facebook-stalking him and I got curious."

"Uh, wasn't that night almost a year ago?"

"Eight months."

"So he has no idea?"

"Nope."

"Surprise!"

"Incoming!" I made a fake explosion noise with my mouth.

"Oopsie!" Mel giggled, and then changed the subject. "Jenny and I had sex!"

"That's awesome!" I knew it had been a while. "Was it good?"

"Yeah, it was," Mel said, as if she herself were surprised.

Hayes looked up and scanned the room, spotted me and grinned. "Here we go," Mel said.

"Oh fuck, what am I doing here?" I drained the last of my whiskey.

Hayes had just put on a Hole song. Courtney Love's tattered voice ripped through the bar. *I am doll parts.*

"Hey, you two." Hayes draped his long, skinny arms around our shoulders like an awkward man-shawl. "It's been forever. You should have told me you were coming."

"We didn't know. Just walking by and then remembered you said you have a nineties show here, so we thought we'd come in." I looked up at him.

Mel pushed her knee against mine. *Liar*, that knee said. I flashed to Courtney Love's long-armed guitar stance, her foot up on the guitar amp, leaning into it, fucking it, the way she owned the stage. I scanned the room at the twentysomethings lounging on the couch. What could these songs mean to them? The nineties were not even nostalgia, but something new and cool.

"You look good!" Hayes squeezed my shoulders. "Have fun! I gotta change the song." He trotted off, back toward his computer.

"Do I look like I'm dying?" I asked.

"Are you?"

"Yes."

"Why are we here?" Mel asked.

"I dunno. I want to see if I can get him again. I was like a virgin when I was married. He broke me out of my spell. He ruined me. I have to see if he'll do it again."

Mel looked down at her phone. "I gave the chef my number. Well, I put it on a napkin and crumpled it up and threw it at him."

"Smooth."

"He makes me act like a fucking seventh grader."

"It's cute," I said.

We drank. Listened to the songs. The calm, living room–like choice to stay all night at one bar. To pick a stool and stick with it. Hayes stopped and chatted some and ignored us too. He talked to everyone at the bar actually. I understood that he was working. At 2:30 a.m. a woman sat down next to us at the bar. Black straight hair with Bettie Page bangs and tattoos. She held a bouquet of balloons above her head and wore a tiara that said *Happy Birthday!*

"That tiara means fuck me," Mel whispered to me. She looked drunk and sleepy.

"Right?!" I sat up.

Hayes came over and hugged the birthday girl.

"Stevie and Mel, this is Georgia."

"Like Stevie Nicks?" Georgia asked.

"The one and only."

"How old are you?" Mel squinted at her tiara.

"Thirty!"

"Such a big girl!" Hayes leaned into Georgia. The energy was all there. She'd come to fuck him too. Maybe she was his girlfriend. What did I know? The Breeders were playing "Cannonball." *I know you, little libertine. I know you're a real cuckoo.*

Georgia giggled as Hayes wandered back toward the booth. She put her balloons in the seat next to her and turned to beam at us. I looked down at my phone. 3:07 a.m. I wanted to write back to my OkCupid messages, feel the heat of unfixed desire, possibility. *I can get others. I am not without potential.*

"So how do you know Hayes?" Georgia shouted at us through the corona of her balloons.

"We met at a bar," I said. The bartender came over and leaned into the three of us. "Let's do shots. On me."

"Not the well," Mel pleaded.

"Nah, it's three a.m. The good stuff." He poured a fancy-looking bottle of rye into four shot glasses. Down the hatch. I felt the room tilt and spin, and then I stood up to pee. Wandered into the back, bumped into a guy. *Sorry. Sorry.* Looked up at the gold stars stapled to the ceiling. The bathroom rocked and swayed as I peed. *It's time to go*, I thought. I didn't say goodbye to Hayes or Georgia. The bar was too crowded. I was too drunk.

Outside it was still sweltering—late August. Mel on the corner trying to hail a cab. Every cab full of drunk bearded men and pretty makeup artists, screaming at each other out their open windows. I jogged up to her. Mel held up her phone screen at my face.

"He texted me!"

I leaned into the screen and read it out loud. "I'm thinking about your ass."

I danced a little fake tap dance next to Mel. Squashed down my own humiliation at having come to Hayes's bar, at having waited so long. Tonight he'd fuck a thirty-year-old, and not me. "He likes you, he likes you, he likes you," I cooed over my clumsy booted tap routine.

We slumped together in the back of a cab. Taxi driver. Plexiglass. The TV for tourists. Jimmy Fallon clip. Broadway shows! A segment about foodies, filmed on stoops!

"Turn it off, with your finger," I slurred into Mel's shoulder. "Thank you for coming to Manhattan. I know it's lame, but my bed is nice and comfy."

Mel was still staring at her screen, the text from her chef. "He likes my ass!"

"You have a great ass!"

"I am not texting back until tomorrow," Mel said. She had resolve, unlike me.

The cab sped over the bridge. Pink scaffolding on the foot and bike path. Puffy graffiti tags. A couple of remaining lofts holding their own against the skyline of metal and concrete condos. Crossing over and coming through. We both stopped talking in the way all non-native New Yorkers do on drunk cab rides between boroughs—to stare at the city's magical lights, the night skyline that reminded us why we came so long ago. To be in a live place! To never be bored! To die trying!

"I'm ruining my life." The view must have sobered Mel up. That, or she was drunk enough for secrets.

"What? No. Why?"

"By wanting to fuck guys and by never having enough money," Mel said.

"But you've always fucked guys. I mean, you took a break for a while, but now you're back. As for the money thing, I don't know what to say. Everyone I love is broke. I mean, like, just barely okay, and crawling, inching, and scraping along. Artists and people in the helping professions have no extra money and no savings. It's America!" I felt my voice getting high and shrill. I still hadn't told her I was being thrown out of my apartment. Saying it out loud to too many people would make it real.

She groaned, but more in the direction of the seat than at me. "But Jenny has a real job and I don't." Of all my friends who taught, Jenny was one of the few who had landed a tenure-track job. It was upstate and so she drove back and forth every week; but still, it was a good job, in a sociology department. She'd also published four books, founded an Asian American minor in her department, and got paid to speak. She was pretty much a rock star. Still, they were often broke.

"You hated adjuncting and so you taught yourself how to bartend and you are surviving and you're writing!"

"I am not writing."

"Yes, you are."

"I am?"

"Yes, you showed me a chapter last month, and I loved it."

"What am I writing again?"

"The novel about your childhood."

"Jenny doesn't like that I want to fuck cis straight men. It's like a political failure for her."

"Well, she's a lesbian. Cis straight men are not her thing, at least not for fucking."

"I guess." Mel raised her head an inch to indicate I was maybe having some kind of positive effect, and then she lurched forward to the window of the cab, pressed the window open, and hung her head out of it like a dog.

"Miss, will you be sick?" The cab driver looked back at us nervously.

I rubbed my hand up and down her back. "Mel?"

No answer. "Melissa?" I tickled her spine with my fingers.

"I don't answer to that," she said. "I'm not going to be sick, I just need to feel the air on my face."

I leaned into Mel's back and wrapped my arms around her. I felt the warm air on my face too. The cab sped off the Manhattan Bridge ramp and up Chrystie Street. Just off the bridge, the lights of a Chinatown Buddhist temple flickered out of the corner of my eye. We sped up the Bowery, across Great Jones and LaGuardia, and lurched onto the south side of Washington Square Park. "Just on the corner is good," I said to the driver.

He stopped the cab and I used my credit card to pay him. I waited uneasily for "Approved" to flash across the screen. I'd just paid the minimum payment on my credit card, but I wasn't sure it had gone through.

It worked! The driver handed me my receipt.

"Thank you!" Mel and I said.

We stood on the corner and watched the cab speed off toward its next fare.

Mel held up her pointer finger at me and walked into the corner of the park. She leaned over a bush and barfed on top of it.

"Melly!" I ran over to her.

"I'm okay."

"No you're not."

I rubbed her back, and she wiped her mouth with the back of her hand. My building lit up the corner like a candy machine. It seemed pointless to pretend anymore. I'd never belonged in Manhattan. My apartment was never mine. I wasn't supposed to get too comfortable.

"I'm getting kicked out of my apartment at the end of the year."

Mel didn't miss a beat. "Come back to Brooklyn?"

"Or maybe I can find a cozy dumpster somewhere."

"Don't say things like that," Mel slurred as I pulled her toward my building.

We stumbled into the fluorescent lights of my lobby and nodded at the guard. Upstairs, I tucked Mel into my bed like she was Sasha. She didn't fight it and fell right asleep.

SECRET

"Come on, lemme drink both bottles!" Johanna grabbed for the two containers of Robitussin that Butch had just pulled the safety seals off of.

"No way, little girl." Butch held them both close to his chest. "All mine." He was getting meaner lately. More dope sick or fed up with her, she couldn't tell.

"But I fucking stole them!"

"It's your fault we lost our stash."

"It was your idea to hide them there."

"Pimp takes all the money."

"You are not my pimp." Johanna fussed with the ratty sleeping bag they hid in the hollow of a tree to use at night in the park. It was too hot to sleep inside of it, but they could use it as a mattress.

"I could turn you out." Butch tipped one of the bottles into his mouth and drained it.

"You said you don't like it when I do that," she begged. They couldn't cop. They didn't have enough money, so this was her only chance to get high. "If you take two you'll OD."

"What are you going to do for me?" Butch looked up at the sky and burped.

"I will tell you a secret."

"Don't care about those."

"I'll fuck you good then," she said and sighed. "How can you be such a sexist anarchist?"

"My mother ruined feminism for me. Besides, I'm eighty percent kidding, always."

"No, you're not."

Butch passed her the bottle and she chugged it.

They lay on the blanket and waited. Nearby some couple fucking like cats in heat, and farther away the hushed murmurs of the dealers who wouldn't give them anything. Johanna got up to puke in the bushes and came back. The sky spun. She said some words but they came out a trail. She pawed at her jean shorts trying to find the seam of the pocket. It took forever. Butch in the background, puking and gagging.

"I tried to keep it down," he said as he flopped on the sleeping bag next to her.

"Where is my pocket?" she asked him.

"You're one fucked-up little lady."

She found it! She pulled out a piece of notebook paper that she'd folded ten times into the tightest little square. She waved it in front of Butch's face. He grabbed for it and missed. She laughed at him.

"What's that?"

"My secret."

"You don't have any secrets from me." He licked at her ear and fell backward giggling.

"I do now."

"What is it?"

"A note from a dead girl. Don't you want to read it?"

But Butch had already lost interest and was tugging at the waistband of her shorts. "You promised."

"I can't," she said.

"Then just let me put my hand in your pussy. It's so warm in there. I love it."

"I don't care."

And when he came inside of her, she clutched the note and thought, *I am a nearly dead thing, a husk of an earlier version of myself, just like the one who jumped.*

"You're so high," Butch said, rolling off of her. "This never happened."

LINES

"Mel!" Tommy the manager yelled from his tiny windowless office next to the freezer.

Carmine winked at her from behind his station in the kitchen. Prepping for dinner. Chopping. Making sauces with subtle flavors she could never approximate.

"What?" She stood in the doorway to Tommy's office, her ass facing Carmine. She felt her phone vibrate in her pocket. She pulled it out and glanced at it.

"When are you going to let me touch it?" From Carmine. Her face flushed.

"Let me see?" Tommy joked, and when she ignored him: "Come in, shut the door?"

Mel sighed, but squeezed herself up against the desk so she could shut it.

Giggling behind her. Greta. Short sleeveless black dress. Strappy high-heeled sandals.

Mel jumped. "Jesus, that's scary. Don't hide!" She couldn't figure Greta out. Was she with management or the workers? She gave off a lame HR vibe sometimes, but was an amazing kisser.

"Do a line with us?" Tommy pulled a little jar out of his pocket and started to tap a thick line of powder out onto the screen of his phone.

"What is it?" Mel played along.

"Addy," Greta said.

"I can't. My girlfriend will kill me," Mel lied. She had no interest in doing lines with her crazy manager.

"Just one can't hurt." Tommy rolled up a twenty and gestured for her to lean over.

"Honestly, I'm already a hyper nervous wreck. I don't need energy," Mel said. "Besides, what is this? A bad after-school special from the eighties?" she joked. "Are you guys, like, peer pressuring me?"

Greta shrugged and leaned over the desk to do the line. Her ass brushed against Mel's thigh. Tommy stared into the *V* of Greta's neckline.

Tommy poured out two more lines—one skinny, one fat. "This will help me finish the schedule. Mel, you want to keep Saturday night, right? If you don't, I could also move you to Sunday afternoon."

Saturday was her best night. She made $400 most Saturdays. She couldn't lose it. Sunday afternoon was hangover Bloody Marys with five different pickles she had to fuss to get on a giant toothpick and brunch eggs on every surface.

"Greta's a bartender too. I want her to pick up a shift soon." Tommy and Greta did the lines Mel wouldn't. Tommy wiped his nose and rubbed the remaining powder off of his phone screen and onto his teeth.

"You could train me?" Greta said.

"Totally." Mel had worked in enough restaurants to know the sexual politics. You played along. You trained the younger girls who would could replace you, but you did whatever you could to keep your shifts. She had a loyal following of devoted customers who came in just for her. Still, she was forty-two—expendable for sure. *I should've just done the fucking line*, she thought.

"How's about a little kiss on the cheek from my two favorite workers?" Tommy stood up.

Mel leaned over and brushed her lips against his beard. Greta stayed for a second or two longer. "Don't we have the best restaurant in all of Brooklyn? Aren't we like an amazing family?"

Mel wanted to punch him. *This is not my fucking family*, she wanted to say. "Yeah, it's super cozy." She winked at Tommy and then turned to open the door. "I gotta go get the bar ready."

In the hallway, Carmine raised his eyebrows in a *what happened?* She rolled her eyes and started prepping her martini glasses.

Later that night, out back by the dumpster, she met Carmine during his cigarette break.

"I don't trust Greta," she said.

Carmine pressed her up against the brick wall and slid his tongue into her mouth.

"What's she going to do, murder us?" he whispered into her neck.

"She's going to steal my shifts!" Mel kept talking through the kiss.

"She can't do what you do," he said. "The vibe you create, the way you make customers feel special. Tommy knows that's a gift."

"You're just trying to flatter me so I'll fuck you," Mel said.

"Maybe."

"You can't trust bartenders," Mel said. "We're vampires."

"So bite my neck?" Carmine took his last drag, flicked his cigarette away, and angled his neck in Mel's direction.

She licked his neck and he groaned.

"You'll have to wait for the bite."

CUBANASWEDE

"You got a dollar now?"

I looked up from my phone screen. A breeze blew across the fountain and sprayed water onto everyone sitting on my side of it. I shielded my phone, let the water hit my face, and then turned away as the crowd squealed in unison. It was just past nine p.m. Sasha was back with her dad. The energy was different than during the day. Fewer little kids. More students. An edgier, druggier vibe as the dealers from the northwest corner spread out into the darkness.

"I mean, did you bring your wallet this time?"

I stood up so I could see who was talking to me.

"Remember me?" she asked.

It was the homeless punk woman. The straps of her pink bra had faded and were stretched down the sides of her arms to her elbows, but her hair looked cleaner, like she'd had a chance to wash and brush it. "I'm going to go to the University and become your student."

"Yeah, I remember you. You waved at me the other day when I was at the playground and you flashed me the peace sign at CVS."

"I did?" She shrugged.

I didn't bring up the cough syrup or the pills. How to finesse that? *Were they yours? Some douchebag lawyer dad made us throw them in the garbage, but maybe don't stash them where the toddlers play? Did you drink the Robitussin? Did it help you forget her body smashing into the pavement?*

I reached into my back pocket. I hadn't brought my wallet, but I'd grabbed a couple of dollars before I'd left the apartment. I gave her the three I had.

"Thanks." She slid the money into her front pocket.

I'd left the apartment because I was hot and bored. I'd been mindlessly scrolling through dating profiles. I typed a text to the guy who'd been shot, but I couldn't bring myself to send it. *No more bad sex*, I told myself as I rode down the elevator and walked to the fountain.

Another young woman peeled off her shirt and bra and began a little topless jig toward the center fountain.

"That's legal now, you know," the woman said to me. She wasn't going to budge.

"Yeah, free the nipple," I said, as if saying the slogan aloud would make it possible for me to never show mine in public again. Breast-feeding Sasha had cured me of that particular desire.

"We should join her," the girl said. I couldn't tell if she was mocking me or flirting with me. She had a boozy, confusing effect.

"Nah, I'm good." I pictured one of my colleagues walking by as I frolicked topless in the fountain. "I overheard you saying in the drugstore that you saw the girl who jumped?" I asked, not sure what I was opening up.

"Yeah, it was a really bad trip," she said.

"I saw her fall too. She jumped in front of my classroom window."

"Let's just stop." She put her hand up near my face and did a five-second hip waggling "Stop in the Name of Love" dance. "You were eavesdropping on me?"

"You were kinda loud."

She laughed until she snorted. "Well that's prolly true." As she stepped out of her dirty jeans and stripped off her shirt, she asked, "Are you sad?" She twirled her shirt over her head like she was a stripper and flung it at me. I caught it and tried to hand it back to her. "Keep it," she said as if she were a rock star who had just thrown me her underwear.

I put the shirt down on the fountain stairs next to us. "No, I don't know, maybe. Isn't everyone a little bit sad always?"

She cocked her head to the side as if she were thinking about it. "Not everyone, no. Not always," she said. "I just want to know if you're one of those sad women who makes everyone take care of her."

"Like a hysteric?" I joked.

"Ooh, see this is why I want to be your friend. You're smart." She took my hand and pulled me toward the center of the fountain with her. I resisted and she let my hand go. "I'm definitely a hysteric."

"About the girl who jumped?" I tried to redirect.

She grabbed for my hand again and gave it a squeeze. "I'm not going to gossip about some dead girl, but I was there when she hit and there were some clues and the police took them away like they always do."

"Clues?"

"The papers that fell with her, from her notebook. They had things written on them, and I took one," she said, and then she ran into the center of the fountain where the water was the strongest, screaming as it hit her.

"What things?" I asked when she waded back to me.

She shrugged off my question. "My boyfriend thought you were cute in a MILF way," she said.

"Um, thanks?"

"I know that's kind of degrading, like porno or something, but he's really picky about women. I just think you're interesting."

"I'm not really." I slid my phone into my back pocket.

"What happened to your husband?" she asked.

"Nothing, we're still good friends."

"La profesora!" her boyfriend shouted from the other side of the steps and waded toward us. Several people looked over at me, as if I were a narc or about to teach a class.

"He's high, just ignore him. I'm high too, but I'm cooler about it."

When he got to us, he grabbed each of our hands and pulled us back toward the other side. "My shoes," I protested.

"They're fine. I want you to meet someone important." He was still wearing his Dead Kennedys T-shirt, but it looked crustier and smelled worse.

"This is the lady I told you about." He put his arm around my shoulder and squeezed me hard. I winced. "This is Arturo. He's the one who told me about taking over Wall Street. Remember?"

"No touching without consent." She smirked.

He let his arm fall off my shoulder and took a step back.

I looked up. I knew I was blushing, but it was dark, so fine, whatever. Arturo, it turned out, was a small, hot nerd. Maybe an inch taller than me, with wavy brown hair and a cute nose. He had on some kind of canvas jacket with big breast pockets where he maybe kept his manifestos, a plaid shirt buttoned to the top, corduroy pants, and the requisite New Balance sneakers, but in bright orange and magenta. He pulled out a flyer from the messenger bag slung over his shoulder and raised his eyebrows at me.

"Profesora?"

"I don't know why he's calling me that," I stammered. "I mean, my grandma was from Cuba, but I don't even speak Spanish, and I'm Swedish and English and a bunch of other mutt stuff."

"Are you a professor?"

"Yeah, and a writer."

"You teach here?" He gestured toward the buildings around us.

"Yep."

"The evil real-estate conglomerate."

"Pretty much." I paused. I wanted to tell him a story and keep his attention on me.

The girl looked back and forth between us and grinned like we were a really good YouTube clip.

"That's the one."

"I teach at The New School part-time," he said.

"That place is a little less evil."

"Just a little."

"I was at a meeting with our president once."

"Isn't he the one who forces everybody to hug him?" Arturo interrupted.

"Totally, I hate it. Anyway, somebody asked him what he thought about The New School, and he got this faraway look in his eyes and stared off into the distance, and then shrugged and said, 'Oh, we'll own all of that by 2040.'"

"Holy fuck!" Arturo said.

"I know, all the faculty in the room were like, oh my god, Darth Vader is in charge of our school."

He pressed a flyer into my hand and I looked down at it. It was a young woman dancing on top of the Wall Street Bull. *Take the bull by the horns*, the flyer said. *Occupy Wall Street.*

"Come! Bring your students," he said.

"I'm planning on it."

"You can radicalize them!" Arturo said.

"Who has Tipsy?" the girl asked her boyfriend.

"Dunno." He shrugged, and they waded off and out of the fountain to look for her.

"You're Cuban?"

"Just a quarter. My grandma left when she was eighteen, long before Castro."

"Funny, I'm Puerto Rican and Swedish. I call it Swederican. I guess that makes you . . ."

"Cubanaswede?" I asked.

"Swed-*an*?"

"Maybe neither?" I cocked my head to the side and laughed.

"Can I get your number?" he asked, and for a stupid moment I thought he was asking for it for himself. "You know, to keep you updated?"

"Sure." I rattled it off. "So what do you mean by occupy?"

"Take over the square. Live there."

"For how long?"

"As long as it takes."

"Like Los Indignados in Spain or the Arab Spring?"

"Totally, those protesters are our heroes," Arturo said. "Shit, duck!" Arturo grabbed my hand and pulled me toward him. A Frisbee from the other side of the fountain sailed through where my head had been.

I hadn't been paying attention to anything else. I felt like Arturo's groupie. Maybe everyone felt this way around him. I knew about the complicated history of political affiliation and sexual desire. I taught a class called Youth in Revolt, for fuck's sake. Jean Genet admitting his homoerotic love for the Black Panthers. Women doing the secretarial work during the meetings for the Students for Democratic Socialism, and then falling in love with the more visible male leaders. And there were the women who stood out too—Bernardine Dohrn of the Weather Underground, Angela Davis with her fist to the sky while on trial, and Kathleen Cleaver's expert leadership in the Black Panther Party. Did I want to be like those powerful women or next to the power? Maybe both.

"I gotta keep moving. My partner and I are trying to cover Washington Square and Tompkins tonight." He let go of my hand and glanced over his shoulder, but I didn't see anyone who seemed to be with him.

"Bye," I said. I wondered what "partner" meant. *Partner as in girlfriend? Partner as in anarchist comrade?*

"Power to the people," he said.

"Power to the people," I said, nervously aware that I was appropriating a Black Panther Party slogan. *Did I want to do that? Was that cool? Not really.*

"Loosen up, chica," he whispered, leaning in close to the side of my face. I felt his stubble for a quick second, and then he was gone.

WANTING

She met him at a bar in the East Village called the Ship Yard, one of the few dive bars left on Avenue B. She wore what was becoming her standard uniform: a navy-blue dress, hot-pink underwear, and black boots with the laces untied. She didn't care if she smelled like sweat and perfume. It was a test to see who wanted to get through. *Am I repellant enough?*

In office hours a couple days before, after an excruciating fifteen minutes of not staring at him while he drew squiggles on her poems, he finally spoke.

"I really think you've got a chapbook here. These poems are better than a lot of the adult writers I know, not that you're not an adult." He looked down at his keyboard nervously. She wanted language, affirmation, a yes—finally, someone to tell her that she was good and that her writing wasn't a waste of time.

"What even is a chapbook?" she asked. She knew, but sometimes for fun she played dumb.

He laughed and rubbed his beard, like he could conjure magic out of it. Clearly, he liked her stupid. "It's a short book of poems and a good way to start publishing."

"You think someone would publish these?" she asked, leaning forward over her poems. She wasn't pretending anymore. She did want a small book with her name on it that she could give to her parents and friends and say, *Fuck you, I have talent.*

"I do."

There was a long silence. He got up and shut the office door, and then sat back down. "Do you want to meet for a drink to talk about how to sequence the poems?"

She knew he shouldn't have asked and so did he, and still it was a thrill. A meeting with a real writer to talk about her poems. A dream come true!

"I mean, of course, we can do that here too, if you want."

"No, let's have a drink. I'm twenty-one," she said to reassure them both.

At the bar, when she showed up, he was already drunk. He bought her shots, which she did dutifully. At some point she took out the poems. They were blurry, but she was determined.

"I was wondering if you have favorites or think any should be cut?" she asked, fanning out the pages in front of them.

He frowned, like poems were the last thing he wanted to talk about. "I think I'm too wasted to think about this right now," he said, and as if the bartender were an extra in the shitty movie that was her life, he exclaimed, "It's not an office! Put your work away!"

She blushed, ashamed at her own stupidity. She wasn't any good. He didn't care about her writing or if he did he was too drunk to say.

The bartender brought them another shot, and she did it to keep from crying.

"Do you want to play darts?" he asked far into the blurry night.

She slurred yes and slid off her stool. He helped her up and she was grateful and they did throw the darts *bang, bang, bang* into the board, but then they almost hit another girl and the bartender yelled, "Get the fuck out of here!" and they laughed more on the street, and suddenly they were in a cab and his hand was up her dress and it was not okay, but she was too drunk to stop him and she felt something warm and wanting and that was better than cold and nothing.

THE WIFE

I found my shoes and started to walk the path back to my apartment. I paused to look at the makeshift memorial that had formed around the spot where the girl's body had landed. There was a printed-out Facebook profile picture of her, framed in pasted-on black lace, several handwritten notes, and a candle, all surrounded by police barriers. Someone had written in cursive chalk on the sidewalk, *Rape + Suicide = Murder.* I tried to look closely at the photo, but I couldn't. I didn't want to add her face to the image that looped in my head since I'd seen her fall.

I kept walking and passed the stage where theater students put on bad versions of *Romeo and Juliet* and skater boys ollied and skidded with their determined, clacking commitment to mastery. I noticed a group of moms from Sasha's school. They were working with a personal trainer in a tight cluster. Doing burpees, clad in yoga shorts and sports bras.

"Stevie!" one of them called out to me. It was the mom of one of Sasha's classmates from last year. We'd been to their apartment for a playdate. They had a backyard in the West Village and more rooms than I could count. Her name was Paige.

I waved, stopped walking, and said, "Hi!" I'd been hoping to get away. These women had so much time and money. They were the reason our public school had art classes and an after-school chorus. I was grateful for their labor, but I had a hard time talking to them. I could never do what they wanted me to.

"Exercise with us?" She gestured for me to join them. The others kept at their burpees. Squat. Jump back. Jump forward. Stand. Their abs were so flat.

"I have a bad knee." I walked closer.

"I hope the girls are together again!" she said. She left her cluster of Stepford moms and jogged down the stairs. *You will never have enough money or time to be that fit,* I told myself.

"Me too! Aren't you guys usually away in August?" I asked. I'd learned from Sasha's poorly attended playground birthday party in July that most of her classmates spent big chunks of the summer in the Hamptons or on the Cape. Some even went abroad and worked remotely from Paris or a Greek Isle. *Hugs to Sasha. We'll be in Provence! Give the birthday girl our love, we're in Sag Harbor!*

"We're selling our Bridgehampton house and the realtor is showing it like every hour, so we decided to rough it in the hot, sweaty city," she said.

"Totally," I said as if I knew what it was like to have a house to sell and a realtor to sell it. I felt a flutter of shame licking at my constricting throat. Soon, we wouldn't even have an apartment. "Maybe the girls can play soon?" I said.

Paige frowned and wiped at the cute sweat that had pooled on her upper lip. "Savannah is at sleepaway camp for another week and when she comes home she's doing an animation day camp."

"Well, we're just kicking around. Sasha is at a day camp on the Lower East Side for artist kids, but we're here."

"Ooh fun, what camp?"

"Abrams. It's at an old settlement house."

"Hmmm, never heard of it."

"It's little and cheap, but good," I added.

"God, I wish Savannah would choose something cheap once in a while."

I laughed like I understood, like *Yeah, sure, we give Sasha a choice about which shitty camp she can go to, and she picks the one at the settlement house.*

I'd recently made the mistake of looking up the median income for individuals in the West Village. It was $127,000. I saw those numbers floating above Paige's head. They were not enough. She was probably worth five times that. I wanted to work on my class rage. *These people are perfectly nice to you. They invite Sasha into their homes and they are kind to her, and you can't stand to talk to them once in a while?*

"So, I came over because I wanted to talk to you about the silent auction this year. I'm trying to spread the word to parents about what kinds of donations we're looking for." Paige pulled at her ponytail. Her teeth were bright white. The kind of white that costs a lot of money. Not strips. Not the shitty little tray full of poison that you do at home.

"Sure," I said. I'd avoided the silent auction. As far as I could tell, it looked like a lockdown on a Hudson River booze cruise with a bunch of miserable couples. Last year, I donated a homemade pie and a manuscript consultation. Nobody bid on my items.

"So, it's great when you can give away like a weekend at your beach house or something quirky like a writer thing, but our highest bidding happened because some parent works at the agency that represents Lady Gaga and they got Gaga to agree to donate a half hour with her in her dressing room!"

"Wow," I said. The girl's falling body flashed in front of me, the yellow of her backpack, a faux parachute. Sasha and me, out on the streets, in just four months. *None of this matters. None of this matters*, I thought as I stared at Paige's superwhite teeth.

"I know, right?! So, just really think outside the box this year."

I felt my face flush with rage, but my head started moving up and down like I agreed, like it made perfect sense.

I thought of all of the moms I used to hang out with in Brooklyn—those sad artists who sometimes even had jobs of their own. I thought of the stay-at-home dads I knew there too. I remembered Mel and how lucky I was that she was my best friend and that I liked the parents in the East Village better than the West because the East Village still had projects and rent-stabilized apartments. Artists, teachers, social workers, the occasional fucking painter or filmmaker. Not many, but some.

"Stevie, you gotta hydrate in this weather," Paige said. "You look like you're wilting."

"I am," I said.

"Go home, get into the air-conditioning." She gave my forearm a tight squeeze and jogged back over to her squad of fit moms.

I stared up at the crane looming above the park, like some giant's arm. I closed my eyes and saw it crash down onto the dog run, the fancy new bathrooms where the junkies still shot up, and land with a CGI splash into the fountain. The girl with her yellow backpack and cloud of loose-leaf paper fell and fell, like my own private trauma GIF, lodged into my brain's hard drive forever. I remembered my father's forearm, thick and hairy, smashing down onto the kitchen table when my brother and I wouldn't eat, milk everywhere. My mother sopping it up with a red-and-white checked dishtowel while we whimpered and begged to not get hit. Splash and wake. "Do you want me to feed you like babies, is that what you want?" he said as he forced giant forkfuls of food into our bird-mouths. Later that night, after my mother had gone to bed, he appeared wild-eyed, seventies hippie shag hair askew, with a belt or a slipper or a wooden spoon, to "finish what we'd started" at dinner. My brother always got it worse than me. Because he was a boy? Because he cried less? Because he was physically stronger? I never knew. But as he whimpered and scratched at his door, a small animal fighting against a big one, I ran my finger along my welts, and stared into the blue glass eyes of my favorite stuffed-animal bunny, and said, "You are a good girl. You are a good bunny. You are a bad girl. You are a bad bunny." The broken part of me, the part of my psyche that made deals with the world so that she could understand it, decided that I deserved whatever I got. When my brother finally cried out for me, "Stevie!" I ran upstairs to wake my mother. Had she been asleep? Was she waiting until it got out of control? I never knew that either, but she made him stop, snapped him out of his violent spell with a couple of words. "Are you done now? Satisfied? Had enough?" He dropped whatever household item he'd turned into a weapon and went upstairs. My mother slept with us on those nights—the three of us crowded into one twin bed. "I'm sorry," she said over and over again until we fell asleep.

I opened my eyes again. The crane still loomed above us. *Who gets crushed and who lives to tell the story? What does it take to survive a fall?* I wondered as I walked back to my apartment.

GETAWAY

"What are you reading?" a man asked me when he sat down on the empty stool next to mine. I'd run away for the weekend. Mel gave me the keys to her father's cabin in Gloucester and I jumped on a bus.

"*The Best American Essays,*" I said, and he didn't flinch or ask me a dumb question about writers or essays or publishing, and then for a full half hour he left me alone.

"Would you like another drink?" He nodded at the bartender.

"All right," I said, because we both knew why I was there. He had on nice pants that fit him well and curious green eyes. He didn't tell long self-involved stories or laugh too loud. Maybe I picked him for what he didn't do. Bars, I discovered in the last couple months, were waiting rooms. Who could wait the longest? Who got seen right away? Who was coming and going?

"What's with the short hair and the pouty lips?" he asked, three drinks later. I'd put my book in my bag. He didn't know that Mel and I had been coming to this bar for years in our twenties—once or twice every summer—before I met Aaron.

"What's with the beard and shaved head?"

"I'm bald." He laughed. "David." He stuck his hand out.

"Stevie," I said and shook it.

He gave me a ride. "This yours?" he asked when we'd pulled onto the gravel by the trees.

"My friend's."

"They say this island will be underwater in twenty years." Once we were inside, he reached for my waist.

"Then it makes it even more special," I breathed into his neck.

"The turtles think so." He kissed me, moved his tongue along mine, and rubbed one hand up and down my back. He was looking for a zipper, the quickest way to get me out of my dress.

From the porch earlier that day before I'd walked into town, I watched women in their fifties and sixties traipse by with little blue flags. They were saving the turtles—putting blue flags wherever eggs had been laid so that no one would step on or drive over them. It looked like a straightforward, meaningful job. I wished for something so simple. Snippets of their conversation floated up to me. *Her granddaughter is so good at biology she got a special award. She had breast cancer, but she kept fighting and she beat it. Her husband, no matter what she says, will not rinse off the dishes before he puts them in the dishwasher.*

"Do you like it when I kiss you there?" he asked, moving down to my clavicle. "Let's just take this off, shall we?" he said as he pulled my dress over my head. He took off his watch and placed it on the nightstand, and then he unclasped my necklace, and reclasped it so it wouldn't get tangled.

When it was over, I stared up at the wooden-beamed ceiling of the cabin bedroom, until I couldn't take the boredom of insomnia anymore. I got up to pee and took my phone with me into the bathroom. Two more real-estate listings had popped up in the night.

This is the only two bedroom in Red Hook priced at $2,000. This is a steal and will not last!

Beautiful gut-renovated 1 BD in full amenities building directly across from Prospect Park! $2,195.

It was already sending me apartments out of my price range. I swiped them away. "I miss you," I texted Aaron.

"I miss you too," he surprised me by texting back immediately. "U ok?"

"I guess," I texted while I peed. "How's Sash?"

"Good. Bossy, but good."

"U r not allowed to call her bossy." I added the cat heart-eyed emoji.

"Oh right, not feminist, huh?"

"U can say she's a leader."

"But she's bossy."

"Ha, I know." I wiped and stared at my phone, at the pulsing ellipsis that indicated Aaron was typing. I thought of the man asleep in my bed, and my soon-to-be ex-husband who I couldn't stop texting. I let my mind drift to Arturo's hand on mine, pulling me into him in the fountain.

"Where r u?"

"Mel's dad's cabin . . . Gloucester."

"I miss that place, so beautiful." Aaron and I had been there together with Mel and Jenny many times. We'd been a foursome for years and had couples' nights out. Now Jenny and Mel saw us mostly on our own. Aaron and I vowed to never make our friends choose sides. "Nice?"

"Yeah, but lonely." I wondered what Aaron would think of this man I'd picked up. Would he care? Would he find him lame? He knew I was dating. He said he wasn't ready and didn't want to go online.

"I bet," he texted back, not quite taking the bait.

I stood up and looked in the bathroom mirror. My face looked redder than usual, more freckled and burned from the sun. I walked back over to the bathroom door and locked it, suddenly protective. I leaned into the mirror and examined the pores on my nose, the flesh of my neck, and the darkening smudges underneath my eyes. I saw a bite mark on the flesh just above my breast—a pinkish cluster where he'd sucked at my skin.

"Have we done the right thing?" I felt the panic of overlaps—of a new landscape on top of an already existing one. Plate tectonics. How land masses shift and grind into one another. I could only text these things in moments when I was raw and opened up, but I couldn't say them to him in person.

"I dunno. Maybe. It's hard to say," Aaron texted back.

Noncommittal. Typical, I thought.

"You are the only good man I know," I texted.

"I feel the same about you."

"R u happier on your own?"

"Sometimes," he texted. "R u?"

"Sometimes."

I sighed and flushed. I put my phone on the back of the toilet and splashed water on my face. I didn't know what to say. It was an impasse of sorts, and it was not like in the movies. Nobody was driving through the rain to declare that we'd made a mistake! That we'd figured it all out! We'd never even called our separation a trial one.

"Tell Sash I love her," I texted as a way to say goodbye.

"I will."

I checked my email and saw a message from my dad. I wavered for a second before reading it. His emails were like tiny poison darts aimed at my heart. My brother had recently put a block on my father's emails. I was close to unfriending him on Facebook, but at this point it was pretty much our only contact, and I felt guilty depriving him of this very curated, voyeuristic view of Sasha and me.

Let's face it. You don't want a dad, you just want an ATM. You have no interest in me or anything about me. You just want me to bankroll your life in NYC, so that you can sneer at all of the little people you've left behind. I quit. I'm retiring from being your father.

I deleted the email. I felt the blood rush to my head in anger. I wanted to type back a million hateful things. *Fuck you! Aside from paying for half of my state-school tuition in the early 1990s, you've never given me a fucking dime. You're threatening to sue my brother and you still want us to be in your life. Wow. You're amazing. What a dad. We really hit the parent jackpot.*

Instead, I texted my brother, "I hate dad," and then I turned off my phone and left it in the bathroom. When I got back into bed, David rolled toward me and wrapped his arms around my body. I wanted to squirm away, but I let him hold me, until eventually I fell asleep.

THE NEXT MORNING, the sun on my face, I got out of bed, walked into the living room, and looked at the top of a narrow bookshelf by the couch.

A Guide to the Common Birds of Cape Cod by Peter Trull

Wading and Shore Birds by Roger S. Everett

Consider the Oyster by M. F. K. Fisher

Cape Cod by Henry David Thoreau

The Famous Beds of Gloucester by D. B. Wright

Unfinished Monsters by Melissa Bale

I moved Mel's book to the facing-out position like I used to do with my favorite books when I worked in a bookstore in my twenties. Other than the books, the house was scrubbed clean of personal effects for renters and guests, except for one photo on top of the TV—Mel and her two sisters when they were in their early twenties. I leaned in to get a closer look. I'd taken the picture myself, so many years ago. Mel was the baby. The three of them, tan and freckled, arms looped around each other's necks, in bikinis, the beach behind them. All blond, all with that same straight nose and their lips set just firm, with a hint of a smile—but in-on-something girls, who could take a joke, and would happily make you the butt of theirs.

Mel's father died of a heart attack when she was twenty, two years after leaving her mother and running off with his secretary, Carol. The cabin had been a present for Carol, and at first Mel and her sisters hated it, but eventually they forgave Carol and shared the cabin.

The bedsprings creaked in the other room. What would I say when he came out? He'd been better than I imagined. We found each other's bodies quickly. He slid inside me and the animal thing in me clicked. I moved my hips, closed my eyes, and forgot about him as an individual, as particular. We were the parts of a perfect machine. Humming along until I broke.

I liked the surprise of a new person, how they used their hands, and what their lips tasted like, the smell of their neck and armpits. Maybe I was trying to never be bored again, to keep myself alive with new men.

The bedsprings creaked again. I put the photo down. *I'll offer him coffee. I'll thank him. No, I'll say that was nice and I'd mean it, but I would have a faraway, preoccupied look in my eyes, and he'd understand that I was a mess, and a busy one at that, and he'd take his well-tailored pants and go.*

I came up to write, promised myself that I would, but so far all I'd done was fuck a stranger. *Once he leaves, I'll write for three hours, and then I'll drive to the pond and swim, as a reward.* I thought about

Sasha's face, the space where her two bottom teeth had fallen out and her long hair snarled into small nests behind her ears. Sasha beaming into the square of my phone, narrating the plot of the new Tinker Bell movie to me. *Mama, I want to be a tinker.* I'd FaceTime her later and her face would remind me that I had work to do. I could not descend into nothingness. After the pond, I'd buy a bottle of rosé and scallops from the stand by the liquor store. I'd cook them in butter and drink just half the bottle of wine.

I heard him pee, and I continued to stare out the window. Two turtlers crossed in front of the house. Each woman wore brown pants and a short-sleeve shirt, and looked to be about sixty. The blue flags they carried to mark turtle nests bounced jauntily behind them.

He came up behind me, put his arms around my shoulders, and breathed into the back of my neck. I felt my shoulders tense up.

"Where did you come from anyway?" David asked.

"New York." I pressed my ass into him, felt his cock harden. This happened a lot lately—my brain had a plan and my body did what it wanted.

"I don't believe you. I think you're a nymph or a sea witch."

"Nah, I'm just a woman who is no longer a wife. The not wife."

"Okay, not wife, but I still think you might be a witch."

"I'm definitely a witch."

The turtlers paused in front of the cabin, squatted down into the mud, and placed a cluster of flags just fifteen feet from where we were standing. One stood up, shielded her eyes from the sun, and looked toward the window. I waved at them instinctually, remembered I was naked, and stepped back from the window. The woman waved back, looked down demurely, and said something to her partner.

"You're scandalizing the island," David said, pulling me back toward the bedroom.

"I'm just a tourist. Nobody expects me to behave." We paused in the doorway between the living room and bedroom.

I stared down at his cock, at the trail of gray hairs that led up to his chest.

"Good to give those old ladies a show." David tugged at my hand.

I looked down at his feet. They were lovely—high arches, well-trimmed nails, no callouses.

"I need to write today," I said.

"That's not a need." His eyes were still that curious green, the lashes long, his bald head shaved close. "Water, food, shelter. Those are needs."

"I should," I clarified.

"How long are you here?" he asked.

"Until Monday."

"That's plenty of time," he said.

"For what?"

"For us," he pulled me through the doorway and onto the bed, "to swim in a pond you *need* to see."

I pretended that I didn't know the pond he was talking about. I rested my head on his chest, ran my fingers through the wiry gray hairs, and breathed into his armpit. I remembered that even half a bottle of wine was too much for me and that I didn't know how to cook scallops. He climbed on top of me, kissed me. I opened my mouth, shut my eyes, and wrapped my legs around him.

LATER, FLOATING ON my back in the middle of the deep pond, the water rushed and whirred its tiny storm in my ears. I tried to imagine I was a skiff, bobbing along the edges of whatever landscapes would have me. Here I am on top of a school of fish, here I am butting up against the tree that's fallen into the pond, and here I am in the middle of it, doing nothing, being no one, and performing nothing. I stopped floating and treaded water.

David waved at me from the shore where he was poking around in the sand with a giant stick. I stared down into the water and panicked when I couldn't see my feet. I felt too far out and I started my lame half doggy paddle, half crawl back to the shore. David waded out to meet me and I thought for a second, *Who is this stranger? He could murder me out here if he wanted to.* My legs got tired and I thought of the girl who jumped—how she'd given up, her arms backstroking into the air, like she wanted to get somewhere. Down, I guess. To the bottom of it. The end.

I shivered in the passenger seat of David's car, a towel wrapped around my wet suit, goose-fleshed arms and legs.

"Where to?" he asked.

"Don't you have anything you have to do?" I asked.

"It can wait," he said, turning on the car.

I let him drive me around all weekend and from the passenger seat I stared at all of the little sea-salted houses and wondered how much they cost.

BREAKING AND ENTERING

She'd always been good at breaking and entering. The laundromat back home when she was eight so she could wash her own clothes in the middle of the night and not get shit about it. The car she slept in the first time she ran away. All the closets and rooms her mother tried to keep her in—she picked those flimsy locks with coat hangers, paper clips, the backs of cheap earrings from Claire's in the mall. The cellar where Butch once stashed her so one of her mom's dumb boyfriends wouldn't beat the shit out of them both. She picked her way in or out of every last one of them. If that didn't work, she started moving her mouth. She talked her way into bars and clubs, and out of apartments and bedrooms. A girl Houdini, except that she didn't need chains or water to show off. When it didn't work, she told herself she hadn't tried hard enough—that was her excuse for feeling stuck.

She saw her from across the park. Walking toward the new fancy building. She'd combed her short hair and was wearing a dress. Still, she didn't look like a professor. No stupid tweed blazer or secretary skirt. No boring dead-fish face, mouthing at everyone. Johanna waited for five minutes and then left Tipsy's leash knotted around Butch's ankle. He was still sleeping on a bench.

The guard was fighting with some brown kid about coming into the building without any ID. *Racist*, she thought, as she hurried past his desk in the two seconds he looked down, glided over the turnstile, and into an open elevator. A girl with long, dyed-auburn hair wrinkled her nose ever so slightly at her.

"I love your blowout," Johanna said to her, tugging at the roots of the matted clumps of hair she sometimes called dreadlocks. "Did you do it yourself or go to one of those places that does just blowouts?"

The floors ticked up. Three. Four. Five. Six. She realized she didn't know where to get off.

"It's not a blowout. My hair is just really straight." The girl looked annoyed.

Some people got on. Some people got off. A blur of fancy backpacks with magnetized buckles and cute patterns and "Can you press twelve? Is eight pressed?"

"Did you know the girl who jumped?" Johanna kept at it.

Straight Hair looked at her as if she'd been punched in the stomach.

"She was my friend and I can't get over it," Johanna lied or said something that was starting to feel true to her. She didn't believe in reality, but in stories—facts blurring into fiction and becoming memories which were true enough. She ran her finger along the sharp folded corners of the girl's paper in her pocket. It was a talisman, a good-luck charm, a spell.

"Madison was not friends with you." The girl looked like she might explode. Ninth floor. Johanna got off too, but let her huff away. *Fine, be that way*, she thought. *I'm the only one who knows what happened.*

It took her an hour of sticking her head into classrooms to find her. *Sorry. Sorry. I left something in this room. My water bottle?*

When Johanna opened the door to Stevie's classroom, she was in the middle of reading a poem out loud to the class. Stevie stopped and looked up from the page. She was sitting cross-legged on one of the long tables arranged in a square.

"Oh hey, hi, are you taking a class here?" she asked, clearly confused.

The students stared at her. One of them had been crying, Johanna could tell. She was a dowser for the tears of sad women. A girl, sapling-boned, dark hair. Another student eyed the clock.

"Our class is almost over," Stevie said. "Did you want to talk to me?"

"Can I take your class?" Johanna asked. "I just really want to learn something today." She felt a flicker of doubt in her stomach. She didn't want to scare this woman. She suddenly wasn't sure why she'd come. Her stomach was sour and empty. She was too sober.

"Um, maybe we can talk about auditing after class, but you can stay today and write a poem with us," Stevie said, her face first a small frown and then a reluctant smile. "What's your name? I realized I don't know."

"Johanna."

"Stevie."

One student whispered something to another and giggled. "We're writing a poem?"

Stevie turned back to the sheet of paper. "Just take one of the lines from this poem and make it the first line of your own poem. If you want to be in conversation with the ideas in this poem, you can, or you can just use the line as a jumping off point."

The students put their heads down and started to scribble away in their notebooks. Stevie gave Johanna a piece of paper from her notebook and a pen. Johanna found a seat and let her eyes pass over the poem. It made no sense to her. She noticed a couple of words and wrote them down on the piece of paper like she was making a grocery list out of someone else's language. She got lost in the process of finding a word and copying it down. *Blood. Jealous. Earth. Salt. Stick.* It felt good to hold a pen, to hold Stevie's pen, and to read a poem intentionally chosen by this woman who seemed both strong and broken. The ink was green and it bled out past the contours of the cursive letters that Johanna formed. She hadn't written anything down in a long time. She fingered the handwritten note in her pocket again. Script from a ghost now. She wondered if she should give it to Stevie.

"We'll have to finish these for homework," Stevie said, looking at the clock.

The class started to pack up their pretty backpacks and a couple of students crowded around Stevie to ask her questions. "When is the first essay due? Are you going to have more office hours? I don't know how to fix it, can you help me?" Johanna listened to the questions and remembered why she'd hated school and dropped out. Too many stupid questions. Babies who couldn't think for themselves or figure it out. Brown-nosers and ass-lickers. Rich kids trying to be perfect as if that would save them from becoming their parents. Nothing that mattered. A waste of time. She folded up her piece of paper, slid the pen and paper into her only empty pocket, and left the room.

"Wait," she heard a faint voice behind her, but she was already gone.

FLIRT

Mel's phone rang. She didn't recognize the number, so she picked up.

"Mel?"

"Yeah, who is this?"

"It's Gabe, Carol's son."

"Oh, hi." Mel got out of bed and let the dogs, Petie and Walt, out of their crates. They whined and stretched. She'd need to take them out soon. She couldn't remember the last time she and Gabe had spoken. Her dad and his mom were only together two years before her father had a heart attack and died. But for those two years, they'd had holidays together and tried to act like a family, like stepsiblings. Mel and her two sisters, Gabe and his one brother. After the funeral, they'd drifted. At this point, they were Facebook friends who happened to share a cabin in Gloucester. "How are you? It's been forever."

"I'm all right. Money is kinda tight, but I'm healthy. You?"

"Same, mostly broke, but Jenny and I are chugging along. I'm bartending and working on a book." Mel fed Petie and Walt and mouthed at them, *I know, I know, we'll go out in a minute.*

"What's the book about?" he asked.

"Our messed-up parents," Mel joked. "Kidding!" The sound of his voice made her feel like teasing him, like he was eighteen and she was twenty, and they were playing Frisbee on the beach and trying to see who could steal more beers from the cooler and hide them in the sand to drink warm later when their parents weren't looking.

"It was weird the way they tried to go all *Brady Bunch* on us," he said.

"I know, suddenly we were smashed together," Mel said.

"And we had no interest in acting like brother and sister."

"Oh, just that once," Mel said. She couldn't believe they were actually talking about it. One of the first times they all went to the cabin together, Mel and Gabe stayed home while everyone else went to a movie. They found an old bottle of Jim Beam in the cupboard, finished it off, and ended up making out in Gabe's bed. She'd never told anyone, not even Stevie. She remembered him sliding his hand down the front of her jeans. It was hot until Gabe threw up on his comforter and Mel snapped out of it to clean up the evidence. "I guess it was our way of telling our parents to fuck off."

Mel was outside the apartment now, in the hot, early September city air, watching the dogs sniff around several garbage piles to find the perfect place to shit and piss.

Gabe chuckled. "Highlight of my teenage years."

"Really?" Mel felt a surge of weird pride. "But you barfed."

"That was the whiskey, not you."

"I thought I molested you," Mel confessed.

"If I recall, I was the one who made the first move," he said. "I was so angry when I met you. Like, fuck, this hot girl has to be my sister."

"You were pretty cute too," Mel said. She liked talking about this, clearing the air, but she couldn't imagine this is why Gabe had called.

"I bet you're still amazing," Gabe continued.

Mel didn't know what to say. Was this awkward? Were they flirting? She had a flash of a fantasy of hanging up, firing up her vibrator, and whacking off to the memory of their teenage make-out session on the couch. *It's hot because it's so wrong*, she thought. Sometimes she felt like the star of her own amateur porn.

"Why do you have to flirt with everyone?" Jenny recently complained. "I mean you flirt with dogs, people of all genders, plants, and furniture."

"I only flirt with really expensive modernist couches," she joked, but she knew what Jenny was getting at. *Why do you have to be such a slut?*

"Oh, I have my days," Mel said, putting a pin in it.

Gabe sighed through the phone and Mel felt guilty for what she'd started. "You must have called for something other than to remember our attempt at *Flowers in the Attic*?"

"Yeah, actually, I have shitty news."

"Is your mom okay?"

Carol lived in Manhattan, on the Upper East Side, and though Mel never visited, she sometimes thought she should.

"She's okay. She has Alzheimer's and needs to go into a home, but for now my brother and I have someone who comes in to check on her a couple days a week," Gabe paused. "Long story short, some fly-by-night bank got her on the phone alone and tricked her into refinancing the cabin, and she lost the paperwork and missed several payments and basically the cabin is in foreclosure."

"What?"

"I know, it's crazy."

"I thought the cabin was paid for," Mel said.

"Not entirely. She refinanced a while back and then this happened. I'm really sorry. I think we're going to lose it."

"No, that can't be," Mel said. She felt tears in her eyes. She thought of all of the summers she'd gone up with Stevie, Jenny, Aaron, and Sasha. It was only ever a week or two, but it was an amazing escape. The way the sun came through the front window. The crab shack along the reedy beach. The plank on the porch where everyone she'd ever loved had carved their name. She'd reconciled herself to never owning anything anywhere, but at least she and her sisters had the cabin. "That's my special place. It's all I have."

The dogs had pulled her toward Gowanus—the pretty, once-polluted, now-gentrifying little strip of a neighborhood between Carroll Gardens and Park Slope.

"Have you called the bank?" she asked.

"I'm getting nowhere," he said. "They say we owe like $75K."

"Can you email me the info? Maybe I can try with them?" Mel allowed the dogs to drag her toward the canal. "I don't have that much money," she said.

"Me neither," Gabe said.

Mel felt her old resentments against Carol, her stepmom. Her father had bought her the apartment in New York long ago, and left the girls the cabin, but it was in Carol's name until she died and she controlled it and now this had happened.

"I'm really sorry," Gabe said.

"Thanks for letting me know," Mel said, and hung up.

She called Jenny, but she didn't pick up, probably because she was on the road to Ithaca, driving for five hours.

She scrolled through her phone to Carmine's number. She could text him something stupid or she could tell him a real thing.

She pressed the call button on his number.

He picked up.

"You doing anything right now?" she asked.

THE WIVES

The wives were supposed to wear red. Or white or black or pink. The wives were knitting and quilting. Some wives refused to sew. The wives went to their tailors to have their pants let out. The wives were so tiny. The wives were always at SoulCycle. The wives told the other wives through the plexiglass spit guard what they wanted on their kale salads. Avocado. Sweet potato. Cucumber. Salmon. Mixed in. Light dressing. The poor wives took care of the rich wives' children. Some wives had cabins and second homes and time-shares, and some had none. The wives were giving away a lot of money. The wives had no money to give. Some wives knew this history of women and this made them angry. Others wives did not. The wives were shopping, everywhere, all of the time, for all of the small and big things that made the houses run. The wives could not imagine a strike. The wives went on strike for an entire day, but it was not enough. Some wives made fifty-five cents, some made sixty cents, some made seventy-nine cents, and some made eighty-four cents for all of the dollars that the husbands made. The wives were so pissed off they could no longer suck all the husbands' cocks. The wives were eating pussy and loving it. The wives were getting their hands wet finally. The wives jumped right in. The wives were kicking ass, frankly. The wives were leaning way far in and also sometimes not at all. The wives underestimated what some other wives would do in the election booth. The wives were getting married at City Hall. They needed witnesses.

PART 2
FALL

THE SIGNS

"I could babysit for you," Johanna said. She wore a fresh change of clothes—baggy overalls cuffed at the knees, an old black Nirvana *Nevermind* T-shirt, a purple bandana tied over her snarled, matted hair, and her scuffed combat boots. Her eyes looked brighter, her pupils less pinned.

"How do you know I have a kid?"

"I googled you. I read some of your essays and your faculty profile. It said you live in New York City with your daughter."

"I don't really need a babysitter. I don't go anywhere unless she's with her dad or at school."

We were standing in the middle of Zuccotti Park. I was waiting for Mel to meet me. The half-built Freedom Tower loomed over us. There was a steady drumbeat and a chorus of horns. Was it party or a protest? The organization, the scale of it, was amazing, even though it was just a couple days old. People, it seemed, from all walks of life, had made this little village of activism. Before I bumped into Johanna, I saw women handing out extra socks to people underneath a Comfort Station sign and a crew of nurses giving free medical advice between two trees linked with a First Aid banner. There were kids and their parents washing dishes near the People's Kitchen and a free library staffed with volunteer librarians and donated books. I heard Spanish, Chinese, German, and Russian.

"I used to babysit for some of the neighboring farm kids before I ran away."

"You ran away?"

"Doesn't everyone basically run away at some point so that they can be an adult?"

"But how old were you?"

"The first time I was ten, but I couldn't make it stick. I finally got away for good when I was fourteen."

"How old are you now?"

"Seventeen."

I took it in. I had more questions, but I didn't want to push too hard.

"My mom used to tie me to a chair so she could get drunk without worrying that I'd wander off or burn down the house, but I always broke free. I was so mad, but then she'd pass out in a pool of her own barf, and I'd clean her up and get her into bed." Johanna said it flatly, without emotion, a fact.

"Sorry, that sounds rough," I said, unsure of how to respond. I was used to comparing traumas, weighing other people's childhood suffering next to my own. It was a bad habit.

"What? I don't fucking care, it made me totally independent!" She brushed me off and stabbed her paintbrush in the air for effect. "Do you want to help me paint signs?"

I looked over at the patchwork quilt of signs on the ground— some she'd painted, but others left behind by other protesters.

We are the 99%.

Loan Sharks Ate My World.

Eat the Rich.

One Nation Under Greed.

Wall Street Built on the Graves of Slaves.

The People Want a Bailout.

"I could, but I'm waiting for my friend."

"The one from the fountain?" she asked.

"Yeah." She seemed to know everything about me. I stared over at the drum circle. One of the bongo players nodded in my direction, like I was supposed to come over and dance, like we all were.

"Is she a professor too?"

"She used to be, but now she's a bartender."

"What bar?"

"It's a fancy place in Brooklyn called Zoe's." I wondered if I should have told Johanna where Mel worked.

"She probably got sick of coddling rich kids," Johanna said. "Your students are a bunch of wealthy fucks."

I thought we might get around to her crashing my class and the dead woman that tethered us improbably to one another. Was she still thinking about her like I was? Was she waking up in the middle of the night sweaty and with a thudding heart from a nightmare in which the woman fell to the ground, her blue dress and bright-yellow backpack always just a foot out of reach? "Some are really privileged, it's true, but some have financial aid and scholarships. In general, I like them. They work hard." I wasn't sure why I was defending my rich students to a homeless girl, here of all places.

"They have no idea what hard work feels like," Johanna scoffed.

"Yeah, you're right," I admitted.

Her shoulders softened and she narrowed her eyes at me. "So you're just going to give up the fight?"

"We're not fighting. You're right," I said, aware in a way that I often was with my students, that I was a stand-in for someone else—a parent, a friend, a lover, a sibling. Teaching had transference too, just like therapy.

"The woman that day?" I tried.

"I'm not ready," she said, and put her hand up. I sighed. Was she serious or just putting me off?

My phone chirped and I pulled it out of my back pocket. It was Mel. "Late! I'm sorry. Just getting on the train! Be there in thirty!"

"La Profesora!" Arturo emerged out from underneath a red tarp in the middle of the park. "Let me have her?" he called out to Johanna. She shrugged me away and squatted back down to paint a sign.

I walked over, flattered that he remembered me, and annoyed Johanna wouldn't talk to me about what I most wanted to know. *Just fucking let it go*, I told myself.

"Welcome to Little Puerto Rico or La Prensa as some of us are calling it." He leaned in to kiss the side of my face. I smelled cigarettes and pot.

He pulled me by the hand back under the tarp. "Es una profesora de la Universidad," he said to two men and a woman.

"Hola," I said, and held up my hand. "Stevie."

They barely looked up from their computer screens.

"They're deep in layout land." Arturo stood close to me. I had to fight the urge to take a step back.

"Are you in charge of some of this?" I asked.

"Me? No, nobody's in charge. There are working groups and I'm helping out with social media and the Spanish-language newspaper, but it's a collective and leaderless. Everything we decide is by consensus."

"It kind of reminds me of when I was a member of my campus women's center. We took over the quad of our upstate campus with a bunch of other student groups to keep the University from giving guns to security officers and letting the police patrol our campus."

"Did it work?"

"Yeah, we won! We actually occupied our president's building for a week." I remembered linking arms with strangers on campus in a hot stairwell, so that we couldn't be separated. "It's nice to do something again. Since I became a mom, I haven't had time to protest much. I mean, I teach about activism and I write, but this is more physical and I miss it. I used to hang out with this gang of squatters when I first moved to New York in 1994. They had this amazing abandoned synagogue way down on Clinton Street. They were mostly painters and they covered the walls in murals about Diego Rivera and Frida Kahlo."

"The ultimate Latino artist power couple!" Arturo laughed. "Can I borrow your students? They could come down and help me do some reporting."

"Yeah, I'm going to bring them."

"I feel awake, you know, that's the best thing. Like, wide open. Ready." He looked up at the sky. He seemed all possibility. All horizon. I felt myself staring at him. He had an energy coming off of him that made me want to stand next to him, walk with him, whatever.

"What?"

"Nothing."

"I'm corny? I'm always looking for la frase justa. You know, the exact right phrase in English."

"No, not corny. Just positive. Excited. It makes me feel better about the world."

"Do you want to see where we're sleeping? Some of the tents? In case you decide to camp out?" Arturo steered me away from the media tarp and toward a small cluster of tents near the People's Kitchen. "My partner and I are sharing this with some friends. Like, sometimes we sleep here and sometimes we go home to Brooklyn."

He unzipped the tent, crawled into it, and then stuck out a finger to wave me in. "Pásale."

I crawled in after him. It was dark and hot underneath the nylon September sun. He leaned back on his elbows and raised his eyebrows at me. "Isn't this the coolest? We're basically camping out against capitalism at Wall Street. We snuck in and now they don't know what to do with us."

"It's super utopian." I ran my finger along a seam of the tent.

"Anarchists are really good at makeshift worlds." He sat up. His face close to mine.

"Are they? I haven't been around anarchists in a while."

"I'm maybe more Marxist than anarchist," he clarified.

"Well, duh, I'm more feminist than Marxist."

"Well, duh, I'm more feminist than Marxist too," he said.

"I should hope so. I mean it's 2011, you have to be." I laughed. My phone chirped.

I ignored it and it chirped again. And again.

"You should check your phone. Where is it?" Arturo asked. I felt his eyes on my face and neck. I liked it.

"My back pocket?"

"May I?" Arturo reached around me and pulled my phone out of the butt pocket of my jeans. I felt his fingers and thumb press against my ass for a second and then he handed my phone back to me. I smirked at him. He raised one eyebrow at me.

All from Mel:

"Where are you?"

"I'm waiting in line to talk to the free lawyers."

"Come find me, but no rush."

"Hallo?" Someone scratched at the tent. "Don't mean to interrupt, but the GA is starting. Do you guys want to come?" Johanna unzipped a corner of the tent flap and peered in at us.

"Yes! You can meet my partner," Arturo said. "She's running this one."

"Mic check!" Someone yelled from the meeting area near the statue at the corner of the park. I looked over. A tall woman in a black shirt dress over jeans and boots. She had messy shoulder-length black hair, flecked with gray. She was holding some loose papers in her hand, and had that same magnetic energy that Arturo had, only in a feminine form.

"Devora used to be in a punk band, so she can really yell," Arturo leaned in to whisper in my ear, squeezed my arm, and then disappeared into the crowd. I looked around for Johanna, but she was gone too.

"Mic check!" the seated crowd called back.

"We are the General Assembly of Occupy Wall Street," she called out.

"We are the General Assembly of Occupy Wall Street," the crowd called back.

"We meet at two p.m. every day!"

"We meet at two p.m. every day!"

"We use our voices—this call-and-response technique called mic check—because the police are not allowing us to have an amplification system." I followed along, repeating the words that Arturo's partner said with an enthusiastic crowd. The effect was powerful, like we were one giant voice, yelling at the fucked-up economy and at Wall Street, who'd taken so much. I thought of that banker I'd seen that day in the park with his perfect, slicked-back hair, clutching the waist of his beautiful bride. I imagined him behind one of these buildings, snickering down at us, and I shouted a little louder. I spotted Mel off near the People's Library and went to talk to her.

"This is even better than I saw on Keith Olbermann," Mel said. He'd started to run a series of sympathetic reports on Occupy with Michael Moore that had gotten a lot of attention.

"Isn't it amazing?" I said, gesturing to the whole park. "I can't really believe it's happening."

"I've just been watching it all unfold from the Legal Aid line," she said. "And you've been flitting around the park, like some manic-pixie activist. How do you know so many people here? Who was that guy you followed into a tent?"

"This organizer I met in the fountain."

"Well, I could feel you guys flirting from across the park. Oh, and also you have a stalker friend." Mel pointed in the vague direction of the sign-painting area, but Johanna wasn't there anymore either. "That girl we met in the fountain. She told me she crashed your class?"

"Um, she's kinda lost," I said as if that explained Johanna's presence in my life.

Mel looked skeptical. "Boundaries, Stevie?"

"What? I have amazing boundaries and so do you," I joked. "What were you talking to a lawyer about?"

"The cabin."

"What about it?"

"I don't want to say too much or I'll sob, but Carol maybe fucked up the mortgage and the banks are foreclosing."

"But I was just there!" I said as if my fucking a stranger in it a week ago could make it suddenly okay. It was the only place I'd ever seen Mel get sentimental about, and when we were feeling low about money and New York, we joked about running away to Gloucester, living the cabin, and starting our own café. In a way, it was a safety net. "I was looking at that picture of you and your sisters on the beach and went to our bar in town and the turtle ladies were saving the lives of baby turtles."

Mel's nose quivered like it always did right before she cried.

"Stevie?"

I knew that meant I needed to stop with the memories.

"That's so terrible. I'm sorry. The banks can do whatever they want. I guess this is why this whole thing is happening," I said as I gestured to the carnival protest unfolding around us.

"Did the lawyer have anything helpful to say?"

"He said we might be able to appeal and be part of one of Obama's programs, but once the bank has sent the foreclosure papers, it's harder to apply."

"Did they send the papers?"

"Carol lost them."

"Shit."

"Right?"

I looked over at the Legal Aid table with its snaking line. The sign said, *We help with foreclosures, student-loan debt, credit-card debt, tax issues, sexual harassment, and immigration.*

MINT JULEP

Carmine dropped an ice cube down the back of her shirt. She squirmed until it fell out onto the floor of the bar.

"You'll pay for that," she said over the din of customers, three deep, waiting to catch her eye.

"Just passing through for a Diet Coke," he said, and pinched her elbow.

"What are you, an old lady?" She grinned at him, but she didn't want to get distracted. She was working on a martini, a new kind of old-fashioned with mulled cherries, and a mint julep that had actual crushed-up mint leaves in it.

"Sort of, but I'm disguised as a hot dad chef."

"So modest." She rolled her eyes at him. The drink tape from the servers spooled out endless requests on the little machine next to the register. She pulled the slips of paper off and hung them up in front of her. *One drink at a time Mel, just focus*, she told herself. She was feeling the rush she loved so much, the excitement of the bar and all of the people who wanted a drink and would tip her if she was nice enough or if she had a halter on that showed the outline of her tits or if they were drunk enough. Everyone behind the bar and in the kitchen goofing off and running around and getting slammed and feeding off adrenaline and flirtation and the rush that all really good bars and restaurants seemed to create.

"You know what I'm gonna do?" Carmine leaned in to her ear.

"Make it fast," she said, but she wanted him to stay pressed up against her face for a long time.

"When you're ready, I'm going to take you back to my place and I'm going to fuck you so good, you won't ever want a fake dick again."

"My dicks are not fake, but I bet yours is all right."

"Oh, it's better than all right."

Mel turned away so he wouldn't see her face get red. "I gotta make these drinks!" And then he was gone, back into the kitchen.

She looked up at her customers and tried to get her stomach to stop doing its little kick turns. She saw Greta watching her from the hostess's station—all cleavage and tight pants. Had she seen Carmine put the ice down her shirt? Were they performing something for Greta? Mel winked at her and watched her blush and get nervous. She grabbed her Boston shaker and turned back to her customers.

"Mint julep, right?" she said to a pretty redhead in a black dress.

She made drinks for another two hours, nonstop, until finally there was a lull. Jenny and Stevie came in and sat at the bar.

"I didn't know you two had a date." Mel made them both dirty martinis.

"We didn't." Jenny sipped and aahed over her drink. "But Stevie texted me because you hog her and I never get to see her." Mel and Stevie met Jenny at a queer bar that no longer exists in Brooklyn, when Park Slope was called Dyke Slope. Jenny was the best dancer that night.

"I totally didn't say that." Stevie bent down to sip at her martini like it was a dog bowl. "I can't pick it up yet."

"I love it when my girlfriend is bartending. Free drinks and made just the way I like them."

"Can I have another?" Tommy's underage girlfriend, who was already drunk at the bar, interrupted them and called to Mel.

Mel rolled her eyes at Jenny and Stevie and walked over to her. "How about a seltzer first?"

"No," she said.

Mel shrugged and made her a weak cosmo. She gave her a seltzer too, which she drank in spite of Mel's attempt to mother her. *At least in the city, no one is driving*, Mel thought to quash her guilt.

Tommy's girlfriend reminded Mel of her students and of why she quit teaching. They were overflowing with need and mess and wanting anyone to fix them, but hostile to suggestions that would actually make them feel better. Mel had never been able to escape the feeling that she was a puppet in the classroom and somebody else's hand was crammed up her ass, controlling her every move. At first, she'd worn weird secretary-like skirts and shirts from Ann Taylor Loft, and later when she'd lost her graduate teaching fellowship and was surviving on adjuncting, pants from the Old Navy outlet on Flatbush Avenue that were baggy and tight in all the wrong places. Once she started bartending, she understood that she'd been looking for a barrier all along, a wooden bar, that separated the people who wanted something from the people who had something to give. The bar was high enough so that no one could jump over, push through, shove past, or ask for too much. There were transactions for clearly stated goods and services, and a bill of sale. You pay me and I give you the change. You tip me, too, because that is the custom. You leave and I go home eventually and I mostly don't think of you anymore. It was clean. Physically demanding, but emotionally pure.

But what she most loved about bars were the tricks. The dim lights, smoky wallpaper, and alcohol were powerful magic. In bars and restaurants, she wasn't in charge of anyone and so age was not as much of a thing. Or maybe she passed better in bars. If she felt motherly and protective about Omar the dishwasher or Greta the hostess or Tommy's pretty mess of a girlfriend, it was out of choice, not obligation. She'd not been assigned the role of school marm or writing teacher. She did not have to correct anyone or anything unless she felt like it.

She pulled at the straps of her tank top and looked out onto the restaurant. The windows were still open. Warm, late September air. Conversation on the street. Magical Brooklyn artisanal luxury quirk—that's what they were selling at Zoe's, at all of the restaurants in this neighborhood. Tommy's girlfriend slid off her barstool and stumbled to the back, probably to yell at Tommy for making her wait so long. Mel looked over at Stevie and Jenny—deep in conversation. She wanted to join, but she decided to give them space. It's true, they hardly ever saw each other. Maybe Jenny was telling Stevie about her new girlfriend, and maybe Stevie would gossip with Mel later.

What would she do if Carmine came out again and slipped an ice cube down her shirt? She hadn't yet figured out how to introduce Carmine and Jenny. She didn't have a plan for that yet.

"Hey! You can't bring a dog in here," Greta said, her voice sweet but firm.

Mel snapped out of her bar reverie.

"We'll tie her up outside." A man's voice.

They came in and sat down at the bar, next to Stevie and Jenny. Greta, flustered behind them. "We have a dress code? Do we have a dress code, Mel?"

"We made it!" Johanna said, and wrapped her arms around Stevie's neck. Stevie looked surprised.

"Not that I know of," Mel said to Greta as she slid the drink menu in front of them. *Stevie's stalker*, she thought.

"Hi, you're Stevie's best friend," Johanna said, pulling crumpled dollar bills out of her overalls and onto the counter. "I'm Johanna from the fountain, from Occupy."

"Mel."

"This is Butch, my boyfriend."

"This is my girlfriend, Jenny." Handshakes, hellos, and nods all around.

The bar contracted around them. Homeless anarchist punks were not the normal customers at Zoe's, but who cared? Butch looked up and down the length bar. "Fancy."

Johanna counted out twenty-five crumpled dollar bills and arranged them in a wrinkled stack in front of Mel. "I'll take a gin and tonic."

"Yep, and for you?" Mel asked.

"Is the old-fashioned good?"

"I like it, but you have to be into mulled cherries."

Butch frowned and rested his forehead on the counter for a couple of seconds, like it was all too much for him, like he might not make it through the ordering. Jenny made big eyes at Mel and then nodded at her for another martini.

"He likes cherries," Johanna took over, whispered something in his ear, and he popped his head back up.

It was dark enough. They blended in, almost. The smell was a little off. Body odor, sweat, and salt, something acidic, but no garbage or shit. They reminded Mel of girl and boy Pigpens from *The Peanuts.*

Greta circled the bar like a shark, shooting Mel dirty looks. *Fuck you, rich girl,* Mel thought, protective of her new customers.

She made the drinks. They each took a demure sip and then drained them. She made them another. "On me," she said, and poured a shot for herself. The five of them—Mel behind the bar; Johanna, Butch, Stevie, and Jenny in front of it—glasses in the air. "To protesting!" Mel said.

"To protesting!" they shouted, and the rest of the customers turned toward them because they were clearly the rowdiest people there and everyone wants in on a party.

"What is a protest anyway?" Jenny leaned into their little group. Mel could tell she was getting buzzed and philosophical.

"It's for reclaiming public space and taking back the street," Stevie said. "Like, reminding us that we are part of democracy, no matter what the outcome."

"It's a party for the protesters!" Johanna stood up and danced a jig next to her chair, and Tipsy barked loudly from the tree outside the bar.

"Shhhh!" Butch said to her. "You're fucking up the dog." He put his head down on the bar again and held up a finger, like *give me a minute*, like *hold up.*

Mel leaned her elbows on the bar, heart warmed from the whiskey shot. "It's to effect change, right? I mean, we protest because we want shit to be different."

"It's for babies and complainers!" one of Mel's regulars called to them three seats down and then winked like he didn't mean it, but Mel knew he did. He was a gay real-estate developer, in his midthirties. Cash dripped out of his hands and onto Mel's bar. He had condos going up all over Brooklyn.

"Don't get mean, Charles, or I'll have to cut you off," Mel joked.

"You're the boss, Mel." He loved being dommed by Mel. It was the reason he came to Zoe's.

"I think it's also about the protesters. I don't think systemic change is always possible, but at least when you protest, you feel different and better. You connect with people and you make a change in yourself," Stevie said.

"No, no, no." Butch managed to get his head off the bar. The women all sensed that they were about to be mansplained at, so they looked down, away, out the windows, anywhere to avoid it. "We protest to cause a revolution, to overthrow the ruling class. Marx. *The Communist Manifesto.* It's simple. Anything else is a waste of time."

"He did read that," Johanna said in case they doubted Butch's credentials. Stevie was glad he'd kept it short.

"I totally disagree." Jenny sat up. She was head of a department full of mostly white male sociologists, and she was used to fighting and winning arguments with them. She called them "her bitches" and somehow they loved her for it.

Tommy came out from the back office, done fighting with his tiny girlfriend, who was probably passed out on his desk, to stare them down. Greta must have ratted them out.

The dog barked and whined on his leash outside of the open window. A table of customers winced in Mel's direction. Tommy raised his eyebrows at Mel and his two dirtiest customers.

"I'm sorry, we have a dress code. No shorts." He came up smoothly behind them.

"We're already fucking out of here, dude." Butch stood up, animated suddenly by the possibility of a fight.

"All right, then. Well, enjoy your night," Tommy said, mock friendly.

"Seriously?" Jenny said to Tommy. Mel knew she was drunk enough to cause trouble.

"Since when does Zoe's have a dress code?" Stevie asked.

Mel shot them all a look. *Don't get me fired*, she thought. "Thanks for coming to say hello." She was trying to diffuse.

"When the revolution comes, douchebags like you will be strung up." Butch couldn't help it. Tommy was too easy of a mark.

Johanna pulled at his shirt. Tipsy barked louder and pulled at her leash. She lunged toward two passing customers and a woman on the sidewalk screamed.

"Oh yeah, loser?" Tommy said under his breath.

Butch shoved Tommy hard and Tommy shoved back. Greta screamed. Jenny calmly picked up her drink and took a couple steps out of the way. Stevie mouthed *I'm sorry* at Mel. Carmine, suddenly out from the kitchen, with a wild look in his eyes. Omar too. As if two shoves summoned a testosterone dog whistle.

"I know them! Don't!" Mel shouted at everyone. "They're leaving. Just let them leave."

Butch lunged again, but Carmine held him back. "It's okay, man, let it go. Not worth it."

"Thanks for the drinks," Johanna called out to the three women from the street. This seemed like a normal exit for her. "Stevie, I'll see you at Occupy!"

"Fuck the one percent!" Butch bellowed from the sidewalk, and the crowd in the bar cheered wildly. Tommy looked confused. His girlfriend stumbled back out from the back office. "Tommy!" she whined and stamped her foot. "You said we could go home!" Mel thought she looked like a pretty foal—all long neck and skinny legs.

"Mel, we'll talk about this tomorrow," Tommy said.

"Totally," Mel said, her face feigning concern, as she watched him steady his girlfriend and walk out the back.

"Wow," Stevie said as she and Jenny settled back onto their barstools. "I can see the *Onion* headline right now: 'Drunk Hedgefund Dudes Fully Support Occupy until Sober.'"

"Or, 'Banker Bros Use Occupy to Get Laid.'"

"Fucking daddy's boy." Carmine straightened his chef's whites and scowled at Tommy's back.

"Um, so you guys, this is Carmine," Mel said, and pulled nervously at her tank top straps.

HOBO GIRL

She left Butch at Occupy with Tipsy. It took forever to get him from Mel's Brooklyn bar and into Arturo's tent. Asleep. Passed out. Whatever. *Shut up*, she thought as she zipped him into the tent.

"We were paying customers!" he shouted up at the steel girders of the Brooklyn Bridge as they trudged across it.

"It was a good drink," Johanna tried to soothe him. She'd panhandled for two hours to raise the money. She'd made a new sign, which was a lie, but worked. *Girl alone. Just trying to get back home to Pennsylvania.* She kept some of the money for herself, folded the bills carefully and put them in the old heroin baggie next to the note from the jumper and the poem from Stevie's class, also folded carefully. She duct-taped the baggie back into the inside of her shorts. Safe and dry. She didn't tell Butch she kept some for herself, and when he snorted three quarters of his bag and waved the rest at her, she shook her head no.

"You sure, baby?"

"I'm good."

They took the train to Mel's bar. Johanna had made a point of remembering it when Stevie told her. She didn't know a bartender anywhere. She was hoping they'd drink free, but she'd been nervous and pulled her money out too soon.

After she ditched Butch, she walked up Church and then West Broadway. She wanted some quiet, to be left alone with her own thoughts. Sure, Occupy was an amazing revolution unfolding in front of their eyes, and there was free, delicious food every day, but it was a constant stream of talk and dialogue and texts and ideas. It made her head hurt to think that much in such a concentrated way, and she missed Washington Square Park. The little makeshift cardboard world they stashed under the pine trees by the dealers, how quiet it got at night, and the birds chirping in the morning.

On the corner of West Broadway and Houston, a black sedan stopped in front of her. The window rolled down. A foreign accent she couldn't place. Russian, maybe. "Where are you going, beautiful? I will take you anywhere." She shook her head no. "Please, we have very good time." She walked around the back of the car and kept walking. Didn't look back. Didn't want to know if he would turn his big, dumb car around and follow her.

She knew Butch protected her. Her pride was too big to admit it to him, but she'd seen what happened to other girls who were traveling alone.

You had to act or be crazy to stay safe, and even that wasn't a guarantee of anything.

By the time she got to the park, it was closed. She ducked under the barricades and found her way to the cardboard they kept folded tightly and stashed up in a tree branch.

"Shit!" she said into the night air. Someone had stolen their cardboard.

She passed a homeless, toothless man she'd never seen before. He had a big branch he was using for a walking stick and an oversize Rangers jacket. He was muttering into his neck, and then at the moment she walked by, he looked up, and said, "I'm sorry that your friend is so sick," as if he were a seer in a Greek tragedy, and could see right into her life.

Did he mean Butch? Dope sick? Her new friend Stevie? The girl jumper? She had loose affiliations, but she considered them all friends in a way. She reminded herself that he was crazy, not a psychic, and kept moving.

She sat on a bench and put her feet up so that rats wouldn't run across her toes. She couldn't sleep without her cardboard and wished she'd done her quarter of the bag. *That bartender had her shit together*, she thought, savoring that moment when she and

Butch had been two regular paying customers at a bar and passed out of their shadow world.

She squinted in the dark at the other sleeping figures. There weren't many. The police did sweeps. Most left at night to lie on top of subway gratings or to sleep in building alcoves. Others walked east and west toward the rivers. Some rode the trains and slept. A few went to shelters or to wait in line for soup kitchens that opened on certain days. She and Butch sometimes went to the Catholic Worker kitchen on First Street because the workers were especially nice and the food was really good.

They didn't think of themselves as homeless. Like Woody Guthrie, Ernest Hemingway, and Hobo Lump, a famous woman who rode the rails and lived to be ninety, they told themselves they were making a choice to be free and to travel. They weren't against doing odd jobs either, but lately they'd gotten into a rut of begging and scoring.

Johanna had her favorites in the park—probably more homeless than hobos, but they were fixtures, people she saw every week, and she cared about their comings and goings, and worried if they disappeared. The woman who wore the neighborhood's fancy cast-offs, talked to herself, and had lice. The woman with a distended stomach, who at first everybody thought was pregnant. The trans dancer who carried a giant white suitcase filled with dirty scarves. The woman who shouted at anyone who passed her, "The world is so fucked up! The world is so fucked up! The world is so fucked up!" The punks in Tompkins who shared their forties. The pigeon man.

She didn't count the musicians because they went home at night, but she still loved them and considered them a part of the park's fabric. The piano man. The banjo and bass boyfriend-girlfriend duo called Coyote, the cheesy saxophone guy she and Butch called Steamy Manhole Cover because everything he played sounded like a bad eighties solo. The lone trumpeter, the Friday night bongo circle, and the countless kids with guitars who were still trying to catch the 1960s Greenwich Village folk-star dream. With the exception of Coyote, she hated most all of their music. Everybody sucked, but she liked that they tried anyway. Somehow—maybe it was in the

New York drinking water—people still knew to come to Washington Square Park to get naked, to score, and to busk.

She lay down on the bench. She didn't plan on falling asleep. It wasn't safe, but as she drifted off, she had two thoughts—for a poem, for signs, for dreaming, she wasn't sure, but she liked them.

Sometimes a girl is a time machine.

Occupy is a storage space for class rage.

WHEN SHE WOKE up. Something, someone poking at her shoulder.

"Butch?"

Squinted her eyes open. Her arms were cold. The sky was light gray, pink around the edges; the sun was just starting to come up.

A grinning stranger. Thirty? Forty? She couldn't tell. Giant pack on his shoulders, wild curly hair, tan, jeans down around his ankles and a dirty gray T-shirt covering his beer belly. He stroked his dick in his hand and grinned at her.

"You want to suck on it?"

"No!" she shouted, and bolted off her bench toward the fountain. "Fucking pervert!" she turned and shouted back at him. Her voice echoed through the quiet of the park. She walked past the memorial and looked at the picture of the dead girl. *Is this what you had to put up with?* she wondered. The papers rubbed against her hips and she felt comforted for a moment. Her heart was pounding. She walked out the park and down LaGuardia. She wanted to sprint, but she wouldn't let herself. *Keep moving, keep walking,* she told herself, *but don't run. You didn't do anything wrong.*

How many times had guys flashed her? It was like she had a sign on her chest that said, *Try me, I like it.* The first time she was eight and in the drugstore with her mother who was wrangling with the pharmacist to try to get free birth control. It wasn't working. Her mother raised her voice and started to make a scene. Johanna heard her use the word *vagina* and then she disappeared down a far aisle to look at toys, magazines—anything to avoid being embarrassed by her mother.

She bent down to pick up a crossword puzzle and when she stood back up, there was a guy standing there with his dick hanging out of the zipper of his businessman slacks. He didn't even look at her, kept his eyes on the rack of magazines, as if nothing out of the ordinary were happening. She stared at it for a second. Purplish red, surprisingly alert, searching for what she could only assume was her. She said nothing, dropped the magazine on the carpet, and walked quickly back to her mother. She imagined sirens wailing up to the drugstore and cops pinning him to the ground and cuffing him, but there was nothing like that. That particular pervert folded back into her memory, like a mirage. But she knew he was real. There was a guy on the subway, a guy on a bus, some lunatic in California who waved his dick at a crowd of women until Butch and his friends tackled him, and now this guy.

She wished Butch would have been there. He would have beat the shit of him.

She kept walking back down to Occupy. She was hungry and there would be breakfast.

THE WOLF

"Um, thanks," I said, panting on top of him. The orgasm's wave and crest. For a second or two, the manhole covering the sump pump of my heart shifted a little to the side. Some steam coming out. Warmth. Tenderness.

I rolled off him and David rested the side of his head in the space between my tits.

"That was nice," he said.

"Super nice."

"Is this okay?" David asked. "Me contacting you?" He had intense green eyes that made me look away. "I'm down in the city for this project and I just couldn't help myself. I wanted to see my sea witch."

"Yeah, I like the way you growl." He'd snarled while I was on top of him and nipped at my neck when I first let him into my apartment. "I wrote a poem a while back about a wolf I met at a bar. I must have conjured you up."

"I knew you were a witch."

"Witches like animals. Hi, Wolf."

"Hi, Red."

"My heart's been dead for a while," I admitted. Good sex opened me up and made me chatty.

"I could be like those emergency heart paddles." He put his palms on the top of my tits and made an explosive noise.

"Wait, lemme play dead." I opened my eyes wide and held my breath.

He made the explosive noise again. "Nurse, I think she's flatlined."

"She's got a cold dead heart," I said.

"Nah, she's okay," he said. "Nurse, please leave me alone with the patient."

I hadn't really allowed myself to cuddle with anyone. I hadn't wanted to since Aaron had left. I wanted to fuck people, and then go home and lick my wounds.

"This whole building is full of eighteen-year-olds?" he asked. Everyone was curious when they first came over. *You live here? With students?*

"My kid and I are the youngest and oldest people in the building and everyone else is eighteen."

"Sweet deal?" he asked.

"For now." I didn't tell him that I was getting kicked out. I didn't need to make him my confidant. *He doesn't even live here*, I said to myself.

I got up to pee and stared out the window in the living room. Some of the leaves were turning red and others had started to fall. Through a bare patch of trees, I spied the makeshift memorial; the candles were burning bright. I was impressed by the students' devotion to the site, and surprised the University hadn't swept it all away.

"Come back, Red," David called from the bedroom. *Would he stay or go?* I felt my familiar urge to be alone creeping back.

I got back into bed. It was ten a.m. on a Friday. *What else am I gonna do?*

"Where did you go?"

"Just thinking about a dead girl."

"Yourself?" he joked, thinking we were still playing.

"I wish. A student jumped in front of my classroom and killed herself."

"That's crazy."

"I know."

"I'm sorry you had to see that," he said, and pulled me close for a hug.

"What are you looking for?" I asked, changing the subject. I hadn't yet asked any guy I'd fucked this question. It was too messy, too much for me to consider myself, let alone ask someone else.

"Openness. Play. Multiplicity. Nonmonogamy," David answered quickly, certain.

"Like, dating a bunch of people at the same time?" I asked.

"Sometimes, maybe, probably not a bunch."

I took it in. I wasn't sure what to say.

"How about you? What do you want?"

"To have fun, to not be sad," I said. It was the most honest answer I could give. "I ruined my marriage. I did a stupid, bad thing."

"I've been married twice. Marriages have lots of stupid, bad things in them."

I sighed. "Maybe."

"I can help with the fun part," he said.

"Yeah, you already are," I said, and looked into his eyes. He stared back at me. I looked down, still shy.

"I see you," he said, and then added, "Is it okay if I stay over?"

"Yeah, I'd like that." But I couldn't tell if I meant it or not.

WILL YOU BE MY LITTLE SISTER?

It was Saturday morning and Sasha was in the tub with her Lego elves. She playacted multiple angry girl voices mouthing off to each other about friend betrayals and the injustice of being a kid. "I'm going to unfriend you. There's no choice time for you this week. Let's have cupcakes for dinner." I sat on the toilet and read a magazine while she splashed behind the shower curtain.

"How do you know about unfriending?" I interrupted through the curtain. She was six. None of her classmates were on social media. Yet.

"Savannah said it to Coco."

"In school?"

"Yeah, when they were fighting at lunch."

"That's not a thing," I said, struggling for the right words. "You can't do that in person."

"The lunch lady said that too."

There was a knock at the door.

"Someone's here. I'll be right back." I left the bathroom door open, so I could hear Sasha splashing and not drowning.

A man in a suit. An adult. There were never other adults in the dorm. "Professor Quinn?"

"Yes."

"I'm Detective Gonzalez. I work for the University." He flashed an ID card at me. "You called in the young woman who jumped in front of your classroom?"

"Yeah." I stepped out into the hallway. "I can't really talk right now. My kid is in the tub."

"This is quick, I promise," he said. "Did you know her?"

"No."

"See her around campus?"

"Not that I remember."

"Anything unusual about her?"

"Other than the fact that she fell from the sky in front of my classroom?"

"Yes, ma'am."

"The papers. She jumped with a notebook and the papers floated down afterward. That seemed odd to me."

"We're investigating the papers."

"What's on them?"

"I can't discuss the details of the case with you." He handed me his business card. "If anything else comes to mind, give me a call."

"Is something wrong? I mean, was it a suicide for sure?"

"We just need to reach legal closure on this case."

"Sure, okay."

He pressed the elevator button and stepped into it.

I shut the door. *What the fuck is legal closure?* I thought.

Sasha behind me, dripping in a towel. "Who was that?" she asked.

"Babe, we didn't wash your hair yet."

"Who was that?" she pressed.

"Students," I lied.

Later that morning, we stepped into the elevator. A student, petite, eighteen, probably homesick but hungover, leaned over Sasha. "I always wanted a little sister. Will you be my little sister?"

Sasha squirmed and turned away from her. "She doesn't really know you," I gently reminded the student. "What's your name again?"

"Sofia." She looked hurt that I didn't know her name, but they'd all just moved in and it was impossible for me to learn 250 new names every year.

"Is she shy?" she asked as if Sasha weren't there.

"No, but there's a lot of new faces and she's just one kid."

She got off on the fifth floor and waved goodbye. "See you soon, little sister!" she said as the elevator door shut.

"I don't know what's up with her, I'm sorry," I said to Sasha.

"Students are so weird," Sasha said as we walked into the lobby of the dorm.

"She's going to fall!" the guard called to me as Sasha crawled over the turnstile. There was a gate we could use, but Sasha preferred a jungle-gym challenge.

"She's okay," I called back. The guards were bored and trapped behind their desk. They loved to tell me what to do as we walked in and out of the building. *She needs a hat! Where's her umbrella? Is she late for school? Where's her father?*

We walked toward the fountain, Sasha flip-flopping next to me in her suit with her towel around her neck.

"Soon they'll probably turn it off," I said more to myself than to Sasha.

"Nonfiction is real and fiction is a made-up story," Sasha said. They were learning about genre in first grade. I was amazed by how much their teachers taught them about writing. They had writing workshops and publishing parties, learned about story structure, and even wrote blurbs and bios for their books.

"Like, facts about butterflies are nonfiction, but stories about fairies are fiction," Sasha picked up where she'd left off.

"But I thought fairies are real?" I asked, and faked a confused face.

"They are, but stories about them are fiction!"

"Totally," I said.

The fountain spray shimmered in the wind. Sasha ran ahead of me and slid into the water.

A sixty-year-old woman in Tevas and an Athleta halter dress looked behind Sasha, bewildered—like, *Where is her mother? Why is this child alone?* I jogged to catch up, nodded at her, and thought, *Got it. It takes a village. Fuck off.* Aaron and I had trained Sasha to never walk or scoot out of our sight; still we both knew you couldn't hold a city kid's hand forever. I marveled at the middle school kids I saw on the subway, alone or in tight packs, with their small bodies and giant backpacks, jostling for a seat like any other straphanger.

It was early enough so that it wasn't too crowded. Mostly neighborhood kids and tourists. And Johanna. With Tipsy, no Butch. I slipped off my sandals and waded in after Sasha.

Johanna waved excitedly and splashed over to us. "Is this your kid?"

"Yeah, Sasha. This is Johanna."

Sasha squinted up at her, mumbled hi, and splashed off.

"How are you?" I asked. She looked tired, like she hadn't slept well.

"Some asshole flashed me this morning, but I'm okay."

"In the park?"

I remembered the time a guy had his dick out on the F train. He was standing, holding the pole that ran along the ceiling, so that his dick eyed all of us women in our seats. I stared down into my book until he got off the train. None of us said a word. That was 1998.

"Yeah, this park, which everyone thinks is so safe."

"Did you tell the police?"

Johanna smirked at me. "You're cute with your belief in cops."

I looked over at Sasha, who had her arms wrapped around Tipsy's neck. Tipsy's tongue hung out the side of her mouth and her lips were curled up in a big dog grin.

"Do you want to play fetch with her?" Johanna pulled a tennis ball out of her pocket. She tossed it and Tispy used her three good legs to bound after it, then she gave the ball to Sasha and let her throw and catch. I kept an eye on Sasha, like I always did, everywhere. Did I trust Johanna with my kid? Not really. But we were all there together, and she had a light touch with Sasha. She didn't say much. She let her throw and catch, and she didn't push for anything in particular to happen. I liked that.

"Stevie!"

I looked up. It was Paige, the PTA mom who made me miserable, waving. She had her daughter Savannah with her.

"Sasha!" I yelled. "Savannah is here."

Sasha and I waded over while Tipsy and Johanna kept at fetch. *Maybe I can get Savannah to come over*, I thought. Sasha and I had no plans today. The day spooled out in front of us. It would be nice to have a friend over.

"Savvy!" Sasha leaned over the fountain wall to hug her friend. "Come in!"

Savannah looked up at her mom expectantly, and Paige made a face. "Honey, you know we don't swim in the fountain," and then more quietly to me, "I just get too freaked out by the homeless people who use it as a bathtub."

"Well, my joke about the fountain is that it's filled with kids and schizophrenics." I laughed, trying to mask my class rage once again. "They get along great!"

"Like that girl with the dog?" Paige leaned closer to me.

"She's actually a friend of ours," I said.

"She is?" Sasha asked.

"Well, mine, but yours too now," I said. "She's an anarchist." I decided to go for it. Fuck Paige and her fear of the fountain. "We've been swimming here for two years without getting any diseases."

"Ha, I love the Village, it's still so weird." Paige was unflappable. I couldn't make her balk. It made me crazy. I wanted to throw her in the fountain or lick her face just to make her scream. "I'm just always going to be one of those germophobe moms. I can't help it. I want to be more like you, Stevie. God, I wish I could relax more."

I didn't believe her. Johanna waded over with Tipsy.

"Johanna, Paige. Paige, Johanna." They eyed each other.

"Can Savannah play later?" I asked.

"I can drop her off after her textiles class," Paige said.

Johanna snorted.

I tried to keep a straight face. "Or I can pick her up from textiles and you can get her from me later?"

"Sure," Paige relented, and the girls squealed with delight. "Just promise me, no fountain."

"Totally, I promise." I held my hand up. *Scout's honor.*

THAT'S NOT LEGAL

"Are you sure this is it?" Jenny asked.

Mel knocked harder and pushed the doorbell a second time. "This is her address. She's been here for years."

They heard the sound of a chair being scraped across the floor and shuffling by the door.

"How long has it been since you've seen her?" Jenny whispered.

"She's not my mother!" Mel whispered back. She felt guilty suddenly. "I don't know. I saw her at the cabin maybe ten years ago."

Jenny put her hands up in an *I'm sorry* gesture.

The door opened and Mel and Jenny moved into hug Carol, Mel's stepmother. She'd wrapped her small frame in a sweater cape and had on loose yoga pants. Her hair was still cut in a chic gray bob. She narrowed her eyes at Mel as if she were trying to make her out. "Madeleine?"

"No, Carol. It's Mel, Madeleine's youngest daughter. We talked on the phone last week and I said I'd come by to help you find the paperwork from the bank. Remember?" Mel realized she was maybe shouting.

"I don't want to fight with you," Carol continued as if it were the late eighties and she'd just run away with Mel's father. Mel remembered her mother, pacing in the kitchen with the phone cord twisted around her arm like a tourniquet, tearfully calling Carol and demanding that she send their father back.

"Carol, it's Melissa," she tried again.

Jenny eyed the apartment. There were piles everywhere. Newspapers. Plastic bottles. Tin cans. Clothes on the couch and in the chairs. Dishes near the sink. The mail in drifting heaps on a long table near the window.

"Mel, you know, the gay one," Jenny said.

Mel wanted to object, but it worked. Whatever memory synapse had just been triggered, lit up, and Carol's expression moved from confusion to understanding.

"Is this your friend?"

"Yeah, Jenny, my girlfriend."

Carol pulled a frown. "That's not legal," she leaned into whisper at Jenny, and Jenny laughed. She was good with old homophobes, Mel remembered from the Chinese New Year celebrations she'd mostly stopped going to with Jenny's family because she couldn't take it anymore. She and Jenny had mostly taken a divide-and-conquer position with their respective parents. Except for Mel's sisters who Jenny loved dearly, they hardly ever hung out with each other's relatives. It was easier that way. Mel was surprised when Jenny said she'd come along.

"I have a girl who comes and cleans and looks after me three times a week," Carol said, as if sensing they might be worried by the mess.

"Do you mind if I start to look through the mail?" Mel asked.

Carol ignored her or didn't hear her. "But I think she's stealing things from me. I have very expensive face creams and they go missing."

"Have you eaten today?" Jenny asked.

"I had some rice and a banana."

Mel moved toward the table of mail and started to sift through it.

Jenny opened the refrigerator and peered in. "Do you want me to make you an omelet?"

Carol nodded. "Just don't use too much butter."

"Can I throw away the old coupons and fliers?" Mel asked Carol.

"No! I need those!" Carol looked alarmed.

"Okay, I won't." Mel rolled her eyes at Jenny.

It was all much worse than she'd imagined. After their father died, Mel and her sisters had never understood what their relationship to

Carol was supposed to be. Technically, for two tumultuous years, she'd been their stepmother, and then they shared a cabin together, like people with a time-share. And then her son Gabe called, and Mel thought she needed to try to reach out to save the cabin and to check in. Still, they mostly were tethered by landscape and a man with a huge personality that they all probably saw as too much of a savior. Mel knew Carol had made her father happy in a way her own mother never had. The joy of sex with a woman who actually liked him stopped his heart. She never blamed Carol for that.

Jenny turned on NPR and fixed lunch for Carol. The two of them chatted while Mel worked her way through the mail drifts. She couldn't find anything from a bank. She wondered if the bank had even sent anything. She doubted it.

She got a text from Carmine.

"Tommy is up to something. Let's meet for a drink and plot his death?"

"Can't we just rub up against each other instead?" Mel texted back.

"Yaz."

She didn't want to think about work intrigue or about making Tommy happy so he'd keep her on the schedule or about having to train Greta so she could eventually replace her. She wanted the bar to be about fun and money and nothing else.

She piled through the last drift of mail and pulled out the table to make sure nothing had fallen behind it.

AFTER LUNCH, CAROL kissed them each on the cheek and went to take a nap. Jenny and Mel let themselves out and walked past the weird mix of nannies, plastic surgery wives, and doormen that comprised the Upper East Side.

"It's worse than I thought," Mel said as they waited for the downtown 6 train.

"She probably needs to go into a home," Jenny said. "We should call her son and maybe we could go visit her once a month or something?" The platform swelled with high school kids and their rowdy, after-school, *we're free!* energy. They scarfed down bags of chips while they talked too loud. *I'm going to fuck her up! Is that what he said?*

"Yeah, we should do those things." The train rattled and screeched into the station and they got on. "I don't want to get old," Mel said as the doors shut.

"You won't, baby. You won't." Jenny rubbed her back and put her body between Mel and the teenagers.

LOST THINGS

While we rode the train to Brooklyn for Sasha's soccer game, I spaced out and she played a game on my phone.

The train rattled aboveground and into the neighborhood of Brooklyn where I first lived with Aaron when Sasha was born. We couldn't afford our rent in Park Slope anymore and so we moved deeper into Brooklyn—two doors down from a fire station, around the corner from a pulsing salsa studio, and beneath a woman who spent three hours a day on the treadmill. For two months, Sasha had colic. It had been the loudest year of my life.

"Three more stops, babe," I said. Sasha showed me a pony she was dressing and using a hair dryer to style. "I like the wig situation," I joked.

"That's not a wig, it's the pony's hair."

"Looks like a big wig to me."

Sasha ignored me and ran her pointer finger over a shampoo bottle. *We've got to download a better game*, I thought as the train lurched into the Parkside station.

"Your phone is talking about apartments." Sasha pointed to the apartment listings that had popped up on my screen.

Penthouse B on Metropolitan epitomizes Modern Living. $5,500.

Fully Renovated SUNNY Studio for rent. Immediate Move In! $1,700.

"Stand clear of the closing doors," the conductor's voiced boomed. I swiped the listings away and spaced out as Sasha played her game.

I made a list of lost things. My marriage. A husband. The earliest version of him—that young man who once loved me so. Dead and gone, or at least lost to me. A girl who jumped. My apartment. Not yet, but soon.

I remembered the baby boy. Sasha's twin. Lost to me forever. Swimming along in the black-gray screen of the sonogram machine. In the fifth month he stopped moving, and there was no fixing it. The technician left the room, came back with the doctor. Some dumb, confusing words. *This happens all the time.*

Outside of the imaging center in the empty wind of the Upper East Side, Aaron clung to the wreck of my body. I was stupidly naive. Did the amnio kill him? Had I killed him? Somehow? Nobody knew. Nobody could or would say. *These things happen all the time,* the doctor said again, and I hated him and knew he was right.

You could lose all kinds of things. Loved things that were becoming people, cell by cell. You could lose your house, your car, and your job. You could lose your girl, too, if you weren't careful and you didn't keep her close to you in the bed at night. You could lose so much that living in a tent in the middle of the park looked good and real and right. You could start to think that was home and you could like it.

We got off at Church Avenue and started to walk.

"Gimme phone," I said, and Sasha handed it back to me.

"Do you want to put your cleats on by this bench?" I asked.

"When we get to the field," she said. "I just want them to pass me the ball today."

"They will, your coach will make them, and also you have to scream for the ball really loud." I made ridiculous waving motions with my arms like a drowning monkey and grunted "Ball, ball, ball!" at Sasha.

"That's weird," Sasha said, but laughed anyway.

"Weird is good," I said, and watched her trot off down the field and toward her teammates. One high-fived her and another put her arm around Sasha's neck.

"Mama, did you bring the snack?" Sasha called back at me.

"Oops. Is it my turn?" I asked the dad who was the assistant coach, whose name I could never remember.

"I think maybe?" My good, cool mom feelings dropped down a notch. I hated SignUpGenius.

"Okay, I'll just run and get something. Clementines or apples, not donuts."

"Donuts!" the girls all shouted back at me.

The dad shook his head no at me, and then he winked. "Watch my kid?" I asked him. I hadn't been winked at since I was in my midthirties. It was nice.

"Donuts!" the girls cheered.

"I'm not allowed!" I called back, and started to jog to the supermarket.

I came back with a bag of clementines and a small box of donut holes. I sat down on the bench next to one of the other soccer moms and started to peel the clementines so the girls could eat them between quarters.

Sasha jogged up and down the field, sometimes kicking the ball and sometimes chatting with a teammate.

"Thisbe, focus honey!" the mom next to me called out, then started to help me peel.

"They mostly cluster up at this age," I said.

"Thisbe is so spacey out there," she said.

We hadn't spoken before. The soccer teams changed every ten weeks, and with Aaron and my co-parenting schedule, I didn't always meet every parent.

"You're Sasha's mom?"

"Yeah, Thisbe is yours?"

"Yep." She added a peeled clementine to the little pile I'd made out of the top of the donut holes box.

"I figure they eat a clementine and then pop a donut hole," I said. I was always the mom who let her kid have more sugar than the other kids. For the kids who only got to have one treat a week, I was like some kind of sugar-god-mama-pusher.

"Perfect!" She smiled. I was just happy she wasn't Paige or another Stepford PTA mom.

"We met your husband last week," she said. "Kick it, Thisbe!"

I looked up at the field. Sasha had fully spaced out and was chatting with the goalie. "Sash, move up, you're halfback!" I called out.

"He's not my husband anymore," I said.

"Oh sorry." She looked flustered. "I didn't know."

"No, it's a good thing. We're friends now."

The mom leaned forward on her high-heeled wooden boot clogs. I couldn't figure out how women walked in those.

"How did you do it? How did you get out?" she whispered as if she were in jail and I'd tunneled out through the wall.

"I did a stupid thing and then he left, but we did couples therapy for a long time first."

"I've done so many stupid things," she said, staring off onto the field.

"You just kind of go, and it's terrible and then it's a little less terrible," I said. I had no magical wisdom to impart about the end of a marriage.

The referee blew the whistle and the girls trotted over to us.

"Oranges first and then you can each have a donut if your parents say it's okay," I said.

The girls stuffed clementines into their mouths, grabbed for a donut, and huddled back around their coach.

"I just don't want to have to sell our brownstone." The mom leaned closer to me, as if this were her most horrible secret. Real estate. I got it. If I had a brownstone, I'd cling to it too. So much for my theory that rich couples were happier.

"Well, my joke about my ex and me is that it's easy to get a divorce when all you have to divide is debt."

She didn't laugh, but smiled tightly and changed the subject.

"Have you been following all this Occupy stuff? NPR did a little thing on it, and then I saw that cop pepper-spraying those girls and I just thought, Jesus dude, back off."

"I haven't watched the video yet, but I heard it's straight in the face."

"Disgusting. I mean, my father was a cop, and I understand the things officers have to do, but even he thought it was too much."

"I went to check it out the other day. It's amazing, a party and a protest rolled into one. You should go and see it for yourself."

"But what do they want? What are their demands?"

"I'm not sure it matters, does it?"

"If you're going to take something over, you have to make demands."

"I dunno. I think they're just changing the conversation." I reached for the box of donuts and stuffed two in my mouth. I held out the box to her, but she shook her head and made a face like I was offering her a poisoned apple.

OCUPADA

To seize. To take up space. To fill up time. To employ. To reside or have one's place or business. To hold a position. To be situated in a hierarchy. To fill the mind or thoughts. To keep someone busy or active. To have sexual relations with. To fill. To transfix. To seize. To take up space. To fill. To fill. To fill. To be situated. To be in a hierarchy. To hold a position. To employ. As in, that television show occupied time. As in, I kept the salesgirl occupied while he stole the necklace. As in, that building occupies two city blocks. As in, those people occupy the position of waiter, of bartender, of adjunct, of clinical assistant professor, of nurse, of doctor. As in, she occupied my pussy all night long.

I'm sorry, this park is occupied. These people are really busy. Occupy peace and love. Occupy my heart. Occupy my head. I said, Occupy this pussy. Get down there. Go ahead. Do it. When you're done, you can occupy that house over there. And then, that one, and that one, and that one. I can't come to the phone right now because I am occupied. Occupy the Bull with his giant balls. Occupy the late-night stars and the early morning sun. Occupy your school. Occupy your church and your classroom. Occupy your food. We got so preoccupied that we forgot. We occupied for as long as we could. We held our ground. We did. We really did.

GOLD STAR

When I got back from teaching and office hours, there were men in hard hats with clipboards in my apartment.

"We knocked and you weren't here, so we keyed in," the tallest of the three of them said. Another one let the tape measure go and it snapped against my leg as it retracted.

"Yow." I lifted my shin and rubbed it.

"Sorry about that."

"God, the University doesn't waste any time, does it?" I said.

"Next time, we'll make sure to get your permission before we come in." He pointed the corner of his clipboard at me like we'd reached some kind of truce.

"You go ahead and do that." I slammed the door behind them and felt a fuming rage to punch through a wall. I took a couple of deep breaths and scrolled through my contacts. H. Hayes. I'd kept it from so long ago, but I'd never used it. I needed many drinks. I needed a body on top of mine. I needed to pretend otherwise.

"You out?" I texted him.

"Come to Gold Star," he texted back immediately.

"What's going on there?"

"Just DJing, hanging."

I changed my clothes and spent a long time applying mascara and eye shadow. I stared at my freckled face in the mirror as I put on dark red lipstick. Mel had bought it for me. "It makes guys think of your pretty red mouth blowing them," she said when she gave it to me.

What am I to him? I wondered as I left my apartment and walked to the train. He texted back! I pushed the question away. I couldn't say.

I bought cigarettes at the bodega next to the bar to steady myself. I smoked one outside as I stared at the water facing Manhattan. More pink skyline. More balmy, thick, late September air. My phone did its chirpy things. I read its headlines while I smoked. I didn't want to look like I'd rushed over, though it had only been an hour since I'd texted.

Africa: More Dangerous to Be a Woman Than a Soldier.
Life for Libyans in Tripoli Returns to Normal.
US Hikers Freed in Iran on Spying Charges.

It was the most terrible way to get the news. A daily drip of horror that fed my anxiety and kept me clicking, swiping, and deleting.

I walked in and waved at Hayes. He beckoned me over, hugged me, and stepped away from his computer in the corner to introduce me to a guy in his band and the bartender.

"This is Stevie. She's a writer. Jaime plays guitar. Kyle, well, he's an asshole who bartends."

I said hello and asked for a shot of Jameson and a can of beer.

Hayes moved back to his corner. Jaime bought me another shot, and I did two more with the bartender. There was a small clutch of twentysomething women on the other end of the bar, deep in their phones. A Buck-Hunter video game and an ATM in another corner. Two old couches. A cute nerd in tortoiseshell glasses, jeans, and a flannel sat on the couch. She smiled at me and I smiled back. Did I remember how to flirt with women? I'd buried this part of myself for so long, and I missed it.

"What do you write?" Jaime asked me. He looked comfortable on his stool, like he understood that a bar wasn't for anything other than drinking and sitting.

"Fiction lately, poetry always, sometimes essays."

"I write songs."

"Those are hard," I said. I meant it. "I can't rhyme or do, like, meter and beats."

I pulled two dollars out of my wallet. "You wanna play?" I asked Jaime, and nodded at the video game.

"Nah, but kill a buck for me."

I felt the nerd on the couch watching me as I moved toward the video game. I put in my two dollars and aimed the cheap plastic faux rifle. The deer ran across the screen. Some had antlers and some didn't. I pulled the trigger a bunch of times, squinting, drunk, and missed all but two. Does.

"Wow, you're terrible." She came up behind me and stared at the screen.

"I got two," I protested, turning just enough so that I had to look up to see into her glasses. Her eyes were dark and pretty.

"Those are your friends?" she asked.

"Kinda."

"Kinda?"

"I mean, I don't know them that well."

"You with that guy?"

"No." I looked over at Hayes who was deep in conversation with the girls at the other end of the bar. I remembered the last time I'd shown up when he was deejaying. My being here meant nothing really.

"Okay, good," she said.

"Good?"

"You heard me."

Jaime looked over from his barstool and waved at us, like a *howdy* thing, like brotherly, I decided.

"Do you want to smoke a cigarette?" I asked her.

"Sure." Outside the bar. Night sky now. Cloudy moon. She had a lighter. Lit mine and then hers.

"What's your name?"

"Stevie. Yours?"

"Adija."

"Oh, it's . . ." I trailed off, realizing I had no idea.

"Nigerian," she finished my sentence.

We smoked in silence. I felt her eyes on my face, but resisted looking back at her.

There was a girl I was in love with for two years in college. Her name was Hope and she grew up in the Bronx and was a women's studies major, and we sometimes slept in the same bed after helping each other with our essays. She had beautiful purple lips and dressed like a skater girl, baggy everything, and she was a fast reader and a tease. She knew I wanted her, but was paralyzed by fear. After six months of cuddling, we finally fucked. My mouth on her pussy, my fingers inside of her, and then eventually my whole hand. I cried when she came—is there anything better than making a woman come? The joy of it! She wiped my tears with her thumbs, and then pushed me down on my back and licked and sucked until I cried again.

We walked back into the bar. "Can I sit with you guys?" Adija asked.

"Sure," I said.

She followed me back over to where I had been sitting and rested her hand on the small of my back. She bought me and Jaime a shot.

I managed the intros: "Jaime, Adija. Adija, Jaime."

I felt warm and fuzzy. I heard them saying something about guitars—brands. Telecaster. Fender. A banjo. I whispered answers to questions in each of their necks. Jaime's beard brushed against my cheek. Adija's lips close to my ear. The passivity of being desired. Doing nothing. Sitting back. I saw that I was a go-between, a wanted thing, and up-for-grabs, and this made me happy in an electric drunk way. I went to the bathroom. It had a slight turn and tilt. I texted Mel. "Hot woman at a bar. So sexy! Maybe too young?! Do I remember what to do?" When I came back out, I saw that the younger women on the other couch had left. The bartender gave us shots and I finished my beer. I'd drunk up the night.

A quick flash. The four of them. Me, the bartender, Adija, and Jaime. An old fantasy. I tell them what to do. I line them up and fuck them one at a time while the others look on and watch. I come and come. They're just dicks. Cocks I can control and use to get off. Adija has a strap-on and maybe I do too.

"You wanna get out of here?" Adija asked.

"Sure."

I waved goodbye at Jaime and Hayes, who barely looked up from his laptop. Adija maneuvered me out into the street by the shoulders and made me hail the cab.

"Lots easier for a white girl to get a cab at this hour." In the back-seat she leaned up against me. Kissing. Tongue. Wet. I rubbed my hand against her tits and she slid her fingers down into the waist-band of my skirt. The cab driver stared straight ahead. We'd all pretend the plexiglass was a curtain.

"You've kept your hair." Her fingers in my wet pussy. "That's nice. Nobody has hair anymore."

We drove and drove to her apartment. The cab driver was lost, but we ignored him. I remembered the bit of *Swann's Way* that I loved the most. Odette, the object of Swann's obsessive desire, her carriage idling in the park for a rendezvous. Cars, carriages, and cabs are all perfect little rooms for fucking.

I unbuckled her belt and pushed my hand down her pants, and she moaned. She was wet, and I wanted to taste her. The driver looked back at us in the rearview mirror. He didn't look away or tell me to stop, but said, "We are lost."

KEEP WALKING

It wasn't like it happened all of the time.

But it was the surprise of it.

The middle of the night. Getting to the know the boundaries of a new park with so many people in it.

Arturo loaned them his tent and some college girl gave them some blow.

"Let's do lines off my stomach?" the girl said. She had on leather sandals that crisscrossed over her feet like they were made on an island by a goddess.

"That's the stuff!" Butch rubbed his hands together.

Johanna shrugged and cut up the lines and licked the girl's stomach like she knew they all wanted her to, and then she let the girl do a line off of her and Butch kept watching and getting more and more excited.

"You guys been together for long?" the girl asked as she undid Butch's belt buckle.

Johanna kissed her perfectly soft lips, but she felt more like talking than fucking and so she sat back and watched and made comments like she liked in porn. *You like sucking that cock don't you? Do you want to eat that pussy?*

"Hey, maybe come over here and talk less?" The girl held out her hand for Johanna to take like they were best friends. Johanna wouldn't, and Butch shot her a dirty look. "It just feels like you're a sportscaster, or something."

And then she was out of the tent, in a red-hot flash of anger and walking. It was annoying and she wasn't in the mood. Once, she and Butch had a plan. They were hobos and artists, people who wanted to see the world on their own terms. Now it was just a grind. Begging, scoring, partying.

There were cops everywhere now. They lived here too. *This protest is a twenty-four-hour job*, she thought. She wanted to pet one of the horses, but cops were the total enemy. Never talk to them if you could help it. Don't look at their piggy eyes.

Wham. Smack. Another burst of red and then black. His hand against the side of her head. She whirled around and shouted, "I fucking hate you!" Holding his pants up with one hand, the other one cocked to hit her again. There were no cops now.

"Why do you have to ruin my shit?" he shouted back.

She felt some sick pride that he'd stopped fucking the girl to smack her.

"You're the one who is ruining everything," she yelled, and then she kept walking. North. Up Broadway. He didn't follow her. Now he could have that girl all to himself. She touched where he'd hit. Felt the blood and took off a sock to staunch it. Kept walking. Away. From him.

When she got to Washington Square Park she found a bench and sat there. Panting and still bleeding. She took out the two pieces of paper that she kept taped inside her underwear in a baggie—the one from the girl who jumped and the list of words she'd written down when she crashed Stevie's class. They were damp from her sweat and folded too many times, but they were her most important documents. She unfolded them, laid them out on the bench in front of her, and studied them. Was there a code? What did it all mean? Artifact and list. The dead and her witness. Corpse and survivor. She read, *Later, he'll kneel / so that you can mount him. / He'll carry you across the / surface of the ocean. / Hold on. / You'll lose your dress. / But right now his horns glisten like eyeteeth. / Calasso says he's gentle like a puppy. / Playful.* The blood from her cut dripped down onto each page. She felt dizzy and wondered who Calasso might be. Maybe Butch knew or she could ask Stevie. The sun came up, and she put the papers back in her underwear.

Lately, Butch reminded her of her mother. She couldn't tell who needed who more. Butch had saved her, taken her to California and back across the country to New York, made her read all of his favorite books, and knew her better than anyone ever would, but it was bottoming out.

Her jaw finally unclenched from the blow and then she saw Stevie, walking through the park, not exactly straight. She caught up to her and saw that she was loaded. Slurring. Red eyes. Not able to stand in one place.

"Wild night?" Johanna asked.

"Your head," Stevie gasped and almost fell backward. She lifted her hand to touch Johanna's bloody cut, but thought better of it. She leaned in too close to Johanna's face and whispered, "You have to take care of yourself."

Johanna pressed her forehead against Stevie's. Their lips touched for a second and then Stevie hiccupped and pulled back. "It's such a cliché to get the hiccups."

People scare so easily, Johanna thought. "Can I crash on your couch for a couple of hours?"

Stevie thought about it for ten seconds too long and then nodded hard. "Yes, of course," she said, as if she were convincing herself by saying it.

BLAST

I woke up to the sound of my phone chirping. *Little bird, where are you?* I thought as I lifted my head a few inches off the pillow. My head throbbed. I squinted at the clock radio, but I couldn't make out the numbers. Sunlight against the blinds.

"You made it home," I said out loud to the room, to congratulate myself. Rudy stood up, stretched, and walked up to my face.

"Don't rush me, I know, I know," I said to him. "Who would I talk to if you weren't here?" I offered my forehead to his cheek for a head-butt. My stomach churned. My phone chirped and chirped again. I felt around under the covers and found it next to my knee.

"9:37 a.m." I pulled it up close to my face. I was tired of being blind without my contacts.

"Ugh, why can't I ever sleep in?" I groaned at it and scrolled through the texts.

"Um, I think you stole my contacts?" from Adija.

"I did?" I texted back.

No response.

I tried to remember how I could have done that, but all that came back to me were flashes. Stumbling out of the cab and up five flights of stairs. Waving hello to a roommate awake and watching TV on the couch. Into a small, dark bedroom. A twin bed with a red plaid duvet. A fish tank against a white wall.

"There's no room for me here," I said.

"You'll fit," she said, steering me onto the bed.

Dress over my head. Tights off. Bra off. Fingers inside me. So wet from the cab.

"Do you have a condom?"

"Yeah."

I slid it over the dick she'd put in a harness. Got on top. Rocked and groaned. She flipped me over.

"Why are you so good at fucking me?" I said as she pushed in and out of me, harder and faster. I knew I was performing something for her. The girl who can take it, who likes it, who knows how to handle anything.

"I don't know. Why are you so good at getting fucked?" she said, and then fell on top of me when I came. Waterfall. Crush. Crash. The wave broken.

My mouth against her pussy forever. Taste of salty water. Taste of tart and sweet. Taste of the world and I held her hips and I remembered what to do and I felt proud like a good puppy, like a good girl. "I just want to be a good girl," I whispered, and she said, "Shhhh, the room is spinning."

A blur then. She handed me a contact case. I fell asleep? I passed out? I woke up? I didn't want to be there. I wanted to go home. I stumbled out. The roommate still watching TV on the couch. I waved again. Sheepish. Down so many stairs. Outside. Chilly September morning. No money for a cab. I managed to find the open, lit maw of the subway entrance. My phone said 5:47 a.m. Still drunk. I put on my headphones. Ignored the people on the train. Found a seat by a door for protection in case I had to run away from someone. Girls and their subway tricks. I couldn't remember the walk from the train to my apartment, except that the sun was coming up and it felt way too bright on my face.

But I didn't shame myself or wonder what I was doing. I wasn't going to have an existential crisis about fucking a woman. Someday I might fall in love with a woman, someday when I met her, and maybe I would love her forever. In the sunlight, I didn't call myself a slut. I thought, *You are just very good at fucking, eating pussy, sucking dick, all of it, and that is a skill.*

Rudy meowed in my face. "Your breath!" I said to him, and scrolled through the other texts. He jumped off the bed and gave me a dirty look.

"You were supposed to go home with me last night." From Hayes.

"Maybe next time?" I texted back.

No response.

"Occupy in full swing. Still space to camp out. Bring food and socks." Another text blast from Arturo. Not personal. Not for me, and still I texted back.

"I'm going to camp out soon!"

No response.

I stood up. I stepped on Rudy's tail and he yowled at me. My stomach lurched, I ran to the toilet and gagged. I started to tear up. Throwing up made me sad and reminded me of my pregnancy when I barfed almost every day for nine months. I became an expert at vomiting quietly and unobtrusively into shopping bags and once my own purse. I learned how to exit subway cars quickly and throw up into a smelly, sticky, overflowing garbage can without touching its sides or rim. I sipped smoothies while I taught so I wouldn't have to throw up in the middle of class. I found trees to hide behind so that I could have some privacy while I yakked. Still, it was an out-of-control feeling. I was entirely at the mercy of my stomach.

Out it came. Burning. Ugh. Whiskey.

I wiped my mouth and brushed my teeth. Gagged again because of the toothbrush and stumbled back into bed. I fell asleep for a fitful hour. I saw Sasha on the Wonder Wheel, our favorite ride at Coney Island, alone in her own sliding car. I was in the car behind her, but I couldn't get to her. I rattled the door of my car, but it wouldn't budge. Sasha ahead of me. Rising and falling. She looked back from her caged car and mouthed, "Mama." I rattled my cage again. Her car slid farther and farther away from me. I woke myself up. My phone chirped again, and I grabbed for it.

"You okay? Checking in." From Mel.

"I gotta stop. I drink too much."

"Let's both slow down, okay?" she texted back.

"It's a pact."

Mel sent me the fist-bump emoji. I didn't tell her about Adija because then she would ask me too many questions.

I sent the thumbs-up fist back.

I wandered out to the living room and jumped. Johanna asleep on my couch. Wrapped up in a comforter I must have given her. Here because I let her in? Her boots right next to her. I walked over and peered down at the tangle of limbs and hair and blanket. She had a bloody gash above her right eyebrow. Maybe she needed stitches?

I let her sleep and took a bath. In the tub, I decided I'd make her breakfast and try to get her to talk to me. What was going on for real? I wanted to know.

But when I came out, she was gone. The blanket folded in a neat square and an empty water glass on the counter.

YOUR GIRLFRIEND

Mel lay in bed and stared at her phone. Their dogs, Pete and Walt, were wrapped around her legs, Walt's snout up against her butt and Pete's butt up against her foot. She scrolled through Facebook and saw that someone she wasn't friends with had tagged Jenny. The new girl. *Maybe I better not,* she thought, and then clicked on the post anyway.

"Out with my new hottie girlfriend." A photo of Jenny with her arm draped over her shoulder. Cocky. Confidence. That same look that had made Mel fall in love with her almost ten years ago. Her name was Stella. She had long wavy hair and was wearing a sheath dress and heels. A necklace made of big wooden cutouts. Earrings that matched. Red lips. Super femme. Mel felt a hot flash of anger, saw red spots around her eyes, and then cried.

Jenny was up and rattling around in the kitchen totally oblivious. "Babe, do you want eggs with me or oatmeal with avocado in it?" she called to Mel.

The dogs both sat up at the mention of food.

"Girlfriend?" Mel yelled through her tears, and threw her phone down onto the bed. "She calls you her fucking girlfriend? *I'm* your girlfriend!"

Jenny appeared at the bedroom door, sheepish, hair rumpled. "Oh shit, I didn't want you to see that."

"Well, I did. Because she tagged you!"

"I have to talk to her about social media," Jenny offered. "But you knew this might happen."

"I know, but it doesn't mean I'm not going to get jealous. And why is she calling herself your girlfriend?"

"Because you're my wife," Jenny said as if it were all so clear.

"Yeah, and I haggle with the bill collectors and clean up dog shit and text you when you're driving for five hours in the snow and I'm worried you've slid off the road and died. Wives go to couples therapy and call banks to try to save cabins from foreclosure. If this is my wifedom, I don't want it to be legal. Wives don't get to do anything fun."

"Yes, they do. Wives are cool and powerful! They run the show. Everything we have and do is because of your vision and planning. You have crazy ideas, but you push me to explore myself and to go on adventures with you and other people."

"You mean your girlfriend?"

"Sometimes."

"Girlfriends get to go on trips and be in Facebook photos and make out with you in bars."

"Wives can do that too," Jenny said. "We need to work on that, it's true."

Mel lay back down on the bed between the dogs, who had their ears perked up like children during their parents' argument. "It's okay, boys." She rubbed both of their heads. "The mamas are okay."

Jenny sat down on the edge of the bed. "We could just hop on the R train to City Hall and get married today if we wanted to. Because it's finally legal in the state of New York!" Mel noticed that she was still holding a frying pan and a sponge, which made her even cuter.

"Is this a proposal?"

"I don't know. Maybe. Yes. It's not like how I planned to ask you, but I've been thinking about it a lot."

"But I'm so jealous I'm going to die."

"Then be my wife?" Jenny asked. She put the frying pan and sponge on the floor.

"Maybe," Mel said. "But I'm still mad at you." She made a little mental note that she needed to move things along with Carmine. What was she waiting for? *It's not a competition*, she reminded herself, but still she wanted to have her own thing.

"I can handle it," Jenny said as she moved the dogs over and rested her head in Mel's crotch.

"Stop it," Mel swatted at Jenny's hair, but she lifted her butt up so that Jenny could pull down her pajama bottoms.

"You smell good," Jenny said, sniffing at the crotch of Mel's underwear before she pulled them off. "Do you really want me to stop?"

"No, keep going."

TIN CEILING

I lay naked on my back next to David, staring up at the white pressed-tin ceiling and network of copper pipes.

"You found an apartment, rented it, and moved here in a week?" I was jealous of his mobility, the ease at which he seemed to sail through the world. In three months, Sasha and I would be lucky to find a studio apartment in a distant Brooklyn neighborhood. By my calculations, I could afford rent between $1,200 and $1,500 a month.

"A realtor showed me two apartments in this building, both lofts, but I liked this one better, and so I took it," David said. "I've been missing New York and I got this big job here for a year, so why not? The company I'm freelancing for pays for it. I've still got my place in Gloucester, so I can come back and forth."

"I wonder if the pipes work or if they're just decorative?" I didn't have a thing to say about companies who paid for their employees to live in expensive lofts. I thought about cataloging all of my friends who were slowly driven out of the loft spaces they'd found in the nineties in Williamsburg to make way for new luxury condos or delivering a mini-lecture on the evils of gentrification, but I didn't have the strength. Did I need to educate this guy or could I just fuck him?

"Look, I get it, I see it in your face. I'm a white guy with money and privilege. I know I'm lucky, and so I try not to be a dick in this world."

"I didn't say anything," I said. "Just use your big dick for good and not evil, okay?"

"Like giving you mind-blowing orgasms? Does that count?"

"Definitely."

David put his hand on my hip and rubbed it. I was having the best sex of my life, and yet it freaked me out that he was suddenly living in my city. How could I keep it light? Separating from Aaron had made me commitment-phobic. Wary. Wanting no ties. And yet, when we walked into his apartment a couple hours earlier from a bar in the neighborhood, I found myself imagining my stuff in his space, living here with him. Was this a relationship fantasy or a housing one?

I turned to face him and looked into his green eyes. A blush spread from my neck to my cheeks to my forehead. I put my fingers into his beard and tugged.

"I love that you blush." David kissed the tip of my nose. "I bet I could make you blush just by telling you to blush."

"Don't." I ran my fingers along his side to tickle him.

He squirmed away and commanded, "Blush."

My face got hotter, redder.

"Ha, this is fun."

"No it's not." I felt the red creeping up onto my scalp and so I pulled the sheet over my head. From inside the weave of what felt like at least one-thousand-thread-count sheets, I said, "I like sleeping with a Wolf."

"And I like sleeping with a Red."

"Have you heard about those protesters who have taken over Wall Street?" I changed the subject. It was all I was talking about to anyone lately. Was he the kind of person who would go to Occupy? I wanted to know where everyone stood.

"Yeah, I wonder how long they'll last?"

"I don't know, but I visited and it's really cool. They've created, like, a whole working city."

"They should probably just get jobs." David sat up on his elbows and smirked at me.

I sat up too, incensed. "They have jobs! One of them is a professor like me—well, part-time, and then I guess the rest of the time he's an activist. His name is Arturo and he's from Puerto Rico." I felt my face turning red, and I realized he was teasing me and I flopped back down on the bed. "Shut up."

"Why? You're cute when you're defending a bunch of hippies."

"They're more anarchists than hippies."

"Sure they are," David teased.

"There are teachers and students and union guys there too. I was thinking about joining them," I said.

"You mean you were thinking about joining Arturo?" David waggled his eyebrows at me.

"Why are you doing that?" I asked, half-annoyed, half-amused.

"'Cause somebody has a thing for a dude named Arturo."

"No I don't."

"You can relax. I think it's hot, and if you fuck him I want to hear all about it."

"I don't want to fuck him. Also, you are so weird. Why do you want to hear about me and other guys?"

"It's hot to me to think of you with other dudes, doing your dirty little Red things. It's just the way I'm wired."

"But I don't want to hear about you and other women."

"That's okay. We can be different."

I sighed. "Anyhoo, I think I'm going to camp there."

"You don't look like the camping kind."

"I could be, if I have a pillow."

TINY DEATH OF THE SOUL

Strapped to my back, I had a sleeping bag I'd borrowed from Mel. I wandered off toward the People's Library, and then toward the drum circle, and then the sign-painting area. I was looking for Johanna or Butch or Arturo or anyone I knew. I couldn't find them. I asked a couple of people. Shrugs. *I dunno. Probably a meeting off-site.*

I took a picture of the Vietnam veteran, in a combat helmet, jeans, and flannel shirt, who had become a social media fixture. His large cardboard sign read, *2nd time I've fought for my country, 1st time I've known my enemy.* He stood staring straight ahead, as if at attention. He reminded me of my stepfather, who had fought in Vietnam and was having health problems that no one except for his VA doctors were willing to admit were probably related to Agent Orange. I took a picture and texted it to my stepdad and mom. "Look, veterans are here too."

"It's just like the sixties," my mom texted back.

"Cool!" from my stepdad.

"Don't get pepper-sprayed!" my mom texted.

I texted her back the woman salsa-dancer emoji, then slid my phone back into my pocket.

"Boo!" Johanna crawled out from under one of the tables in the People's Library.

"You can borrow anything as long as you keep it in the park," she monotoned. She looked more like her fountain self—dirtier and with sleepy, sped-up eyes. She stood up and bounced a couple times on her heels before doing a full pirouette to face me. "I hate working in the library. Yawn attack. I'm trapped here talking to whoever walks by. Thank god it's you!" she said. Her voice was manic now. Bored. She couldn't sit or stand still. "Did you bring Sasha?"

"She's with her dad," I said. The cut above her eye had scabbed over, but there was a deep, plum-colored bruise forming around it. "Are you going to tell me what happened to your eye?"

"Drug fight with Butch," she said.

I felt my stomach tighten. Little alarm bells. I must have looked worried.

"I'm fine!" She stuck her arms out in the air and slid down into a Warrior Two pose. "You should see what he looks like!" She bounced back up and made little boxing jabs in the air space around my ears. I winced.

Somebody tapped me on the shoulder. I turned around to see Arturo.

"Stevie!"

"Hi!"

"Did you bring students?"

"Not yet. I was thinking I would bring them on Tuesday, like, instead of class, and I could give them a writing assignment and a couple could go with you guys to La Prensa." I thought of the ridiculous gleaming-cube classroom we'd tried to reclaim since the woman jumped. It still felt haunted to me and I didn't ever want to go back. A castle in the sky. The illusion of safety. My students would be better off on the streets.

"Tuesday is good."

"I brought my sleeping bag, though." I shrugged my shoulders at my backpack. "My kid is with her dad. We split our time with her fifty-fifty. It's my time without her, so I thought I'd try to camp out tonight in solidarity."

"I get the whole co-parenting thing. My partner is doing that with her ex, but they still fight a lot about the arrangements." Arturo looked tired too. His stubble had grown in and his face was flushed. His hair was wilder today too. Thicker. Uncombed. I loved it. "You didn't have to bring all that. We're not staying tonight. You can have our tent."

Johanna had slid back down under the table, probably bored by us. Was she napping down there? Camping out? I couldn't tell.

He gestured for me to give him my backpack.

"It's okay, I'm fine."

He gestured again, and I relented and shrugged it off. "Just put your backpack in our tent, and then you can sleep wherever you want." I followed him back to the center of the park and into the labyrinth of tents.

"It's bigger now?" I asked.

"Yeah, since the cops pepper-sprayed our comrades and it went viral, way more people have come. The march on the bridge also really galvanized people. We've been getting a shitload of donations, but it's also getting a little edgier too, more people we don't know and who are probably in need of some good mental health care."

Arturo somehow found his tent and stashed my bag in it. "Do you want to come inside for a minute? Just for a breather? I get overwhelmed by all the people sometimes."

"Okay." I crawled in behind him.

Red glow from the nylon tent. Hot from the sun. We sat on the ground inside the tent and for an awkward thirty seconds no one said anything. Someone had hung up a postcard of Kathleen Hanna from Bikini Kill on the tent wall.

"I loved her when I was twenty," I said, tracing my fingertip along the outline of the postcard.

"That's Devora's."

"We probably have a lot in common. Moms who are hanging out at Occupy and like riot grrrl."

"Yeah, you probably do. Probably pretty different too."

"Totes projecting." I laughed. "Sorry." I stopped touching the postcard. "How long have you guys been together?"

"A couple of years now. We have our ups and downs. We're open. We see other people."

"Like everyone these days."

"Really? I know a ton of hardcore monogamous people."

"I used to, but not anymore." I sighed.

"Does that annoy you?"

"No, not at all. I mean, sometimes, um, I don't know. Ha."

"Confused much?" He smiled at me, and I noticed his eyeteeth were a little crooked and that it was cute.

"Every second," I said, and looked back up at the Kathleen Hanna postcard as if she could guide me. "But I have a thinking problem, like, too much of it."

"I read some of your essays. They can't be bad for thinking."

Oh god. I was getting better about this—having readers, fans occasionally who read something of mine and liked it, but I still sometimes had an initial gut feeling of shame for exposing myself.

"The one about online dating and the other one about getting lice out of your kid's hair. You're really good. You have this funny slash sad thing in your writing. Like, hilarious next to, like, ugh, tiny death of the soul."

"Tiny death of the soul? You gotta review me on Amazon if I ever publish a book."

"No, it's a good thing!"

I looked down at his jeans, which were dirty and ragged at the ankles, and then at his hands and fingers. His knuckles were hairy and his nails were bitten down to the quick like mine. I didn't quite know where to put my eyes.

He leaned in a little. The cross-legged sitting thing was feeling way too much like the final scene of *Sixteen Candles*, when Jake picks up Samantha from her sister's shitty wedding and brings her a giant birthday cake.

"Maybe you could write about all of this?" He leaned back again as if he might be having second thoughts.

"It takes me about five years to process the shit I do, so maybe a long time from now."

"I can see it. Like bourgeoisie divorcing mom radicalized by Occupy Wall Street."

I felt my face get hot. "I'm not just some bourgeoisie mom divorcée, and this is not radicalizing me. I was already radical."

"No, no, not like that. I mean, it's a good thing. Lots of regular people are getting turned on by this thing."

"I'm not regular. People think moms are boring and not political, but some of us are broken, queer, crazy, loud, sex-positive poet single mamas so don't underestimate us or call us regular."

"You're right, you're not." Arturo sighed. "I've been drinking all day. Sorry, sorry. I know you're not regular or normal. I've been messing up a bunch of shit today. Naming when I should just listen. Talking instead of waiting my turn, you know?"

I nodded, but I didn't quite. He seemed like he needed a nap.

"What's a sex-positive poet single mama?" He raised his eyebrows at me.

"I think you can figure it out," I said.

"Me encantan las poetas," he said.

"Lo supuse." I remembered my undergraduate Spanish.

He started to crawl past me to get out of the tent. I smelled sour whiskey on him and a bit of sweat. He squeezed my knee and then let it go. "You just seem kind of together, like, organized, and not falling apart."

I followed him out and pulled my backpack with me. "I am together, I guess, because I have to be, but I am also falling apart. I just hide it."

"Well, you don't really have to hide it here," he said. "We are all falling apart and keeping it together, sometimes in the same minute." He paused and looked around at the park. "It's still kind of crazy to me that this is happening."

"You guys are really changing the conversation."

"Amazing, right?" Arturo's face lit up again like I'd seen it do in the fountain and as he watched Devora speak. "But you came to work today, not just bullshit with me, right?"

"Yeah, where do you need me?"

"Probably the kitchen." He walked me over to the center of the park.

"Marissa?" he called out over the kitchen din.

A woman in pink scrubs, a tight bun, and no-nonsense lips looked me up and down. "Do you have any special skills?"

"I'm a writer and a teacher." I suspected as soon as I said it that this was not what she meant.

"That's awesome, but I mean, like, in the kitchen?"

"I'm a great baker."

She shrugged. "Just scoot over to the other side and you can peel potatoes."

I crawled under the table and a man about my height with wide shoulders and short black hair gave me a paring knife. Arturo waved goodbye and disappeared back into the chaos of the park.

"Habla español?" the man with the paring knife asked.

"Un poquito."

"I speak English too."

"Why are you here?" I asked, taking the knife from him and picking up a potato.

"I came from Mexico, I work three jobs, and I'm still living in one room with four guys. You?"

"I'm tired of how unfair things are, and I think capitalism should be regulated."

"Sí, sí." In the span of this short conversation, he'd already peeled two potatoes. I had cut off one slice of skin. "You are terrible." He nodded at my potato.

I laughed. "I know."

"I'm Diego," he said, brushing off his hand on his jeans so that I could shake it.

"Stevie."

We peeled potatoes for the next three hours, taking a fifteen-minute break to eat. Marissa brought us plates full of chickpea stew with rice and beans. It tasted better than anything I could have made.

When it was dark Diego helped me find a place to set up my sleeping bag. I looked around for Johanna or Arturo, but I didn't see them anywhere. I didn't feel like sleeping in Arturo's tent.

Marissa set up her sleeping bag next to mine. She took her hair out of its bun, and it fell to her shoulders in curly ringlets. "Thanks for all your hard work today," she said, and then zipped up her bed into a little cocoon.

I lay on my back and looked at the flashlight screen of my phone. I'd posted earlier that day a cryptic FB status, "Might camp out tonight," but the only person I told that I was sleeping here was Mel.

My father had left me a Facebook message: *You think you're more powerful than the police, but you're not. They will crush you. They have horses and guns. Don't be stupid. You're a mom. Watch this video to see what I'm talking about. I love you.*

My mother must have told him I was here. I deleted the message without responding, but felt a rush of anger rise up from the pit of my stomach up to the tips of my ears. I never watched the YouTube videos he sent. They were usually about Asperger's syndrome, which he didn't have, but used as an excuse for being an asshole. Sometimes they were guesses at videos for songs he thought I liked or used to like when I was a teenager. I sometimes felt like my father was my own personal internet troll, invading my inbox with shitty ideas and bad advice.

I aimed my phone at the starry sky, took a picture, and sent it to Mel. "Occupied. All okay."

I sent the same message and picture to David and Aaron and Hayes and Adija.

"Badass," Aaron texted back.

"Did you fuck a hippie yet?" David texted back.

"They're anarchists," I texted back.

"Still stinky," he responded, then added the nose and pile of poo emoji.

"Ha."

"Can't wait to hear all about it," David texted.

No response from Hayes or Adija.

I turned off my phone and shoved it down into my sleeping bag. I lay on the cold, hard granite of the park and looked around me. Bodies everywhere, snuggled into their sleeping bags, some still lit up with the glow of laptop screens and phones, but many more asleep. There were probably about 250 of us sleeping there that night. The scaffolding of the Freedom Tower loomed overhead; its partially affixed, mirrored exterior wall made it look like an ice sculpture in the night. It was the first time I'd looked at it up close and felt something—like hope, like freedom, like these two things belonged to me and to all of us.

THE WIVES

The wives were carrying around this thing that had no name. Once in the sixties, it was called the feminine mystique, but that sounded dated to most wives and to some other wives it sounded like a douche brand. The wives didn't really douche anymore. The wives were also carrying actual things like strollers, diaper bags, groceries, laundry, books, children, free weights, firewood, luggage, toys, breast pumps, bicycles, scooters, backpacks, purses, takeout, recycling, stinky bags of garbage, cans to donate to the homeless, and all the objects that were somehow always in the wrong room or strewn about the floor like there was a god called Entropy and only he reigned. Sometimes the wives were carrying all of these things at once, up the stairs of a five-story walk-up or down the stairs of a subway entrance at rush hour. A lot of people sighed behind the packhorse wives. Fuck you, the wives thought and slowed down. Fuck you, the wives thought and sped up. Mostly the wives were very good at the carrying of many things, though sometimes they dropped something and somebody whined about it. Later, when the world had really gone to shit, the wives would learn that the things they carried was not only a groundbreaking short story collection about the Vietnam War by Tim O'Brien, but also something much smaller, but equally political. The wives learned that they'd been carrying "the mental load," and it wasn't just the things, but it was all of the ideas and the feelings and worries and plans of the households they had somehow become the bosses of. The wives felt like office managers. They had their big wall calendars and chore wheels and lists on whiteboards that nobody looked at except for them, and the husbands and the children were more like wayward employees. They had to be told what to do and they were super bitchy and foot-draggy about it and so the wives lay on couches in dark rooms and they pretended to be hysterics who had to be left alone or their uteruses would explode and that worked for about an hour.

THE BATH

Carmine put two beers on the table and Mel made a face. "Beer?"

"So you're an alcohol snob and you're married to a lesbian?"

"I'm a bartender who is sometimes made to wear suspenders. I'm supposed to be an alcohol snob, and I'm not married." She almost said, "Yet," but stopped herself. It was the first time they'd been outside of the restaurant or his apartment. They'd agreed to call it a date in air quotes only.

"So you hate beer?"

"I'm a top-shelf tequila girl."

"Well, Gold Star is a dump." Carmine shrugged. "Unless you want to drink Cuervo, this is it."

"I've been here before. My best friend is obsessed with the DJ."

"Obsessed, like, with his music or hot for him?"

"Hot for him, but it's a long story and I'm not allowed to tell it."

"Intriguing." Carmine raised his glass and gave her a look that made her want to take him to the bathroom stall and slide her hand down his pants. "To going outside."

"To not making out by the freezer." Mel clinked glasses with him, and took a big gulp of her beer.

"So, this is nice," Carmine said, and slid in closer to her in the round booth and put his arm around her. She felt the urge to shake him off. She wasn't used to such public gestures with him, but she let the back of her neck rest against his arm. "Is your girlfriend going to run in here with a steak knife and stab me?"

Mel slid her hand onto his knee under the table. "We're not like that. We get jealous, but we talk about it. Or we try to, at least."

"Modern," Carmine said.

It was a Saturday afternoon. The bar was empty except for them, the bartender, and a couple sitting at the bar nursing big cans of PBR. Mel was happy not to see Hayes. She hated him for making Stevie so crazy.

"You just gonna keep your hand on my thigh all night?" he asked.

"Yep, and other places maybe," she said.

"So, how do you do these date things?"

"What do you mean?"

"Like, what do we talk about?"

Mel laughed. "I have no idea. I usually just cram my tongue into your mouth and you move your hands up and down my body in some dark corner of the restaurant. I don't know what the fuck to talk to you about."

"Talking is overrated."

They finished their beers in what felt to Mel like electric silence. The bartender brought them another round.

"On me," he said, raising his eyebrows at Carmine. "This your new girl?"

Carmine looked at Mel and raised his eyebrows. "That's up to her."

"It's just a date," she stammered.

"Playing hard to get, I guess." The bartender winked at her and took their empties back to the bar.

"You know him?" Mel asked.

"A guy from forever ago, before this neighborhood was full of hipsters and was mostly Italian and Irish and Puerto Rican."

She hadn't been out in public like this with a man in years, not since Andre when she was in her twenties—before she met Jenny, before she felt like she had to choose sides. Lesbian or straight. But could she be Carmine's girl? What did that mean to him? What would it mean for her and Jenny? *If Jenny has a girlfriend, I can have a boyfriend*, she reasoned. *But Carmine is an old-school guy. He's always going to want things I can't give him.*

"I'm sure you saw the schedule?" Carmine interrupted her worry fest. "Tommy took you off the next two Saturdays."

"What? He posted it early?" Mel drained her beer. "Fucker."

"Who's on?"

"Him and Greta."

"He can't train her on a Saturday."

"You still have Friday."

Mel put her head down on the table for a quick second. "There goes three hundred bucks a week. This is totally happening because I won't fuck him and do lines of Adderall off his phone."

"You better not fuck him," Carmine said, all guy-guy, all straight.

"I mean, I can if I want," Mel said. "But I don't want to."

"Dude," Carmine called out to his bartender friend. "You guys got any open bartending shifts?

"Who's asking?"

"Mel's looking for a Saturday night and she's the best bartender, besides you, I've ever met." Carmine gave her shoulder a squeeze.

"I can try you out in two Saturdays," he said.

"Just like that?" Mel looked back and forth between the two of them. *Straight guys rule the world*, she thought. *They do whatever they want.*

"I'm the manager and Carmine wouldn't lie to me."

"Okay. Cool. See you in two weeks."

Back at Carmine's apartment, she took off all her clothes and stepped into the tub. He had one of those apartments that hardly existed in New York City anymore with a bathtub in the kitchen and a little toilet closet with a sink in the hallway.

"I think you're a dirty girl who needs a bath and a snack," Carmine said from the kitchen. He was cooking something. She smelled cheese and bread and dill. She leaned back into the sudsy water, closed her eyes, and rested her hand between her legs.

In her daydreams there was always water. She'd been on a swim team from ages six to twenty-one when she got kicked off for drinking too much and sleeping with nearly every one of her teammates who didn't have a boyfriend and even a couple who did. She still swam laps almost every other day—the splash, kick, turn, paddle of lanes was like breathing to her. She never showered if she could help it. She loved bath salts and staying in so long her fingers pruned. She thought of the marsh in front of her father's cabin, the salty brine on her skin as she dried off on the beach down the road. If Carmine meant something to her, she'd want to take him to the cabin. Everyone she cared about went there eventually. But she and Jenny were getting nowhere with the bank. A Gloucester neighbor, one of the women who saved baby turtles, sent her a photo of the foreclosure sign the bank had nailed into the ground in the front of the cabin.

"What happened?" she asked.

The photo made Mel so mad she had to delete it, and she wallowed on the couch for an hour and yanked down an old photo album from her childhood—one of the ones that she kept on the highest shelf of her closet. She found the photo she was looking for—she and her dad standing next to each other on the beach, each holding a can of beer, the cabin off in the distance. Mel, nineteen, impossibly fit and tan. Her dad, beaming and with his wild, too-curly hair. He looked like he'd escaped something; Mel's mother, she figured. Carol must have taken that picture.

She opened her eyes. Some of Carmine's daughter's toys sat on the rim of the tub—a little plastic sailboat and one of the fish from *Finding Nemo.* She'd watched it with Sasha, but couldn't remember any of their names.

"What's the confused fish named?" she said.

Carmine slid a crostino into her mouth.

"Dory."

"Right." She chewed.

He set the plate on a chair by the tub, stripped down, and got in.

He reached for her nipples and rubbed the suds off of them. His lips against her neck and then his tongue against her tongue. His hands on her hips moving her closer. She wrapped her legs around his waist. Water sloshed out of the tub and onto the floor.

"I keep it really clean," Carmine said.

"Your dick?" Mel laughed.

"The tub. But yeah, my dick too."

"Let's go slow," she said, and scooted back so they were at opposite ends of the tub, legs still entwined.

"You're making me crazy," he said.

"I don't know what it is about you," Mel said. "I haven't liked a guy in a long time." She felt around in the soapy water and squeezed his cock in her hand. He groaned. "I just want to see what this can be."

"But it can't be anything more than fucking," he said.

"But I can love you if I want to," she said, and then covered her mouth. "I did not say that word."

"Yes, you did!" Carmine seemed pleased with himself.

DIRECT ACTION

Johanna must have found me in the night. When I woke up, her body was pressed up against mine like Sasha's. I fought the urge to move a strand of hair off her face and inspect the cut next to her eye. I scooted over a bit and Tipsy, her dog, yawned at me and then settled his muzzle back down on her hip. I sat up and rooted around for my phone. Forty-two percent charge. I'd have to plug it in somewhere soon.

I texted Mel, "Come march with us today at noon!" I rolled my sleeping bag up, and shoved it into the backpack I'd stashed under a bench.

"Hija." I turned around. It was Diego.

"I think I'm actually older than you."

He held up a plate of eggs and what looked like a side of guacamole and turkey bacon. "But you have a young spirit," he said.

"Not in my lower back." I took the plate of eggs and sat with him on the bench.

"Do you want to work with me again in the kitchen?"

"Yeah, sure." I devoured my food. I badly needed to pee. "Where are you from?"

"Mexico City. Have you been to Mexico?"

"No. I'd like to go, but it's hard for me to travel."

"Why?"

"I have a kid and no extra money."

Diego took out his wallet and pulled out a picture of two little kids standing on the beach. "That's Lili. She's seven now. That's Nestor. He's four."

"Awww, so pretty and so handsome. They both have such beautiful eyes. Lili just lost her top tooth! Nestor has such a tough expression!" I took out my phone and showed him a recent picture of Sasha.

"She looks like her mama," he said.

"Are your kids here with you?"

"No, they are with my parents in Mexico City. Their mom died when Nestor was born."

"I'm sorry." I looked down at my picture of Sasha. I couldn't imagine her life without me in it, all of the little things that mothers do—rubbing her back before she fell asleep, moving her hair off of her forehead when I woke her up for school, putting notes in her lunch box.

"It was terrible." Diego stared off at the red sculpture that loomed over the park. "After this," Diego waved his arm toward the many sleeping bodies, "I think I am going to go back for good. America is not what I thought it would be, and my kids need me."

"They will be so happy to see you."

"They will probably not remember me." He stared at the picture for another couple of seconds and then shut his wallet.

"It could take some time," I managed.

"You should not be here, as a mother," Diego said. "If you were my wife, I would not let you come."

"But that's the great thing about me!" I laughed. "I'm not a wife!" I was starting to love my freedom. On the days when Sasha was with Aaron, I could go anywhere and do anything. I didn't have to ask permission, figure out childcare, be home at a certain hour, or even check in with anyone.

Marissa called over to us from the kitchen. "Ready to cut tomatoes for lasagna?"

I went to a nearby Starbucks to pee and then joined Diego and Marissa and the rest of the kitchen workers for lasagna-making. Diego entertained us with stories from the student marches in 1999 in Mexico City. "They shut down the campus for 292 days! When they marched off campus, traffic came to a standstill!"

"Were you a student there?" Marissa asked.

"No, I had a friend who went to university and kept me informed. I should have gone. I probably wouldn't be here today with you cutting tomatoes for anarchists if I went to school. Back then I thought the students were lazy rich kids. Now I think differently."

We managed between the fifteen of us to put together twenty-five giant trays of lasagna, which would then be driven out to bake at a local church's kitchen in East New York that had donated its space to Occupy. Once they were cooked, the truck would drive them back to serve for dinner. Every day, volunteers prepped and cut and chopped and drove and cooked and drove it all back so that everyone who wanted food could eat it. I liked the simple hard work of our task. It was so much more straightforward than teaching or writing or even parenting. People were hungry and we fed them. I liked the community of the kitchen too. So often as a writer and now as a single parent, I worked by myself. I got lonely. At Occupy, there was endless, fairly easy companionship. It reminded me of the record store/arcade/drug den I used to hang out in as a teenager after school. There was always someone there and usually something going on.

"I'm not an anarchist," Marissa clarified. "I'm a nurse who grew up in an activist church, and I know how to cook massive amounts of food. So there you have it."

"Where did you grow up?"

"Charleston."

"I've never been there," I said. "But why are you here, really? I mean, did you know people who decided to camp out?"

"There are a lot of strong women in the nurses' union and we started to talk about it on breaks. My parents recently lost their home. They'd been living there for twenty years, making steady mortgage payments, and they tried to refinance and they got a shitty rate and they fell behind and within six months the bank kicked them out. So I'm just fed up, like a lot of working-class people of color." I wanted to tell her about Mel's father's cabin, but she scooted down the line to begin to assemble the noodles in trays for lasagna before I could say anything. We followed with tomatoes, sauce, and cheese, and then we all helped load the trays of uncooked lasagna into the van.

Diego waved goodbye so that he could go to one of the two restaurants where he worked. As he untied his apron, he said to me, "Mami, don't sleep here again tonight."

"Don't worry so much about me, I'm fine," I said as I hugged him goodbye.

Johanna wandered over. Her eye looked worse than yesterday. I couldn't help but wince at her.

"Where's Tipsy?"

"She's staying with the librarians, so we can march to the Bull."

I saw Mel up near the corner of the park, looking for me. I held up my hand and waved. "Mel!"

She jogged down to us. "Am I too late?"

"Just in time!" I linked one arm with her and Johanna linked her arm into mine too. Marissa linked up with Johanna.

"Sorry about my douchebag manager," Mel said to Johanna.

"That guy is your boss?" Johanna asked.

"Mostly, I ignore him," Mel said.

I introduced Mel and Marissa and then we joined the growing crowd of protesters set to march up to the Bull in front of the Stock Exchange. I looked at my phone. It was only ten a.m. I had plenty of time before three when I had to pick up Sasha from school.

Mic check. Mic check.

I saw Arturo and Devora up near the front of the crowd. They carried the giant waving blue flags that had come to symbolize Occupy: "Revolution Generation" and "Debt Is Slavery." I wondered what he and Devora had done last night. Had they cooked dinner together, just the two of them? Had they fallen asleep wrapped in each other's arms or was he out in the living room typing away on his laptop while she used her vibrator? I wondered what it was like to wake up next to Arturo. I imagined him pulling me close, his chin rubbing up against my lips.

My phone chirped. A text from Aaron: "Be careful! Don't get arrested!"

I was tired of everyone worrying about me. My mother's parting words to me my whole life were always "Be careful!"

The drummers and dancers were out in front leading us with a fantastic beat and endless catchy chants, like *This is what democracy looks like. Get up! Get down! Democracy is in this town! Wall Street, no thanks! We don't need your greedy banks!*

It felt great to shout in the streets! I loved being part of a giant organism for change. I took out my phone and aimed the camera at the heads of the crowd. Marchers flooded in from side streets and we swelled out onto the sidewalks and farther into the streets. Cabs and buses honked in solidarity with us, even as we stopped their movement. A tourist bus stopped in front of us and the tourists waved and cheered at us. "We love you!"

I saw the horns of the Bull and a wall of police officers. I linked arms even tighter with Mel and Johanna. There were several blue corrections buses parked and waiting to cart resisters off, and a wall of stoic, giant, all-male police officers with grim expressions. No women. No smiling. The front line of marchers stopped as they hit the police wall, and sat down. We all followed, a ripple in a pond. Traffic had stopped completely.

"I can't get arrested," I said to Mel. "I have to get Sasha from school today."

"I think it's okay," she said. "They can't arrest this many people."

Mic check. Mic check.

Our goal just like it is every day. Our goal just like it is every day.

Is to march to the Bull. Is to march to the Bull.

The symbol of wealth and greed. The symbol of wealth and greed.

And disrupt business as usual. And disrupt business as usual.

I took in the people closest to me. College students who had painted their faces with dollar signs and wore matching T-shirts that said, "We deserve a debt-free future." African American women in scrubs who had signs that said, "Health Care Needs a Bailout Too." A lesbian couple in their fifties with bandanas around their heads, and a sign that said, "Dykes for socialism!" Several bearded white men with various Marxist accessories—Che caps, wire-rimmed glasses, armbands, and knapsacks. A couple of heavyset, union guys with UAW T-shirts on, who looked very uncomfortable sitting on the ground. Johanna's fucked-up eye made her look badass, I had to admit. Maybe she had given as good as she got. I wanted to believe she could stand up to Butch. Mel had dark circles under her eyes. She'd given up her postbartending sleep to march with us.

"This is a public street and you are blocking traffic. If you do not move, we will have to arrest you," a police officer with a bullhorn shouted at us.

Link arms. Link arms. Link arms. Link arms, the crowd chanted.

The police started to wade into the crowd.

"I do not actually want to get the shit kicked out of me," Mel said.

I felt some deep fear rise up in the pit of my stomach. I felt queasy and dizzy. I wanted to get up and leave.

I repeated my concern to Johanna and Marissa, "I don't think I can get arrested today. I have to get my kid from school."

"Just get up and leave," Marissa said. "It's okay."

"They're not going to arrest us." Johanna seemed annoyed by my panic.

Lie down. Lie down. Lie down. Lie down, the crowd chanted. And slowly, like the sea rising back on itself after a wave, fell onto their backs. Mel, perhaps sensing that I felt stuck, pulled me up, and we stepped carefully over several bodies. I felt ashamed that I was giving up so quickly, and annoyed at myself for not being political enough. We walked toward the line of expressionless police officers who were standing in front of a police barricade. We bent down to duck under the barricade, still holding hands.

"Oh no you don't," a police officer said to us. "You're one of them now."

"This is a peaceful demonstration, and I'd like to leave now."

He looked over at the uniformed officer next to him. "You two should have thought of that before you started marching."

Let them go. Let them go. Let them go. Let them go. The crowd of now-prone protesters chanted on our behalf. I heard Johanna's clear throaty voice in the midst of the chanting. The police officer nodded back at the direction of the crowd, and then went blank in the eyes.

"You can't trap us here," Mel shouted.

I sat down on the ground and put my head between my knees.

"I feel dizzy," I said to Mel. She sat down next to me, we linked arms again, and she rubbed my back. The police began to pull at protesters' legs and arms to separate us.

"Get ready," Mel said.

Go limp. Go limp. Go limp. Go limp, the crowd chanted.

The air rushed out of my lungs. I held tightly to Mel's arm.

"You're okay," she said. "We're okay." I looked out of the corner of my eye through a crevice in my elbow. The police were separating bodies, they had their batons up in the air, and were using pepper spray. There was more chanting. *Shame. Shame. Shame. Shame.* I saw someone get hit. Screaming. The edges of my vision went gray and then black.

My brother and me, alone in our rooms, waiting for punishment. He was angry about something—dinner, our toys, his special pens he said we had stolen, the time we ripped the chair, the time we spilled the grape juice, it didn't matter. It was after dinner. It was before bedtime. It was always dark. Other children on the street, playing sneaks outside. There were no words. This was happening without language. Silence. Whimpering. Scrambling. My brother tried to get away. I always took it. Fight or give up. Go outside yourself. Fly up into the sky and look down at yourself, the little animal wreckage that you are. Or go inside yourself into your heart's chambers, the ventricles can be used as rooms, more places to hide. He used a belt or a slipper or a wooden spoon. His hands were not enough. He needed a weapon for the badness of his kids.

"Stevie." Mel's voice. Her hand in mine. Squeezing it, trying to pull me back.

It went gray again. My mother. Distracted. Late. The bus let me off in a blizzard. I couldn't see through the swirling clouds of snowflakes. A girl on the bus said you can walk home with me and then we'll call your mom. We have potato chips and pop. "I don't know my phone number," I said. I was afraid to go with her. I thought I was in a fairy tale and this was the witch's lure, the easiest way to kidnap me. The girl left me. I stood there waiting. My mother emerged out of a snowbank. "Here I am. Here I am." Another time we had a substitute bus driver who missed my stop, and I didn't say anything because my mother wasn't standing there on the corner to stop the bus, to wave him down. I couldn't speak. My mother later frantically drove through town looking for that bus. I remembered how tightly I hugged her when she found me.

My childhood. The beaten kids. The girl who got left behind and then ran away. I forgot to take my brother with me. He didn't want to go. A silent girl. A sullen boy. Why couldn't our parents keep track of us? Scramble. Scratch. My arm pulled from his. He has me by the shoulder and then the scruff of my neck. Bad kitty. Bad girl. Bad mommy. Tumble down into the rabbit hole. Alice. Alice. It's dark in the crook of my arm. It's dark when I press my eyes with my fingers to make them stay closed. It's dark in the bedroom, in class, on the pavement, and in the street. The world is a darkening, ending thing, a planet with a sun in a vast, unknowable galaxy, with a shrinking atmosphere, and way too much methane. I don't feel my body anymore. I've lost Mel and Johanna. I surely lost my brother a long time ago. We were forever in the woods. Confused and defiant. Silent and secretive. Why were we such lost and silent children? Why couldn't our parents keep track of us?

I see Sasha with her giant turtle shell of a backpack waiting in the schoolyard for me to pick her up, craning her slender stem of a neck: "Where's Mama?"

Sasha, I have to get her.

"Wow, you're not very good at this, are you?" I woke up staring up at Arturo, who was waving something foul under my nose. He put his hand on my forehead and moved my bangs to the side with his thumb. Mel still had my hand and was kneeling on the sidewalk next to me. Johanna was there too, but staring off into the distance, looking for someone or something—probably Butch, but who knew?

"Am I arrested?"

"No, you passed out, and a police officer took pity on you and carried you to the side."

"Sorry," I said as I looked back and forth between Mel and Arturo. I felt guilty that they had to take care of me.

"Don't be. It was rough today," Arturo said.

"Stevie." Mel gave me a look of concern.

"I have office hours and then I have to get Sasha." I sat up on my elbows. "I'll come back, I promise."

"I believe you," Arturo said.

Mel and I walked to the subway. My legs felt shaky. Johanna was gone again, disappeared into the cracks of the city where I couldn't find her. Mel kept hold of my hand.

"I think I might be more of a visitor to Occupy than a protester," Mel said.

"Yeah, it's intense," I said.

"What was that? What happened to you?"

"I had a panic attack."

OFFICE HOURS

"What if you turn this into a scene?" I bracketed off a paragraph of dead writing.

My student, Emma, nodded and wrote something I couldn't make out in her notebook. We were sitting in my tiny, windowless office.

"Remember, we talked about scenes in class—they have tension, dialogue, details, imagery," I continued.

She nodded and wrote down a couple more words in her notebook—tension, dialogue. Words that I knew later would not help her. She looked up at me, and I saw it was coming. Tears. Just one or two maybe, but yes.

"It's okay. Essays are hard, but I know you can do it," I said, and pushed the tissue box I kept on my desk closer to her. I wanted to cry too. I was so tired from camping out at Occupy. "Is there something going on I need to know about?" I asked. My students could be so tamped down, such diligent overachievers. They'd learned to keep it all in, to get ahead, and to win. They took drugs to stay focused rather than letting go. It was probably good she was crying. What if I started crying too? Did we all always have to keep it together? Had any of us recovered from the trauma of watching that student fall? That class, unlike my other two, was eerily silent. I could barely get them to talk or look at each other.

She yanked a tissue out the box and dabbed at her eyes. "This is so embarrassing."

"I don't believe in TMI and I'm not embarrassed. Lots of people cry in here. I cry all of the time," I admitted.

"That student who jumped in front of our class?"

"Go ahead."

She stood up and closed my office door.

"I know why."

"Why?"

"I was raped in high school," she said.

"I'm so sorry."

"That's what everyone says."

"I know, but I mean it. Are you okay? Have you told anyone?"

"I'm telling you."

"That's really brave." This wasn't the first time a student had told me she'd been raped. As a writing teacher of small classes, students confessed to me and wrote about all kinds of trauma—rape, child abuse, sexual abuse, anorexia, addiction, bullying. There wasn't much I hadn't heard.

She shrugged. "I don't want to focus on me, but I understand the suicidal feelings that it can trigger." The tears fell down her face and onto the page in her notebook. The words she'd written down smudged. I pulled another tissue out for her, she took it, and blew her nose.

"Do you know that Madison Reilly was raped?" I willed myself to use her name.

I thought of the chalk letters next to the makeshift memorial for her in the park. *Rape + Suicide = Murder.* Did I believe that particular equation?

"I was at this party and everyone was really drunk," she continued. I felt queasy about what was coming. "These girls were talking about her."

A knock at my door. I ignored it. Emma eyed the door. "Is someone out there listening to us?" She closed her notebook.

"I doubt it."

A knock again. I opened it. Another student. One of the dudes in a baseball cap. I remembered he was on the golf team and loved poetry. I still hadn't learned everyone's name. "Can you give us a couple more minutes?"

"I have to see you now because I have my barista shift in a half hour."

"I think you're going to have to come back next week," I said.

"No, it's okay. I'm going." Emma shoved her notebook into her backpack and stood up.

"Wait, this is important, don't go," I begged.

"I made a mistake. I don't know anything." She was still crying. "Don't block the door."

"I'm not," I said, and stepped aside. She hurried out the door and down the hallway.

"Emma!" I called out, but she didn't turn around.

"So can I come in?" my other student asked. I sucked in a breath and tried not to say something truly awful.

"No, next week."

His face fell, and he walked off toward the elevators.

I closed my door and put my head down on my desk. I felt overwhelmed and panicky. My phone chirped.

"Occupy sux without u. Butch is sorry. Should I forgive him?" A text from Johanna. "Arturo gave me your number."

I can't be everybody's mom, I thought, and then I remembered something my therapist had said in one of our early sessions: "Teaching stresses you out because you feel like the kid and your students are your parents, and no matter what you do, how perfect you are, you can't make them happy."

"Well that's for fucking sure," I'd sobbed, because it was one of those stealth therapist moments—*Oh! I'm a kid again, not an adult!*—that stabbed you with pain because it made perfect sense.

I rooted around in my backpack until I found it. The card the campus detective had given me. I stared at the number and at the phone in my office that I hadn't once used since they'd installed it. Who used an actual phone anymore? Still, it seemed like the official thing to do. I'd never once been helped by a police officer. I wanted it to be different, but it never turned out that way.

I picked up the phone and dialed the number anyway.

TURN AND TALK

"Do you believe in God?" Sasha paused the computer and took a bite of her frozen pizza.

I stood over the sink, washed out the French press, and put two plates in the dishwasher. "How come you ask?" I needed a minute.

"Katie and Denis told me during 'turn and talk' that God made the world."

"Well, I don't believe in God, but I am a spiritual person." The French press slipped out of my hand and into the sink. I gasped the way my mother did, like someone had sliced off their entire arm. I felt addled from my office hours. I'd left a message for the police officer, but I hadn't heard back. I was trying to be present, to compartmentalize, and to be a good mom.

"Owww!"

I picked up the French press. A shard of glass was missing from the rim. My index finger sliced at the tip.

"Mama cut herself," I said as I walked into the bathroom, squeezing my finger and trying not to look at it. I ran it under the faucet.

Sasha followed. "Can I put the Band-Aid on?"

The blood trickled off the side of my finger and into the sink. I got out the box of Band-Aids. "Can you unwrap the big ones, babe?"

I felt that same gray-around-the-edges-of-my-eyes sensation I had at Occupy and on the street that day with Sasha. My panics. I sat down on the toilet. I didn't want to scare Sasha. She pulled at the wrapper with her teeth until she got two open.

"Good girl," I said. The gray closed in until I saw just a tunnel of the bathroom floor.

"Mama?"

"Yeah, I'm okay." The gray receded a little and I looked at Sasha to steady myself. I put the Band-Aids on. The first one got soaked through with blood, but the second one stopped it.

"Mama, I saved you." Sasha danced a little triumph jig back out to the kitchen.

"You did!" I lay down on the couch.

"I believe in fairies, dragons, ghosts, witches, and trolls," Sasha continued.

I took a couple of breaths to steady myself. "Me too, but Daddy and I also believe in evolution."

"What's that?"

My brain card cataloged back to one of my high school science textbooks to try to attempt some recovery. I saw pictures of monkeys, but no words. I thought of PBS shows I'd watched with my father in elementary school, and his useless phrase whenever I expressed adult frustration at some shitty person or unkind bureaucratic procedure: "We're all just a bunch of fucking monkeys, what do you expect?" "I expect better!" I muttered, full of my usual righteous and useless rage. I taught *On the Origin of Species* badly during graduate school to some unsuspecting first-year students as part of a mandatory hybrid literature and science unit. The text seemed to be mostly about birds.

"It's the scientific idea, er, fact, about how humans began."

"So, how did they?"

"Come snuggle?" I needed a hug. She came over and wedged herself in the space between my body and the back of the couch. "Mama, your butt." I shifted.

"So, the universe used to be all matter, like just galaxy and stars," I started. My vision had cleared, but I hadn't planned on going all Carl Sagan. "This was, like, billions of years ago. And then there was a huge explosion, and the earth was full of dust and lava. Out of the lava, the tiniest creatures formed."

"What creatures?" Sasha interrupted.

"I don't know, like, so small you can't see them with your eyes. Like cells and bug-like cell things."

Sasha looked over at the computer. The Netflix home screen had switched to *The Apprentice*. Donald Trump's cheesy smile and comb-over glared at us. I imagined him shouting "You're fired!" at me.

"Why is he so orange?"

"I don't know. That's just his skin, I guess."

I plugged ahead. My finger throbbed through the two Band-Aids. "Eventually those tiny creatures evolved, like, changed, into bigger animals like fish and frogs and sharks, and some of those fish crawled onto the land and turned into other animals, and eventually there were monkeys and after a while those monkeys turned into humans."

"Monkeys became humans?" Sasha looked shocked.

"It took a really long time, like, billions of years." *The fuck?* I thought. *This shit sounds crazy.* "We should get Daddy to tell us the story of evolution. Or a book. We really need a book for this question."

"Katie said God is also an angel."

"I'm not really an angel person."

"Can I have cookies?"

"Eat your peppers first."

Sasha got up from the couch, stuffed five peppers into her mouth, and chewed loudly. She clicked the space bar a couple of times to replace Donald Trump with cartoons. When she finished, she held her plate up in my direction.

I gave her two cookies and flopped back down on the couch to zone out and stare at my phone while she watched her shows. I felt woozy again from the cut. My phone chirped.

"Hey, this is weird, but do you care if I pick up a shift at Gold Star?" It was Mel.

"We can reclaim the space!" I texted back. "And I can keep almost fucking him!"

"Perfect!"

An hour later, as Sasha wrote in her diary from my bed and came out every fifteen minutes to ask for something, I turned on NPR and listened from the couch. *Mayor Bloomberg toured the encampment today. He arrived with an entourage, and didn't speak to anyone currently living and protesting in the park. Before he ducked back into his limousine at the northernmost corner of the park, he did pause to talk to a reporter. He said, "The citizens of New York have a right to make a living. Right now the owners of the park are rightly concerned about safety and hygiene."* Soterios Johnson continued, *The police have issued an eviction notice to protesters to vacate the park by October 15th for mandatory cleaning.*

Once Sasha was asleep, I peeled off the two Band-Aids and looked at the cut. Half a centimeter across the pad of my index finger. I felt like gagging. I'd always been terrible about blood. I squeezed Neosporin onto it and covered it back up with two fresh Band-Aids. "Heal already, would ya?" I whispered to myself.

I'd never planned on being a single co-parenting mom. I sometimes didn't feel strong enough to make it through my five-day stretches with Sasha on my own. I wanted another adult around to take over when I nearly cut off my finger or was having a panic attack or needed to run to the drugstore for toilet paper. I couldn't admit to myself, but in these moments when something went wrong, I realized I was lonely and that I wasn't keeping it together.

A knock at my door. I sighed. I was in my nightgown and Sasha was asleep. Probably a student. I opened the door a crack. The same detective with his gray suit and shaved head.

"Give me a minute." I threw on yoga pants and stepped out into the hallway. A student down the hall opened her door, wide-eyed us, and then slammed it shut.

"I was hoping you'd just call me. My kid is asleep, but it's stressful for her to see her mom talking to the police."

The detective pulled a picture out of a folder. "Did you know Madison Reilly?" It was a school picture, maybe from senior year when students take cheesy pictures in photography studios. She held an umbrella and there was a fake backdrop of raining London behind her, complete with a double-decker bus. Wide smile. Too much mascara. Much longer hair. Prep rather than punk.

"We've been through this. I saw her fall, but I didn't know her and hadn't seen her before that day."

"You need to cooperate with us," the detective raised his voice.

"Why are you yelling at me? I'm an adult who is trying to help you."

He took a step back. "The girl, your student, won't talk to us. We don't think she knows anything anyway."

"Did you yell at her too?"

"What did she tell you?"

"Nothing, she was about to tell me about something she heard at a party, but another student knocked and she left."

"We'll be in touch."

He pressed the elevator button and we both waited awkwardly. Another student on my floor opened her door, waved sweetly at me, and then closed it again.

Back in my apartment, Sasha was standing in her underwear by the door.

"Why are you in the hallway?"

"I had to talk to someone for a minute, but it's fine."

She pulled me by the hand back into bed.

"Mama, I need you," she said.

"I need you too."

DON'T DIE

She ran through the maze of tents looking for Arturo's. Was it red? Green? Black? Everyone was zipped up tight for the night.

"Arturo!" she yelled. "Arturo!" Louder this time.

His girlfriend, Devora, popped her head out of one of the tents. Somebody from another tent yelled, "Shut up!"

"My boyfriend overdosed, I think, up near the sculpture. He won't wake up."

Devora slipped back into the tent and then Arturo crawled out with his phone. He held up a finger at her—to be quiet, to scold her, she couldn't tell. He dialed 911 and followed her to where Butch lay twitching on the ground.

"Hi, yeah, I'm calling from Zuccotti Park on behalf of the medical working group of Occupy Wall Street. We have a homeless person who has overdosed near the southeast corner of the park and we need an ambulance."

Johanna hated it when someone they knew, a friend, called them homeless.

Devora was just behind them. "Didn't one of the nurses say she had some Narcan?"

"I'm not about to pull a *Pulp Fiction* tonight," Arturo said.

"Grow up, babe, we're not in a movie," Devora said.

Johanna couldn't believe they were talking about *Pulp Fiction*. She kneeled down beside Butch and shook his shoulders. "Babe, babe, come on."

Arturo grabbed Butch's wrist to feel for his pulse. His legs and arms kept twitching.

"His lips are turning blue!" Johanna stood up and jumped up and down. "Where is the fucking ambulance?"

A crowd had formed around them. Some of them leaders of the working groups. Johanna felt their tsking, scolding vibe behind her. "Makes the movement look bad," one voice said.

"The media will say we're a bunch of addicts," said another.

Sirens wailed up to the corner. Ambulance. Stretcher. EMTs. "Clear a path please," one of them shouted.

Johanna took hold of Butch's hand and squeezed it. "Don't die," she said. "We have to get back to California, to City Lights." It was their favorite bookstore. The home of the Beats, their hobo icons. They hadn't talked about books or ideas in a long time. He, or whatever idea she'd once had about him, was slipping away from her.

"Ma'am, can you give us some space?"

Arturo stood up and pulled her back. They all watched as Butch got a shot in the arm.

He came to and threw up. "Jo?" he called to her.

"You're such a stupid asshole," she said.

The EMTs strapped him onto the stretcher and wheeled him into the back of the ambulance. "She's coming, right?" he said to the EMTs, but Johanna couldn't bring herself to get in the back of the ambulance. The bright lights, the hospital, there would be paperwork and questions. She was high too. Butch squeezed her hand. She squeezed it back and then let it go.

"Not unless she's your sister or wife."

Butch leaned back on the gurney. He was still so high. She knew it. She also knew he'd be out by morning. He'd rip out every IV and walk out of the hospital when no one was looking. He'd done it in Pittsburgh a year ago. He'd find her tomorrow.

Johanna ran a thumb along the cigarette burn scar on the inside of her arm. *I hate New York*, she thought. *Everything was fine until we came here.*

"Where are you going to sleep?" Arturo asked her. The ambulance sped off.

"Can I have a cigarette?" She didn't answer, like anyone ever really cared where they slept. They all just wanted them out of sight and out of the way. He lit two, one for each of them. The crowd dispersed. Back into their tents. It was three a.m.

"You guys can't use here. This is a protest, not a party," Devora said.

"We don't use here," Johanna lied, and then started to walk north. She'd never liked Arturo's girlfriend. She was hoping Stevie would steal Arturo away from her. *That would show that righteous bitch.*

"Johanna?" Arturo called after her.

"Let her go," Devora said.

She didn't stop. She knew that she and Butch weren't wanted, that they were fucking up the utopian vision of the Occupiers. But didn't their stories matter too? Hadn't they been just as fucked over, if not more so, than so many of the protesters?

When she was a couple of blocks away from Zuccotti, she leaned against the granite wall of a fancy building, took the last long drag of the cigarette, and put it out on the inside of her arm. Her flesh singed and she whimpered at the pain of it. She did it once more so that she had a triangle of three burns.

"See, you're still alive," she said out loud to herself.

DEAD STARS

Aaron and I crossed St. Mark's toward the construction that had taken over Astor Place. I was surprised the cube was allowed to stay next to the new Starbucks, a Walgreens, and the condos which, when finished, would resemble a giant tube of glass lipstick. He put his hand on the small of my back as a cab lurched into the crosswalk. He was still protective of me sometimes, chivalrous in a way that I missed. We were only able to be out together because Mel had Sasha for the night. Co-parenting only threw into relief our previous existence. Never in the same place at the same time, like Clark Kent and Superman, but we fought over who got to be the worker and who got to be the superhero.

"Which train are you taking?" We stood at the mouth of the N/R.

"I can take this one." I knew it wasn't his train.

Aaron wrapped his arms around me for a goodbye hug. His grip was tight, unlike our usual postseparation hugs, which had become the limp remains of the no-longer-fucking. He rubbed my hair and moved his hand down my back almost to my butt. My body responded instinctively and I pressed my breasts into his chest. I felt his cock through his skinny jeans. He lost weight since he left. We both had, but he felt slighter to me in the waist than ever before. I felt a familiar wave of relief, followed by a mounting panic. I breathed in his smell—coffee, always coffee, and something that was just Aaron. Soap and a hint of body odor, which I loved. Salty skin. Chest hair. All of it. He moved his hand back up my spine and to my neck, squeezed. I leaned back to get a look at his face. I wanted so badly for us to backslide, to fall into bed somehow together, our bed, the one I now mostly slept in alone, but that was ours, belonged to the both of us, in some way, forever. He kissed the top of my hair. Brotherly almost, but then he rubbed his hand back down to the top of my butt again, so not. We stood there, clinging to one another at the mouth of the N/R. I wondered who would let go first?

"I miss you," he breathed into my neck.

"I miss you too," I breathed back.

The train lurched and screeched from down below. He pressed his lips onto mine and opened his mouth. I felt his tongue against mine and responded by opening my mouth wider and kissing back. He rested his hands on my ass where they clearly belonged. We stayed like that for a minute, and then he took a step back. "I'm not sure what that was," he said, and smiled.

"Me neither. Do you want to come over?"

"What if we confuse Sasha?" He looked down. I felt the sting of rejection, and I wanted to kick myself for even trying. Fucking Aaron. One of the reasons we separated was because we couldn't fit together. My action. His passivity. I always felt like he was turning away from me.

He leaned in again and kissed me for longer this time. I wanted to melt back into him because I missed him and he was the most familiar and stable and best man I'd ever known.

"There's this new person." He paused. "My therapist says I have to tell you, but I'm afraid. I don't want you to be mad. She's younger."

"How young?"

"Twenty-five."

I stepped back from him. "Why don't you just get a sports car and put her in it?" I knew I was being nasty. I couldn't help myself. "You're not a feminist," I added. I knew that would hurt him the worst of all.

Aaron put his arms around me. "Don't say that. It's mean."

I raced through the rolodex of insults flipping around in my hot skull. I wanted to scream them all, but I knew it was pointless and I'd regret it. I couldn't really bear for Aaron to be mad at me. The only thing making our separation okay for me was our friendship. I needed him too much still.

"I want you to be happy," I said, and I meant it. "But I'm not ready. It will make me too jealous and it will kill me." I held up my hand to keep him from talking. I knew I was being a hypocrite. Adija was definitely not a day over twenty-eight and I looked at guys online who were much younger than me, but those were not relationships.

I walked away. When I turned the corner, I looked up at the nine p.m. Manhattan sky over lower Broadway. There were no visible stars, dead or alive, just the crescent moon, squinting at me.

"Stevie!" I looked up. It was Butch. He lurched toward me and bent forward to give my waist an awkward hug. I noticed he had a hospital bracelet still tied around his wrist. He held me tightly and alternately patted my stomach and ass.

"Where's Johanna?" I looked around. People streamed by. Nobody stopped to see if I needed help or protection. Did I? It was Butch. I knew him. A little.

He stood up and let go of me, but he kept his face close to mine. "She left me in the hospital. I took too much." He mimicked a shot to his arm and grinned. "But science brought me back to life, and now I'm out here with a beautiful woman and I'm free."

He planted his lips on my neck.

"Okay, okay," I said, and took a couple of steps back. "No kissing." I started to walk the other way. He wove around a couple of people and tried to block me. "Come on, Johanna wouldn't want this," I said.

"You're no fun." He bent over and hugged my waist again. I patted his back. I just wanted to get away. "I want to get an expensive coffee drink," he said.

"I'll give you money for one, but let go of me," I said.

He dropped his arms and stood up again. I noticed he'd lost a tooth. It looked bloody and raw. Had someone punched him? I fished around in my purse. My hand shook a little. I found a five and I gave it to him.

He kissed my neck again. I stood there and waited for it to be over. He lurched away. "I really do like you," he called over his shoulder. "We could fuck and it would be good."

I watched him go. I felt outside of myself. Aware that I should be afraid, but not quite feeling it.

I texted Adija with a still shaky hand, "You at a bar?" I slowed my pace down to wait for a reply. I looked over my shoulder to make sure Butch wasn't following me. I couldn't bear to go home to my empty apartment and my big bed, and I needed to be out of this borough, nowhere near the park, Butch, any of them.

No response. I was just a hookup to her.

And I needed a sure thing to put on top of my rejection. Because I knew Aaron. He was serious. If he was telling me about someone, she was real and not a trophy girlfriend. I didn't want to have to flirt or beg or wait or be coy. I texted David. "Can I come over and fuck you?" I added the smirky face emoji.

"Yes, please," he texted back.

TIED UP

He chased me up the stairs of his loft that led to the alcove where he kept his bed. I stopped on the fourth stair so that he could admire my ass. He put his tongue between my legs and licked. I spread my legs and groaned and then he spanked me hard.

"Ouch!" I cried out, but I giggled too. "What did I do?"

"I'm sure if you think hard enough, you'll be able to figure it out."

I looked over my shoulder at him. His cock was hard. He grinned and then frowned as he settled into his role.

"You might have to spank it out of me."

I gripped the stair. He slapped my ass again. I laughed harder.

He leaned over and whispered in my ear, "Red means stop, yellow means slow down, and green means go. Do you understand?"

I whispered a breathy yes into his neck.

"I can see that you are a bad, bad girl."

"I can't help it. I try to be good, but things get in the way."

He slapped my ass again and then rubbed the cheek he'd hit with his palm. He put his finger inside me and I pushed up against it.

"Things or men?"

"Men usually," I conceded. "I just kissed my future ex-husband, which is a big no-no."

"That is very naughty. Get upstairs," he said.

I crawled up the remaining stairs, still on all fours, and lay face-down on his bed. "I'm also hanging out with anarchists and drug addicts and I don't care. I like it."

"Oh, so you're a bad mommy. A real fuckup," he said.

"Yes, I am." I wasn't sure if what he said was liberating or true or sad or not. It just felt good to have the bad thoughts out in the air, like in therapy, but better because it was sexual. There was no boundary here. I could touch David all I wanted.

"And I like men who are completely unavailable to me," I continued.

"Awww." David made a mock sad face at me. "I think you like these unavailable men because you're afraid of commitment, and this means you can do whatever you want."

"That's not true," I said.

"Oh, you want to talk back, do you? Maybe you need to be tied up," he said as he reached the top of the staircase.

"With what?" I asked. I'd never been tied up or spanked, and I'd never had anyone tell me what to do in such an explicit way. My clit was hard.

"I have restraints."

"Where?" I looked up and back at him.

He bent over and pulled at the restraints attached the frame of his bed.

Before I said yes, I heard my voice in my throat. "I'd rather tie you up," and then I peeled off into a laughter that I hadn't experienced in months. Deep. From the stomach. I couldn't stop it. Almost a cackle.

"That sounds like something that makes you very happy."

I tried to talk through my laughter, but it doubled me over for a moment. David looked on and grinned. "Ah, well, maybe I'm crazy," I managed finally.

"I think you're having fun."

I stroked his cock and then put the tip of it in my mouth. He groaned. "Well, if you're going to tie me up, you better start telling me what to do, and stop sucking on that cock."

"I can do both."

He grabbed the scruff of my neck and pushed his cock deeper into my mouth. I took it in.

"Lie down," I commanded.

He did, and I fastened his ankles and wrists into the restraints. "Sometimes you have to tie up wolves to keep everyone safe," I said.

He whimpered and pulled at the restraints with his arms, but they held tight. I laughed again. I wasn't quite sure who I was. I felt like the actual witch I'd joked with Arturo that I might be. Powerful. A dom. I could do whatever I wanted to this big giant man. Giddy.

"Green," he said.

"Ah, okay." I remembered what that meant. His cock waved in the air at me. He really did have a perfect dick.

"Why don't you sit on my face."

I climbed up. He licked it like he wanted to stay there forever. "You can smother me with it," he mumbled underneath me.

I stayed until I thought I might come and then I scooted off and grabbed a condom from his headboard. I slid it over his cock and then sat on it as quickly as I could. I was so wet it slid right in. Deep. Straight to my heart maybe. I didn't know, but I cried out and then I laughed again and rocked my hips back and forth for a minute or two. I undid the restraints on his wrists with a resounding Velcro snap. He grabbed on to my hips. *I am made for this*, I thought. *The thing I do best is fucking. Mine is an animal joy. I am riddled with fears and anxieties and fucking is my only way out. I will never, ever stop. Never, ever.* Everything went red around the edges. Red like my pussy. Red like blood and cervix and vagina and the insides of the insides. The deep red core of me that was mostly hidden and that I'd always wanted to keep a secret.

"Oh fuck!" I cried out as I came, and then I fell down on top of him. I stayed there for a moment and he kissed the side of my face. He reached down to untie his ankles and then flipped me over and fucked me until he came. We lay there in a heap for a minute or two, panting.

"I haven't done anything like that before," I managed when my breathing slowed down. "I didn't know I could be both submissive and dominant."

"I think you're what's called a switch."

"Ah, new lingo. I like it." I stared at the ceiling, at the elaborate network of pipes that ran the length of David's loft.

And then it came. Rising out me. A feeling. Again. Shit. Fuck. Joy.

Happiness. Sadness. What. Tears. Yes. Again. I wiped my eyes and sniffed quietly. I didn't want David to see.

He sat up on his elbows. "You all right over there?"

I couldn't help it. I sobbed and hid my face in the crook of my elbow.

"You are opening me up, teaching me new things, and I'm grateful for it," I said, but was that what was happening? I wasn't sure.

"You're teaching me things too," David said, and pulled me closer. "Thank you."

"You're welcome."

"Well, this is all very polite," he said, and then he drifted off to sleep.

PORTALS

The day before, she did all of her favorite things. She spent two hours in the vintage clothing store on Thompson trying on old hats and dresses from the seventies and then she walked to Lucien, the old-school French restaurant on First and A, and ate a steak frites and a chocolate pot. She drank three glasses of wine and she let the pretty French waitress fuss and coo over her. She'd heard that Rene Ricard and Gerard Malanga used to drink and fight there.

"Did they?" she asked the waitress.

"You're sitting at their table," she exclaimed. "But then they had a fight that lasted twenty years, and one sat at the table and the other at the bar until they made up. You are a poet or an artist then, no?"

She nodded and downed the last of her wine, but she couldn't bring herself to say yes out loud. The word was stuck in her throat like a hairball.

In the bathroom, she wrote on the wall with a Sharpie at eye level with the toilet. Some of her own lines, *You look back, but it's way too late. / You're in the middle of the ocean now. / They're gone and you've started a new life. / You now live on the continent of after-the-fact, / of long ago, of I did it and it kind of hurt.*

She bought the waitress and bartender a drink and paid with her father's credit card—one final *fuck you.* They toasted her and she felt like a big shot.

On the walk home, she smoked the rest of her cigarettes, lighting one off the butt of another until she felt queasy. In her apartment, she got her papers ready—the poems and the goodbye letters she planned to take with her, arranged in a particular order in a folder. She packed her yellow backpack and laid out the clothes she'd wear the next day, down to her pink underwear.

Using the Sharpie and masking tape, she marked some of her favorite things and who would get them. *Records go to Jonah. Poetry divided between Claire and Willa. Jewelry to Mom. Plants to Nana. Clothes to Beacon's Closet and whoever takes them gets the store credit*, she wrote on the door of her closet.

She took two Valium she'd scored off of a boozy Tinder date and masturbated. She texted him one last time, "I thought you were cool," and then she turned off her phone because she was a believer in portents, omens, and auguries, and she didn't want that text to mean anything.

Then she walked into the Coal Yard on First Avenue next to the McDonald's to sit with the winos and get drunk enough to pass out.

After six shitty well whiskeys, she went to the bathroom and stared at herself in the gritty mirror until she became a blur. "I never said yes," she said to the tangle of hair, pink flesh, and eyeliner in front of her, and then she pressed her nose against the glass and shouted, "No!"

Was she practicing for the future or the past? She wasn't sure.

In her daydreams of jumping, there was always a portal, a hidden trapdoor into another galaxy, a fiery rip in time, or a trick panel sliding open into a lush garden.

She managed to stumble home. No one followed her because no one gave a shit, she told herself. On her laptop, she googled portals and clicked and clicked and clicked until she passed out.

REWIND

I woke up with a jolt in David's bed. I looked at my phone. It said 5:05 a.m. It was still dark out, so I let my brain go over its little catalog of home movies about the last weeks of my marriage when everything had fallen apart. Our own *Scenes from a Marriage* or *Take This Waltz*.

First this:

"I love your boots," I said to Bess, our couples therapist, as Aaron and I stationed ourselves on opposite corners of the loveseat couch in her office. We each grabbed for an embroidered lumbar pillow and clung to them like they were all we had.

"Thank you." Bess smiled warmly at me and I managed a rictus smile—frozen and fake—back in the direction of the floor. What I meant was, *I'm jealous of your shoes because they remind me of a time in my own life where I cared about weird, artsy objects, and I could shop impractically because I was childless and blissfully in denial about my impending financial doom.*

"Can we go back to the pattern conversation?" Bess began.

"Like, I'm active and he's passive?" I blurted, leaning way too forward on the couch.

Aaron stared down into his lap. Bess nodded, waited for him to respond. He said nothing for what felt like a full minute. I bit my tongue. One of our problems was that I spoke so much that Aaron didn't have a chance to say anything.

"I notice you're pretty quiet today, Aaron," Bess said gently.

Aaron shot her a dirty look. He hated it when people "named" something he was doing. Bess was young, thirty, maybe thirty-two, if we were lucky. We decided after our first session with Bess that we had a rookie, a person who'd never been married, trying to save our marriage, and a new therapist on top of that. Sometimes we felt sorry for her. She was empathetic and kind, but in way over her head with us. Usually, when we left, we bonded over something stupid she'd said.

See! I wanted to shout. *These are not patterns! They are personalities! I talk. He waits. I lean forward. He looks down.* But I waited and looked kindly at Aaron. Sometimes I felt sorry for us, for the people we had become. Before I started couples therapy I naively assumed that we would have the kinds of therapeutic breakthroughs I'd seen in movies. Like when Robin Williams finally cracked Matt Damon open in *Good Will Hunting* and he said, "It's not your fault," a couple of times and there were muffled man sobs and then it was all over. All better. Or at least better enough.

"Maybe we could use this silence to talk about silence," Bess ventured. I shot Aaron a conspiratorial look. A new Bessism! He didn't return it.

"Last week, Stevie said she feels alone, like, you're always out at night without her, and that you don't want to spend time with her," Bess said.

Aaron looked up at Bess, but not at me. "I know that she's sad."

"You can talk to her," Bess said gently.

Aaron winced and looked toward me, but more at my arms than my face. "I know that you're sad, and I feel really bad about that, but I can't be responsible for your sadness, and I don't want to give up what I've made for myself."

He was talking about the little space he'd carved for himself in the poetry world. The small clatch of readings and young poets he'd started hanging out with in the last couple of years. Before we'd become parents, I'd been part of this world too, but I drifted away into other people and projects. Mostly, at night I felt too tired to go out and see anyone or hear anyone read, and if I did I felt like I had a sign around my neck that said Grouchy Wife.

"But don't you want to spend more time together?" I asked. I felt the heat of Bess's stare, and her wheels turning, trying to figure out what to say next.

Aaron stayed focused on a fixed point, somewhere near my elbow. He could not, it seemed, look at me. "Actually, I don't."

I felt my face flush. It was something I knew in my bones, from his choices, and from the way we had come to divide our time. We tag-teamed everything: childcare, teaching on opposite days because we couldn't afford a sitter, nights out alone but rarely together. And yet, those three words—*Actually, I don't*—felt like a death blow. My worst fear was true. My husband, the one person who was supposed to love me best, did not enjoy my company. I was someone to escape. It was not a fear I had invented out of my usual cocktail of insecurity and rage, but a fact, straight from the horse's mouth.

And then this:

We danced at someone's apartment. We all went—Mel, Hayes, me, and maybe half of what was left at the three a.m. bar. We did one more bump in the bathroom and one last shot at the bar.

Hayes stayed by my side, touched my knee and shoulder, and whispered into my neck. Jokes, mostly about Duran Duran.

"I'm so hungry," I said on the walk back to the strange girl's apartment. Hayes on one arm and Mel on the other.

"I want nachos or an omelet," Mel said, squeezing my elbow.

"I'll make pasta with butter and parmesan cheese," Hayes said, squeezing my other elbow. I shut my eyes. I imagined I was on the yellow-brick road with my misfit, broken friends. *We're off to see the wizard, the wonderful wizard of Oz! Because, because, because, because, because—because of the wonderful things he does.* Mel and I used to sing this song in college, walking back from parties in the dark, small-town night—arms linked, kicked-out feet, a dance that couldn't be stopped.

"Butter," Mel said up at the night sky.

It turned out that Hayes knew the girl who decided to throw the impromptu dance party. They were former roommates or lovers or something. Whispers and looks, camaraderie of eyes. We all danced to the computer's tiny speakers and we ate pasta out of the pot. The girl gave us an air mattress and Mel passed out on a couch in the hallway. I told myself it was nothing, just sleeping next to another man. Somebody turned off the lights.

He reached for my hip, put his hand there, and didn't move it. He kissed the back of my neck. I felt the surprise of someone else's lips and mouth—not Aaron's—moving down my neck. He pulled my hip into him. He was hard through his jeans. He'd left them on. I thought that was gentlemanly. I lay there like that forever it seemed. I was at a crossroads. I thought of what Aaron had said to me and to Bess. *He doesn't even want to spend time with you*, I told myself over and over again, until eventually I turned around to face him, pressed my mouth into his, felt his tongue against mine. The room was spinning and then it was incredibly still.

Press. Give. Chest against chest. Shirt off. Dress off. Bra off. Warm mouth. Lips. Press. Give. He ran his hands through my hair. His mouth moved down my neck, onto my breasts, and down my stomach. I hadn't been touched like this in so long, I realized. He pulled off my tights and grabbed at my underwear with his teeth. I lifted his chin up to meet my mouth. Kissed it. Opened my mouth. His tongue. I felt myself breathing, panting, at the shock of it. The heat of him, of us together. I pressed my forehead against his.

"I can't. I mean, I want to, but I can't," I said.

He slid on top of me, pressed down on me, and kissed my neck gently and slowly. He paused.

"Okay." He rested his head on my breasts. "Your heart is beating really fast."

I ran one hand through his hair.

"I'm married and I have a kid," I blurted.

"Oh, wow, I didn't know." But he didn't move. Kept his head between my tits. "You should maybe have told me that."

"I know, I am, right now, but, before, yes." I felt the room spin and tilt again, and wondered when the blow had stopped cutting through the shots.

"Not that it would have stopped me from trying." He looked up and grinned.

"It's not a good marriage. It once was, but obviously I wouldn't

be here if it was happy," I stammered. "I like this, I am happy tonight
. . ." I trailed off.

Hayes kissed me again. Tongue. Hard. He meant it. He talked
through his kissing of me. "We can stop. I don't want to put you in
a bad position."

"I'm not, I want to." I kissed him back.

"Is he a big man?" Hayes asked and smirked.

"I don't think he cares," I said into his lips.

"I bet he does."

"I'm going to pee." I pulled away, stood up, fumbled down the hallway toward the bathroom, and heard Mel breathing on the couch. I
peed in the dark, couldn't bear to turn the light on, felt my heart in
my chest, listened to the voices in my head.

*Don't stop. You want this. You've been so lonely. He wants you. You
need this. A man at a bar thinks you're hot. You exist. Nobody has to
know. Not even Mel. You'll fuck him. You'll wake up. You'll go home.
You'll cure yourself of this longing for connection, for someone else. Go
home. Get dressed. Wake up Mel and leave now while you still can.
Find your dress, your tights, your shoes. Stay. You can just sleep next
to him. That's enough. Skin against skin. Just touching.*

I felt along the wall and made it back to the air mattress. I slid into
him and he slid into me. Body met body. Lock and click.

And afterward, this:

He grabbed me by the neck when I came through the door. Bad
kitten. The scruff.

"Sash?" I asked.

"Asleep. Don't talk."

"But what I did," I whispered. I'd told him the night before. I
wasn't a liar.

"You've already said way too much," he hissed into my ear.

Lights off. Facedown on the bed. His lips down my spine, my ass,
and between my legs. He stood above me and then flipped me over.
He was not exactly looking at me, but at a point on the dark horizon just past my shoulder. That darkness, I knew even then, was my
future. The two of us alone, on separate planes. We faced each other.
I was willing. I wanted to be punished. I was a very bad girl. I broke

a major rule. Snapped it in two. I still belonged to him. I was a wife. He leaned into me, pressed me down, and slid into me. We became each other, one-moving-together-thing, one organism, intent only on pleasure. For once, a thing that made sense. Joined together. Fitting. He ran his fingers through my hair. I pulled him down on top of me and pressed my chest into his. Moving deeper still. Pushing.

"Can I?" I climbed on top of him and pressed his shoulders down into the bed. He grabbed my hips and arched to meet me.

We rocked back and forth. We became waves and particles of waves. Bits of ocean. The sea churned up against itself. Crashing. Crashing. First me, then him.

And I thought, *We were a boat with a minor mission. We were orphans and we found each other. We built the boat together, but we had shitty tools and it was flimsy. We bobbed and crashed finally into a rocky shore. What did we know?*

I panted on top of him. Short breaths he knew so well. I stayed there sweating, this animal sometimes called a wife.

"It doesn't change what you did," he said. But he held me tightly because he hadn't yet let me go.

It was the last time we fucked. A month later Aaron moved out.

DAVID STIRRED NEXT to me and opened his eyes. I looked out the window. The sun was up. I guessed it was at least seven.

"What are you doing over there?" he asked.

"Feeling like shit about the end of my marriage," I said.

He rubbed his eyes and yawned. "The ends of all marriages feel like shit. I should know, I've been through two."

"But the things I remember are not really the end, they just feel like it because we need a narrative to understand how things come to life and then die. I mean, I did a shitty thing, a wrong thing, but the end was already coming. It was just one way to make it happen."

"Don't be too hard on yourself, Red," he said, and pulled me closer to his warm, naked body.

"Too late for that."

NAVIGATOR

Mel closed the bathroom door and stared at her reflection in the full-length mirror. She was naked except for her big gold hoop earrings. She had bikini lines from the summer, and a neat little bush because she'd just splurged on a bikini wax.

She opened the medicine cabinet and looked inside. An old-school razor, shaving cream, a comb, Tylenol, a kid's SpongeBob toothbrush and bubble gum–flavored toothpaste, and an adult's electric toothbrush.

There was a small window in the bathroom which looked out onto a narrow Brooklyn backyard. Red fall leaves brushed against the window. Mel made a wide-eyed expression in front of it and snapped a selfie. She kept the tops of her nipples in the shot and sent it to Stevie. "At my chef's place. It's so hot I had to take a break and hide in the bathroom."

"Yer beautiful," Stevie texted back. "Have fun!"

"Are you using my toothbrush?" Carmine knocked. "'Cause that's a no-no."

"I'll be out soon," she said. "But I did just stick it up my cunt."

He chuckled on the other side of the door and flopped down onto his bed.

When she came out, he was lying on the bed stroking his cock. "It's not nice to make me wait for so long," he said.

"You like waiting." She crawled on top of him and rubbed her clit against him.

"You like to torture me from behind the bar, don't you?"

"Yes, that's my job. I'm a bartender. Look, but don't touch."

"I'm touching."

"Special permission."

He put on a condom and slid into her. She sat up, held on to his shoulders, and moved back and forth. She hadn't fucked a man in almost a decade. She had feelings about it she couldn't explain to anyone—it wasn't a homecoming. She wasn't Odysseus returning to Penelope after years of whoring and adventuring with the damned and lost. This wasn't about gender or dicks or pussies, though she knew both he and Jenny thought it was. It was about skin and connection and traction and lift. It was about smell and hair and eyes and cells. The stupid things he said, the way he watched her from the kitchen, and then pretended he wasn't looking at all. Each body had its own landscape, a vast terrain that only lovers get to know—a scar here, a dip in the hip there, a birthmark near the shoulder, the pretty fat where ass meets leg. Mel wanted to explore them all.

"Jesus," he said. "We're a perfect fit." He held on to her waist.

"Right?" She leaned down to kiss him.

She moved her hips and ground into him.

"Can I fuck you from behind?" he asked.

"Yeah."

He flipped her over and slid inside her. She rubbed her clit while he moved in and out of her, faster and harder.

"Can you come this way?" he asked.

"Maybe," she said. He felt so good.

She rubbed herself. The bed shook and creaked. Her head banged against the headboard. She didn't care.

She collapsed back into him. A wave of pleasure from pussy to spine. She moaned and arched her butt back. He slid into her even deeper.

"Jesus," he said, and then fell on top of her panting.

"Did you come?" she asked.

"Um, yeah," he said, and pulled out of her.

They lay there panting on their backs.

"Well, that was terrible." Mel laughed.

"We should definitely never do that again." He sat up on his elbows and grinned.

"Absolute major mistake."

"Where did you come from?"

"I live around the corner with my girlfriend."

"Shhhh." He kissed her on the mouth.

He sat up to peel off the condom.

"Shit," he said.

"What?"

"It ripped."

"Stop joking," Mel said.

He held up the shredded condom. "Are you ovulating right now?"

"I have no clue." Mel felt a wave of panic and then reason. "I'm forty-two, it's really hard for women my age to get pregnant."

"Piece of shit condom."

"Jenny and I do sometimes talk about finding a baby daddy," Mel said. It was true—well, it used to be true like three years ago, but this wasn't at all how it was supposed to happen.

"I can't have another kid. I'm barely hanging on to the one I have," Carmine said.

Mel jumped up out of the bed and did a little jig. "Look, I'm shaking all of the sperm out of me. It's running down my legs and away from my old and inhospitable womb. Your sperm is jaded and tired too. I can feel it. It's giving up right now, dying or turning around to quit." She waved her arms over her head and then crossed her knees back and forth like she was in a vaudeville show. She did a quick Charleston and then collapsed onto the bed in a fit of hysterical laughter.

"You're fucking crazy," Carmine said, but he was laughing too.

"I'm not pregnant. I've never been pregnant and I never will be," Mel said to his ceiling, but she could already see herself in the feminine aisle at the drugstore, staring at the boxes of pregnancy tests.

"All right. I believe you."

MY TEACHING ASSISTANT

He'd led me down some little side streets and into a dark Irish dive bar.

"Well, if I'm going to be your TA for the day, you have to compensate me for my labor." We'd come from Occupy where Arturo spent the day teaching my students about independent newspapers and the secret inner workings of Occupy while I worked in the kitchen. He nodded to the bartender. "Four shots of Jameson and two cans of Tecate. She's paying."

"Jesus. It's only three in the afternoon."

"So?"

I pulled two twenties out of my wallet and slid them over to the bartender.

"Quick, do the shots," he commanded.

I did one right after the other and tried my best not to gag. "Attagirl," the bartender said. He had a comb-over and a small belly. I noticed pictures of kids taped up by the cash register. "Yours?" I asked him.

"My grandkids."

"Cuties," I said, and he smiled.

"Troublemakers mostly, now that they're teenagers."

Arturo downed his shots and we took our cans of beer to a booth in the back. The place was empty except for us, the bartender, and a guy on a Blackberry at the other end of the bar.

"Don't you want to be at the GA?" I asked.

"They don't need me there," he said.

"Thanks for talking to my students," I said. "That was really cool of you."

"They're cute. They seem rich as fuck, but the one percent can change."

"I'm sure some of them are, but the University has some kids on scholarships and loans." I pushed the lime wedge down into the mouth of the beer can and then licked the lime and beer off of my finger. My chest felt warm from the two shots and my head buzzed.

"I'm sure more loans than scholarships."

"Prolly."

"Prolly? Aren't you an English professor?"

"I teach writing and I hate grammar snobs. I love slang, puns, made-up words, silly prefixes and suffixes. When I was married I had a pretty elaborate house patois with my husband."

"House patois?"

"You know, like, the private jokes and slang that's unique to the culture of the family, apartment, or house."

"In Spanish we have a lot of nicknames and suffixes."

"My grandma had a nickname for everyone," I said.

"What was yours?"

"La gringa."

"Ha, that's fitting." Arturo drained the rest of his beer and stood up to get more. "Another shot?"

"Um." I paused. I pressed my lower back into the soft, cushioned back of the booth. I felt like I could curl up and fall asleep there.

"I think that's a yes."

I looked down at my fingernails. Chipped and bitten, as usual. Arturo returned with another shot and can of beer for each of us.

"I'm still finishing the first beer."

"Quit whining," he teased, and picked up his shot. He gestured for me to do the same and I did.

The last shot gave me courage. "So, what's your deal?"

"What do you mean?"

"With your girlfriend?"

"I told you. We have an open relationship."

"Yeah, but how do you do it?"

"Well, if I like someone, I take them to a bar, and we get drinks." He smiled at me like he was winning me over.

"No, I mean, do you tell each other about other people. Is it don't ask, don't tell? Is there a hierarchy?"

"She's my primary partner, if that's what you mean, so whoever else I see has to be pretty cool with that and understand that she comes first."

"What's in it for the second person?" I asked.

"Fun, adventure, amazing sex." Arturo raised his eyebrows. "Are those things that appeal to you?"

"Maybe. I don't know. I'm seeing this other guy right now and it's open and I go on dates with other people, but I've never been with anyone who has a primary partner. I don't think it would work for me. I think I'm too jealous."

"That's a lot of thinking." He set his can down and came around to my side of the booth.

"No." I laughed. "Why are you coming over here?"

He slid next to me and put his arm around me. "Let's just put our heads together and think about this," he said, and leaned his forehead against mine.

"I don't think that's a good idea," I said, but I kept my forehead pressed to his, the tips of our noses just touching. His whiskey breath against my lips. Mine against his.

"I like your reformed riot grrrl thing," he said.

"I like your commie scarf," I said, and tugged at the black-and-white patterned scarf wrapped around his neck.

"It means I support Palestinian liberation." He kept his forehead pressed against mine.

"Duh, I know." I sucked a breath in and out.

He kissed me and I kissed him back. He ran his tongue along my lips and up my cheek and into my ear. I put my hands on his shoulders and pushed him back a couple of inches.

"What?"

"I don't want to be second. I want to be special."

"But you are special. You're Stevie."

"And I don't want just fucking. I have a lot of that right now, and it's fun, it's great, but I . . ." I couldn't finish my sentence because I felt like I might cry. My voice cracked a little and so I swallowed a big gulp of my beer.

"It's not going to be just fucking," he said, and squeezed my hip for emphasis.

"I don't believe you."

He let out a big sigh and slid over to give me a little space.

My phone, which was lying facedown on the table, chirped.

"Kid stuff?" Arturo asked.

"Maybe. Let's just take a minute and stare at our phones and collect ourselves, okay?"

"Do I have to go back over to my side?"

I didn't want him to, but I said, "I think so."

"Fine, make a boundary," he said, and slid back over onto his side of the table. He pulled his phone out of his pocket. "Boundaries are good for me."

I looked at my text. It was from David. "Thinking about you Red."

I read the alerts that had popped up on my phone. *Amanda Knox stunned to be home after dramatic trial in Italy. This is a brand-new two-bedroom apartment for rent with DINING ROOM! $2,500.*

My phone said 3:47 p.m. I remembered where I was supposed to be. "Shit. Fuck." I reached for my jacket and stood up.

"What?"

"I forgot, I have therapy today. I've got to go."

"Therapy? Like with a therapist?"

"Yeah." I tugged drunkenly at the zipper of my coat and gave up. "Are you making fun of me for having a therapist?"

"No, I have one too. I just started. Does yours talk a lot? Because I can't figure out what mine is thinking and it's making me crazy."

"Mine is active. It's like a conversation."

Arturo stood up and put his arms around me. "Just don't overthink it, okay?"

"Thinking is my thing." I hugged him back. "But I gotta go," I added, wriggling free. "I can't believe I'm going to therapy drunk. This is a new low."

I waved goodbye to the bartender as I scurried out of the bar and into the afternoon sun.

THE WIVES

The wives were just fine, thank you very much. The wives didn't feel like doing the practice tests. The wives were having big daydreams about old boyfriends. Some wives had threesomes because why not? And some didn't because tacky! That wife was wondering what her life would have been like if she'd stayed with her girlfriend. The wives just wanted a moment to themselves and they were willing to lock themselves in the bathroom to get it. The wives didn't understand the "mommy wars," but they kept reading articles about it, until it became true. The wives were working all the time. The wives didn't get why anyone would choose to camp out in a park. The wives wanted to run away and join the protesters, but they knew they couldn't. The wives were sure that LGBTQ people should have the right to marry, and yet sometimes they thought marriage was overrated. The wives were always on Facebook and Twitter and Pinterest and Instagram. The wives cried when their iPhones fell in the toilet. They put them in bowls of rice to dry them out, but it didn't work. The wives were so, so hungry. The wives were starving themselves to be "beach body ready." All the wives could carry their own strollers up the subway steps. They wives were ripped, but they had small tummies that sometimes stuck out. They felt fanatical about these tummies. They didn't believe any of the husbands or not husbands when they said it was cute. The wives were composting on the terrace. Or not. The wives were eating the leftover nuggets from their children's plates for dinner. The wives were worried about climate change, BPA, real estate, public schools, gentrification, and affordable day care. Some wives were worried every day that the police would shoot their sons, but the other wives weren't listening. The wives weren't really thinking about the big picture because they had to make the doctors' appointments and pack the lunches and take the barfing cat to the vet and grade the papers and find a babysitter. The wives didn't have time for your shit. The wives were totally busy. The wives were so fucking bored. The wives started a co-op. Some worked for 350.org and volunteered at the soup kitchen. The wives picked the Whole Foods rotisserie chicken clean. It was delicious. Especially the skin.

YOU AND YOUR LITTLE DOG TOO

"Tipsy!" Johanna called out to the park.

"Tipsy!" she shouted louder as she walked the curved paths that led to the fountain.

"Have you seen my dog?" she asked a group of students. "She's a pit bull mix, black-and-white spots, like a small cow?" They shook their heads blankly at her, like she wasn't speaking English, like she was a ghost they were staring through.

"You lost your little dog," someone singsonged at Johanna. It was the crazy lady who sometimes shouted at her and Butch about the apocalypse.

Johanna took a long look at her. She had a stiff gray helmet of hair, full of lice. Probably thirty, but looked fifty. Tanned, hard, leather face. New Doc Martens boots that one of the richies who lived in the townhouses on the north side of the park must have given her. Old black cocktail dress. Pink puffer jacket stained with piss. She had a kind of chic hag street style that Johanna admired, but she was utterly fucked. No friends. Batshit. In need of major meds.

For a second, Johanna wanted to steal her boots. She remembered her name was Cathy.

"You lost your little dog," Cathy cooed, and patted the bench for Johanna to sit next to her. She scanned the park for Butch's lanky, lately skeletal frame. Butch had said he'd look too, but he'd probably left to score. He lied about everything now. He'd come back from the emergency room like nothing had happened, like he hadn't nearly died while she stood over his twitching corpse. He wouldn't even talk about it with her. She sat down next to Cathy.

"You and your little dog too," Cathy said. "Do you remember the witch in the *Wizard of Oz*?"

Johanna shook her head no. They were having a lucid moment.

"'I'll get you, my pretty, and your little dog too,' the witch said to Dorothy."

"I never saw that movie," Johanna said, but she knew about the yellow-brick road and "Somewhere Over the Rainbow," a song she hated so much she'd never been able to listen to the whole of it. Her mother had once played it and she'd run out of the cabin and into the snow to get away from the despairing hope of it.

Cathy put her hand on Johanna's back and patted, patted, patted. Johanna heard a voice in her head, *You suck. You're a failure. You can't do this alone.* She heard it sometimes when she was alone, when she wasn't using, when things were getting fucked up. It was more persistent lately, a hissing in her ear, rather than an occasional aside. *Yousuckyou'reafailureyoucan'tdothisalone.Yousuckyou'reafailure youcan'tdothisalone.*

Johanna winced. She didn't want any comfort. She didn't want lice either, but here they were.

"I used to be like you. I had a dog too," Cathy said. "A poodle. He had a purple bandana. I made a lot of money because of that dog."

"She was a good dog." Johanna hunched over her knees and cried into her hands. For Tipsy and all the strays. For the idea that she could become Cathy or that Cathy had once been like her. How easy it was to go from beatnik hobo to homeless hag.

Cathy patted, patted, patted, and shouted at a woman jogging by with a stroller, "The world is fucking ending, don't you know!"

DEAD BIRD

The guard called, "There's a girl here for you. She says her name is Johanna."

I let her in. She'd been crying.

"I lost Tipsy." She hugged me and I hugged her back. Regular eyes. No slurring. Not high. I decided she could stay for the night.

"Hey," Mel said sympathetically from the kitchen. She'd just made dinner for Sasha and me, and was cleaning up. Since Aaron left, Mel and Jenny were the only ones who cooked for me. "Do you want me to fix you a plate?"

"Yeah, that would be great."

Sasha peered out from behind the couch. She did this with strangers. Hid until she felt like coming out.

Johanna got down on all fours and pretended to be cat. "Meow," she said in the direction of the couch. "I'm shy."

Sasha crawled out on all fours too. "Prrrr . . . I'm a cat too. Do you want to meet the other cat that lives here?"

Johanna looked up at me for permission, I guessed. I nodded, and then she followed Sasha into the other room to find Rudy.

Mel raised an eyebrow at me. She was protective and territorial and it made sense, but Occupy had opened me up, made me less worried about boundaries. I'd decided to stop fighting it and just help Johanna when I could. I didn't want to witness another lost girl fall. Besides, I had a feeling about her. She was a good person, I knew it. Mixed up, bad boyfriend, drug problem, yes; but at heart, okay. She wouldn't be interested in me if she weren't. I attracted overachievers, writer nerds, queer kids, smart punks, and budding feminists. Those were the young people who wanted to be around me, came to my dorm events, and took my classes.

From Sasha's bedroom, I heard the murmur-whisper-yells of the Lego elves as they fought off an evil dragon. Johanna played along.

"I'm Faira, and I've brought my dragon," she said.

"No, you're going to be Emily," Sasha corrected her.

"I'm Emily, and I've brought my giant fire-breathing dragon." Johanna took kid direction well.

"What?" I shrugged at Mel. "She'll sleep in Sasha's room tonight and I'll have Sasha with me in my bed. No biggie. Why can't I help this person?" I whispered.

"You can, but just . . ." Mel shrugged hopelessly at me. "No strays. No losers, Stevie." She put the plate on the counter for Johanna and grabbed for her bag. "I gotta go meet Jenny."

"Things okay with the cabin?" I asked.

"Nope, not at all, but I'm in denial now and not officially talking about it."

"Fair enough." I kissed Mel on the cheek at the door. "Thanks for dinner."

"Anytime, babe."

I opened my laptop on the table to the livestream feed from Occupy, while I kept an ear trained on Sasha and Johanna. It was pure elf talk and kitty play. I was hoping to see Arturo's face flash across the screen. He hadn't texted me since that afternoon at the bar. Maybe I'd been too clear. Maybe I scared him away. Maybe that was a good thing. I was addicted to the livestream. Its shaky cam view of the park. The people who sometimes stood in front of it to announce updates. The tops of the tents, and the red metal sculpture looming in the background. No matter what mundane thing I was doing, a bunch of radicals had taken hold of a public park and wouldn't let it go, and that was oddly comforting to me. The live cam let me know that everyone was okay. Position held. Park occupied. Protesters busy. Police, for now, at bay.

I shut my laptop.

"Johanna, come eat. Sasha, time for bath," I called to them. I felt like I had two kids for the night and I didn't mind. Long ago, I was supposed to be the mother of twins. I could pretend, couldn't I?

I gave Sasha her bath while Johanna ate and leafed through a book she'd pulled off my shelf. She asked to take a shower, I gave her a change of clothes to sleep in, and we all went to bed.

IN THE MIDDLE of the night, I heard my front door shut. I felt around for Sasha next to me. Warm. Safe. Yes. I went into Sasha's bedroom, and whispered, "Johanna?"

No answer.

I padded out into the living room and looked at the blue clock in the kitchen. It was three a.m. I opened the door to the dorm hallway and looked out. It was empty and quiet, but the door to the roof was propped open with a book. The roof was off-limits, had an alarm attached to it, and a giant sign that read: *Are you in the midst of a crisis? There are people who can help. Call the University Wellness Hotline at 212-555-5555.*

"Johanna?" I called down the bright hallway. I walked toward the door and pushed it open. Still no alarm. Had she disengaged it somehow? I'd never been onto the roof. I sometimes jokingly referred to the roof as "the terrace I'd never have," but it wasn't a part of the building I knew at all. The University's secrets. Landscapes the University wouldn't let us touch or see or access. Since the spate of student jumpers in the last two years and the most recent suicide, the University had installed plexiglass over the high fences in the library. The effect was jarring, like a police barricade. The new student center had several terraces for students, but none of them were higher than the third floor. They'd installed alarms on all the roof doors, but had they checked to make sure the alarms were working?

For what felt like the hundredth time since I'd seen her fall in front of my classroom, I saw Madison's body again. Her dress flapping in the wind. Hair wrapped around her face and neck. The papers from her notebook trailing behind her. Feathers to her rock.

I stepped into the crisp fall air. I wrapped my arms around my body and squeezed. It was getting colder. I thought of the Occupiers asleep in their tents, and I hoped they were warm. "Johanna?" I called again, louder this time. I felt pulled in two directions—to find Johanna and to stay close to Sasha. What if she woke up and I wasn't there? Still no answer. I walked farther out onto the roof and away from the door. The view, not unlike the one from my windows, was stunning, but from here I could see the full sky, a dome of clouds, and one or two distant stars. The student center was lit up in the distance like a slot machine. The condos gleamed from within—lights they'd recently installed that seemed always on.

"Johanna, are you out here?" I asked into the air. I stared out onto the tops of the trees. I saw more branches than leaves. The bones of winter, emerging. "Please talk to me. I'm worried," I said.

"Watch out for the dead bird."

I turned toward her voice and squinted in the dark. She was sitting on the edge of the roof at the far corner, her legs hanging off the side of the building, as if she were about to slide into a swimming pool. She turned her head around, just enough so that I could see the side of her face. I looked down and saw a mass of feathers and entrails, and stepped over it.

"You're too close to the edge," I said.

"I'm not gonna jump. I just want the best view possible," she said, and swung her legs alarmingly.

I gasped. "Johanna, please."

"Stevie, dude, chill," she said.

I sat down on the bouncy asphalt rooftop. I needed to figure out what to say or just keep her talking. I scanned the roof's horizon. Her body dangled like a comma in the sky. I wanted to pull her off the ledge, to grab her under the arms and give her a good yank, like she was Sasha up too high on the monkey bars. But Johanna was tall and lanky, and I knew I couldn't wrestle her down. Also, maybe I was overreacting. Maybe she did just like the view.

A terrible vision flashed in front of me. I could say the wrong thing. She could jump. Another woman lost as I stood staring. Someone I couldn't save. I wanted to catch all of my students. A good teacher is like a safety net. I remembered the one or two professors who saved me as an undergraduate—one invited me to eat with his family on Sundays and called me a writer. Another let me babysit her son and gave me food to take home when I was broke. Still, Johanna wasn't my student. She was a runaway, a drifter who wandered into my life and gave me someone to fix so I wouldn't have to fix myself.

"What are the voices saying?" I asked.

"You can't make it without him. He saved you. He's like the father you never had, but in the form of a boyfriend." She paused and leaned back to look up at the clouds, which had just drifted over the crescent moon. "Other times, it's just a bunch of garbage thoughts in the voice of my mother, but worse—sped up and all scratchy like the devil in a dumb horror movie. Things like, *You suck, you're a failure and a whore.*"

"But those are just voices," I said. I heard a siren wail down Fourth Street and stop on what sounded like my corner. The flashing red lights made a kaleidoscope pattern against the few remaining red and gold leaves. "They aren't real."

"Sometimes they wake me up. Tonight they said, You need air. You want to be higher."

"I didn't mean they aren't real, I just meant they aren't right," I clarified.

"It's better if I'm outside or under the stars. It's why I keep sleeping at Occupy. The voices are quieter there, maybe because there's so much other noise. Sasha's room is too small. I had to come out here and look at the sky."

"Sasha will be jealous. She's been begging me to come out here since we moved here a year and a half ago."

A university police officer pushed the door open and stepped onto the roof. His walkie-talkie crackled and beeped. "Professor, step back, let me take over."

He wasn't among the regular guards I knew from our building— Clara, who grew up in a big Dominican family on the Lower East Side and brought Sasha flowers for her hair; and Cleveland, who immigrated from Jamaica and was stern, but had the most infectious laugh if you caught him in the right mood.

This guard looked like he spent his time off doing deadlifts while congratulating himself in the wall of gym mirrors. I'd seen him before in the lobby of another building, flirting with eighteen-year-old female first-year students, but we'd never spoken. He couldn't have been much older than Johanna and he kept his eyes fixed on her, like he would tackle her if necessary. Was he equipped for the nuance of this particular moment? Was I?

Two EMTs stepped out onto the roof behind him, pulling an ambulance gurney behind them, with arm and leg restraints dangling from the sides of it.

"Ma'am, are you a student here?" the guard called over to Johanna. She ignored him.

"She's my guest and she didn't know about the roof policy. We're just about to go back inside," I said, trying to diffuse the situation. *Did Johanna need to go to the hospital?* I wondered. Maybe, but I didn't want it to be like this, against her will.

"Professor, how's your daughter?" the guard asked me. I hated this generic name of professor. They might as well call me Teach or Coach.

"She's good. Asleep in our apartment, just down the hall."

"Go back to your kid. We've got this," the guard said. He still had his eyes fixed on Johanna.

"Ma'am, you're trespassing on university property. I'm going to have to ask you to climb down."

"I'm sorry. I didn't know that the roof was off-limits. Stevie and I were just headed back inside," Johanna said, but she didn't move an inch.

The officer moved a couple of feet closer to us. I smelled his spicy chemical deodorant and sweat. He gestured with his head that I move back, but I didn't.

"If you come any closer, I will jump," Johanna said to him. He stopped moving and took a deep breath.

"Johanna, I'm just thinking about the people who love you and don't want you to do this. Butch and me and Arturo. That's just who I know about, but there are so many more."

"Butch doesn't love me. He just wants to control me and you don't even know me. I've just wormed my way into your life."

"I care about you. I would be really sad if something happened to you," I said, trying to be accurate about my feelings. "We're just becoming friends, and I want to know more about you." I couldn't get into the complicated stew of guilt and horror I would feel if this happened on my watch, in my building, because Johanna had stayed overnight in my apartment and felt trapped there. What would I say to Sasha? How could I forgive myself?

"I am a failure. I don't know how to do anything," Johanna said.

"But you're young, and something is shifting, and you have plenty of time to learn new things. You're trying to get clean and leave Butch and it's super hard but I believe in you." I took a step forward and reached out my hand for her to take. It was the same gesture I made to Sasha before we stepped into the crosswalk. *Gimme. Hold Mama. Where's my girl? My hand is lonely.*

"When I saw that girl's body hit the sidewalk, every cell in my body was like, 'You're next. That should be you. If a college girl with her whole future in front of her jumps, why should you live when you have so little?' "

"But you can have more," I pleaded, and stretched my hand closer to her.

She looked down at it and swung her legs back down onto the rooftop. I noticed her bare feet and that she wasn't wearing pants, just the long T-shirt I'd given her. Before she could stand or take my hand, the officer lunged at her, put his arms around her waist, and pulled her toward the EMTs. Johanna started to kick and thrash. "Get your fucking hands off of me!" she shouted.

"Don't!" I yelled at the guard and EMTs. "She's not going to jump. You don't need to do that!"

The roof door opened again, and Anna, the RA who lived on the floor and who was in charge of the residents, stuck her head out.

"Get back inside," the guard yelled at her. Johanna kicked and squirmed as the three of them struggled to fasten the restraints around her arms and legs.

"Stevie, Sasha is out here in the hallway," Anna said to me.

"Can you just take her back into the apartment and tell her I'll be right there? Put on one of her cartoons?" I shouted.

"Sure thing," Anna said in her shockingly chipper RA voice.

"Fuck you!" Johanna yelled at the EMT who tightened the restraints on her legs. The other one readied a syringe.

"No!" I shouted. But I realized it was a losing battle. They were going to sedate her and take her away. "Where are you taking her?" I asked, trying to focus on what was next.

"I fucking hate you fascist pigs! Corporate stooges! Fucking rapists!" Johanna bucked and arched against the restraints.

One of the EMTs stuck her with the needle in the thigh. Their faces were red, but they said nothing, showed no emotion.

"Where are you taking her?" I asked again.

"Bellevue."

I groaned. "Can't you take her to the University Hospital instead?" Aaron and I had a friend in graduate school who was bipolar. During a manic episode, he holed up in the Chelsea Hotel for three days and sent status updates from his Facebook page as Walt Whitman. Eventually, his girlfriend had to call the cops and he was taken to Bellevue. It was a labyrinth of New York City bureaucracy and paperwork. It was days before we were allowed to visit him.

"You said she's not a student, so we have to take her to Bellevue," the other EMT said to me matter-of-factly.

"Well, I'll get a babysitter and follow you guys in the cab," I said, thinking out loud. I could call Aaron or ask Anna to stay overnight.

"Don't bother," the EMT who was still holding the syringe said to me. "You won't be able to see her until she's been processed, and that takes a day or two."

I looked down at Johanna, who had stopped writhing and had a serene look on her face. It wasn't unlike the expression she had on the day I met her in the fountain. It suited her. She stared back at me with her big, blue-green eyes.

"I'll come and see you as soon as they let me," I said. I was afraid for her, but I didn't say it.

"This is all your fault, Stevie," she said to me. Her tongue seemed to slacken in her jaw as she spoke. "You called them."

"I didn't," I said, and I put my hand on her forehead for a second before the EMTs hoisted the stretcher up and started to wheel Johanna toward the roof door. "There are cameras everywhere."

The guard's walkie-talkie burbled and he unclipped it from his belt. "We got her. Coming down now," he said into its staticky mouth. Had he saved her? Or made the situation worse? Could I have talked her down by myself? I hated his brute force, but I felt relieved we were no longer sitting on the cold roof together, me begging and Johanna making fun of me.

In the hallway, I expected to see Sasha's worried face, but instead we were met by the twenty pajama-clad first years who lived on my floor. A couple of them had their phones out, ready to take a quick pic.

"Back into your rooms," the guard yelled, and the students groaned and padded back into their well-appointed rooms. I was about to step into the elevator when I heard Sasha's voice.

"Mama," she said.

I squeezed Johanna's hand and let the elevator go down without me.

NARC

I found Butch passed out at the base of the red metal sculpture in the corner of Zuccotti Park. I'd gone to Bellevue after dropping Sasha off at school, and had been turned away by a bland-faced nurse who barely looked up from her computer to say, "She hasn't been processed yet."

I felt like I needed to tell someone where Johanna was and he was the only person I knew who might care.

I kneeled down and nudged Butch's shoulder. His black jeans smelled like pee, but he was wearing a new bright-red Patagonia down jacket and thick, gray wool socks pulled over the ankles of his jeans. He opened his eyes and stared at me.

"The fuck?"

"Hey."

"Stevie!" he slurred, and his leg jerked like he was a dog running through a field in a dream. He reached up to put his arms around my neck. I was afraid he'd kiss me again, so I stood up.

I decided to get right to it. "Johanna is at Bellevue. She tried to jump—or, er, was maybe going to jump off the roof of my building and the security guards took her away," I said.

His expression changed. He sat up and glared at me. "You fucking did this, you narc." He reminded me of a boy I liked in high school, a skater dropout from a rich family who spoke French and knew how to sail, who had a pert nose and a strong jaw, and spent the days huffing and playing video games before meeting the rest of us after school at the local record store/arcade/drug den. I could never quite figure out how he fit in either.

I took a step back. In the five days I'd been taking care of Sasha, the population of the park seemed to have doubled. I looked around for familiar faces—Marissa, Diego, Arturo—but I didn't see anyone I knew.

"I didn't call security. I was trying to talk her down, but they have cameras on the roof and they came anyway. I tried to stop them from taking her to Bellevue too, but they wouldn't listen to me."

"You think you're so much better than us." He waved his hand around in a grand drunken gesture. I knew it would be impossible to argue with him. "And she thinks you're her savior."

"I'm just wondering if there's anyone we could call, like her mom or dad or a sibling?"

Butch laughed so dramatically I thought he might choke. "She doesn't have a dad or any brothers and sisters and her mom's a fucking cunt. She used to tie Johanna to a chair when she was a kid so that she could drink and not have to be bothered. I'm her family." He pointed his thumb at his chest.

"I know, that's why I'm telling you," I said, trying to diffuse, but I already regretted telling him. Hadn't Johanna been trying to get away from him? Or was that just something I wanted to believe because she'd been staying with me?

He stood up and stumbled. "Stay out of it," he said, and walked out of the park.

"He's actually okay when he's sober," a voice behind me said. I turned around. It was Devora, Arturo's girlfriend. She had a girl next to her, maybe ten or eleven, looking bored in skinny jeans and a tie-dyed hoodie. That must be her kid. Did she know about me? Did she and Arturo have one of those open relationships where they told each other everything, like Mel and Jenny were trying to do?

"Yeah?" I asked. I wasn't sure I agreed. "I don't think I've ever seen him sober."

"We keep banning him, but he keeps sneaking back in and Arturo has a soft spot for him," Devora said.

"Do you know his girlfriend, Johanna?" I asked. I didn't want to get too far into it in front of her kid.

"Dreadlocks. Overalls. Pretty?" Devora asked.

"Yeah, well, she's in the hospital, and I'm trying to figure out who to contact."

"She okay?"

"I think so, but I'm not totally sure yet."

"Well, we have a hospital fund if she needs money."

"You do?"

"Yeah. We set that up early, along with the legal fund."

"I'll tell her if I can ever get in to see her," I said. "I'm Stevie, by the way. I don't think we've officially met." I stuck out my hand.

"I've heard a little about you. Devora." She took my hand. "This is Sid."

"Sid, like Sid Vicious?" I asked, half joking.

Sid looked up for a second and nodded. "Hey. Yeah, or Siddhartha."

"Whoa, that's cool." I thought about saying I was named after Stevie Nicks, but I didn't think my pop diva namesake could compete with a punk guru one.

"Are you in a working group yet?" Devora asked.

"Nah, I do the kitchen, which I like," I said.

"Yeah, but we could use you in a working group. You're probably a good facilitator."

"Sometimes." I heard myself being noncommittal. I felt completely drained from the night before, and now I was running around the city trying to find Johanna. I'd sent my kid to school exhausted, full of questions about why she couldn't find me in the middle of the night, and how I'd managed to get out onto the roof when she had never been allowed.

"No pressure, just a thought." Devora turned ever so slightly away from me. I felt like I'd failed some kind of activist test. Was I here to do real work or was I here to volunteer in the kitchen? Was I a tourist or an Occupier?

"Mom," Sid said, pulling on the sleeve of her mom's shirt.

"Yep, gotcha, I know," Devora said to her. "We've got soccer practice in Brooklyn," she said to me.

"O's waiting for us," Sid said impatiently.

"O's what she calls Arturo," Devora said. I got the sense that she wanted me to know that, to understand the intimacy of their arrangement, that they were a real family, a tight little unit of three—not four or more.

"Do you stay overnight here ever?" I asked Sid.

She wrinkled her nose a little.

"You've stayed with us a couple of nights," Devora answered for her. "You could bring your kid. I mean, maybe not every night, but it's not so bad."

Arturo must have told her I have a kid. I waved goodbye to them and stood by the statue for five more minutes trying to decide what to do with my day. I knew I could find Marissa and Diego and spend the morning or the whole day in the kitchen if I wanted. Sasha was headed to her father's. I had fifteen students coming over for dinner and to write poems with me, but that wasn't until six. I looked at the screen of my phone for guidance, for a text to come in, for someone to tell me what to do, but there was nothing except a short one from Aaron.

"Okay to swing by and get Daddy bag?"

"Yeah, it's by the door. I'm not there, but go in." Aaron had his own key to my apartment and I had one to his though I hardly ever used it.

I looked up and saw two young women dressed up as superheroes—a DIY combo of Wonder Woman tights, boots, and red corsets, topped with white-blond Storm wigs—walking by with giant signs, hand-lettered in glittery gold paint. They were tall and confident, and they reminded me of the women who held up signs in between rounds during boxing matches. Their signs read: "Guilt is not action" and "Your guilt makes you complicit."

I took a picture on my phone and sent it to Mel with the caption, "Now they're just reading my mind."

Ugh, I get it, I thought, and I got on the subway so I could hold impromptu guilt-ridden office hours and prep for my classes.

ADMITTING

"I don't want to be here!" Johanna shouted. "I don't belong here!"

"If you calm down, we can undo the restraints," a nurse said. Animal-print scrubs. She fell back asleep. Came to. Waited. Asked for water. An orderly brought her water. She decided not to yell. Yellow hospital walls. A man jerking violently up and down on a gurney down the hall, while three burly orderlies tried to restrain him. Two police officers in another corner drinking coffee out of Styrofoam cups. Cops always made her nervous. Another woman wailing down by the nurse's station: "The medicine isn't working. The medicine isn't working."

"She's not a student, but the University brought her in. She was on one of their roofs, trying to jump." A nurse came over with a chart, the doctor followed.

Johanna groaned. "I wasn't."

The doctor came around to look at her, moved a clump of her hair off her forehead gently.

"How old are you?"

"Nineteen," Johanna lied.

"Why were you on that roof?"

"I needed some air," she lied again.

"You can tell me the truth," the doctor said. She wasn't wearing a dumb white lab coat. Eyes that looked at her. She had an accent—Russian, maybe?

"Where are you from?" Johanna asked.

"Romania. Do you like photography?"

"Sometimes." Johanna worried she was being tricked with kindness. Lately, it made her weak.

"Brassaï is from my hometown. He photographed a Parisian underworld."

"I am the underworld," Johanna said defiantly, like she was Persephone standing up to Hades.

The doctor raised her eyebrows and laughed. "Can't we undo her restraints?" she asked the nurse.

The nurse untied her. Johanna stretched her arms over her head and then instinctively patted at her hips to make sure her papers were still there, taped inside her shorts.

"You have heroin in your system. Are you an addict?" the doctor asked her. "What's in your pants?"

"I use, but I'm not an addict," Johanna said. "My papers." She knew that made her sound like she had scraps of paper in a plastic bag to prove the CIA was following her, like some of the other homeless women in the park. She and Butch had once watched a man step onto an A train and unpack five plastic bags full of plastic bags. He pulled them out, one by one, like a magician with multicolored scarves and pressed them flat onto the subway floor, until they were arranged like a patchwork quilt around him. The passengers watched in stunned silence, stepping around him and his bags. At Utica Avenue, he swept it all up in a violent flourish, and stuffed the little bags back into the giant one. "It's a fucking piece of performance art," Butch said. "He's just batshit," Johanna disagreed, but now she felt just as protective and methodical about her papers. She couldn't wait to lay them out and read them, and she'd fight any 250-pound orderly who tried to take them from her.

"How often do you use?" the doctor asked.

The nurse took notes in the chart.

"I don't want her to write everything down," Johanna said, sitting up on her elbows.

"She has to, it's her job," the doctor said.

"Every couple of days."

"Well you can't leave because you're a suicide risk and I'd like to get you to rehab. There's a bed in Queens for you. You're lucky.

Someone just quit. Usually, you'd have to wait two months."

"Will you be there?"

"Yes, once a week."

"I don't want to go." She thought of Butch somewhere nodding off on some bench. Who would help him? Who would get money for him so he wouldn't get sick? She remembered Tipsy limping along on her three good legs. Who knew where she might be? She hoped she wasn't dead and she wanted to find her. Stevie's face flashed in front of her, worried—like she cared, like this wasn't her fault.

"You have a couple hours to think about it," the doctor said, and walked away.

She slid her hand down the front of her pants to feel the outlines of the poem from Stevie's class and the dead girl's paper. The duct tape seam she'd made around the edges felt smooth and comforting. She loved that about duct tape—tough and soft at the same time, the next best thing to a needle and thread. The woman continued to wail down by the nurse's station, "The medicine isn't working! The medicine isn't working!" Johanna fell back asleep. The sedation hadn't entirely worn off.

She dreamed she slid off the roof and into the pool of sky. But there was no water and no one there to save her, and she fell and fell and fell. Through branches and leaves, past birds and squirrels, and when she hit the ground, it cracked and parted and she kept going. Through warm dirt and walls of worms, past tree roots and subway tunnels. She fell until she hit the hot core of the earth. Red lava. Red magma. Red center. The end of her heart.

She woke up again with a start. Sweaty, vomit feeling. The Romanian doctor's hand on her forehead. "What do you say, hon? Shall we go to Queens?"

She had a look on her face that reminded her of Stevie—warm, concerned, open to whatever, like mostly she gave a shit—and so Johanna surprised herself and nodded yes.

FAMILY

"She's no longer at this facility." The woman slid my driver's license back through the plexiglass hole.

"What do you mean? The ambulance brought her to Bellevue, and yesterday when I called they said she hadn't been processed yet." I slid my license back into my wallet. "Where is she?"

She sighed at me and moved her mouse up and down. Was she reading the screen or just trying to get rid of me? "Are you family?"

"No, I'm a friend. A teacher of hers," I added a lie.

"I can't tell you where she's been transferred unless you're related to her. I'm sorry, ma'am."

"But nobody has relatives anymore. I mean, like not close by. We're all transplants—we make our own families, out of friends and people we meet on the street." I wasn't wrong; for most of the queer outcast artist types I hung out with, this was basically true.

"My whole family is born and raised in Queens. We all live in the same neighborhood—aunts, uncles, cousins, grandparents."

"Lucky for you," I said. The rest of my family in western New York felt this way too. I might as well have been getting a guilt trip from my mother and I wasn't getting any information about Johanna.

"Has a guy come to visit her? He, um, looks kinda homeless. I mean, like a skater punk. With a mohawk, and a red Patagonia jacket?"

"I can't tell you that," she said.

"Right, I figured."

As I left the building and walked toward the subway, I thought, *Maybe this was a good thing. We didn't really know each other. I wasn't her family. I was just some weird mother-teacher proxy.* Still, I wanted to find her. I needed to know she was okay.

PART 3
WINTER

BUSTED

"I want to know what I'm being arrested for," I demanded. He didn't answer, pushed my face down onto the hood of the car, and cinched plastic handcuffs onto my wrists. I saw Marissa on the ground with a police officer's knee on her back. Arturo and Butch were facedown too.

He pulled me off the hood of the car and started to march me toward the white corrections bus. "Where's your phone and wallet?"

"In my backpack," I nodded at my bag, which he was holding in his other hand. "I need to call someone and let them know," I wriggled my wrists against the too-tight plastic handcuffs.

"You can make a call once we book you."

"Can you loosen my handcuffs?"

"Can you shut up?" he said into the side of my face. I felt his rage—at me, at all of us, at the chaos of the scene. I was the only one standing. Around me, a sea of black and brown people on their stomachs in handcuffs as a bunch of white police officers stood over them with pepper spray.

"What are you doing?" people on the ground shouted as those hit started to cry out in pain.

"The whole world is watching. The whole world is watching. The whole world is watching," the crowd started to chant.

I was the first one in the corrections van. There were small cages near the driver's seat and two long benches in the back along each side of the window. He put me in one of the cages and slammed the door shut. I sat down awkwardly with my hands cuffed behind me. "Please, can I sit on the bench? I don't want to be in this cage." I begged. No answer.

Nobody knows I'm here. I felt a wave of panic in my stomach. I hadn't texted anyone that morning. I wasn't teaching today, and I didn't have Sasha to pick up from school, though I'd made a tentative plan to meet Aaron and Sasha for dinner at Whole Foods.

The chanting continued outside, *This is what democracy looks like!* and a call-and-response, *Whose streets? Our streets!* but it was quieter, as if the crowd of protesters was starting to get the message that we were all going to jail.

The back of the van opened again, and Arturo and Butch got shoved in. "Bench!" the police officer shouted at them. Butch's face was bloody either from where he'd been hit or fallen and Arturo had his eyes closed tight from pepper spray.

"Fucking pigs!" Butch shouted. Blood dripped down his chin.

I looked away.

"You okay?" he asked Arturo.

"That shit burns," Arturo said. I looked at him through the metal of my cage. His face was sweaty and he had a red rash around both of his eyes. He'd lost his green worker's cap during the arrest.

"I'm in here too," I said, not sure if they even saw me.

"I see you, narc," Butch said.

Arturo sighed. "Can we not do this now? She's not a narc. If it weren't for Stevie, Johanna might have jumped."

"She would never try to kill herself. Stevie panicked and called her security guard friends who protect her ivory tower, and they took her away." Butch spoke through bloody lips. He was so over-the-top, so fucked up, I knew it was silly to argue, but I hated him for blaming me. I felt guilty enough on my own.

"Stevie is a comrade. She got arrested. We need to stick together," Arturo reasoned.

"It's her fault Johanna is in some rehab lockdown in Queens."

"She's in Queens?" I sat up against the wire mesh of the cage.

"Yeah, they transferred her from Bellevue to some twenty-one-day lockdown treatment center in Forest Hills."

"Really?"

"Now nobody can see her until they let her out," Butch said.

"She wanted to get clean," I said, but it worried me too.

I looked over at Arturo, who was still wincing in pain. I wanted to help him, to clean out his eyes, and stroke his forehead. "Arturo, your eyes," I said uselessly.

We sat there for a while. Nothing happening. Arturo wincing and blinking. Butch dripping blood onto the floor and me stuck in the cage.

"How long before they release us?" I pressed my forehead against my cage.

"It depends on how many of us they decide to arrest. If there's a lot, the paperwork takes forever and it could be a while," Arturo said.

"Like a couple of hours?" I asked.

"More like ten hours."

Butch groaned. "The point is not paperwork and time lost. It's about disrupting a system that isn't working and confronting the police state head-on."

I wanted to agree, but all I could think of was missing dinner with Aaron and Sasha. I knew it had nothing on mass incarceration, and still I felt like shit about it. Would Aaron wonder why I'd flaked? What would he tell Sasha? I never missed anything with her. I was always there when I said I would be. It was my job. I imagined him texting me and then calling me and getting no response, and he and Sasha eating their pizza, chicken tenders, and lemonade without me. I pictured her swan neck craning in the direction of the Whole Foods stairs as she waited for me to show up. What would she think when I didn't?

My jean jacket was ripped at the shoulder from where the cop had grabbed at me. My scarf was still wrapped around my neck, which was a comfort of sorts. *You are a shitty mom*, I said to myself as my eyes welled up. And then I had the opposite thought: *You're a good mom because you're fighting to make the world better for your kid.* Which was it?

I was used to my heart's drag and tether. I was a woman, alive in the twenty-first century and trying to do all of the shit, and so I was tugged at and pulled apart—by Sasha, by Aaron, by Arturo, by

David, by Hayes, by Mel, by Johanna, by my students, by activism, by writing, by reading, by pleasure, by work, by exercise, by cooking, by cleaning, by laundry, by all of it. I used to think my job was to stay whole, to keep it all humming along like the vaudeville act with the spinning plates, every plate just about to fall and break, but still miraculously whirling. But I was wrong, my job was to let the plates crash and shatter. My job was to fall apart spectacularly, and then to make a new self out of fragments.

So what if I'm fucking a bunch of guys and the next day I'm watching cartoons with my kid and the next day I'm getting arrested at a protest? The through line is me. I am the link between these activities. I make my own days, I tried to convince myself as I stared through the wire mesh.

The cage and the handcuffs were making me sweat. I sniffed to keep myself from crying in front of Butch and Arturo, and tried to wipe my nose on the shoulder of my jacket.

"You got sprayed too?" Arturo asked.

"I'm claustrophobic and I hate this pen," I said. I couldn't convey the mash of thoughts in my head to either of them.

"Cheer up, Stevie. It's your first arrest. It's a rite of passage," Butch said.

We stared out the window at the city skyline as the van rattled over the Manhattan Bridge.

"Why are you taking us to Brooklyn?" Arturo called out. The cops didn't answer.

We pulled into a parking lot and slowly filed out of the van and into a low-slung concrete slab of a building where we spent the next three hours waiting in lines and getting yelled at. Still, I was happy to be out of my cage.

The officer who arrested me reappeared so that I could have my mug shot taken. Out of habit, I smiled until the flash blinded me and I remembered that this was my mug shot and I didn't need to act happy about it.

"You think you're at the beach don't you, princess?" the officer teased.

"Do you know when I'll get my stuff back?"

He didn't answer and then disappeared again.

A female officer led me to another cell. There were three other women in mine—Marissa and two spaced-out girls in their twenties who monopolized the cold metal bench and wouldn't speak to us. I was happy to see Marissa. There was a larger cell across from us with nearly forty men in it. They were packed in tight with virtually no place to sit. One man, not from the protest, rocked violently back and forth near the door of the cell, while another kept his hand firmly down the front of his pants and cupped around his dick, shouting, "Fuck you, motherfucker!" whenever a police officer walked by.

We looked on as several men were taken out of their cell. Arturo and Butch were still there.

"I bet they're taking them to Rikers," Marissa said. "You wait, they're going charge all the brown people with felonies instead of misdemeanors."

"Legal's gonna have us out of here soon," Arturo called over to us.

I looked at the clock on the wall. It said 9:30 p.m. I'd long since missed dinner with Sasha and Aaron. I hoped Aaron would make up something convincing.

At 10:30 p.m. the women were released with papers for a future court date. We were not given our phones or bags, but told we could come back to get them tomorrow.

"But we don't have any money, how are we supposed to go home?" Marissa asked the female officer who opened our cell.

"You'll figure it out," the officer said, and led us to the phone where we could finally make our one phone call. Then she disappeared back into the labyrinth of doors and hallways where we were being held.

"It's about slowing you down and tripping you up, making protesting just enough of a pain in the ass so that you won't want to do it again or you'll think twice," Marissa said.

"It's also about reminding you who is in charge and that they can lock us up if they want to, and they can take their time and drag their feet," I said.

"But we have lawyers! Think about what happens when you don't," Marissa said.

Marissa called a good friend who'd heard from her girlfriend.

She'd been booked in Manhattan and released over three hours ago and was already back at Occupy. She decided to walk back to Zuccotti Park to find her. She hugged me tightly.

"Who are you going to call?" she asked.

"My baby daddy."

"Don't get cute," she said, and I watched her walk out the door of the precinct and into the cold November night.

THE HUSBANDS

The husbands, let's face it, were winning. Because they had wives. The husbands lived longer and were happier. The husbands were, like, "Dude." The husbands went to the cheap old barbers in the East Village or they went to the new hipster barbers in Soho. The husbands never had enough pants. The husbands had too many shirts. The husbands were so grouchy. The husbands were always vaguebooking. The husbands loved to cook. The husbands were loud and then they were quiet. The husbands wanted to email while the kids were playing and they didn't think too much about it. They were fair trade and all about NAFTA. Some husbands worked at Goldman Sachs and they had sleek black cars take them home. Other husbands were anarchists or freegans or conspiracy theorists. The husbands had terrible headaches, but they were not allowed to say. Many of the husbands were poets. A few husbands were bartenders. A few more decided to go to law school. The husbands were in the zone. The husbands played soccer in the green fields of the city. Some of the husbands were dead—from heart attacks or from getting shot at in the street and in their cars and sometimes in their own homes. The husbands worked three jobs. The husbands ran loops around the perimeters of all boroughs. The husbands would never, ever forgive you for cheating. The husbands were cheating too. The husbands loved you so much it hurt.

QUEENS

In detox, there was a room with a mesh-covered window. The sunlight filtered through it and made a crosshatch pattern on the institutional blue-gray blanket. Johanna lay on her scratchy blanket and figured out how she could use the spork that came with the food to undo the screws. It was a two-story window. She could jump. She'd stay a week, not the mandatory twenty-one days, she'd already decided.

The best thing was that they gave you meds and three meals. The worst thing was the rest of it—her roommate, the talking, the group therapy where people cried and told the saddest fucking stories ever, and the TV droning on all day to the most terrible channels.

"Look, I brought that book I told you about." The Romanian doctor slid it across the desk at Johanna.

"You said you worked here." Johanna ignored the book.

"I do, I come once a week and I added you to my roster of patients even though I'm not supposed to." She had greasy shoulder-length hair and gray, winter-ocean eyes. She was looking at Johanna. Closely. Taking her in.

"I thought you'd be here every day." Johanna picked up the book and flipped through it. It was better than the stupid TV. Everyone wanted to watch reality shows or something called *House Hunters International,* which was total bougie capitalist trash. She never wanted to live in a house, and reality TV was like living with her mom again. Angry women screaming at each other about meaningless shit.

She kept turning the pages of the book. Hidden queer nightlife in underground Paris. She ran her finger along the black-and-white world of butch and femme, couples kissing in cafés, and shadowy cobblestone streets.

"Do you feel like I abandoned you?" the doctor asked.

Johanna rolled her eyes at her.

"Yes, you're too smart for that question. I will have to be clever with you." She leaned back in her chair. "My name is Helena," she said. "I don't think I formally introduced myself."

"Hey." Johanna didn't look up from the book.

She stopped at a photograph of a woman in the shadows near a streetlamp, underneath a "Fromage" sign. She couldn't see her face or hands. No expression. Just high heels, slim legs, fitted dress, jacket, and hat. The light was like a spotlight on a stage, but the stage was the street.

"So, that's your favorite?" Helena asked. "Do you know why?"

"Fine, I'll talk about art," Johanna said. "I like how the wash is almost brown and that we can't see the woman's face at all and that she's alone."

"It's likely she was a prostitute," Helena said. "Brassaï was famous for capturing brothels and their customers."

"You don't know she's a sex worker."

"Maybe not. Does it bother you that I made that leap?"

"No."

"Do you like seeing a woman alone like that?"

"Why?"

"Just curious."

"Fine, yeah, she looks free or at least comfortable enough to stand alone in the dark by herself."

"Have you been alone in the dark a lot?" Helena asked, her gray eyes resting gently on the book instead of Johanna.

"Hasn't everyone?" Johanna shrugged.

"Who is Butch?" Helena looked down at the file in front of her.

"My junkie boyfriend who saved me from my mother. I ran away from her when I was fourteen and he picked me up on the side of the road."

"And now you're homeless and using together."

"We're not homeless. We're Occupiers."

"The Wall Street thing?" Helena leaned back in her desk chair and waved her hand in the air.

"It's not a thing. It's a revolution." Johanna put her boot up on the desk, since they were both getting comfortable.

"I believe that. It reminds me of Poland in the eighties. Everything coming apart. Ideology breaking down."

Johanna nodded. "Exactly."

"You know I'm psychic sometimes," Helena said. "And I have some thoughts about you that came to me just now in flashes. May I say them and if I'm wrong you can tell me?"

"Whatever, sure." Helena's quiet office with the art book was better than sitting with her roommate Diane, who kept a file of loose papers about aliens that she was always trying to get Johanna to look at.

"You had to be your mother's mother and you saved yourself by running away, but you've outgrown your boyfriend, Butch. It's just that you don't know how to get away or where to go, and so that roof seemed like as good of an option as any."

"Can I go now?"

"How did I do?"

"Fine," Johanna said. She wasn't going to let on that this woman, a stranger, had read her like an open book. It gave her the chills. "I like the photographs."

"The book will be here for you, and I'll see you next week," Helena said.

I doubt it, Johanna thought.

As she opened the door, Helena said to her back, "People do get clean and you can keep seeing me even when you leave. You can go to school." She handed Johanna her business card, like she knew she wouldn't be here long. "My number, in case we lose track of each other."

Johanna took it and shut the door.

EMERGENCY CONTACT

Aaron showed up an hour later. He wrapped me in a big bear hug. I tried not to cry with gratitude.

"I think you'll be my emergency contact forever," I said. I thought of the overworked nurse at Bellevue who wouldn't give me any information about Johanna. *Family is complicated*, I'd say to her if I could go back in time and make her give a shit.

"You too," he said.

"Who's with Sasha?"

"Anne, she's my . . ." He paused.

"New girlfriend?" I said it for him.

"She came over," he finished. I felt a surge of jealousy. It was possible that Anne would come to know and love Sasha. Sasha and Anne were closer in age than Anne and me. Was that depressing or comforting? I imagined it would be cool to have a stepmom who was more like a big sister than a parent, one who didn't have a bum knee and complained all the time about her lower back. Maybe Anne would someday give Sasha a sibling.

"Is she good with kids?" I asked. "I need to meet her."

"She doesn't have expectations, she lets Sasha take the lead, so, yeah, I think so. Do I have to pay bail or something? I brought five hundred bucks. It's all I have."

My eyes welled up again at his sweetness, that he would give me his last five hundred dollars, and that he left his girlfriend with our kid to come and get me. "Our lives are so complicated," I said. "You didn't tell Sasha where I am, right?"

"She's fast asleep. She knows Anne from the Antic, so if she wakes up she won't be scared."

"There's no bail, just a summons to come back in a month."

"So it's not a big charge."

"I don't think so."

Aaron smiled and put his arm around me. "Good because you are weak and you can't cut it in jail."

"I did okay," I protested.

"Oh babe, that wasn't real jail."

"Shut up."

We left the building and wandered vaguely in the direction of a subway. I thought of all the men still in that cell and felt angry.

"Can you maybe take a break from the marching now?" Aaron asked.

"Why?"

"Because you're a mom and I can't come and get you out of here again."

"Why can't moms be radicals?"

"Because they're moms," Aaron said as if it were the most basic thing in the world.

"I knew you were always just pretending to be a feminist," I joked back.

We were at the mouth of the subway again, our perpetual portal away from each other. Sometimes the hardest part of separating was breaking the habit of going home together. The familiar routine. The dip in Aaron's shoulder where I used to rest my head. His body on the couch. Two figures in a shitty living room of a railroad apartment in Brooklyn at their laptops ignoring each other. The luxury of that! To take him for granted. I missed it.

"Could you love Anne?" I asked. A group of tourists with Century 21 bags walked slowly around us and down the subway stairs.

"I think so. She's young and a little high-strung, and I wonder what kind of future we could have, but she's a good person."

I used to be young and high-strung, I thought. *Now I'm anxious and middle-aged.*

"What about you? Have you met anyone?" Aaron asked.

"Met anyone?" I repeated as if that were an answer.

"Yeah, like a man you like a lot."

"I see some men," I managed, and then Aaron got that worried look on his face. I added, "I go on a lot of dates, but it's hard to find someone who can be all that I want him to be."

"Isn't that an Army slogan?"

"Yeah, from the eighties or something. That's me, the boot camp of women," I said.

"I want you to be happy," Aaron said.

I felt my nose tingle and tears welling up in my eyes again.

"Happiness is not attainable. You know, the pursuit of it. Like, the American dream," I said, and wiped the tears off my cheeks. "Is my mascara all fucked up?" I asked.

"It's okay, no smudges."

"I'm okay," I sniffed. It was the best I could do.

"I want you to be more than okay."

"But I might be at a *just okay* part of my life. I have to be cool with that."

"I understand."

I pulled my ripped jean jacket tighter around my body. November chill. The mouth of the subway felt warm. Aaron took out his wallet and gave me a hundred dollars. "Until you get your wallet back. Is this enough?"

"Yeah, I think so. Thanks. I'll pay you back."

He waved his hand at me. "I don't want it. Consider it my Occupy donation."

We walked down the subway steps. Aaron hugged me and swiped me through the turnstile with his card. I watched him jog back up the stairs so he could cross the street to the downtown side. We waited for the R train, across the tracks on our separate platforms—him deeper into Brooklyn and me to Manhattan. His train came first. "Write to me on FB until you get your phone. Let me know when you get home?" he called out just before the train rattled in front of him. I stared at him through the windows of his car as he found a seat. He waved at me and I waved goodbye back.

I waited for the R train as it crept out of Brooklyn and into lower

Manhattan to pick me up. I stared at the passengers. When I walked through the turnstile of my building and nodded hello at the guard, I looked at the giant placard of Sasha and me that hung in the lobby. I imagined replacing it with my newly minted mug shot, a final *fuck you* to the dorm before I had to move out. *Professor Criminal in Residence.* Ha.

JUST PEE ON A STICK

A couple days later, Stevie knocked on Mel and Jenny's bathroom door. "How is it going in there?"

Mel opened the door. Her belt hung from her jean loops. "I'm just going to walk away from it for the five minutes and when I come back it will be white and not blue and we can go to Gold Star and have a drink and talk about your lost homeless girl and the fact that you're a convict."

"You're not pregnant. It's much harder to get pregnant than people think." They sat on the couch in Mel and Jenny's apartment. The dogs jumped up and sat on their laps.

"Guys, elbows," Mel said. "They each weigh seventy pounds but they think they're cats."

Petie put his paw on Stevie's forearm to keep her from moving. Walt stared into her eyes. "God, you're such their little bitch," Mel said.

Stevie laughed. "That's the way I like it, right boys?"

Mel picked at some skin around her toenail. "God, this is excruciating. How did you ever do this? Didn't you pee on a thousand ovulation and pregnancy sticks when you were trying to get pregnant?"

"I wasted a lot of money on those," Stevie said. "Were you ovulating when the condom broke?"

"Carmine asked me that too. I don't have a clue."

"There's like a period app for phones, you can keep track of it."

"I haven't been in contact with sperm for ten years, why would I need to keep track of that shit?" Mel scratched behind Walt's ear and kissed him on the snout. "Can you go look at it? I can't do it."

"Yep." Stevie got out from under Petie and stood up. "But before I go check, do you want to be pregnant? I mean I know you and Jenny had wanted to get some sperm like three years ago and have a baby, but we haven't talked about it in a while."

"Stevie!" Mel pleaded.

"Well, it will help me with inflection and tone when I tell you what the stick says."

"Maybe, yes. I don't know. It's complicated. We did want to, but then we got bogged down in our relationship stuff and couples therapy and being nonmonogamous and we stopped talking about it. This wouldn't have been the way we planned."

Stevie walked into the bathroom, picked up the stick, and brought it back out into the living room. The dogs barked, jumped off the couch, and ran to the door. Jenny opened it and stared at the two of them. She had no idea what they were doing, but those two were always up to something. Mel was huddled in a ball, knees up to her chin, while Stevie held the pregnancy pee stick.

"Um . . ." Stevie stammered.

"Just say it!" Mel writhed on the couch.

"Congratulations?" She held up her hands. "You're pregnant." She shrugged her shoulders and made a crazy grimace happy face.

Jenny looked back and forth between the two of them, stalked into the bedroom, and slammed the door shut.

"Baby? Jen?" Mel called out.

A terrible crash through the door, like Jenny had knocked over a bookcase or kicked through the wall. Stevie sat down and hugged Mel on the couch. "Is she going to kill us?" she asked.

"She's not violent!" Mel said.

"I wanted to get Chinese sperm!" Jenny opened the door and yelled at them. "So the baby would at least have some resemblance to me and not be a total fucking ghost." She slammed it shut again. A silent thirty seconds passed. Jenny opened the door. "I can hear you. I didn't knock anything over. I tripped on my backpack and knocked over Mel's giant fucking book pile." She shut the door again, this time more gently.

"I think I should go." Stevie started to put her shoes on. The dogs looked back and forth between her and Mel, like, *Is everything okay? What should we do? What should we do?*

"I'll text you," Mel said, and hugged her.

"Sorry, I fucked that up."

"There was no way to do that right."

Jenny opened the bedroom door again. "Just stay, Stevie. You're the only person we know who is a parent, you can help us figure this out."

"But you guys need alone time."

"Just have tea in the kitchen for a while and text your little boyfriends and then you can talk to us when we're done processing in the bedroom," Jenny said.

"Mel, what do you want me to do?" Stevie asked.

"Stay."

Stevie sat in the kitchen and looked at her phone.

A text from Arturo. "?"

"?" she texted back.

Ellipsis. "You said you'd think about it."

"I have been."

"Good."

MEL AND JENNY shut the door to their bedroom and started what would become a weeklong fight.

"You broke a rule," Jenny yelled. "You didn't use a condom. You're sneaking around with Stevie to pee on a stick. Were you ever going to tell me?" Jenny was standing by the dresser and Mel sat on the bed and took it because she was always the bad one who messed everything up. And then came the jealousy and rage. "So, you're just going to have some random white asshole's baby? Are you guys going to run away together? Maybe I can be your Chinese nanny!"

Mel cried and listened and patted the heads of the dogs who didn't like it when their moms fought. She knew she had to let Jenny get it all out, all of the terrible shit she needed to say, and then she could speak. Maybe she was shutting down too. She did that when Jenny got mad.

"Are you even fucking gay?" Jenny finally sat down on the bed.

Mel felt angry enough to speak. "Remember, the therapist said there are certain topics that we should make off-limits for now?" she snapped.

Jenny surprised her and said, "Right, that's one. I'm sorry."

"And I *did* use a condom. It broke," Mel said. "I'm queer, bi, remember? I love you and I also like fucking men sometimes and other women."

Jenny stuck her tongue out at Mel.

Mel stuck hers out at her.

"This isn't the plan, I know, but we did want a baby."

"I don't want a white man's baby," Jenny said, starting to cry. She hardly ever cried.

"But it's free." Mel leaned in to hug her.

"Stop trying to make jokes."

"I can get an abortion then. It's my body and ultimately only I get to decide, not you or Carmine."

Stevie knocked softly. "Can I come in? I made tea."

Mel and Jenny looked at each other. Jenny mouthed, "She stayed?"

Mel mouthed back, "She does that. She's good."

"Come in, fine," Jenny said.

Stevie put the mugs on the nightstand and walked over to the fire escape to stare out the window. The big Brooklyn sky, sun setting. Daylight savings, gloomy early nights. She heard her friends sip the tea behind her.

"You know, whatever you decide will be okay," Stevie said, and Mel knew she was lying to them because parents always lied to potential parents. They had to, to keep the dumb species going and to have company through all of the shit of parenting. "Aaron and I love babies and will help you, and soon Sasha can babysit and we will treat this Frankenbaby like our own if you decide to have it. If you don't, I will go with you to the clinic and love you both forever, and a fetus is not a baby. It's just a bunch of cells. I know because when they implanted Sasha into me they gave me a picture, and you know what, it was just some cells called a blastocyst or something like that."

Jenny sighed. "Stevie, you can go home now."

"Totes!" Stevie chirped. "I can get the fuck out as I would have preferred."

Stevie left, and Jenny and Mel moved around the apartment in various positions of silence. Mel poured them each a glass of wine. Jenny drank hers, hugged Mel tightly, and left.

She didn't come back until the next day.

THE FISHERMAN'S WIFE

I woke up and stared at David's back—at the giant tattoo that covered it. It was a full-color reproduction of a Japanese woodcut by Katsushika Hokusai. In it, a woman with long black hair reclines on her back as an octopus with an exceptionally large head eats her out. Another smaller octopus kisses her. She's entangled in their sixteen arms and her face is ecstatic. She looks deep in the throes of orgasm. Perpetual pleasure. All release.

I decided that the fisherman's wife was me or any woman who liked David. In ecstasy, but going nowhere. Perpetual, cyclical, but no forward movement. No plan. Just be here now. *There are worse things*, I told myself. I thought of Arturo's forehead pressed up against mine in the dive bar booth, and then I pushed that image aside. I ran my fingers up and down David's big back. I traced the outline of the octopus's giant head. "You're smart, aren't you?" I whispered at it. Was it possible to make one boyfriend out of several distinctly non-boyfriend-like men?

David stirred and turned around to face me.

"Hi," I said, pulling myself closer to his chest, wrapping one knee around his legs. "You were away for a while, I thought maybe you weren't coming back."

"Did that make you sad, Red?" He frowned at me.

"Nah," I said. "But if you weren't coming back, I'd squat in your apartment and bring all my dates here."

"Oh, and then fuck them in my bed?"

I felt his dick get hard underneath the sheets. "You'd like that wouldn't you?" I asked.

"I would," he said.

I reached under the sheets to grab his dick, but he swatted my hand away. "That's for later."

"Later?"

"We have all day. What do you want to do with it?"

I reached again for his cock and he arched away from me. I pouted. We were playing my favorite game. Chase. Keep-away.

"Awww, poor little Red Riding Hood has to wait for the wolf," he teased.

"I have other wolves," I said. "Some of them have a lot of fur."

He growled at me and bit my shoulder. "Owww," I squealed. "No biting!"

"I know you have other wolves in your forest," he said. "That's one of the reasons I like this particular Red. She's very bad and she likes to tease a whole pack of wolves."

I lay on my back and stared at his tin ceiling. Sometimes the game was too much for me, and I wanted to break out of my character.

"There's another wolf who could hurt me."

"We wolves are quite dangerous."

I felt a tingling in my nose, like I might cry. David sat up on his elbows and looked at my face.

"What's going on over there?" he asked.

"I like him too much already, and Aaron and I are finally going to the mediator so our divorce is really happening, and my homeless drifter friend girl is in rehab and I can't find her, and my best friend Mel is pregnant but it's an accident and it's really all a mess."

"Your friend will be okay," he said, and pulled me in for a hug. "Who is the other wolf? The Occupy guy? I forgot his name, Jaime?"

"Arturo. He's really intense and I'm afraid I'll sleep with him."

"That's great!"

"No, it's not! He's not available!"

"Availability is overrated."

"That is such a David thing to say."

He laughed. "It is, isn't it? About your divorce then, that's a good thing! Congratulations! No one ever says that to divorcing people. You and Aaron had a good run and when it was time to shift, you figured it out without too much toxicity."

"But I won't be anyone's wife anymore," I said.

"Do you want to be?"

"Not really," I admitted. "I suck at being a wife."

"That's right, you're the not wife." He kissed me and I felt his tongue against mine. "You're doing good," he said.

"Don't be proud of me," I said. "It's like you're my therapist."

"Okay, I'll stop that."

"Before you woke up, I was staring at the woman in your tattoo."

"How is she doing?"

"She looks pretty happy actually, even though she's cheating on her husband with those octopi?"

"I suppose she is," David said. "Next time you're looking at her, tell her I said hello."

"I will."

David pulled me closer to him. I felt his cock harden against my belly. "Why do you have so many clothes on?" he asked. I was wearing only my underwear and an old T-shirt of his that I pulled off the floor last night after we'd fucked. He reached under my shirt and cupped a hand around one of my breasts. "I love your tits."

"I think the gods must have known that I'd be single again and so they made me fail at breastfeeding so I could have these pert boobs."

"They are quite alert." David ran a thumb along one of my nipples and I felt it harden. I arched my back slightly.

"I thought we were waiting," I said, and squirmed a couple inches away. "Do you believe in marriage? Like do you think it's good for people as individuals?"

"I just don't ever want to be codependent," David said.

"What does that mean?"

"Like dependent on someone else for my happiness and well-being."

"But isn't that what love is?"

"I don't think so."

"But if you love someone, you feel like you need them, don't you?"

"I think need and desire are two different things and we confuse them," David looked down at his hard cock and raised his eyebrows at me. "I clearly desire you, but I don't need you to be happy."

"That makes me kind of sad," I said, and then I licked the tip of his penis.

"Why? You want me to need you like I needed my mother?"

"Ugh, gross, no." I ran my tongue up and down the shaft of his cock. "But I do want you to want me so badly it feels like a need."

He groaned and placed his hand on my neck. "Keep sucking my cock like that and I probably will."

I paused for a second, but kept my tongue hovering just above the tip of his cock. "Do you think you'll ever want to live with someone again?"

"It's not something I fantasize about, frankly," he said. "I like living alone, and I think when couples move in together or get married, that's when it all goes to hell."

"It doesn't have to be like that," I said.

"But it often is."

I wanted to argue, but I didn't. I had no convictions anymore about marriages and living together, just some random garbage thoughts that shifted and changed as often as my moods. Couples baffled me. I wanted someone to dream with me, but lately I figured it could be Sasha.

I'd been mad at Aaron for so long because he wouldn't dream with me—other landscapes, apartments in neighborhoods we could never afford, and houses in dumb towns we'd never actually want to live in. I just liked to fantasize. What about building a tiny cabin in the woods? What were those giant apartments on the Grand Concourse like? Maybe someday we could all live in a yurt in the desert? *I was never sure.* Aaron hated that—said it made him feel like a hopeless failure. *Why can't you enjoy what we have right now?* he'd say testily. Why couldn't I?

David extricated himself out from under me and pulled his cock away from my mouth. "Don't try to distract me with magical blow jobs. We were talking about my tattoo and how skilled I am at licking your pussy."

"Oh right, I forgot," I said, and I leaned back and spread my legs wide open. David put his mouth between my legs and sucked and licked. When I looked down, I saw his beautiful bald head and pretty eyes. He winked, I closed my eyes, and imagined myself in the woodcut. My husband, the fisherman, was always away—at sea or at the market, and when he was home he treated me like a servant. *Fix me supper! Mend my net!* I remembered how we met. I was a just a girl, really; a shell diver, sent down into the deep by my father to look for pearls. On a day unlike all of the rest, I came up with a clam to my breast. I'd found a pearl! My father's boat was nowhere in sight. In its place was my soon-to-be-husband's boat. He took my pearl in exchange for passage in his boat. I never saw my father again. One day, long into our marriage, I snuck away to dive into the waves. Underwater, I danced with the octopi, entangled and enmeshed until we found ourselves nearly dashed upon a rock. I couldn't resist their long arms and suction-cup mouths, and I didn't want to anyway. *Love is a swell dashed upon a rock*, I thought. David groaned with pleasure as I did. I opened my legs wider and shoved my cunt deeper into his mouth.

I came in waves. Crest. Ridge. Awash in the sea of myself. *So what if none of these men need me?* I thought. *Do I have to be needed to be whole? What if I don't take care of anyone but Sasha?* I asked myself.

David rested his head on my stomach.

"Thank you," I managed.

"You're quite welcome, madam," he said.

My phone vibrated on David's nightstand and I reached for it. The number on my screen wasn't one I knew. "I gotta get this," I said to David, who nodded and walked down the stairs and into the bathroom.

"Hello?"

"Just tell Arturo to let us back into the park." It was Butch's angry voice. Slurry. Loaded. Not clean.

"Where are you?" I asked.

"Nowhere. Everywhere."

"Where's Johanna?" I pleaded.

"Why do you want to know, so you can lock her up?" Butch shouted.

I held the phone away from my ear.

"Just tell Arturo to let us back into Occupy," he said.

"You're kicked out?" I asked confused. "Why?"

"Just tell him," Butch yelled into the phone.

"Okay, I will." I gave up arguing.

A siren wailed in the background and I heard a voice in the background, soothing, female. "Okay, hang up now. Come on baby, hang up."

"Is that Johanna?" I asked. "Can you put her on the phone?" Was it her? I couldn't tell. The voice was far away, barely a whisper. I had no idea what I would say to her. I flipped around in the rolodex of useless thoughts I kept in my head, stock phrases I said to students and Sasha, which always felt empty, but which I meant. "You're going to be okay," I said into the phone. "You're going to make it." I meant it for Butch. I meant it for Johanna. For whoever was listening on the other end of the line.

Butch sucked in a breath and hung up on me.

SIGHTING

I left David's and came home. It was almost midnight. The elevator door opened onto my floor. There were two students lying in front of it, wrapped in blankets with their laptops out.

"Hiya." I waved at them.

"Can Rudy come out and snuggle with us while we work on our papers?" one of them asked. Her name was Whitney and she lived next door to me. I sometimes worried that she overheard me having sex.

"Lemme feed him first and then I'll let him out," I said as I unlocked my apartment door.

Rudy meowed loudly. I opened a stinky can of wet food and put it onto his mat. He gulped it down and looked up at me. *Is that it? Is that all you got?*

"Come out and see the students?" I said to him, and opened my door. He wandered out and over to the students, who were all on their laptops, huddled in pajamas under a nest of blankets. The students cooed. They rubbed behind his ears and along his back. He pushed his cheeks against their hands. Cat heaven.

"There was a girl here for you," Whitney said.

I stepped back out into the hallway.

"She was pounding on your door, but she ran down the stairs when the guard came."

"What did she look like?"

"Overalls. Weird hair, blond, all kinda clumped together," she said.

"Um, those are called dreadlocks," the other student said. Her name was Chandra. I liked her. She came to all of my dinners, snack hours, and outings. She'd recently friended me on Facebook and shared everything I posted about LGBTQ writers and activism.

"Did she say anything?" I asked.

"Just that she really needed to talk to you," Chandra added. "Whitney and I were the only ones who saw her."

"Is she your sister?" Whitney asked, sitting up, eager maybe for gossip.

"No, just a friend," I said. "Thanks for letting me know she was here."

Rudy followed me back into the apartment and I shut the door. I looked at the clock. It was almost midnight. I lay down on the couch. I was exhausted, but I had a feeling that Johanna was close by and that I should look for her. I scrolled through the Occupy page and squinted at the Occupy cam to see if Johanna was anywhere in the frame. She wasn't. I saw Diego in one grainy corner of the screen, bustling around in the People's Kitchen.

"Diego," I said to the screen. "I miss you!"

I texted Marissa, "Is Johanna there tonight?" but she didn't respond. She was probably asleep long ago.

I grabbed my bag and jacket and left the building. I was too wound up to sleep. I passed the lone police car parked at the southern entrance of the park and slid through the police barricades that went up at midnight when the park closed. I walked quickly, checking often to see if anyone was behind me. My breath sped up and my nose ran from the cold. I followed the path to the fountain and looked inside. Empty. Two rats skittered past me and I envisioned the mama hawk circling above. No wonder she lived in the park. Rat paradise! Food bounty! The wind picked up and the water sprayed against my face. I followed another path toward the northwest corner, where the drug dealers and homeless men hung out. It was empty too. I squinted at the nearby lawn—at the bases of trees and on the dark ground.

"Johanna!" I said softly into the night air. No answer. I walked back toward the fountain and the chess tables. I saw bodies asleep on the grass and under bushes near the bathroom. "Johanna!" I called again.

"Shut up!" a man's voice called back from the bushes. The police car's siren stuttered awake and the bullhorn voice of a police officer echoed through the park, "The park closes at midnight. Please exit the park." I pushed past another barricade near the arch and left. *If she was in there, I couldn't have found her,* I told myself as I stood under the streetlight near the arch. My phone chirped.

"We got out of jail free! Come over, have a drink, and celebrate your first arrest?" A text from Arturo. Another attempt to lure me over.

"So tired. I dunno," I texted back. It was true—so much had happened in the last couple days. I'd been in jail! My best friend was pregnant! I was hunting in the dark for a girl I barely knew! I was exhausted, and still I wanted to see him. Maybe I didn't need to be anybody's girlfriend or wife. Who had the time anyway? That was a whole other job. Maybe I could just do this and not worry about what it meant.

"Just one drink."

"You're lying."

"Maybe." He added the winky emoji face and sent me his address in Sunset Park. I thought of the men who were walking away from me, Aaron and Hayes, and the men who weren't exactly walking toward me but were at least around, David and Arturo. I decided that was good enough for now. I didn't count my one-night stands, the men who texted me in the middle of the night, my OkStupid messages—those were neither coming nor going. They were a space of pure present. Occupation. Diversion.

I hailed a cab. I told the driver the address and then I checked my credit card balance on my phone. Just $200 of available credit. $10,800 in credit card debt. *That's terrible,* I told myself as I stared at the screen. *But it could be a lot worse,* I counterreasoned. I knew I'd be using my credit card for this very cab ride.

When I got out of the cab, Arturo was waiting for me on his stoop, smoking.

"Can I have one?" I asked.

"Yep." He lit it for me with a Zippo.

"Cool lighter."

"It was my dad's. He died two years ago."

"I'm sorry." I inhaled deeply and let the smoke out through my open mouth. "I don't speak to my dad, but my best friend Mel's dad died when she was in her twenties and it always makes me feel guilty—like I should work on this relationship, well, since he's alive."

"Is that weird?" Arturo asked. "Like not speaking to your father, ever?"

"Not really, because he's an asshole. I've tried to be a good daughter for a long time, but I just got tired of it," I said. "Were you close with your dad?"

"In a distant, respectful Latino son and father way. I loved him. He didn't fuck with me." Arturo finished the last drag of his cigarette and put it out on the heel of his sneaker.

"I would just like my dad to not fuck with me. That would be enough."

"What did he do?"

I finished my cigarette and felt light-headed from the nicotine. "He tried to sue my brother, he called me a bad mother when I separated from my ex, he frequently accuses me of being gay, he beat us when we were kids. You know, the regular dad stuff."

"Jesus."

"Right?"

"Come up?" He held the door for me.

I walked into what was clearly a home, not a bachelor's pad or a convenient share. I noticed the framed pictures of Devora, Arturo, and her kid hung up on the wall. At Disneyland! Camping! Sitting on the very stoop where we'd just smoked!

He must have seen me looking at the photos. "Devora knows you're here and she's cool with you," he said.

"Good, yeah. How do you guys do this stuff? I mean, be poly? My friend Mel, who I was just telling you about, and her girlfriend, they don't have anyone over to their space."

"We talk about it, and sometimes it doesn't work, and sometimes it does," Arturo said, as if that was reassuring. "But we started out with a bunch of hardcore rules and then those kind of fell away for the sake of convenience. Like Sid's with her dad and Devora is at Occupy and I got arrested today, and that makes me feel sad and weird and also kinda fuck the police, so I'm going to have someone over."

"Someone? Just someone?" I asked.

"No, you, not just someone."

"Just making sure," I said. "I was hunting in the park for Johanna. Some students in my building saw her and I thought she might be close by, but it was dark and I couldn't find her and then you texted," I added, as if to explain why I'd come.

"She'll turn up when she's ready," he said, and poured us some whiskey. He was so sure about everything. I followed him into what he called his office. The walls were lined with history and sociology books and covered in collages. There was a futon in one corner, opened and made up like a bed.

We sat on it. I looked at the collages. Giant magazine-scapes, carefully cut with an X-acto knife, rearranged and pasted together.

"You made those?"

"Yeah, I just do it for fun and to help me relax. It's so different than writing, and I can get high and listen to music."

"I love the one with the eighties Madonna in it."

"Yeah, she's so hot."

"I just rewatched *Desperately Seeking Susan* on TV, and I'd forgotten how much I loved that early Madonna, like what she meant to me. She was kinda punk and so sex-positive for her time," I said.

"I was in love with her because she sang in Spanish," Arturo said.

"La Isla Bonita!" I got up and picked up books off of his shelves. Books I knew well from graduate school and teaching, and books I'd never heard of or had read about but never got around to reading.

"In my next academic life, I want to be a sociologist," I said as I sipped my whiskey. He was staring at me. I could feel it. "It's just so cool to work with people instead of texts."

"No more academic lives for me," he said, but then he told me a little bit about each book that I picked up and I liked that. It was so rare that I got to be a student. If nothing else, my father had trained me to be the perfect listener. The girl who mirrored him and nodded and said *yes, yes, yes, Daddy,* and though I no longer wanted to be that girl, I was still a good audience for a man who wanted to show me things. Such a relief to have the tables turn and to not teach anyone anything. To answer no questions from students, to do nothing but take it in and ooh and aah. The deep joy of passivity.

Eventually, he took a book out of my hand and steered me back toward the bed. We lay down on it. He wrapped his arms around me and squeezed tight. He turned off the light. I wriggled out of my dress. He stepped out of his pants.

"I've wanted to do this for a really long time," he whispered in my ear.

"Me too," I said as he kissed my neck.

"It's not just sex," he said.

"I know," I said, but did I?

"I feel this strong connection with you. I want to get to know you."

"It's just because we got locked up together," I joked.

He unhooked my bra, rubbed my nipples, and slid his hand between my legs.

"You get so wet," he said.

"I know, it's just one of my things."

"One of your talents?" He laughed, and made his way down to my pussy with his tongue. He stayed there for a while until I pulled him up. I didn't want to come that way. I wanted him inside me. I unbuttoned his shirt and pulled his underwear off. I put his cock in my mouth and sucked on it. He groaned.

"You like that?" I looked up at him.

"Very much," he said. I kept sucking and licking until he said, "Get up here."

I straddled him and rubbed my clit against his cock. I pressed my chest against his. My cheek to his ear. We were breathing so hard, the both of us. *Take a breath*, I told myself.

"We should use a condom," I said.

"Yeah, I have one," he said.

He reached over to the desk by the futon and grabbed one and handed it to me, but I didn't open it. Instead, I angled myself so that he could slide into me.

"Oh my god," he groaned. "You feel so good."

"So do you," I said. *This is stupid, you'll regret this tomorrow, hadn't I just watched Mel pee on a stick?* I thought, but I didn't care.

He breathed into my neck. I breathed back into his. He put his hand on my hips and slid into me even deeper. I gasped.

"Are you one of those crazy girls?"

"Definitely."

I folded over him and rocked back and forth over and over again.

In the dark, I wanted to say the crazy things, like, *I think I could love you.* And, *Let's do that forever.* But I didn't.

Instead, I got out of bed, peed, and examined the spider veins on the top of my thighs. *Those are never going away*, I thought to myself objectively. Arturo's sperm dripped out of me as I sat on the toilet.

"We have to use a condom next time," I said to him as I crawled back into bed. He nodded, but was dozing off. I pinched him on the arm. "Did you hear me?" I asked as I stared at his face in the dark. I was trying to see him—who is this man who I can never really have?

"Yeah, I always do. I don't know what happened. Something about you, Stevie," he said. "You make me reckless."

"Sperm is bad for all women," I said.

"I know, sperm is terrible," he said. "I broke a rule. Devora's going to be pissed," he said, and then fell asleep. I got dressed and snuck out.

MY CATALYST

Once I was outside, I breathed deeply. November crisp. I scanned the street for scary men and saw no one. I wondered suddenly what Sasha and I would do for Thanksgiving. Would I cook a turkey or would she go to Aaron's parents with him? *Maybe both, that would work*, I told myself. On the walk to the subway, I kicked the leaves on the sidewalk and watched them blow off into the gutter. "It's okay, leaves," I whispered. "That's where you go."

I looked at my phone. It was just after four a.m. I'd fucked two guys in the last twenty-four hours. I felt both proud and disgusted with myself.

When I looked up again, I saw Hayes lowering the metal gate of a bar to lock up. *It must be another place he deejays.* He had his bicycle hoisted up over one shoulder and a giant bike chain across his chest. Should I cross the street? Should I say hello? I couldn't decide. I was surprised to see him alone, without a woman next to him, holding his bike chain adoringly.

What was he to me? He was a mistake, a regret, a pang, a one-night stand who I kept bumping into because I sucked at letting go and moving on. He was a catalyst, a man who happened to be there when I needed to blow up my life, and he was brave that night. He helped me do it. He didn't flinch. But more than anything, he was a portal into another world, and into another iteration of myself, the not wife.

I thought of Arturo alone in the bed I'd just left. I imagined my own bed, empty and waiting for me. I felt drunk and exhausted, raw and exposed, and still I crossed the street and walked toward him.

"Hey," I said.

"Hiya." He turned around. He looked startled and tired.

"You work here too?" I asked.

"Just trying to make rent." The wind picked up. A pile of leaves and a plastic bag swirled up between us. *Being a DJ is just another job that both does and does not pay the bills*, I thought.

I realized I had no idea what to say to him. I wanted him to want me again. I wanted to go back to that night in the bar when we were strangers. I liked that he'd read me all wrong—thought I was single, not a mom, and definitely not forty-two. It was flattering to be seen as someone else. Had I been in disguise all along? He reminded me of the types of guys I'd dated in my early twenties—musicians, skaters, and painters—bad boys mostly, who were dicks to me but who I worshipped because my proximity to them meant that I was cool too. Those guys tended to tire of me quickly, and there was always another girl waiting in the wings, ready to fill my Doc Martens with her petite feet.

"I'm gonna head home and crash," Hayes said. He took his bike frame off his shoulder and set it down on the sidewalk. He looked very much like he wanted to get away. It was fine to flirt with me in a crowded bar or send me a drunken text, but it was another thing altogether to face me on a dark four a.m. street. No stakes versus high stakes.

"Me too. I was just headed to the subway. Have a good night." I held up my hand and did a stupid bye-bye wave, trying to save face. *You don't want me, well fine, I don't want you either.*

"You too," he said as he hopped on his bike and sped off down the street.

THE SUN WAS coming up by the time I got off the subway and walked through the park to my apartment. I needed to sleep for a couple of hours before I taught.

Near the base of a tree I saw the mama hawk—regal, white feathers flecked with gray and black—calmly dismembering a squirrel and eating its entrails. She was in no rush. Kept her talon on the squirrel's body the whole time. Pulled out a piece of bright red flesh, swallowed, waited, pulled at another. A bloody show. I was mesmerized.

THE SACK

They kept having the same fight when Jenny came back.

"I can't believe you had unsafe sex!" Jenny said. She'd had a big glass of wine.

"We used a condom! It broke," Mel said. "We have to move past how it happened."

"I feel betrayed."

"It was an accident." Mel was getting dressed for work at Zoe's. She pulled on her jeans and rooted around in her dresser for a sexy shirt. She hadn't told Carmine. She didn't know what to say. She didn't feel any differently about anyone. She loved Jenny and she was maybe falling in love with Carmine. Was that possible? Was her heart big enough? *Yes*, she thought, fumbling with her earrings. "But I know, you're right. It's not what we talked about ever and I can see how that would feel like a betrayal." She was practicing what they'd been working on in couples therapy—mirroring what Jenny was saying, honoring her feelings, even if she didn't agree with them.

Jenny sat up straight on the bed. "Do you want it?"

"I don't know, do you?"

"No fair, I asked first."

"Well, I think all three of us have to talk before we can decide anything."

"I want it," Jenny said. "People have babies all kinds of ways. Who cares?"

"But you just said I betrayed you."

"You did." Jenny crawled over to the edge of the bed and wrapped her arms around Mel's waist. "But I love you anyway."

"I think you're tipsy." Mel let Jenny pull her onto the bed and unzip her jeans. "But I'll be late for work," she said.

Jenny slid her finger inside Mel. "Fuck that job."

Mel grabbed Jenny's tits and unbuckled her belt. She was seized with a desire for connection, a bodily way to fix the rift she'd made with Jenny. She wanted to be forgiven and move on to the next messy thing, whatever that was. She slid her hand into Jenny's boxers and Jenny moaned. "I'll teach it all of the Chinese holidays," Jenny said as she slid her tongue along Mel's.

"But you hate most of them," Mel said.

"Shhhh," Jenny said as she reached over to the nightstand drawer and pulled out their new dick.

"We have to be fast," Mel said, stripping and sliding under Jenny so she could lick her pussy. "Take everything off," she commanded.

"I'm going to take my time with you," Jenny said. "To punish you good."

"I'm going to get fired." She lay back and closed her eyes.

"You can't work there anyway. You're pregnant."

"I've seen pregnant bartenders."

Jenny slid the dick into her harness and jumped up and down a couple of times for effect. "It's a little floppier than the old one," she said.

"I just want your hand and mouth!" Mel sat up on her elbows. "I can't deal with that robot dick right now."

Jenny unbuckled the harness and let it fall to the floor. "All right baby, all right," she said.

Their hands deep inside each other. Jenny's expert fingers and perfect flicking tongue. Waves of red and purple and blue. Mel sucking on Jenny's clit until she cried out. On their backs, exhausted and sated. Mel thought for a fleeting minute about the cells inside of her, growing. She remembered the photograph Stevie had shown her after IVF of the little light gray cluster that would eventually grow to become Sasha. Stevie had a miscarriage too, lost that second batch of cells that had turned into a fetus, but Sasha made it from blast to birth. They'd held each other and wept on the shitty couch in Stevie's old Brooklyn apartment. *I could lose this too,* Mel thought. *I'm not strong enough to be a mom at forty-two. Maybe I don't want it.*

"I love you," Jenny said.

"I love you too," Mel said as she hurried to get dressed.

When she got to work, Greta was behind the bar, doing a fair imitation of her—black halter, dangly earrings, hair up so that it looked messy and short.

"I swear to god, Mel, if you didn't have so many loyal customers who'd kick my ass if you weren't here to flirt with them and listen to their sad gay stories, I'd sack you today," Tommy yelled at her from her office as she passed by to sign in.

She flipped him the bird from farther down the hallway where he couldn't see. Carmine winked at her. She put her head down. *How can I tell him? What should I say?*

The chaos of the bar took over—customers five deep at the bar and an endlessly spooling tape of drinks for the waiters. Greta stayed with her and she wasn't half bad at it. Bartending loosened her up and gave her something to do, instead of getting in everyone else's business.

Finally, at midnight, she managed to sneak out to the side alley with Carmine while he smoked.

"I have to tell you something," she said.

He took a long drag and flicked the butt onto the cement. He didn't look at her. "I already know. My guys are champion swimmers."

"I don't know what I want." Mel tucked a strand of hair behind one ear, her one nervous gesture.

"Well that's good, because I don't either." She watched the tendons in his neck tighten for a second and then release. "I gotta go make a bunch of sauces, but obviously this is your choice and I respect that." He kissed her on the cheek and walked back into the back of the restaurant.

Mel watched him and the other cooks move around each other in an expert unchoreographed kind of dance through the open back window. *What happened to my fling?* she thought.

PLAYER TWO

Johanna followed Butch around one last time.

She went to Bushwick and watched him fix up in the dealer's apartment, but she didn't go in the bathroom and she shook her head no when Butch offered her a small line.

"Whatever," he said, and turned his deepest attention on the spoon, the lighter, and the syringe.

When he lay back on the futon, feeling the first wave of high, he said without malice, "You think you're better than me now."

"No, I don't. I just think we can get clean together and get back on track, like start traveling again, or go to school." Johanna put her hand on one of his arms.

The dealer sighed loudly at them. He was playing a video game in a war zone. Bodies blew up as shooters wandered through abandoned mosques and fired rounds of ammunition. Sometimes a goat or a child ran across the giant TV screen. If he wasn't getting a blowie for free, he was way less interested in hosting them.

"I don't want to go to school. I've taught myself enough social justice theory and history. I know more than most professors," Butch bragged, and then let his head loll back onto the futon.

"I have this therapist and she can get you a bed in rehab." Johanna had taped her card into her pants along with her poems. She'd broken out of rehab just like she planned, but she'd already called Helena and made an appointment. They'd discussed a halfway house where Johanna could sleep. "I wish you wouldn't have run away, but I know that place is hard," Helena had scolded her.

"I don't need therapy," Butch said. "I can talk to you."

The dealer snorted and threw a video game controller at Butch. "Player two!" he said without looking away from the screen.

Butch grabbed for the remote and started to play. Johanna sat back on the futon. She knew she could stay here all afternoon. She could give in to it like she always did and go into the bathroom with the skinny dealer whose name she could never remember because she didn't want to know his name. They'd order pizza and wings and convince the dealer to share a six-pack. Butch would nod off eventually and she'd do a line because she was bored and she'd pretend that she never met Stevie or her bartender friend or Helena. She could pretend that she never saw a woman jump eight stories from a balcony and smash her life apart, and that her first thought when she hit the ground hadn't been, *Well, that's one way to do it*. She could slip back into the underground and disappear with Butch.

But she didn't feel like slipping. She'd been clean for a week and she felt clearheaded and focused, like there was a flame in her stomach or her heart, lighting the way. She wanted to be her own pilot light.

She watched them play for another hour and remembered the best things about Butch. The way he'd opened the door to his band's minivan that day when she was fourteen and scared shitless and hitchhiking and said, "Get in, we need someone who can play keyboard." His contagious, manic energy about travel plans, maps, and the open road. How he knew the histories of weird subcultures, and how he always insisted that they were adventurers and not homeless. The smell of him in the park on moonlit nights. How he got Tipsy to trust them by giving her chicken he stole from the bodega hot bar three days in a row. That he told her it was okay to hate her mother forever. The way he loved her when no one else would. His total belief in revolution.

She realized that most of that was before the junk got to be an everyday thing.

She draped her arms around his neck from behind and hugged him. "I gotta go," she said, kissing his cheek.

"See you in the park, babe," he said.

"Yep," she lied. She let herself out and started walking. She wasn't sure where she was going.

FUNBUTT

Sasha came back to me so I could stop running around.

I looked at Sasha's bedroom. I meant to clean it when she was at Aaron's but never got around to it. Legos everywhere! Jewelry and tiny people all over the bed.

"Sash, we gotta clean up in here. It's crazy!"

Sasha was oblivious, fully into her third episode of *My Little Pony*. I checked my phone.

A missed call. An unknown number. 212. I called it back and got no answer. Was it Johanna calling from a payphone?

A text from David: "I'm thinking about you, Red."

A text from Arturo: "Hey funbutt."

I texted Adija for the last time. "Want to get a drink sometime?" Ugh, why was I so lame with women? It was getting embarrassing. She never responded.

An email from my father. I opened it. *I know you're planning a vacation with your mother next summer. You treat your mother and brother like your family and me and Elaine like your distant second cousins. That's okay, I'll just keep getting kicked in the teeth. It's what I do best.*

I deleted the email and put my phone facedown on the kitchen counter. *Too much incoming!* "Sasha, let's go to bed."

Sasha shut the computer and we made our way into my room. I pulled down the covers and we climbed in.

"Did you pee?"

"No."

"Go pee."

I turned the light back on and waited for her. Maybe Sasha would just sleep with me until she became a teenager. Maybe we'd be like that mom and daughter duo I'd seen on the taxi cab television who lived together in a one-bedroom studio in Astoria and slept in bunk beds so that the daughter could pursue her dream of becoming a Broadway star.

"Can I do the light?" Sasha asked when she came back from the bathroom.

I watched her struggle with the switch until it caught. Dark. Her body next to mine. "Do scratch rubbies," she commanded, and I ran my fingernails up and down her back. I'd been doing this since she was two.

"You're better at scratch rubbies than Daddy."

"I know," I said. "His hands are too big."

"His nails are too sharp," she said. I felt her shoulders relax. Maybe she'd fall asleep quickly. I shut my eyes.

"Mama, why did you go to jail?"

I sat up and turned the light back on. I couldn't talk about this in the dark; I needed to see her face. Sasha rubbed her eyes. "Who told you I was in jail?"

"I heard Daddy and Anne talking, and Anne said you were lucky to not have to stay all night in jail."

I thought for a second that I should lie, but then I realized I couldn't.

"Remember where the people are camping?"

"Yeah."

"Well, I was there helping serve food and the police made a mistake and put me in jail for a couple of hours."

"What did you do?" Sasha looked like she didn't believe me. "The police came to our school and they taught us about 'stranger danger' and arresting the 'bad guys.'"

"Sometimes the police make mistakes," I reasoned. "You know I'm not a bad guy."

Sasha settled back down onto her pillow. "I know." She wrinkled her forehead. "I have a bad feeling."

"What is it, doll? You can tell me all the feelings." I set my hand on her forehead and pushed her hair off her face.

"I worry about you and Daddy."

"Why?"

"Because you went to jail and Daddy fell off his bike last summer." Aaron had been upstate with friends and hit a gravel patch. His face was scratched up, but he was fine.

"I understand why you would worry, but I'm not going to jail ever again and Daddy is better now."

"I have another bad feeling," Sasha said.

"I can handle it."

"I liked it better when you and Daddy used to fight because at least then we were living together." Sasha sat up and then buried her head in my lap.

"I know you miss us living together. I miss it too sometimes."

"Is Anne Daddy's girlfriend?"

"Yeah, I think so."

"Do you have a boyfriend?"

"No, not right now."

Sasha lay back down on her pillow.

"Do you have any more feelings to talk about?" I asked.

"No, not yet," she yawned.

I reached up and turned off the light.

"I wanted to do it," Sasha said. I turned it back on so that she could turn it off again herself.

Sasha's breath soon fell into a sleep rhythm, and I lay in the dark and stared at the ceiling. I wondered if this would become a salient memory for Sasha. Talking to her mother about going to jail? I felt that familiar tug and pull—the same one I felt that day in the police van cage. Good mommy. Bad mommy. Good wife. Not wife. The desire to make a safe, comfortable nest for my little bird kid, and the hope that I could teach her about the world and turn her into a fighter. *No, it's not a good thing for your mother to go to jail. But it was just one afternoon. It's not like I robbed a bank. I'm here. Sometimes I'm distracted, but I'm here in bed with her, rubbing her back and talking to her. That counts, doesn't it?* I listened to the sounds outside my window. The wind blowing against it. Rain hitting the pane in hard, fat drops.

The next morning, the radio woke us up. It was the smug, dickish voice of Kai Ryssdal from *Marketplace. Today marks the fifty-third day of Occupy Wall Street. Across the pond, London halts its legal actions against Occupy London protesters outside of St. Paul's Cathedral, in an effort to increase dialogue.*

A text from Adija: "Why did you leave in the middle of the night without saying goodbye?"

"Because I was afraid," I texted before I could stop myself.

DISCERNMENT

Aaron and I sat across the table from our mediator. It was our first appointment. Cardozo Law School offered a free mediation clinic to anyone who was willing to be videotaped for future use with students. We were those people. Broke teachers who believed in education and needed a cheap divorce.

"So, we're almost to the end of the list here," Bill, our mediator, said. He looked to be about sixty with salt-and-pepper hair and a gentle grandfatherly way about him. His voice was even and calm. He wore an expensive-looking navy suit and a red bow tie. I liked him so far. We'd already made it through most of the categories on the checklist: *Parenting Decisions, Property Allocations, Expenses of the Child, Spousal Assistance, Tax Ramifications,* and *Standard Provisions* which covered issues like estate waivers and how to deal with future debts. We'd figured out a lot of it already on our own, and the rest we joked our way through. We had no property to allocate! We each made the same shitty salary! Spousal support! Ha! We still had our joint checking account, which we called the "Sasha Fund." Mostly it was empty.

"I guess it's a good thing we were never able to buy an apartment anywhere," I said, and looked over at the camera set up on a tripod in the corner. Its red recording light stared back at me.

"Yeah, because now we'd be fighting over it in court," Aaron agreed.

"Or maybe we'd both be living in it together and hating each other," I said. "Like you'd have Anne over and I'd be full of rage, and I'd bring some random guy over and it would be awkward."

Aaron smiled and then looked up at the mediator, who had a confused look on his face. I remembered suddenly where we were, and said, "Sorry, we're ready for the next thing on the list."

"It's quite all right." Bill took off his glasses and set them down on the legal pad in front of him. "I have a question for you two, and it may feel like an impertinent one, but I feel it's my responsibility to ask it."

I looked nervously over at Aaron. He was busy picking at a very important cuticle on his thumb.

"Go ahead," I said.

"I see a lot of couples in here, and usually within the first fifteen minutes one or both of them tells me why they can't be married anymore or they are at each other's throats, and it's clear to me that they make each other profoundly unhappy. But you guys clearly have a great affection and even love for one another, and so I have to ask, are you sure that you want to get a divorce?"

I looked over at Aaron, who was now looking up at Bill.

The tears started to roll down my cheeks, and I couldn't stop them. "Why are you asking us that?" I wanted to mouth to the camera and to the future mediators who would eventually watch this shitty, low-budget production, *Don't do this! He's out of line.*

"I'm sorry, I feel it's my job to check in and notice what I see."

"Don't you see other couples like us? I mean, this is mediation, not litigation?" Aaron asked. He had that angry, I'm-going-to-punch-you-for-hurting-my-girl look on his face that I'd always found deeply hot and compelling. I missed that look.

"Not that many," Bill said. "Look, it's just something I want you to do for homework. Just make sure, okay? I am also going to send you the name of a therapist who specializes in these kinds of tough decisions. He's called a discernment counselor."

"It's not ever going to be like a one-hundred-percent thing. More like sixty or seventy percent for us maybe on the worst days," I said.

"We were really unhappy in the last couple of years of our marriage and we went to a therapist. I mean she sucked, but we tried," Aaron said.

"Sometimes I think that maybe I'll remarry you like when we're in our sixties and we've both had some time to explore," I said to Aaron, and started to laugh through my tears.

Aaron and Bill both looked a little stricken when I said this. I was kidding and not kidding. Part of me found that kind of romantic. Weird, but it happened. It was very Elizabeth Taylor, but so what?!

"We're best friends again, and that's what's most important I think," Aaron said. I knew he was right, but part of me wanted him to say, *You know what, I'm not over you, and I probably never will be.* And what if he did say that out loud and then I said, *Me too!* What would that mean? Would we slide the paperwork off the table and fuck each other in front of our bow-tied mediator? Would we mouth through hungry kisses, *I'm sorry. I'm sorry. I made a terrible mistake. I missed you so!*

You see, I wanted to explain, *we were orphans when we met. I was twenty-eight and he was twenty-six and we were lost. We were strangers from our families, more adult in some ways than our parents could ever be, but neither of us knew how to do much. We were poets. The only shared dream we ever had was the city. Us in it. Together. Making stuff.* I remembered the first time I saw Aaron. We were graduate students with the same teaching fellowship. He was standing by a cubicle with his hand on his hip, a feminine gesture he made impossibly masculine. He had his beautiful nose and his bright blue eyes. I wanted to know him. It was that simple.

"Do you mind if I go to the bathroom?" I said, and I got up and grabbed my purse and left without waiting for an answer. Down the hallway and past the secretary's desk. Her kind eyes. Too much for me. She was a blur of tears. I walked through the bathroom door and into the room of pink-and-black eighties tiles and into the stall. I pulled my dress up around my waist and yanked my underwear down. As I peed, I let the tears really fall. I cried into a wadded-up clump of toilet paper. It was the inevitable legal end of us, the marriage of

Stevie and Aaron. The couple everyone loved and looked up to, the ones who got married under a giant white tent in someone's stupid backyard and DIYed most of the wedding because their friends kept volunteering to deejay, arrange the flowers, cook the food, bake the cake, and perform the ceremony. Aaron would never be my husband again, and I wouldn't be his wife anymore either. Why was it so shocking to me, still?

I sat there for as long as I could with my underwear around my ankles. I wadded up another hunk of toilet paper and tried to staunch the tears. I blew my nose a couple times and slowly stopped crying. I pulled my phone out of my purse and stared at the picture of Sasha on it. Gap-toothed, wild unbrushed hair, beautiful hazel eyes. I smiled at the screen until it chirped at me.

A text from Arturo: "I can't stop thinking of you, but I'm in trouble. For some reason, Devora is flipping out about you. Might have to slow us down for a bit."

I felt my face get hot again and new tears coming. A flush of anger. *Fuck you. I fuck you without a condom and now you want to slow down? Also, you said this was okay. I've already agreed to be second, or whatever.* I deleted his message so I wouldn't have to see it again.

A missed call, another 212 number. I called it back. It rang and rang. Johanna. My ghost. The girl I'd never find again. The girl who maybe didn't want to be found, but wanted to leave me an exasperating trail of breadcrumbs that led to nowhere.

I thought of Marissa and Diego working in the kitchen that day. Cooking. Doing something that mattered for people who needed to be fed. Diego who left his hometown in Mexico. Marissa who watched the bank take her parents' split-level ranch in Florida, the house she grew up in. Mel's cabin, underwater, in more ways than one. Sasha and I out of our apartment soon.

All of us in the back of that police van. All of us in that cell. Small boxes for holding us and keeping us still. All of us eventually out on the street. What I loved most about Occupy was that it was a provisional home; a public dream made manifest by determination, planning, and a refusal to move out of the way or be swept aside.

Maybe we've reached the end of all homes, I thought as I pulled my underwear back up. The banks took so many homes. *Domesticity, as we knew it, is dead,* I thought. *I am not a wife. I am the not wife. Maybe we'll all form communes in parks and live together forever in new spaces. Maybe we'll break all of the institutions and that will be okay. Maybe. Just maybe.*

THE WIVES

The wives were real and they weren't just housewives, thank you. The wives were dreaming about spring break! The wives were in Tulum or Vieques or the beach in Croatia. The wives were in love with the president. The wives weren't going anywhere. The wives were having stay-cations. The wives were at work. They had three to five different jobs. The wives spent the day on the train. They were commuting to Long Island and Westchester and New Jersey and DC and Buffalo and Los Angeles and Phoenix and St. Louis. The wives were on food stamps and Medicaid and the ACA. All of the wives were freelancers and they were hungry. The wives did everything they could for their kids. The wives were in jail. The wives were crossing borders everywhere all the time. It was called migration. The wives were in detention. The wives were being watched and under surveillance. The wives had perfected the gluten-free cupcake and they had a two-tiered BPA-free cupcake carrier. The wives didn't give a shit. The wives got a kiddie pool and later a swimming pool with a slide. The wives rolled the best blunts and the other wives smoked them. The wives got their kids to school every day no matter what. The wives hated kids, especially yours. The wives were getting beaten and raped. The wives told. The wives had their secrets. The wives were drunk at noon because you could do that now. The wives were working on campaigns. The wives had the best Go Bags. A couple of wives knew that the shit was going to hit the fan. They tried to warn the other wives, but they wouldn't listen.

I GET LONELY

I left my apartment to get Sasha from school. I read the posters in the hallway while I waited for the elevator. *Do you have consent at every step? LGBTQ Film Series! Join the Interfaith Halls Council! Introductory Meeting at 8 p.m. Tuesday in the Lounge! Insomnia Cookies for all! Study Away Informational Session. Do you suffer from an eating disorder? Participate in this study and receive free treatment and a Barnes & Noble gift card.* I stared at the emergency exit door that led out onto the roof, the one that Johanna had pushed open that night. It was locked as always and plastered with a sign that read, *Do you need help right now? Are you in the midst of a crisis? There are people who can help. Call the University Wellness Hotline at 212-555-5555.*

I made my way through the park and toward Sasha's school. I stopped for five seconds at Madison Reilly's memorial. It was still going strong. There were new candles and more notes taped up. She was a symbol for something—loss, campus rape, being a teenager, depression, artistry, a whole bunch of intersections that maybe didn't have much to do with her. There was newly chalked writing on the ground, *Investigate sexual harassment,* next to the older *Rape + Suicide = Murder.* Somebody on campus clearly knew something I didn't. I hadn't heard from that detective again. I knew my university well enough to know that the goal was not transparency or honesty, but legality and ass-covering.

I stared up at the now bony, bare branches of the tree, and scanned the sky for the mama hawk. Would she bring her baby any parts of the squirrel? Or did he hunt on his own now? The pigeon guy sat on his usual bench as a tour bus emptied out and took his picture—seven or eight pigeons spread out along his outstretched arms. His hair was pigeon colored and his coat was too. Do we all become our animals? I zipped up my coat and wished I'd worn a hat. I exited the park, walked past the doggie day care, down Eighth Street, crossed Sixth Avenue, and slowed my pace as I waited with the parents and nannies. The guard unlocked the gate, and we filed in slowly.

"Mama! Can I get a pop-tart?!" Sasha asked the second she saw me. She fist-bumped her teacher goodbye and handed me her backpack. I waved at Ms. Lu and mouthed, "Thank you." Sasha was talking about the artisanal pop-tarts that cost four bucks at the overpriced coffee shop, filled with bearded baristas. I thought of the $329 I had to get through the last week and a half of the month.

"Yes!" I said anyway. At the café, we were lucky enough to get a table from one of the grouchy freelancers. He packed up his laptop and pile of notebooks while Sasha danced impatiently around him.

"Thanks," I said to him when he left, but he didn't say anything back. *You know*, I wanted to say, *you once came out of a vagina.*

"I went to prize box today," Sasha said as she half sat on her chair.

"That's cool! For what?" I asked.

"Listening."

"What did you get?"

"A sparkly pencil."

"Can I see it?"

"I'll show you at home." Sasha bit into the fruity middle of her pop-tart.

I held out my hand. "Mama gets a bite."

"A small bite."

I took a bite and handed it back. "I wish it tasted better," I said to Sasha, who ignored me. "I mean for four dollars, it should be like a pie." I wiped the crumbs off the table and held them in my hand as Sasha finished.

"Why do I have to be the only kid in our building?" she asked. I saw that she had tears in her eyes. It was Wednesday, the day she transitioned from Aaron's house to mine, her hardest day emotionally. She cried on Wednesdays more than any other day and got mad at me more easily too. I got it. How hard it must be to have two apartments, to shuttle back and forth between two spaces, and to miss one parent all the time. But I also knew firsthand the misery of growing up with two parents who hated each other, who stuck it out for the kids, but only made my brother and I unhappy. *There was joy in having two places too*, I told myself. When one parent got annoying, you could see the other. You got cool stuff in each place. When Sasha got tired of the bustle of Manhattan, she got the quiet of Bed-Stuy, Brooklyn.

"I get lonely," she added.

"I know, lovey, it's hard to be the only kid. I get lonely for other adults too, you know."

"We're talking about me," she clarified.

"I know. You wish there were other kids around. I get that."

She put her head down on the table and sighed. I reached over and rubbed her head with my hand. *Shitty bad-mom feeling, go away*, I thought. I wanted to tell her that soon there would be no more dorm or students, and she wouldn't be the only kid, but I wanted to have the place picked out before I told her so that it would be certain and not scary.

"Wanna come snuggle?" I asked.

"Later, Mama," she said, and stood up to walk back home.

My phone chirped and I looked at the message. It was from Marissa. "Getting slammed today. Need servers! Can you come down?"

"Got my kid today," I texted back, but I felt guilty. I knew what the kitchen was like understaffed and it was brutal.

"Bring her. I've got brownies!"

I looked at Sasha and her skinny girl neck. I put my hand on her shoulder and pulled her closer to me. She leaned in like she needed it, like she would melt back into me if she could.

"I dunno. Let me ask her," I texted.

CAMPING

"Do you want to go to a protest with me and help out in the kitchen? Marissa, my friend who works there, says there will be brownies." We'd left the café and finished the math worksheets she had for homework on the counter at home. The rest of the afternoon and evening yawned in front of us. I hadn't yet brought Sasha to Occupy. I'd kept that part of my life separate from her. It was easier that way.

"Do the brownies have frosting?" she asked.

"Not sure."

"Will that girl Johanna be there?" We hadn't talked about Johanna since the day after she'd been on the roof. I'd told her she was sick and had to go the hospital, but that she'd be okay.

"I don't know about Johanna," I said. "But there might be other kids. We'll just have dinner and dessert there and come home."

"Okay!" she said.

"Do you want to bring any toys? Maybe your Lego people?"

We grabbed her Lego elves and got on the A. On the ride down to Chambers, Sasha's elves chatted in high-pitched whispers about a coronation in a castle and whether or not the queen would be there. *Will she be angry?* one elf asked from the subway pole. *Will she for-give us?* another chimed in from the subway seat.

"You made it!" Marissa said. She looked relieved. The food line was the longest I'd ever seen it.

"Mami, you brought your hija!" Diego said.

"The last time I saw you, you were on the Occupy cam," I said.

"Me?"

"Pretty sure," I said.

"I hate that camera, it's like a big eye," he said.

"Sash, this is Diego and Marissa," I said. She looked up and mouthed a silent, "Hi."

Sasha and I ducked under the table to get to the serving side of the kitchen. I put on an apron and found a seat for Sasha on a milk crate right behind me. She settled back into her elf coronation.

For the next hour, I spooned brown rice and collard greens onto plates. Marissa gave out salmon and tofu while Diego ran back and forth with several other workers to refill trays and unload a food truck from Brooklyn that was idling on the street and about to get a ticket. The cops were making it harder and harder to stay in both small and big ways. Ticketing everyone was one of the small ways. I tried to look up and make eye contact, but the line was moving too quickly and there were just too many people in it. As the donations to Occupy poured in from around the world, the food got better and better, and the word had spread on the street. Homeless people and the working poor knew it was a good meal and that they could avoid the hassle of the shelters. The line finally ended, and I fixed a plate of food for Sasha and me. The dancing and drumming circle had taken a break, and the park was quiet with eating. A communal hush. A meal, mostly with strangers, but a nice one still.

"I don't like fish," Sasha said to me.

"That's all there is, so you should try it."

"I caught the fish with my own hands." Diego sat down next to Sasha. She leaned her face into my arm.

"It's okay, Sash. Diego is my friend. You can talk to him." Growing up in the city had turned Sasha into an ice-cold native New Yorker. She objected to any conversation from anyone who she didn't personally know. I admired her badass stone-cold attitude, but the upstate New Yorker in me—the kid who was raised on chitchat and small-town gossip—wanted her to be nice to people I knew.

"But he was a big fish, and he fought me, so I had to smack him around." Diego made little punching gestures into the air above him and Sasha giggled.

"Start with the rice and then just taste the fish," I said.

"If it's all right with your mom, there are at least two frosted brownies with your name on them," Marissa said.

"Yeah," I said. "But first she has to taste her fish."

"You doing okay?" I asked Marissa. I wanted to ask her so much, but we never had time to really get into it. *How is your girlfriend? How is this place? Have you seen Johanna? How much longer do we have here before the police kick us out?*

"My crew!" Arturo walked up to the table and interrupted. I hadn't seen him since our one night together. "Is this Sasha? Our littlest protester?" He held up his hand for Sasha to high-five. She ignored it.

"That's cold." Marissa laughed.

"She knows you are no good," Diego teased.

"Mama, brownies?" I looked at her plate. She'd taken a bite of salmon and eaten a big pile of rice. Sasha ate just enough calories to get her through the next couple of hours.

"It is time for brownies!" I mock shouted.

Marissa and Diego unwrapped two giant trays of brownies and put them on the table. Marissa took two for Sasha and put them on her plate.

A crowd formed around the brownies and then they were gone. I stood up and crawled out from under the table so I could talk to Arturo. Diego and Sasha were whispering about her elves.

"Hi," he said, but he looked jumpy, nervous.

"You okay?" I asked.

"Yeah, tense working-group meeting today. The police are putting a lot of pressure on us to pack up before winter, and Devora, you know she's mad at me a lot." He hopped back and forth on his New Balance sneakers.

"About me?" I asked.

"No, not exactly. I mean, yes, but mostly it's about my bad character and shitty Marxist ideals."

"Well, you are a shitty Marxist," I said.

"Aren't we all." Arturo grinned. His stubble had grown in and he almost had a patchy beard. I felt like kissing him. I knew I wouldn't.

"Have you seen Johanna or Butch?" I asked.

"I haven't. Butch called me too, but I don't have the power to get him back in. The Disciplinary Working Group banned him and they have to decide."

"Could you hear Johanna in the background? Was she with him?" I hadn't given up on finding her.

"No, it was just him," Arturo said.

"Mama, can we camp here tonight?" Sasha had her coat zipped up and her hat on, chocolate frosting on her chin.

Diego shook his head at me and waved goodbye to all of us. "Adios!" Off to work another one of his jobs. I knew how he felt about me staying over. Marissa was busy unfurling her sleeping bag right under the People's Kitchen sign.

"I don't think so babe, it's too cold and we don't have a tent and you have school tomorrow," I reasoned.

"You can sleep in our tent," Arturo said. "We've got sleeping bags too, and we're going back to Brooklyn in an hour."

I shot him a dirty look. *I'm trying to parent here.*

"They are both from L.L.Bean and really warm."

"Please, Mama. Daddy took me camping last summer, but I haven't done that yet with you."

"Sasha, you have school."

"Please?" she begged, and did her best puppy-dog eyes.

"Please, Mama." Arturo batted his eyelashes at me. "It will be an amazing story for her to tell her kids one day." I rolled my eyes at him. *No one is listening to me.*

"Mama?"

"I'm thinking," I said. I envisioned some future version of Sasha smoking a bong in a college dorm room and saying to a group of wide-eyed suburban kids, *Oh yeah, my mom and me slept with the protesters at Zuccotti Park*, and then I flashed forward to the middle of the night, a freezing Sasha and me, barely asleep on the concrete while several police officers ripped through our sleeping bags and arrested us all.

"Please, Mama?" Sasha kept at it.

"It's really warm and safe tonight too, no police activity is being planned," Arturo whispered to me. "And if you don't want to be in my tent, there's the new women-only tent that we set up last week."

"Okay fine," I relented. "But as soon as we wake up, we're going home and changing and then you're going to school."

Sasha did a little jig of triumph and scooped up her Lego elves. "We're sleeping in the forest!" she said to them.

"Good night, littlest worker," Marissa said from deep in her sleeping bag.

"If you ever have a kid, I'm going to show up one day when you least expect it, and fuck with your parenting," I whispered to Arturo as he led us toward his tent.

"I already have a kid," he said.

"I know, I mean"—I stammered—"your own kid." I finished the sentence, but I knew I was wrong. He was a stepparent. That was real.

"I have a family," he said to me.

"I know," I said. "Sorry, that didn't come out right." I felt the sting of what he was saying. The real boundaries of his life. My second-place status. My invisibility. *You can use our tent when Devora and I don't need it.*

Neither of us said anything. We couldn't get into it in front of Sasha. He was enough of a parent to get that at least.

He waved goodbye and zipped us into the tent. "I'll try to come back in the morning to have breakfast with you," he said. I didn't believe him.

I peeled her out of her coat and got her zipped up in her sleeping bag, and then I realized we both needed to pee, so I got her back into her coat and we walked over to the pizza place a block away that was letting Occupy workers use their bathroom.

I had second thoughts on the way back. It was cold and the park was full of people I didn't know. "Sash, let's just go back home and sleep in our big bed?"

"Mama, you said we could camp here!" she wailed.

"All right, all right, we'll stay."

Back inside the tent, we got zipped in and cozy. Sasha's elves talked among themselves. I tried to get comfortable on the granite. I wrapped my arms around Sasha in her sleeping bag and pulled her close to me. I wasn't going to let go.

"No getting up and going anywhere without me," I whispered into the top of her sleeping bag. I wondered if I should text Aaron and let him know what we were doing. I was pretty sure he wouldn't approve. *This is a one-time thing*, I said to myself. *An adventure.*

I didn't let myself fall asleep until I was sure that Sasha had drifted off. I felt her chest rise and fall through her sleeping bag, the familiar hum of her steady breath next to me. The park, even at eight p.m., was a busy, bustling place. The wail of a siren. Glass bottles in the gutter. Two Occupiers just outside my tent talking loudly.

"Once upon a time, there was a group of protesters who got the shit kicked out of them in the middle of the night," one said, and laughed.

"That's not funny," the other one said.

"I'm just kidding, sort of. Sorry," the first one said.

"How much longer do you think we can last?"

"If it's like the Hoovervilles during the Depression, it could be a while. Seattle's lasted for almost ten years."

"I just want things to change. I don't care how long it lasts."

They walked away. Boots on the granite. I thought of David asleep in his beautiful, well-decorated loft. It looked like a page from the catalog of CB2. *He'll get a kick out of me doing this*, I thought as I started to drift off. How much of my life did I live in story? How many things did I do so that I could write about them afterward? Didn't I love making my friends laugh at the stupid, sad shit I got myself into? Or was it just my way of making my life mean something? To turn it into material for something beyond the day-to-day?

I woke up in the middle of the night to the sound of glass breaking and two men screaming at each other.

"I'll fuck you up!"

"No you won't, motherfucker!"

I pulled Sasha closer to me. The men wandered off and faded out. I fell back asleep. I dreamed of the hawk standing over me, shadowing and swooping, until I realized I was her prey. I crouched down. I ran. It didn't matter. She found me. I looked down at my legs. I was no longer a woman, but a squirrel. Running on all fours. Fast. Faster. My legs wouldn't stop moving. I ran and ran. When I looked up again, there was no shadow and no hawk.

PREDATORS

When I woke up my face was cold. I reached for Sasha's warm body. My hand groped around in her sleeping bag for her hair, her shoulders, her back, but I felt nothing. I sat up with a jolt and said, "Sasha?"

"Sasha!" I sat up and called out loudly. I stood up and shook off the husk of a sleeping bag. I unzipped the tent and looked around. I didn't see her. "Sasha!" I yelled.

"Sasha?" I called out again, louder still, but still trying to hide the frantic feeling I felt in my stomach. I walked down the base of the park and across the street, calling her name. Other Occupiers started to notice me.

Marissa was next to me. "What's wrong?" she asked.

"Sasha's lost," I choked out, and then started to walk away. She grabbed my arm.

"Why don't you go left and I'll go right and we'll meet at the top of the park."

I nodded and moved toward the left side of the park, the People's Library, the sign area, the drum circle, and the police on horses.

"Sasha! Sash! Sasha!" I called out as I walked up toward the People's Library. *She's up there, by the books*, I told myself. *She found the one kids' book they have in that stupid fucking Marxist library and she's reading it.* But when I got to all the card tables holding the books, she wasn't there. I crossed the top of the park and walked toward the Vietnam veteran who was just setting up his post. He'd be there all day with his sign. He'd become a celebrity of sorts.

"Have you seen a kid about six? Long brown hair?" I asked. "Purple coat."

He shook his head. "I'll help you look. I'll go north and up toward the Bull, okay?"

"Thanks." I nodded. "Sasha! Sasha!" I called out louder and more frantically. I moved toward the giant red Calderesque sculpture and met up with Marissa who looked worried now too. "I didn't see her anywhere," she said, and then put her hand on my back.

"What the fuck is wrong with me!" I put my head in my hands for a quick second and then started moving again.

"I'm going to wake people up to start having them search," Marissa said, and slipped back into the center of the park. I listened to her rouse the remaining people from their bags, "Hey, we've got a lost kid in the park and we need help finding her."

I marched toward the media station, hoping to find Arturo. There were just two twentysomething guys huddled over their laptops. "Have you seen my daughter? She's six, about up to here." I gestured toward my chest. "She has long brown hair and is wearing a purple jacket."

They shook their head no with the dazed look of people who spent more time talking online than face-to-face. "Do you want me to tweet about her?" one of the younger men asked me. *No, you fucking child!* I wanted to scream. *I want you to drop that useless computer and run the streets with me until we find her!* But I said nothing and walked away. I didn't have time to teach them how to help me.

I scanned the now mostly awake crowd of Occupiers for Sasha's purple coat, her small frame. *She's here. She's here somewhere. She's gotta be here.* I saw nothing close to the color purple. Plenty of blacks, army greens, browns, grays, and the occasional flannel shirt, but bright purple was not the color of Occupy. "Sasha!" I called out as loud as I could. "Sasha!" I called again. "Mama is looking for you!" In her six years of existence in the city of New York, I'd never once lost track of her. *You idiot. You let her stay overnight in a park with a bunch of people you don't even know and now she's gone.*

"Sasha!" I walked and walked. I circled the park two more times. Nothing. *No. My. Girl.*

I spotted Marissa talking to two police officers and pointing at me. I walked over. "Can you help me find my kid?"

"She just told me that you slept in the park with her and now she's gone," the older of the two officers said to me. He looked to be about forty, probably a dad himself. I felt his judgment burning off his badge and onto my entire body.

Marissa nodded. It sounded so stupid. "Yeah, basically," I said.

"You should be in jail," the older officer said. He looked bored though, like he didn't even really care about me or my kid, even enough to insult me, let alone help us. The younger officer, who was maybe in his midtwenties, looked down at his boots and let out a long sigh.

"She already was," Marissa shot back. "You guys arrested her last week."

"I'll find your kid," the younger officer said to me. He led me by the elbow away from Marissa and the other officer, who was growing red in the face as Marissa continued to talk to him.

"I apologize for my partner. He's working a lot of overtime, and it's getting to him." The officer pulled a notebook out of his back pocket. "What does she look like?"

"Long brown hair, pale skin, freckles, a purple jacket." I continued to scan the park for any sign of her. I saw a flash of purple out of the corner of my eye and turned toward it, my heart leaping out of my chest with anticipation, but it wasn't her. It was someone unfurling and rolling up a sleeping bag, probably the only other purple fabric in the park.

I pulled my dead phone out of my back pocket. When would I call Aaron to tell him that I'd lost Sasha? It was the only thing he'd trusted me not to do, and it was the only thing that mattered, and I'd failed.

We circled around the park three more times without finding her.

"I'm going to go talk to some officers outside of the park and get them on it," the young officer said to me, then walked away. I sat on a bench and put my head in my hands. I pounded my fists on my thighs. My stomach churned and churned. Marissa reappeared and sat down beside me and put her hand on my back again.

She kept it there, and I didn't shake her off. A warm spot on my spine.

The images came. The fears and dark thoughts of every parent. Someone, a man, a pedophile, a predator, took her hand and led her somewhere. To an apartment, to a dungeon of some kind, to a closet, to a basement. He tricked her or he talked her into it. He had a treat. He said he knew me. He said it was okay. He said get in the van. He picked her up. He held her hand. He led her by the small of her back until she was out of sight, and then and then and then. I gagged. Marissa kept her hand right where it was.

"This is annoying, but I have a feeling. She's close by. We're going to find her. I can be psychic this way," she said.

I turned and stared at her. I wanted to say, *You have a feeling? A feeling is nothing. A feeling is not a fact.* Instead, I asked, "What time is it?"

Marissa looked at her watch. "It's 7:45."

"She's been gone thirty minutes," I said. "This is not good."

I stared at my feet and the images started again. Maybe no one took her, but she wandered off. I saw her walking toward the Freedom Tower because it reminded her of an ice castle, jostled by the bigger bodies around her, sure that she knew where she was and that I was just asleep over there inside the park. Then she turned a couple of times and got disoriented. She started to cry. She got on the subway for some reason. No one noticed her. Or someone did and that person wasn't good, didn't want to help. She told them my number. She had it memorized, but they didn't call me. They took her to an underpass or a car or another borough. Hands on her. Pressing her down. Hurting her. Stop. Stop. Stop.

You have a baby. It comes out of you and it is slick with blood and so tiny and weak that it can do nothing. It's this way to train you. To scare you into taking care of it, until you love it. Or maybe you love it right away. Either way you see that you must do everything. Because a baby is a crushable thing. And a kid is just a bird that can be destroyed. A small thing with too many bones. A delicacy for predators. A piece of candy. A lure for a witch.

I remembered my recurring fear was losing track of her on the subway. Of having the door shut between us. Me standing on the platform panicked while she hurtled on the A train uptown. "You're holding my hand too tight," she sometimes said to me. I tried to let go. Eventually we wouldn't hold hands at all. She'd be too old for that, and she'd ride the subway by herself like all city kids eventually do.

"I think I'm going to throw up," I said to Marissa, but instead of doing that I stood up again and willed the queasy feeling away. I knew it was time to call Aaron.

THE CHILDREN

In fairy tales the children were lost or they were running away because they had a shitty stepparent who wouldn't give them any butter and so they took off in the night. Some of the children were clever and so they left a breadcrumb trail and they tricked the witch into getting into the oven herself. The less clever children got lost by the banks of a river and were pulled underwater by a creature, who had long yellow fangs and stringy hair. The children who got away went back to school or into the fields. At school they took all the tests and they carried the ridiculous heavy math workbook home on their turtle-shell backs. In the fields, they worked so hard their fingers split open, but they liked the sun and the way it felt on their faces and backs. All of the children spoke to their parents every day because they didn't want to get lost again or hear those little whispery voices in their ear canals that told them, That's not fair. We'll show them. Let's go. Because they were children they believed in their own power to change the story. In their little kid brains they envisioned maps instead of breadcrumbs, trails instead of the deep, dark woods, and flashlights and candles for all. Next time, they said, we will be better prepared.

Los. Lucian. Lose. The computer said it was from the Old English for "perish, destroy," and "become unable to find." A lost sock. A lost puppy. A lost ship. A lost child. Have you seen my husband? I lost him. I let him go. We had to let some people go. We were downsizing. Because of unforeseen budget cuts. Ours is a lost world. Mama, I looked everywhere, and I couldn't find you.

MISE-EN-SCÈNE

She planned it. She picked the highest floor, fussed over her outfit, and chose the time of day when the most people would watch. She'd been an intern for a fashion designer for one painful semester, and even though it was clear that this woman of talent, starvation, and clean lines hated her guts, she'd learned a thing or two about staging and drama. She wanted to fall from a sunny sky. She wanted to be backlit. She planned to make a pretty shadow and a terrible corpse. She wanted props and a beautiful set. She hoped to humiliate her parents for all the ways they had crushed her dreams. The endless hours of tutoring, the insistence on one kind of college, a major they chose, and a career they approved. She hated her father's name, Reilly, because it erased that her grandmother came from Hong Kong carrying just one suitcase after weeks of throwing up on a ship. She hated her mother for acting like this was a boring story.

There had been the brain-chemistry-altering medications and the stupid bland shrinks and the affair with a man who smelled so different than her that he was a kind of medication himself. She tried to overdose on him, but he wasn't strong enough. He never asked. He never asked anyone anything and he called that teaching. After that she decided she was a woman, and entitled to all of the pain. After that, she started talking to herself and her roommate moved out. After that, there were many nights of obliterating blackouts. After that, she missed her parents. She knew bad things happened in the dark, but she hadn't been prepared for how bad. She decided to tell no one. Ever. Instead she wrote poems about being a little girl.

She missed herself. She was trying to remember the grass outside her window, the baby bunny she rescued from her cat and the way it twitched and shivered on her comforter after she'd saved it, and her first kiss. She put the poems in a folder that she planned to open like a parachute. She read about the Tibetan monks who set themselves on fire and the Afghan girls who'd rather burn than marry an old man. There was a fruit vendor named Mohammed who changed the world. She admired them all, but she wasn't stupid enough to see herself as a spark. She wanted to say something with her body that she could never say with words. She wanted to embarrass the school and make a spectacular mess. She wanted to run out of pain, to empty herself of it, to obliterate it. She wanted to be a part of something and so she jumped.

I GET IT

I was waiting for Aaron to pick up when I heard Sasha's birdlike voice. "Mama!"

I looked up. Marissa took her hand off my back and waved her fist in the air in triumph. "I knew it!" she said.

Sasha skipped toward me. She was holding a chocolate milk from Starbucks and a muffin. Johanna, of all people, was walking behind her.

"Sash!" I held out my arms and then burst into tears.

"Why are you crying?"

"I didn't know where you were, and I've been looking around for almost an hour."

Johanna looked at us sheepishly.

"This had better be good," Marissa said, leaning back on one sneakered heel and crossing her toned arms.

"I was hanging out on a bench and Sasha popped her head out of your tent, and I came over to say hello and hug her, and she said she had to pee so I took her to Starbucks and bought her breakfast," Johanna said. She wasn't slurry. Her blue eyes were bright and unpinned. She'd shaved off her dreads and had a short pixie haircut, not unlike mine. She had on her signature overalls, but they were clean. Her coat was vintage faux fur, ratty, but still somehow stylish.

I wanted to punch her! I wanted to hug her! *You took my kid! You brought her back! You're alive!*

"You can't just take someone's kid and not tell them!" I said.

"Mama, I asked you and you said yes," Sasha said. "Can you put the straw in my drink?" She held up the carton of chocolate milk at me.

"No, I didn't," I said.

"Yes, you did. You were asleep but you nodded," she said.

"Sasha said she checked," Johanna said. "I wouldn't just take your kid like that. I thought it was okay. I'm a babysitter. I'm not a total fuckup."

Was it possible? Was my sleep so deep that I'd said yes to Sasha without knowing it? I remembered my hawk dream, and that I'd been running like the squirrel. Could that explain it? Sasha stuck the chocolate milk closer to my face so that I'd do the straw. I relented, took the box, unwrapped the straw, and jabbed it through the foil. The milk spurted up and onto my hand.

I stared at Johanna. I was trying to take it all in. I'd been worried about her for so long. "You're alive," I managed. "You're not just a missed phone call."

Marissa sucked in a breath. "Where's your boyfriend?"

"He's not my boyfriend anymore," Johanna said.

My stomach was no longer in my throat. I took hold of Sasha's hand.

I looked around at the park, at both the chaos and order of Occupy. The people like Arturo, Marissa, Diego, and Devora who made it hum with work and progress, and then the people like Johanna and Butch and the hungry and strung out who made it wild and free. It was a total marvel, a real live utopia in a city that had once been that for me. Squatters on the Lower East Side! Old records and antique furniture rotting on the street! Affordable neighborhoods! Where had it all gone? Occupy made it okay to want it all back again. Its very existence gave me hope that the country could change and we could make something better. I'd always loved makeshift communities.

I squeezed Sasha's hand and she squeezed it back. I was happy to have helped out in my own small way, but I knew now it was no place for Sasha. I remembered that I was always weak on Wednesdays when Sasha came back to me after five days with Aaron. I let her do all kinds of things that I wouldn't on a Friday or Saturday. Four-dollar pop-tarts! Camping out with protesters! On a school day!

"Everything is okay now," Johanna said.

Sasha bit into her muffin. "Mama, it's corn!"

The police officer who told me I should be in jail started to walk over to us. He had that same smug bored look on his face. "Is this the woman who took your kid?"

"It was a misunderstanding," I said.

He walked back over to the barricades and spoke into his walkie-talkie. To call off the search? To report me to social services? Who knew?

"I really am sorry. I didn't mean to scare you. I was so excited to see Sasha and she needed to pee and I thought I was just helping."

"I know." I forced myself to say it. It was over. Sasha was back.

"I'm going to go tell everyone we found her and they can stop looking," Marissa said.

"Sasha, when we get home, we have to talk about never going anywhere without my permission."

"But you nodded," she said. "Are you mad?"

"You can't go anywhere unless I'm fully awake and using words. I'm not mad, I was just so worried. Come on, let's go home. I have to get you to school."

"Are you okay?" I asked Johanna. I hugged her. She hugged me back hard, like she needed it. Sasha hugged both of our legs too.

"Group hug! Group hug!" she sang out.

"Yeah, I met this therapist. I've been clean for over a week. I'm going to sleep at Occupy until I get a spot at this outpatient place. I want to apply to community colleges," Johanna said.

"You should!" I said.

"Can I come see you sometime?" she asked.

"Yeah, you have my number. You know where I live."

"Will you let me in?"

"Yeah, but no roof stuff," I said.

"Got it, that's fair."

Sasha and I walked to the subway and waited for the train. As the A train rattled its way back up to West Fourth Street, I gripped Sasha's hand in my own until both of our palms were sweaty. I thought of the parents who just three months ago dropped their children off in a dorm in New York City and then drove back home. Did they feel like their hearts were walking around outside of them, wholly separate, but somehow still tethered? I remembered the hawk calmly dismembering that squirrel, and I decided she was still bringing food to her kid. Why not? I saw my own parents, each in the split ranch houses with their new partners. My mother quilting and reading, her joy at telling me about a new HBO show. My father playing his guitar in the basement, high and not sorry about it. I knew they were clumsily reaching out to me and I willed myself to reach back.

THE PLANK

Mel stepped to the edge of the deck and stared out at the salty marsh. The other gray-brown cabins were closed up tight for the winter. Petie and Walt tumbled over each other in a ball of dog freedom. Gray, wet sky. She zipped up her windbreaker, but unbuttoned her jeans. They were starting to get tight.

"Walt, don't eat shit!" Jenny called out to him, and he looked up and cocked his ears like, *What, who me?*

"He's just going to do it when you're not looking," Mel said. Stevie, Sasha, and Johanna were inside the cabin, building a fire and making the beds. It was the last weekend they'd have there, before the bank officially took it over. Stevie and Sasha wanted to say goodbye too, and they brought Johanna to keep her out of trouble and away from Butch, who kept crashing Occupy and demanding to see her.

They'd driven up from the city, got stuck on I-295 for an extra two hours, and stopped in town for dinner. Chowder. Lobster rolls. The whole journey took eight hours. It always did. Johanna had never eaten a lobster roll before. She was totally blown away by it.

"I won't miss the traffic," Mel said.

Jenny threw a giant stick to Petie. He watched it fall like a good hunting dog, ran for it, grabbed it, and brought it back to Jenny. "Good boy." She scratched behind his ears. "Yeah, me neither."

Mel found the board near the back of the deck and waved Jenny over. "It's really more like a pirate's plank. At least that's how my sisters and I thought of it." She pointed to a part of the deck, a piece of the wood that jutted out past the rest. It was a mistake or a quirk of the builder, but they'd loved it because it was impossible not to bump your hip against it. In college, they'd carved their initials into it, and whenever anyone came to visit who was special and who they loved, they let them carve their initials too.

"There I am." Jenny leaned over Mel and traced her own initials with her pointer finger.

"And there's Stevie and Aaron," Mel said. "We were going to do Sasha next time she came up."

She sucked in a breath and started to cry. Jenny hugged her tightly. The wind picked up sticks and leaves around them. "Let's just get the plank out."

Mel nodded. She couldn't speak. Jenny pulled the hammer out of her backpack and started to pry at the nails holding it in place. The wood was old and battered and the nails were rusted. She pulled and pulled, careful not to damage any initials.

"You've always been so handy," Mel said.

Sasha and Johanna came out onto the deck as Jenny continued to pry and pull. "Can we sign it?" Sasha asked.

"I have a Sharpie." Johanna pulled one out of her coat pocket. Jenny took a break and sat on the edge of the deck while Johanna and Sasha doodled their names in girly cursive script.

"It's like when I signed Thisbe's cast," Sasha said, adding a heart to the end of her name.

Stevie came out carrying a broom. "I ended up sweeping." She shrugged. "It's like we're taking the graffiti from the bathroom of the CBGBs—so much history, the story of three sisters and all of their loves and friends."

The sky was pink as the sun set on the horizon. Mel stared at it, fixed it as a point in her mind, the not-so-distant future when she would be different, her life changed completely. She felt queasy. "I shouldn't have eaten a lobster roll," she said into the salty air. She felt impossibly grouchy and tired, put-upon because Johanna had come, but surprised by how unobtrusive she was. She had a kind of cat's energy about her when she wasn't high. There, but not there. She mostly focused on Sasha and left the adults to themselves.

"There was no stopping you," Stevie said.

Johanna looked confused, but decided not to pry. Sasha didn't know what they were talking about. She'd started doodling on another plank of the deck.

"I grew up in a cabin," Johanna said. "I mean ours was more like a glorified shack. It was me and a bunch of spiders and mice, all kind of nested together with my mom." Everyone looked at Johanna, like they knew she could say more, and they wanted to hear it. Since she'd been clean for a couple of weeks, there was less bravado, she was quieter, but there were cracks in the rebel girl facade, moments of opening up. "This place has a much better vibe."

"Sash, come inside and help me unpack the stuff to make s'mores?" Stevie said. Sasha and Johanna trailed after her.

"I think it's all going to work out," Jenny said once they were gone. Since she'd decided that she wanted to have the baby, she'd become weirdly positive. She was talking about applying for jobs closer to the city so she wouldn't have to travel so much. She pulled and pried at the plank again until it came unstuck. "Got it!" She wrapped it in a blanket and put it in the trunk.

"You don't know that," Mel said when she came back. She wasn't in the mood for positivity and she wasn't used to Jenny acting this way. It was like an old version of her had come back to haunt them. Jenny at thirty, when they'd first met. Full of bounce and spring, the woman danced all night at that bar and then took Mel and Stevie to breakfast without so much as a yawn.

"We'll have another cabin somewhere, someday, and Carmine will come around to decide how involved he wants to be, and we'll be mamas."

"Can I just be by myself out here for a minute?" Mel asked.

"Sure, babe." Jenny called to the dogs who bounded into the cabin with her.

Mel walked out into the marsh and let all of her questions tumble around in her brain. *Could I be ambivalent and have a baby? What if one person wants it and the other isn't sure? What if two people aren't sure and the other person wants it? Is it good for a baby to have three parents, one who isn't as involved as the other two? Is that confusing? Could I bartend while pregnant? Would I even want to? If I become a mom, will I keep writing? What happens to my sex life? Why hadn't Occupy, with all of its force and creativity, changed the fact that I was losing the only home I ever loved? What's in a lobster roll anyway?*

She'd watched Stevie navigate some of this, and the results were mixed. She and Aaron stopped having sex for a long time after Sasha was born, but Stevie still wrote, lately more than ever. Sasha came out onto the deck. "Melly, I made you a s'more!" she yelled.

"I'm coming," she said gently to Sasha. "Did you burn the marshmallow, like I like it?"

"Yeah, it's black on one side."

Mel put her hand on Sasha's neck. "Love you," she said.

"Love you more."

EVICTED

A week later, I stared at the live feed on my laptop. Police in riot gear—black helmets, plexiglass shields, batons out. I couldn't see their faces. Protesters lying down on the ground—linking arms or covering their eyes to protect them from pepper spray and the glaring lights the cops had turned on. Someone started to sing "We Shall Overcome," and I swore I heard Marissa's sure voice among them. More cops in the background pulling down tents, kicking through the park to get to the People's Kitchen. *Those are people's homes*, I thought, my nose prickly with tears, and then the feed went dark. It was one a.m.

I waited for the live feed to come back on, but it didn't. I texted Arturo and Marissa and Johanna. "Are you there? Be safe!" but heard nothing back. I switched to Twitter.

Flood Wall Street now. Send reinforcements. The cops are trying to tear it all down.

Riot gear! Fuck the police!

Bloomberg says we can come back. We don't believe him. #WallStreetLies

Holding the People's Kitchen until the very end!

They're destroying the People's Library!

Police have barricaded all entry points to Zuccotti. We can't get in. #OccupyEverything!

I closed my computer. Sasha was asleep in my bed. I wanted to hop on the train and run down there. I wanted to resist and get arrested for it. I wanted to fight forever for that utopian, improvisational, messy, loud idea called Occupy, but I couldn't. Not that night. I'd promised myself I wouldn't take Sasha again.

I shut off the lights and got into bed next to Sasha. She pressed her foot into my hip. I moved it gently away. I lay there for a long time, staring at the ceiling and out the window onto the horizon of buildings.

People in the streets—protesting, speaking, marching, camping, living, eating, shitting, fucking, dancing, reading, talking, all of it. It had been the best dream because it came true, and for a time, it kept me busy.

CURTAINS

Johanna and Marissa ran to the People's Kitchen to protect it. It was the center of Occupy, and so the safest and most important place to hold. A couple other campers had already chained themselves to a tree.

"Wake up, they're coming. Tweet everyone you know!" Johanna heard a voice shout from the media tent. "Come and help us! We need more bodies!" She didn't have a phone. Butch had taken it from her.

"Link arms with us!" Marissa shouted, and they waited under a tarp in the cold rain.

Then the zombie-voiced loudspeaker police robot recording shook through the park: "You must evacuate so that we can clean the park. You will not be allowed to return."

"I have to go, they'll deport me. I don't have papers." Diego grabbed his backpack and they hugged him goodbye. Johanna watched him duck out of the corner of the park and into the city night.

Mostly, they had to sit there and listen to the chaos. First, the cops blasted music to shake them out and up—stupid eighties metal that nobody liked. And then they brought in hoses to spray. Crying and shouting. "This is our home! You can't do this!"

Marissa and Johanna looked out from under their tarp. The People's Library demolished. Protesters pepper-sprayed and facedown on the ground.

"Here, eat this!" Marissa passed around cloves of garlic for them to chew to cut the effects of the pepper spray. They chanted at the cops, "You are the ninety-nine percent too!" and "Disobey your orders!" but they were either stone-faced or gleeful in their destruction of what had been built. There was no getting through to them.

There was this steady stream of people trudging up Broadway with all their stuff strapped to their backs with nowhere to go, just out.

Finally, they got to the kitchen, tore it down, and put Johanna, Marissa, and the few remaining kitchen workers in handcuffs.

"Johanna!" Butch cried for her from far away.

"Butch!" she cried back.

"Shut the fuck up!" A police officer's boot on her back. A black man with a bloody face next to her. Another woman crying, "I need my meds. You can't arrest me without my medication."

Marissa's calm voice: "We're okay. We're okay. We're okay."

RADICAL MOMS

Later that December, when Johanna came to sleep on my couch for a couple days before making her way to San Francisco to go to school, she told me all about it. I was putting my books in boxes and trying to pack up my kitchen, but I sat down and listened.

She paused and took a sip of the tea I'd made for her.

"Where's Marissa now?"

"She went back to Florida to help her parents. They're moving into an apartment and she wanted to help them get settled."

"And Diego?"

"He said he's going back to Mexico. He wants to see his kids and he's not making that much money here lately, the economy is so shitty."

"I think that's good. He was really missing them," I said. "I wanted to say goodbye!"

"Arturo asked about you."

"He did? What did you say?" I was surprised. I hadn't texted him, and he hadn't texted me.

"He just wondered how you were doing." Johanna stood up and walked over to the windows that looked out onto the park. "Pretty fucking posh, prof," she said.

"I'm leaving," I said. "They're kicking me out soon and I'm scared, but I know it's a good thing. I need to find my own space so I can prove to myself that I can do it. I moved here with my ex-husband and now he's gone and it's time for me to go too."

"Can't you just move into another faculty apartment, like in those towers over there?" She gestured toward the towers across the park where the tenured faculty lived. "That one looks amazing!" She squinted at the condos. They were almost finished. Two of the giant walls of windows even had curtains on them.

"Not eligible because I don't have tenure."

"That sucks. You're a good teacher."

"Thank you."

"Wanna move to Oakland? That's the next Occupy, you know."

"So I hear."

"We can start a revolution."

I stared out the window. I didn't know what to say. "I've got my kid and my job."

"I know, I know. You're a mom," Johanna said.

I opened my mouth because I wanted to object. I could think of all kinds of radical moms—the home-birth crusaders, the breast-feeding warriors, the moms against guns and nukes and rape and racial profiling and stop-and-frisk, the moms who screamed and cried and marched when their children were shot, my own mother who quietly wrote grants and created programs for the lost children in my small town, the lesbian separatists who made communes in Maine and upstate New York, the moms who made childcare cooperatives and formed radical poetry listservs, the moms who would later take over the House and Senate, the Occupy Moms, and all of the moms who whispered in their children's ears, *It's going to be different. It has to be different.*

But I couldn't speak. I couldn't get it all out. It was too much to list, too many women to explain. She'd find out anyway. On her own. When she was ready.

THE FIRST TIME

Johanna stayed again the next night. Stevie had spent the day packing up her books and finishing her grading. Before they went to bed, Johanna convinced Stevie to smoke a cigarette with her.

"Come on, it's my only remaining vice," she said.

"I smoke occasionally. You're not corrupting me." Stevie got a bowl to use as an ashtray and pulled two chairs closer to the window. Winter had stripped the branches bare and you could see the fountain, paths, and people, all lit up by the streetlamps.

"Remember when I told you I had one of the papers from the girl who jumped?" Johanna blew a stream of smoke through the screen.

"I didn't believe you. I thought you were high." Stevie put her cigarette out.

"I was high, but I did have one of her papers."

"Do you still?"

She pulled a folded-up piece of paper out of her pocket. "Do you want to hear it?"

Stevie looked around the apartment at all of the boxes she'd packed. Two of them were her old journals. Everything she'd ever scribbled down since she'd moved to New York. Class notes from when she was a graduate student, to-do lists, freewriting, and so many lost poems. Poetry was her first genre and for a long time, poetry was the only language that made any sense to her as a writer. She started writing poems when she was thirteen as a lost girl who needed to translate the world into a shape and rhythm that fit into something manageable.

"Yes."

Johanna took one last drag of her cigarette and stubbed it out. Moving away from the window, she cleared her throat.

The First Time
after Europa

Never get on something.
If you do, never get thrown off.
He's white.
He comes with other bulls,
but he separates himself.
Later, he'll kneel
so that you can mount him.
He'll carry you across the
surface of the ocean.
Hold on.
You'll lose your dress.
But right now his horns glisten like eyeteeth.
Calasso says he's gentle like a puppy.
Playful.
You're by the shore.
You're with your friends.
You're always with your friends.
This is the break we all make.
You want to leave your friends,
but you'll always look back.

His breath is full of clover.
You notice the hard shell of his hoof
and if you're really paying attention
the shimmer of his haunches—the muscle.
But you're not.
You're texting or rooting around in your basket
and he's talking to you
which is weird for a bull.

And it seems like everyone (your friends and the other bulls)
are watching but from really far away.
You look into the ocean.
It's blue enough to mimic the sky.

You get on.
You realize he's huge.
You look back, but it's way too late.
You're in the middle of the ocean now.
They're gone and you've started a new life.
You now live on the continent of after-the-fact,
of long ago, of I did it and it kind of hurt.

"God, it's a rape poem," Stevie said.

"'He's white. He comes with other bulls.' 'He'll kneel.' It's like being at a party and meeting a rich douchebag who wants to slip you a roofie," Johanna said.

"That kinda describes Zeus." Stevie tried to remember her Greek mythology, which she never studied in graduate school. She'd read Calasso though; he was one of Aaron's favorite writers. "But Zeus didn't need roofies. He disguised himself as a bull to trick Europa into going for a ride, and then he carried her thousands of miles building the continents as he crossed the land."

Johanna widened her eyes at Stevie. "Mythology is insane."

"'You look back, but it's way too late.' That's pretty eerie. Some people who commit suicide regret it, the instant they jump. But is she writing about herself or Europa?"

"No idea." Johanna flopped down on the couch. "Both?"

"Do you think you should go to the police?"

"Oh, me reciting a poem that I claim she wrote will *definitely* convince them that she was raped." Johanna snorted.

"All right, all right. I have a ridiculous sense of justice. I'm working on that. It's just that I sometimes used to think of poems as proofs—like in geometry, the only math I was ever good at. Statements. Reasons. Givens. Definitions."

"Do poems prove things?"

"In their own way, yes. Europa was the cover for her own rape story. Young writers, all writers, need covers, stand-ins, characters, proxies."

"I'm not a writer, I wouldn't know," Johanna said.

Guiltily, she imagined Butch out there in the cold park. She'd been visiting him every day, sitting on a bench with him, bringing him whatever extra piece of food she had, and watching him turn more fully into a junkie. He had a new crew—a stumbling, messy group of five or six people, whose only job was to get high every day. He'd find a new girl soon too. She knew that. It was one of the reasons she wanted to leave New York. Watching that would make her relapse. She was sure of it.

"That poem and the poem I wrote in your class kept me alive."

"Really?" Stevie sat on the end of the couch by Johanna's feet. "Why?"

"I don't know. Maybe it's like you said, some weird take on a geometric proof of my existence, or my ability to make something."

Johanna looked at Stevie, who looked like she wanted to cry or maybe hug her, which she didn't think she could handle. Helena had been telling her during her last session about transference, and that sometimes in therapy patients learn to have a healthy relationship with a mother-like figure, the kind with their own abusive or absent mothers. She realized she'd been thinking of Stevie as another possible mother, a good one, a woman who kept letting her in—to the classroom and to her home. Mel too—that night she'd made drinks for Butch and Johanna at her posh bar and fought for them to stay— had meant something. And now Helena with her weird accent and art books that she used to trick Johanna into opening up. She needed to be tricked, and maybe she'd be looking her whole life for other mothers to replace the one she'd never had. If the world were full of territories, landscapes, and boundaries, she wanted to cross as many as she could.

"Can I?" She lifted her feet up and Stevie scooted closer.

"Sure."

Resting her feet on Stevie's lap, Johanna closed her eyes. Stevie placed her hands on her ankles. It wasn't a hug, but the smallest bit of touch. She fought the urge to jump up, make a joke—anything to get away. Instead she willed herself to ask, "Can I sleep in your big bed with you?" It was a child's request she was making, she knew.

If Stevie thought that was a weird question, she didn't let on. "Sure, everybody sleeps in there."

PART 4
SPRING

JOHN DOE

He stayed underwater until April. The river had its drag and pull. He bobbed along like bait and tackle. Bumping against rocks and garbage, he became fish food, waterlogged, a sunken wreck. Sometimes the water was three feet deep, sometimes sixty. He never knew what had pulled him in—a vision of a mermaid or a treasure he conjured up in a nod. Maybe he got pushed or stabbed. Homeless drug addicts had a way with dying.

The *Post* reported, "The badly decomposed body of a man was pulled from the Hudson. Police have no information about his identity. The medical examiner will determine the cause of death."

He'd been looking for her for months. She'd told him she was going to college in San Francisco. Every day, she talked about getting clean and what it felt like. He ate the food she brought him and tried to convince her she was wrong. He didn't believe her. "You sound like the system got to you. You talk like that college professor," he said, and leaned over to kiss her neck. She let him do that, but then she stopped coming to the park. It was cold and he found warmer places on the West Side. Subway gratings and the occasional broken sidewalk with a steam pipe underneath. There was a new girl who had a nest in an abandoned building and wanted to partner up. But he always had an eye out. He was waiting for her to come back, to give up, and to miss him. His little runaway. His girl. The one who he lost track of when he wasn't paying attention. Until he slipped. Until he got pushed. Until he decided to take a cold swim so he could wake the fuck up.

It would be years before Johanna learned what happened. Back in New York for graduate school to become a librarian, she decided to try to find him. For closure? To check in? She wasn't sure. She talked to homeless people until she found someone who said something that reminded her of Butch. *He had wild hair and he wouldn't shut up about Marx. He was living by the water with the queer kids.* And then she found one of them. *We haven't seen him, but yeah, I remember that guy.* Finally, she went to the police and everyone ignored her and sighed loudly for days until eventually a cop took pity on her and went through the John Doe cases. He brought her into an interrogation room, threw a file on the desk, and stayed in the room. The photos made her gag.

"Their intestines fill up with bacteria and that's how the bodies float up. Gas," the officer said.

There was a photo of his ripped Dead Kennedys T-shirt. That's the only way she knew.

"You know this John Doe?"

"Yeah, he was my boyfriend. A long time ago. His name was Butch Campbell."

She looked at the rest of the file. "Cause of death unknown."

They made her fill out paperwork. They gave her a horrible box of ashes.

When she left, she bought a ten-dollar bag of heroin and went to the New York Public Library. The reason she'd chosen to become a librarian was because libraries had always accepted her—taken her in and let her rest when so many other spaces wouldn't. She went to the bathroom and fingered the bag and stared at it for an hour until she accidentally dropped it into the dirty toilet. She took this as a sign and stomped on the flush with her boot. She texted Stevie, "I'm here!" and left a message for her therapist Helena. "I almost used, but then I didn't."

NIGHT LIGHT

"I'm stressed out," Sasha said from the perch of her loft bed.

"You can do it. It's hard, but I believe in you," I said from the nest of pillows I'd arranged for myself on her *My Little Pony* carpet. "I'm going to sit in here with you for a while until you feel comfortable."

"I don't like my bed," she said. Her hair hung down onto the wooden ladder like Rapunzel waiting for her suitor.

"I know, but this is a good bed and it's cozy and you've got all of your animals," I said. "Now lie down and close your eyes."

Sasha sighed loudly and flung herself backward. I lay on my back and read my book. She squirmed and tossed and turned.

"Mama?"

"Yeah?"

"What is the beginning of language?"

"Oh god, no idea," I said.

She frowned down at me.

"I think someone was grunting and eventually it became a word, like, *ugh, er, ugghhh,* and then suddenly, *Mama!*"

Sasha laughed and started to climb down the ladder. "Can I be with you down there?"

"No, you have to stay in your bed. We both need to have our own beds."

"Can I have a prize if I stay in bed?" she asked, and stepped back up into the bed.

"No, we're just going to learn how to do this, both of us."

"It's easier for you," Sasha said.

"No, it's hard for me too," I said, and put my nose back inside my book. "You're doing a great job staying in your bed though. I see a person who is determined and trying hard." I'd read in one of my parenting books that it was good to praise attributes rather than offer up an empty *I'm proud of you!*

Sasha flopped and kicked some more, but she stopped talking. I wondered if I would ever meet a squirmier kid? Were all kids this way? I couldn't say because I only had this one.

Eventually, her breathing settled into a rhythm and I knew she'd fallen asleep. I gathered up my pillow nest and went into my own bed. The sheets were cold. I moved into the middle of the mattress and spread my legs and arms out wide. I took up as much space as I could and then I turned off the light.

In the middle of the night, Sasha tapped my shoulder. I lifted the duvet and she snuggled up against me.

"Sorry, Mama," she said.

"It's okay. You tried. In some countries, everyone sleeps in the same bed," I said, and then we fell back asleep.

THE SWIMMER

On the day that Aaron and I signed our divorce papers, we took a selfie in front of the giant gold Cardozo School of Law sign. I posted it on Instagram without a caption and tagged him. Afterward, we wandered into a Verizon store to try to separate our phone bill. Apparently, it's easier to get a divorce than to switch out of a family plan. We picked up and put down the latest beautiful new models of iPhones that we couldn't afford and then left without changing our bill. On the street corner, he hugged me tightly.

"See you soon," I sighed into his neck.

"Probably tomorrow." He squeezed me tighter.

"I don't like goodbyes," I said without looking up at his face.

"You're not saying goodbye, nobody's going anywhere," he said into my hair.

"You're still one of my favorite people." I held on.

"You're mine too," he said, and I started to pull away. It was time, we had to let each other go. The lights had changed from green to yellow to red several times over, and New Yorkers had streamed past, stepping around us and ignoring us. Most were lost in the drama of their own lives or deep into the screens of their phones. One or two may have wondered what our embrace was about and made up a story. Probably they were writers or just nosy. *They're in love. They're grieving. They're saying hello after a long separation. This is their final goodbye.* But nobody bothered us. It was one of my favorite things about New York—its anonymous public theater, how private lives played out on street corners, bodegas, and subway platforms. It was our unspoken contract, to leave each other alone.

"Where you going now?" he asked.

"Mel's ultrasound appointment."

"Can I come?"

"I think so," I said. I couldn't remember the etiquette around watching babies through stomach portals. Besides, Mel was Aaron's best friend too. Why shouldn't he come?

"WHOA, LOTTA PEOPLE in here," the technician said as she came into the room. "Who are the parents?" We all raised our hands and she shrugged. "Okay, Mom, you're cool with this?"

"Yep." Mel leaned back on the examining table. She slid the waistband of her pants down and settled into the crinkly paper.

"The gel might be a little cold." The technician moved the wand along Mel's stomach and we stared at the black-gray screen. First, we heard the *gurgle chug gurgle chug gurgle chug* of its heartbeat.

"Oh my god," Jenny said.

"There he is," Carmine said, smiling at the screen.

My eyes filled with tears and I looked at Aaron who had placed his hand gently on Mel's shoulder.

"Oh," Mel said to the screen. "Hi."

"Do you want to know the gender?"

"Gender is a construct," Jenny said, maybe for the thousandth time in her life.

"Is that a yes or a no, Mom?" the technician asked.

"Not yet," Mel said.

"I see his ribs." Carmine pointed.

The technician narrated as she moved the wand around Mel's belly. "Heart sounds good and strong. There's its legs and here's the umbilical cord. There's its spine. Amniotic fluid is fine, and there's the placenta. Baby looks healthy." Its heart continued its *gurgle chug gurgle chug gurgle chug.* I remembered Sasha's heartbeat and then her twin whose heart stopped on a monitor just like this one.

We all stood there transfixed by the screen as if it were a roaring fire or the cliffhanger to a really good show. It, she, he, xe, they did a little kick turn and floated to the other side of Mel's stomach.

"Mom, you've got a swimmer," the technician said, and then turned off the monitor and gently wiped Mel's stomach clean.

Carmine and Jenny each took an arm of Mel's and helped her off the table. Out on the sidewalk, we huddled awkwardly around Mel until she couldn't stand it anymore. "Too many people! Trying to touch me!" she said and swatted at us.

Carmine took the cue first. "I gotta get my kid from school." He hugged Mel and kissed her on the cheek and jogged off toward the F.

"Me too," Aaron said, and walked toward the 6.

"Bye," the three of us who remained cooed.

"I don't think I have time to drive you to work." Jenny looked at her phone. "I need to get on the road to Ithaca." She and Mel hugged each other. "I'm really proud of you, of us, of what we're doing."

"She's in there, swimming around," Mel said.

"Oh is *she*?" Jenny laughed, and then we watched her go too.

"Do you want me to come to the bar and keep you company?" I asked into the cool April air. Maybe I needed to weep into a tumbler of whiskey about my divorce or toast that little creature we'd seen on the screen. Maybe both?

"It's okay. I just want to get through my shift and ignore everyone. Tommy took pity on me and gave me a stool, and Greta is working too, so it should be easy."

"You okay?" I asked.

"Yeah, it's all just super intense and real. It's what I want, but I don't know how our lives are going to change and shift."

"Nobody knows that until the baby comes and then you figure out a little bit every day and I'm going to be there helping just like you helped me."

Mel teared up. "Ugh, the hormones make me do embarrassing things."

I rubbed her back. "It was cool that Carmine came."

"He's the dad. I mean, that's what he's been saying. And he wants to be involved, but we haven't figured out how much yet."

"Aaron and I always used to say that the optimum number of adults to raise one child is three, and she'll also have Sasha and Carmine's kid as siblings."

"I don't even know his kid. What if she's a total asshole?"

"Very possible, but Sash is nice."

We started to walk toward the subway, and for the second time that day I clutched a person I loved on the street corner while New Yorkers dodged and sighed their way around us. "I love you!" I called to Mel as she walked down the subway stairs. "Love you too!" she called back.

And then I wandered from the imaging center in Midtown to the West Village. I wasn't in any rush. I had nowhere to be, so I stopped to look in store windows and bought my first iced tea of the season. Acting like a tourist, I dawdled on corners and looked at the tops of buildings. I saw gargoyles, elaborate cornices, and script. Eventually, I walked through the arch of Washington Square Park and stared at the fountain. I didn't live there anymore, but I missed it. It had just been turned on for the spring and the water sprayed onto my face in a light mist. I looked over to the building where I lived for two years and felt a dull ache in my chest. I was nothing if not a creature of habit. I didn't like change. I walked the same blocks and followed the same men. Mel had been my best friend since I was eighteen. My marriage ended, but I texted Aaron every day. I'd taught at the same school since I was a graduate student. I fell in love with New York in the early nineties and so I stayed. I didn't know where else to go.

The mist made my face wet, but I stayed put. Maybe I wanted a baptism or a mikvah or some kind of cleansing. I kicked off my shoes, rolled up my jeans, and waded into the cold water. I was the only one except for a scruffy homeless man in his thirties, who was busy having a conversation with himself. There was no Butch or Johanna. No bride or kid to keep me company or distract me from myself. I waded in deeper and had one of those thoughts that is simple, but feels like a revelation: *You're not entitled to anyone or anything. Just because you had a shitty dad and a bad childhood doesn't mean the gods owe you a husband or a partner or a wife.*

It was obvious, but it hit me hard. Maybe everyone else knew this, but I didn't—or maybe I'd known it but never really believed it. I felt released from some cosmic pressure—to couple, to be taken care of, and to care for another adult. As the water lapped up around my jeans, I saw that I was healing and I could finally, maybe, let it go.

WINNERS

She came out a Leo—the cord wrapped dramatically around her neck like a feather boa until the midwife expertly unfurled it—and then she screamed herself red on Mel's chest. She smelled like blood and animals, and for a tripped-out, high-on-the-pain moment, Mel decided she was made out of stars and had traveled across galaxies and through black holes to be born.

Outside was a heat wave and the asphalt rippled and split under a squinting gaze. The world was watching the Olympics on their small and big screens. Mel saw it all from her couch because she was breastfeeding every two hours. Depending on her mood she felt either happily rooted or impatiently tethered. Her favorites were the swimmers with their flapping muscles, broad shoulders, and fishtailing hips. The medaling ceremonies made her weep.

Because everyone had tried so hard and they all deserved to win.

IN THE END

In the end, I found a one-bedroom rental in the Bronx in one of the giant old apartment buildings on the Grand Concourse. It felt right to me because my first favorite poet and professor was Milton Kessler, and one of his books was called *The Grand Concourse.* He was the first man who believed in me and told me to keep writing no matter what. The apartment was $1,100 a month. Cheap for New York, yet still too much for me.

In the end, I moved upstate and into a little cabin near Beacon or Hudson or Tivoli or Germantown. I commuted into the city twice a week and I bought an old shitty Toyota. I learned to shovel the snow in my driveway and scrape the ice off the windshield in the winter. I missed everything and everybody.

In the end, I sold a book and I managed to scrape together a down payment for a condo in Long Island City. When the book came out, a reviewer called me "Elena Ferrante's dirty and manic American niece," and I was so happy that I cried.

In the end, we moved in with Jenny and Mel and the baby for a year. They had a guest bedroom and we bought bunk beds and put them next to the crib. It was too crowded, but Sasha loved it and I became the unofficial night nurse.

In the end, I moved in with another single co-parenting mom. Her name was Erin or Amy or Caitlin. We joked that we were like *Kate & Allie*, the sitcom from the eighties, only messier and grouchier.

In the end, I moved into a communal house in the Lefferts Gardens section of Brooklyn. Sasha and I had a big room with a tinier room off of that one. Most of our roommates were full-time employees of a world-famous Brooklyn food co-op. We ate well, but the bathroom was always a mess.

In the end, there was Occupy Sandy and Black Lives Matter and the Umbrella Movement and Gezi Park and the Debt Collective and Occupy the SEC and the Slut Walks and Ni Una Menos and Iguala and the Sanctuary Campus and the Water Protectors.

In the end, there were protests on a scale we couldn't have imagined. Pushing back. Taking space. Saying no. Hands off this body. Hands off this house. Hands off this land. Occupy This Pussy. The Women's March. Scream Ins and Flash Mobs and Dance Parties and Sit Ins.

In the end, we protested all of it.

In the end, I moved to the desert like all of the crazy women artists. Aaron was pissed at me, but we worked it out so that he had Sasha all summer long and on the holidays. When new friends asked me, "Why Santa Fe?" or "Why Taos?" or "Why Sedona?" I said, "There was something about the sky that split me open and told me what to do."

In the end, Arturo moved back to Puerto Rico. Devora went with him. They joined a group of students and teachers to help create worker collectives for start-ups and microbusinesses.

In the end, I saw David from the other side of the street. Sasha and I were walking down Broadway, and he was stepping into a cab with a pretty woman in a short turquoise dress and tall brown boots. He had his hand on the small of her back. In that moment I saw him guiding and protecting her, and I knew she was probably having the best sex of her life. I wanted to shout out. To wave to him. To cry for myself. To warn her. Instead, I looked away and then I pulled Sasha into a candy store called It's Sugar. I let her buy whatever she wanted, and she picked a giant Hershey's bar that cost fifteen dollars. We opened it in the store and I took a big bite and I felt a little bit better.

In the end, David stayed. He texted and I texted back. I went over to his apartment and he came to mine. We met for lunch and dinner and we went to the movies. Through it all we kept talking.

In the end, Arturo broke up with Devora. For a long time, he was lost and sometimes he came over.

In the end, there was someone else. He was a dad. She had a

motorcycle. He was a video archivist with a full head of wavy gray hair that I ran my hands through. She worked for the Department of Education and was a widower. She was a woodworker or a physicist or an essayist or a volleyball player.

In the end, I didn't go far. I found a place on the Upper East Side.

In the end, I moved to Hoboken and Jersey City.

In the end, I found a place in Staten Island with a backyard.

In the end, there was Sasha, wholly separate from me. A girl, a teenager, a young woman with her own dreams. In the end, she'd turn away, like all kids do, and find her own place. First, with a gaggle of filmmakers from school on the West Coast, later with her band on tour, and after that with a lover.

In the end, I couldn't leave the city, even though it was a stupid, expensive, loud, dirty, and smelly place to live.

In the end, I knew it was about the lights, and the potential drama of every street corner. Clever graffiti tags, some surprising street, a new pocket park, or a tucked-away public pool. It seemed that I couldn't really ever know all of New York, and so I stayed and kept exploring.

In the end, there were so many keys and locks. Some fit and some didn't.

There were strong wooden doors and cheap particleboard ones. There were windows that faced sunny streets and ones that looked out into a shaftway full of garbage. Some of the walls were already painted seafoam green or eggshell white and some I painted myself. I chose pale blues and deep reds. The rooms were too narrow! That room was so big! Once there was a fireplace. It worked! There were high ceilings and wood floors. Tile in the bathrooms. Clean, dirty, and dirtier. Shower stalls and bathtubs. So much I couldn't change! Molding and fixtures. A mirror that I loved.

Sometimes there were people in these rooms with me and other times I was alone. I'd like to say that I got used to the people and the solitude, but I'd be lying. Every day was a little bit different and that was enough.

ACKNOWLEDGMENTS

Thank you to Malka, who teaches me more about plot, movement, action, dialogue, grace, problems, and resolution than anyone I've ever met. The way you dance, bounce, feel, think, argue, and cuddle your way through our days is something I didn't imagine was possible.

Thank you to Matt Longabucco and Jason Nunes for giving me permission to do so much of what I feared I couldn't and reading countless drafts.

Thank you to my mom, Judy Haller, who keeps doing the work.

Thank you to Madeleine George for deep friendship, radical godmothering, and time to laugh and play.

Thank you to P. G. Kain for phone calls, work shit, and giggle fits.

Thank you to Jamie Newman for loving and taking care of me.

Thank you to my therapist, Josh Jonas, who said, "Write the Carley novel"; to my neurologist, Dr. Rachel Saunders-Pullman, who listens deeply and recently taught me the Yiddish word *shpilkes*; and to my psychiatrist, Dr. Mark Groves, who said two summers ago, "I think you're depressed." He was right! I am lucky to have insurance (and honestly, this book wouldn't exist if I didn't). I believe quality, affordable medical care is a human right. Let's keep fighting for it!

Thank you to my dear friends who keep me afloat, text, check in, get me out of the house, honor when I can't go anywhere, come to readings, let me read things to them, and call me: Alex Baker, Martha Conner-VanDyke, Jill Dearman, Arielle Greenberg Bywater Simone, Joelle Hann, Stephanie K. Hopkins, Caitlin McDonnell, Rosa

Mazzurco, Lynn Melnick, Suzanne Menghraj, Amy Touchette, and Karen Weiser.

Thank you to all of my artist, writer, and teacher friends who show me the way through their own mind-blowing work and day-to-day living: Anselm Berrigan, Jacqueline Bishop, David Buuck, Nicole Callihan, Kristen Dombek, Diana Goetsch, Adjua Gargi Nzinga Greaves, Jennifer Firestone, Ariel Friedman, Ifeona Fulani, Jenny George, Alfie Guy, Grace Halverson, Kelly Harris, Ileana Jimenez, Rami Karim, Madhu Kaza, Erica Kaufman, Seth Loftis, Lisa Kron, Andrea Lawlor, Karen Lepri, Brendan Lorber, Jessica Lynne, Jenna Marotta, Gala Mukomolova, Dawn Lundy Martin, Idra Novey, Jonna Perrillo, James Polchin, Susan Rogers, Theresa Senft, Sejal Shah, Amy Shearn, Laura Sims, Smoota, Sarah Jane Stoner, Lauren Sanders, Stacy Szymaszek, Rachel Valinsky, Nicole Wallack, Bill Webb, Simone White, and Aaron Zimmerman.

Long before writing this book, like many New Yorkers, I visited Occupy Wall Street. Though I knew it wasn't a perfect utopian space, I found it radical and empowering in ways I hadn't experienced before, even as a longtime intersectional feminist, protester, and scholar of youth subcultures and activism. Occupy ignited new conversations around class, gender, race, and privilege that were long overdue, and pulled together coalitions in vibrant and surprising ways, all the while holding on to a working structure that was a unique, sometimes messy marvel. Like many scholars who teach and study social movements have noted, I believe that Occupy laid the groundwork for later movements, uprisings, and protests. Protests speak to each other across history, and protesters borrow and change their tactics as they learn from mistakes and wins. Can we listen enough to hear these echoes? I was never able to stay overnight—my toddler and disability made that difficult—but I returned several times to bear witness, march, and show solidarity. Some of my own memories helped me form a fictional portrait of that political moment, but I am also grateful to two books in particular for their detailed descriptions and vivid historical work: *The Occupiers: The Making of the 99 Percent Movement* by Michael A. Gould-Wartofsky and *The Beginning of the American Fall: A Comics Journalist Inside the Occupy Wall Street Movement* by Stephanie McMillan. I was lucky enough to become friends with Pablo Benson, an Occupier, who shared his experiences and helped me with my rusty Spanish.

Thanks to Amy S., Lynn, and Laura, who read versions of this and told me not to quit.

Thanks to Caroline Zancan for the book-changing notes.

Thanks to Genevieve Elam for early, free, twenty-four-hour, door-to-door copyediting.

Thank you to all of my dates—good, bad, and in-between.

Thank you to Kate Greene for the soft and hard tackles out of the closet.

Thank you to Dia Felix for pushing me to send this book to Michelle Tea.

Thank you to Michelle Tea for choosing this book to be part of Amethyst Editions and for recognizing that queer narratives are not just about coming out. You've been my writing and life hero for many years, and I'm honored that my book spoke to you.

Thank you to my brilliant editor at Feminist Press, Lauren Rosemary Hook, for understanding and loving this book and giving me genius revision ideas. Thanks too for being patient with me while I tweet too much.

Thank you to Jamia Wilson for your steady and fierce leadership of Feminist Press and for making our meetings so fun.

Thank you to Jisu Kim for publicity and courage.

Thank you to Nick Whitney for the kind and generous copyediting.

Thank you to Lucia Brown for your social media grace.

Thank you to Drew Stevens for typesetting and font joy.

Thank you to Suki Boynton for the radically sexy cover.

Thank you to my students who give me hope and write with me.

Thank you to all of the teachers everywhere who work hard and are mostly underpaid.

Lastly, thank you to my tenacious and kind agent, Jesseca Salky, who responded to my query while reading the first five pages of this book on the subway. God, that was a thrill! We did the long haul on this and your stamina is wowza! I'm grateful for your vision and belief in my work.

The Feminist Press publishes books that ignite movements and social transformation. Celebrating our legacy, we lift up insurgent and marginalized voices from around the world to build a more just future.

See our complete list of books at **feministpress.org**